PRAISE FOR *THE BA*

"Liked *The Backup Asset* so much, I just bought the other two books by Leslie Wolfe."

"The characters are fantastically written, and the suspense is unrelenting."

"I can definitely say it ranks right up there with the best names in the business like Crichton, Suarez, and Preston."

"A riveting tale of modern espionage, skillfully plotted and meticulously researched, I found it impossible to put down."

"Awesome characters that are human with flaws and strengths."

"Just the right amount of action, character development and general background."

PRAISE FOR LESLIE WOLFE

"Leslie Wolfe is fast becoming one of my favorite authors."

"The writing is first class and the characters are very intense."

"The precision of strategy and character development on both sides, at all levels is mind boggling."

THE BACKUP ASSET

BOOKS BY LESLIE WOLFE

TESS WINNETT SERIES

Dawn Girl
The Watson Girl
Glimpse of Death
Taker of Lives
Not Really Dead
Girl with A Rose
Mile High Death
The Girl They Took

DETECTIVE KAY SHARP SERIES

The Girl From Silent Lake
Beneath Blackwater River
The Angel Creek Girls

BAXTER & HOLT SERIES

Las Vegas Girl
Casino Girl
Las Vegas Crime

STANDALONE TITLES

Stories Untold
Love, Lies and Murder

ALEX HOFFMANN SERIES

Executive
Devil's Move
The Backup Asset
The Ghost Pattern
Operation Sunset

For the complete list of Leslie Wolfe's novels, visit: LeslieWolfe.com/books

THE BACKUP ASSET

LESLIE WOLFE

II **ITALICS**
ITALICS PUBLISHING

$\displaystyle{\prod}$ **ITALICS**

Italics Publishing Inc.

Cover and interior design by Sam Roman

Editor: Joni Wilson

ISBN: 978-1-945302-02-2

DEDICATION

For my husband, for everything.

He stared at the back of his hands in disbelief. They were shaking so hard it made for a difficult task to get another taste of coffee. Using both hands, he grabbed the mug and took a sip of steaming liquid, warming his frozen hands on contact with the white glazed ceramic. He smiled a little, as his eyes focused in passing on the message written in red lettering on the side of the mug. A gift from his coworkers, it read, "I do math well, what's your excuse?" *How appropriate*, he thought, *I don't do* this *very well, and I need to get better at it. Grow a pair, for Christ's sake,* he admonished himself, giving his trembling hands another disgusted glance.

He made an effort to set the mug on his desk without spilling any coffee, but that didn't work as planned. His hands were shaking too much. A few droplets stained the scattered papers on his desk, most of which bore the stamp TOP SECRET.

"Shit," he muttered, under his breath, and rushed to get some Kleenex.

He patted the papers dry, cleared his desk of everything else, and spread the top-secret files on the glossy surface, carefully going through every piece of paper. He finished sorting through each piece of documentation; then paced his office anxiously for a couple of minutes, clasping his hands together, trying to steady himself. *Can't back down now,* he thought, *and I wouldn't even if I could.*

He looked up at the digital weather station hanging on his office wall. His rank within the organization gave him the privilege of a private office, decorated to his taste. Hanging close to the large window overlooking Norfolk Harbor, the device told the time and the weather. It displayed the forecast, showing the high and low temperatures expected, indoor temperature, humidity, and also showed barometric pressure as a yellow chart. In the middle section of its display, a small graphic depicted the sun peeking from behind some clouds, all drawn in blue. It was going to be a nice day, with partly cloudy skies, barometric pressure steady, and reasonable temperatures for the season. None of that mattered, though. He had less than three hours to make the drop, and he wasn't ready yet.

He refocused and wiped his sweaty hands nervously against his suit pants.

"Let's get this done and over with," he mumbled, removing all papers from his desk except a single pile he had just put together. He spread out the contents of the pile and started organizing the documents in order, placing them facedown in an unmarked manila folder.

The first document was an evaluation memorandum regarding the compatibility and readiness status for laser cannon installation aboard USS *Fletcher*, DDG1005, a Zumwalt-class destroyer. Marked TOP SECRET. It was several pages long, and he made sure he had them all and in the right order.

The second document was a capabilities assessment for Zumwalt-class destroyers, complete with technical specifications, class overview, and general characteristics, including weapons array, sensing technology, and vessel performance. Marked SECRET. Nine pages long.

The third document was a performance and capabilities assessment for the laser cannon itself, the most recent and groundbreaking technology developed for the US Navy, the successful and eagerly awaited result of seven years and $570 million worth of research and development. Marked COMPARTMENTED—ABOVE TOP SECRET.

Satisfied, he turned the carefully constructed pile of documents face up and closed the folder.

He was ready for the drop.

Henrietta Marino came a few minutes early for her 10:30AM appointment with Director Seiden. His assistant, a sharp-looking young man in his thirties, barely made eye contact with her before asking her to take a seat and wait.

She didn't follow that invitation. She stood, pacing slowly, feeling uneasy and awkward in her professional attire, and checking her image in the pale reflection of the stainless steel door leading to the restricted communications area. She straightened her back, trying to project the confidence expected of an analyst if she wanted anyone to take her seriously. There was no way she could improve her average, almost plain looks, her dark brown hair tied in a ponytail, or her freckled complexion, but at least she could project some confidence.

Henrietta Marino, Henri for short, was a senior analyst with the CIA's Directorate of Intelligence—Russian and European Analysis. Thirty-five years old, she held a master's degree in political science, and had a twelve-year record of accomplishment as an analyst for the CIA.

For the past eight years, her work had focused on Russia, Russian affairs, and the repositioning of Russia on the world power scale. She understood the Russians really well, or at least she hoped she did.

Her latest report illustrated Russia's concerted effort to reinvigorate its nuclear stance, unprecedented since START I in 1991. The signing of START I, the first Strategic Arms Reduction Treaty, by the United States and the USSR, had marked a historic moment. The USSR was still a federation back then, but the treaty encompassed all former Soviet republics and remained in effect after the federation dissolved.

START I, and later START II, limited the number of nuclear warheads and intercontinental ballistic missiles, or ICBMs, on both sides and mapped the road to arsenal reductions. It marked the beginning of a new era, where peace was becoming a possibility. It marked the end of the Cold War.

Henri had anticipated her report would cause some turmoil, being the first report ever to document and argue the rekindling of the arms race, the first of its kind in fifteen years. Within minutes after she had filed it, her phone had started ringing. Colleagues asked her if she was sure. Her boss followed suit immediately and grilled her for an hour on the report facts. Even the CIA's general counsel, whom she'd never met, reached out and asked if she knew what that report meant. He also encouraged her to withdraw it if she wasn't 100 percent sure. Finally, Seiden's chief of staff asked her for more details and her degree of confidence. Now Seiden wanted to see her.

At first, her confidence had been high, the full 100 percent everyone expected from an analyst of her seniority. However, after so many confidence-eroding phone calls and meetings, she wasn't that sure anymore. Still, she knew not many people were able to spot patterns as she could. She had the ability to identify patterns from the fifth data point, in some cases even from the third. It didn't matter what she was analyzing. People's behavior, global events, communication, actions, legislation, she was able to pinpoint immediately what her data points had in common and project a trend based on her observations. Her ability to predict the evolution of the Islamic State of Iraq and the Levant, infamously known to the world as ISIL, although she had never worked in the Middle East Analysis Group, had brought her the promotion to senior analyst. That, of course, had happened only after everyone stopped thinking she was crazy and started seeing her point. She wondered if the same people were thinking she was crazy this time too. She wondered how long it would last.

"You can go in now." Seiden's assistant made eye contact for more than a second, making sure she went straight in.

She took in a deep breath, straightened her back one more time, and walked through the door displaying as much confidence as she could.

Director Seiden sat behind a monumental desk, reading from a report, most likely hers. Heavily built, wearing the frame of a former athlete or weightlifter, Director Seiden looked intimidating in his charcoal suit, white shirt, and loosened silver tie. In his sixties, the director had a receding hairline showing a tall forehead and permanent frown lines. His role, most likely one of the most stressful leadership roles in the US government, must have given him plenty of reasons to frown throughout the years, carving those deep lines in permanent testimony of who knows what crises he had dealt with.

Bushy salt-and-pepper eyebrows shaded his eyes. He focused intently on his reading material, while his right hand absently touched his teacup, probably considering another taste of Earl Grey.

Henri hadn't interacted with Director Seiden that often. Such a visit was an exceptional occurrence, considering there were three levels of leadership between her pay grade and his. She felt anticipation anxiety creep up on her. She wanted to make a good impression, and she only had one shot at it.

"Sir," she said, after clearing her throat, turned dry and scratchy all of a sudden.

"Take a seat," Seiden said, not lifting his eyes from the pages.

She sat in one of the large leather chairs in front of Seiden's desk, careful to not make a sound and break the director's concentration.

"Interesting theory you have here," he said, finally looking at her. "How sure are you?"

For some reason, Henri instantly forgot her carefully rehearsed exposé and blurted out unfiltered thoughts.

"I was very sure when I put that report together, but now I don't know anymore. Everyone doubts me, questions my judgment. I hope I'm right. I thought I was."

She cringed hearing her own words. She sounded like an insecure child presenting her math homework and still somehow questioning whether two plus two equaled four.

"Are you a leader, or a follower, Ms. Marino?"

"Umm... I aim to be a leader, sir."

"Then you shouldn't let your self-confidence drop because people are asking questions. It's their right. But you do have a brain of your own, right?" Seiden's voice was almost encouraging. He wasn't smiling or anything, but Henri didn't sense any disappointment or anger in his voice.

"Yes, sir," she acknowledged, aware she was blushing.

"Let's try again. How sure are you, Ms. Marino?"

"It's Henri, sir." She blushed a little more. Maybe offering her first name was inappropriate? She had no idea, but she was going to worry about that later. She was clumsy with people, always had been. "Yes, very sure."

"On what basis?"

"I have profiled President Abramovich. His detailed profile is on page five, I think. That profile, combined with several actions he's taking, all listed in the summary section of the report, led me to believe he is preparing for war, or for a renewed arms race, at least."

"I can read, you know," Seiden said, tapping his fingers on the report cover. "What can you tell me that isn't in the report?"

"Sorry, sir. Yes, well, Abramovich is a pure sociopath, of the worst kind possible. He's a malignant narcissistic sociopath, who would kill millions over his bruised ego. I started my report from that evaluation and from analyzing several actions the Russians have recently taken. They correlate really well; they form a pattern that spells arms race to me, possibly even changes in Russia's form of government."

"How so?" Seiden took his reading glasses off and massaged the bridge of his nose with the tips of his fingers.

"His entire background speaks to that. He was KGB. No, even worse, he was political KGB. He was a KGB general during Mikhail Gorbachev's reign at the Kremlin, but Abramovich's contempt for Gorbachev was common knowledge. He hated Gorbachev for his glasnost and perestroika, for his pro-West attitude and his willingness to end communism in Russia and bring freedom to the Russian people. Abramovich climbed to power under the self-proclaimed mission to restore Russia's greatness, and he started working on that since his first day as president of Russia, in the typical manner of a sociopath."

"Meaning?"

"Meaning his actions are disrespectful of anyone else's values, human rights, or the law, for that matter. He is the most dangerous kind of sociopath one can imagine. Absolutely no conscience, no scruples whatsoever, combined with holding the supreme power in a powerful country. After all, when did President Abramovich start being on everyone's mind again?"

Seiden didn't answer; just continued looking at her, waiting for her to resume her analysis. He'd probably heard these things before and had no interest in dwelling on them, nor cared to play question–and–answer games with her.

"Right," she continued. "He invaded Crimea, because he needed faster access to the Black Sea, a waterway shortcut. He didn't care that it was in a different country; he just annexed Crimea, erasing the border that stood in his path. Nothing mattered to him, not even another country's sovereignty. Then what happened? We applied sanctions. Abramovich, whose ego knows no limit, found the sanctions insulting. He fought back with his own sanctions, but he's hurting. Along with him, his financial backers are struggling. The Russian oligarchs, who paid him immense bribes in exchange for favorable legislation and the unofficial permission to do whatever they pleased, now are facing bankruptcies and are demanding action. His personal cash flow has almost dried up. That's why President Abramovich doesn't want the sanctions lifted anymore. He wants much more than that. He wants revenge; he wants blood. He wants us to pay for his bruised ego and tarnished image."

"Interesting," Seiden said, "but not all that new. What else do you see?"

"Several other things that correlate. The Russian people like him a lot. They, too, are sick and tired of poverty and uncertainty. Their support for him has created a unique circumstance that allowed him to start on the road of becoming a dictator, to remain in power until he draws his last breath."

"How come?" Seiden's interest was piqued.

"Well, after Russia became so-called 'free' from communism," she said, making quotation marks with her fingers in the air, "one of the first legislative changes was the amending of the Constitution, limiting the number of consecutive presidential terms to two, just like we have here in the States. The first few terms were four years long, until 2012. Then, they amended the Constitution to make them six years long, all during Abramovich's tenure at the Kremlin. Once his first two terms were consumed, no one thought he would be coming back to lead the country, but he did. He was elected again after a short hiatus, the single-term intermission required to satisfy the Constitution limiting him to two consecutive mandates. Very soon after he returned as reelected president, the Constitution was amended again, extending, as I said, the terms to six years. With these changes in place, he already had twelve years ahead of him, during which time many things could happen. That might include, I am postulating, another amendment to the Constitution, opening the door for more consecutive terms. Because he is well supported by the desperate Russian people in search for stability and sustainability, that amendment will be easy to vote in. This is how I see him paving the road to dictatorship."

She stopped talking, swallowing with difficulty. She was painfully aware she spoke too much and too fast.

Seiden whistled and leaned back in his chair, interlocking his fingers behind his head.

"You definitely have my attention now, Henri. Why an arms race though?"

"In the past year and a half, several incidents involving the Russian military took place around Europe and even here, in North America. Forty-seven, to be exact. Near misses, some might call them, or provocative, as others have labeled them, nevertheless they are quite a few. Way too many to be slipups, mistakes, or random acts. These data points form clusters. My analysis isn't finished yet on these specific actions, though."

"Yet you filed a report?" Seiden frowned, the lines on his forehead becoming more visible.

"My report is focused on Russia's nuclear stance, and I've finalized that part of the analysis. I was just giving you conjuncture."

"I see. Then let's talk nuclear threat."

"Well, going back to the forty-seven incidents I mentioned, and how apparently random they were, well, I am positive they're not. I will finish the analysis on those events and substantiate my point. But keeping those so-called random incidents in mind, I will now list nuclear-related, apparently random events that took place in the past few months. A cleanup and restoration operation of their ICBM sites, in no particular order, took place during the past few months. Satellite shows it clearly; they've dusted off the majority of their ICBM sites, even some we didn't know existed. Our satellites tracked the cleaning crews once we knew what they were doing."

"How did you know to look for those? Do you normally track via satellite every convoy they move around?"

"No, but it was what I would have done. I would have cleaned up my existing arsenal, get it ready, train my people, and produce more weapons. Makes sense. So I had satellite surveillance on a few top ICBM sites, and bingo! One day they showed up. Then I followed the convoys."

"Hmm... What else?"

"A few months ago, an exercise drill was conducted, involving 25,000 armed forces in a simulated massive nuclear attack. You'll find the details in Appendix 2."

"That's worrisome," Seiden said, frowning some more. "Keep going."

"Their top nuclear research facilities received some new funding recently. The Moscow facility is building a new wing. They've increased their uranium extraction rate at Priargunsky, Khiagda, and Elkon, their biggest uranium ore deposits. The plan is to double their extraction in the next ten years, under the guise of green energy. And Abramovich recently made changes in the leadership of the RVSN RF, their Strategic Missile Command."

"I see. Keep going, if there's more."

"Yes, there is. They're building a large center, partly buried underground, relatively close to an enrichment facility, the one in Novouralsk. We're not sure what that facility will be housing, not yet. On the political side, they've forged a troublesome alliance with India, another nuclear power. Finally, President Abramovich made a bold statement in the media, stating that North American defenses, specifically NORAD, cannot stop his new and improved nuclear missiles anymore. By his count, we're defenseless. That's unconfirmed, though. The fact, I mean—"

"Henri, we need to get a task team going. I'll assign some more analysts under your supervision. Find the underlying correlation behind those incidents you haven't finished modeling yet, and get me some working scenarios. I'll deploy a resource in the field to find out what's going on at that center they're building. Maybe even find out what the extra funding is supposed to buy them. We need to get ready."

"For what, sir?"

"World War III, most likely. We've already entered Cold War II."

Alex liked her rental home, a comfortable three bedroom in the heart of Carmel Valley. It had a peaceful backyard she often enjoyed, where she could work on her laptop until late in the evening, in almost complete privacy offered by several dense bushes and mature trees. She enjoyed the deep, heady scent of flowering citrus trees, especially at dusk, when cooler air came rolling in from the ocean, bringing a little moisture with it, to enhance the sensation of peaceful, comfortable paradise.

She'd had that house since she'd started her employment with The Agency, a small, private, investigation firm working exclusively with high-profile corporate clients. Founded by Tom Isaac and his wife, Claire, The Agency had become Alex's second family. With an IQ of more than 160 and a driven, assertive nature, Alex found her work for The Agency quite enjoyable and fulfilling. It supplied the fast-paced challenge, the reward, and offered a politics-free environment where she could thrive.

It was a great team at The Agency. She'd been lucky to find it. Tom carried all the wisdom of the business, and the experience of doing this kind of work, for more than twenty years. He was always willing to share that knowledge with her or any one of her peers.

Claire Isaac was adept when it came to figuring out how someone could infiltrate an organization that The Agency was hired to work with. She found the right open spots on the organizational charts and wrote amazing résumés that fit client job openings, getting a team member inconspicuously hired.

Brian Woods was an expert in procedures, protocols, and systems, and he was a top-notch strategist.

Richard Fergusson, a financial and business genius, normally started his work after the culprits had been identified. He helped CEOs and boards of directors with the cleanup, serving as a senior executive on an interim basis. Richard was also Alex's personal fashion advisor, having taught her how to dress for every role or cover story she needed to fulfill.

Louie Bailey, ex-SEAL and expert computer hacker, broke though firewalls whenever they'd get stuck using other methods. She had recruited Louie from her first job at The Agency when she worked with NanoLance and had him to thank for her self-defense and handgun proficiency.

And Steve Mercer, corporate psychologist, was the one who assisted clients navigate the rough waters of their investigations, managed everyone's expectations, and profiled suspects and other players based on their actions and methods. But Steve was more than that to her. She had fallen in love with Steve, despite her better judgment and her determination to follow the unwritten rule forbidding any type of romantic involvement with a coworker.

Yes, they were a great team, that's why she thrived at The Agency. She had a strong sense of right and wrong, and native investigative skills that helped her navigate the intricacies of undercover investigations in corporate environments, where entire fortunes were at stake, and the perps were highly qualified and knowledgeable.

Alex didn't hold any official function; she didn't wear a badge. She infiltrated organizations at the request of business owners, CEOs, or boards of directors who had reasons to suspect malfeasance within their corporations. Her clients preferred their concerns to stay quiet, private, yet to be investigated just as thoroughly as any official inquiry. Over time though, she had forged good working relationships with the authorities. In a couple of cases, some of the wrongdoing she had exposed had crossed the line from corporate misconduct well into criminal code territory.

When she had a new client, she immersed herself in her work, and the effort was quite considerable. Her cover, typically a newly hired leadership employee starting at the company she was investigating, was a fulltime job in itself. In addition to that, she had The Agency team to work with, a client to update, reports to write, and actual investigative work to handle. No wonder she didn't spend a lot of time decorating her home or picking out new furnishings.

She didn't have a lot of furniture; just a few items she needed to feel comfortable and function effectively. A large leather sectional occupied the living room, together with a huge TV and stereo surround she'd bought the night she moved in. The master bedroom, painted in a light shade of green, held a king-size bed, two nightstands, and two lamps with tabletop dimmers. It wasn't much, but she was most comfortable in open, clutter-free spaces.

The second bedroom was another story altogether. Painted in light blue, it had track lighting installed on the ceiling, holding many powerful light bulbs. Thick, dark blue velvet curtains, not allowing a single shred of that powerful light to be visible from outside, covered the windows.

A huge corkboard covered almost an entire wall. Another curtain railing hung above it. If needed, matching thick velvet drapery could cover the corkboard completely, leading any visitors to believe there was just another window behind it.

Post-it notes, knitting yarn in four colors, scissors, multicolored pushpins, markers, and tape cluttered the two tables in the blue bedroom. A small coffee machine and scattered coffee pods in various flavors completed the inventory of apparently disorganized items. A large armchair stood in the middle of the room, facing the corkboard. Despite the sunny day, clear sky, and perfect temperature, Alex chose to close the heavy drapery and curl up in that armchair rather than go outside and enjoy her backyard. There was one thing she couldn't take with her outside: her crazy wall.

Numerous pictures, clippings, and Post-it notes covered the corkboard, pinned down with colorful pushpins and tied with yarn. Every color she used had a meaning. Green yarn reflected a verified connection between two people, events, or pieces of information. Blue was for plausible, most likely to be true, yet unverified connections. Yellow marked a suspected connection, while red was for surprising, unverified, wild hunches.

Pictures of several individuals were pinned to the corkboard, together with country names, maps, locations, dates, all organized on a timeline illustrating events that had started taking place roughly two years earlier and had stopped in November of the previous year. That was the timeline of her most recent case: a corporate investigation that had uncovered a terrorist plot. She hadn't been able to paste a whole lot of information after that November date. Just scattered Post-it notes with single words followed by question marks, her guesses, and hunches, all unverified, pasted on the timeline wall to stay at the forefront of her attention.

Focused intently on the upper midsection of her timeline wall, Alex stared for minutes at the yellow Post-it marked with the X and a question mark. The position of that Post-it with the letter X showed that he was the leader of the entire structure reflected on her timeline. Underneath that Post-it, there were several others listed facts, conclusions, and hypotheses, using the appropriate marker color. She knew he was Russian, rich or well-funded, mobile, and a male. Those facts were written in green. She wondered whether he was working for the Russian government—SVR maybe? The Foreign Intelligence Service of the Russian Federation, or SVR, was just as powerful as the KGB had once been. After all, it was led by mostly the same people and had the same agenda. That Post-it held the letters SVR and a question mark written in yellow marker. Then a little lower, another Post-it held the initial V written in blue. During The Agency investigation, she had learned this valuable piece of information. His initial was V. His name most likely started with the letter V. Last name or first name? Unknown. She knew nothing more. Not a shred of information, nothing. In almost four months.

Absentminded, she almost missed the doorbell chime. *Steve's here*, she thought.

"Come right in!"

She started getting up from her chair, extracting her long, slender legs from underneath her and looking for her missing left slipper. There it was, almost buried under the armchair.

When she looked up, Steve was leaning against the doorframe, a look of deep disappointment clouding his blue eyes.

"Hey," she greeted him happily, "good, you're here! We can leave in just a few." She had to reach up and stand on her tiptoes to peck him on the lips. He didn't meet her halfway, and his kiss wasn't all that warm.

"Come right in? Seriously?" Steve's frown was prominent. "In how many ways is that just plain wrong? How can you be so careless?"

She looked at him sheepishly. It was gonna be one of those days, when he treated her like a child. She hated that more than anything.

"Look, I knew you were coming. I had unlocked the door just minutes before you came, really."

"But that doesn't make it OK, Alex. Not in our line of work."

"Yeah, I know." She sighed, and tried to deter his attention. "You're right, and I'm sorry. Won't happen again. Let me grab my bag and we can go."

She tried to pass by him through the door, but he stopped her in her tracks.

"Not so fast, Alex."

She turned to face him, feeling her blood starting to boil.

"And this?" Steve pointed at the timeline corkboard. "Didn't we talk about this?"

She sighed again, trying to calm herself and salvage the evening. She wanted them to have a good time, to enjoy their weekend at the cabin, but she also needed to make a point.

"Look, Steve, this is my home. I do what I want in my home, in my time."

"I agree," he conceded, "but it's unhealthy, and I'm worried about you. You're obsessing over a case we closed four months ago. It isn't good for you. You have to move on."

"I'm not obsessing; stop being a shrink, all right?" Anger tinted the pitch of her voice.

"I can't," he smiled bitterly. "I *am* a shrink, and I can't just turn that off and pretend I don't see you heading in the wrong direction, although sometimes I wish I could. The case is over, let it go."

"It's not over, not until we find him!" Alex pointed at the Post-it note marked with the letter X.

"We may never find him, Alex. Sam told you it could take years! You can't live like this. Have you been to work today?"

She blushed and ground her teeth angrily, repressing a groan. She remembered the sweatpants and wrinkled T-shirt she was wearing, her unkempt hair, and lack of makeup. *Yep, busted*, she thought.

"Brian said he didn't need me today, so I took the day off."

Steve paced slowly toward the window, and then pulled back the thick curtains, letting the sunshine in through the sparkling white sheers. She squinted.

"What's wrong, baby?" His voice was warm, concerned, and almost parental. "Talk to me."

She stood quietly, unwilling to have that conversation. It wouldn't be the first time they'd had it, and it would probably be a waste of time again. He just didn't get it.

"You used to like your job," Steve continued. "Just two years ago, when you came to work with us, you couldn't get enough of it. You were so excited, so happy to have the opportunity to do the work we do. What happened?"

"Almost three years," she said.

"All right, almost three years. But still... You are a fantastic computer engineer, you're a great investigator, you have this super-intelligent brain, you're analytical, brave, and bold. Do you remember what you liked the most about working for The Agency?"

She stood quiet, uncooperative. She'd been through this before. *Oh God... make the preaching end already*, she thought.

"I'll tell you if you don't remember." Steve continued unperturbed. "You liked that you could go inside organizations and right the wrongs you found, making people's lives better. You liked you could make a difference for so many. You loved to dig around, chase the facts, and find the corrupt, greedy, evil individuals who made everyone else suffer. You loved saving lives. And you loved taking a new client every few months, keeping your mind challenged and alert, helping you learn new things and celebrate the achievement with every closed case and happy client. Where did all that go?"

Silence engulfed the room for several seconds, interrupted only by chirps and trills coming from the birds in her eucalyptus tree. The world outside was alive, was filled with sunshine, life, and happiness, while she was buried here, with her ghosts. Maybe he was right.

"It didn't," she finally spoke.

"Huh?"

"It didn't go anywhere. I still love doing all that; I wouldn't change it for the world. But my case isn't over, that's why I can't let go."

"Do you trust me professionally?" Steve asked.

"Sure I do, with my life."

"Then trust me when I say you delivered your case successfully. The client was happy. You saved the day. You made us all proud: me, Tom, Brian, Richard, Claire, and Louie. Louie would follow you into a burning building; did you know that? And you made Sam proud too, and he's hard to impress."

"But somehow I can't let go. I'm still twisting my mind looking for clues, and there are none. Did we overlook something? Who knows what *he's* up to next, our Mr. X? Will we even see it coming? He is scary brilliant!"

"Yes, he is. But if you can't take any of our advice for it, take Sam's. We're all corporate investigators, I agree, but Sam's ex-CIA. He knows the spy-and-terrorist business better than we'll ever know it, and he said the same thing. Keep your eyes open, but move on with your life. We might never get to him; he might never resurface again. He might be busy doing time in Siberia for failing his mission, for all we know. Who the hell knows?"

"We're definitely never gonna find him if we stop looking, that's how I feel. Someone's gotta keep on looking. No one knows we've worked this case. Sam's retired CIA. He's not active anymore, so he's not looking either. So, who is? Or who should be?"

She knew she had a point, and he didn't argue.

"All right," he said, "what if you continue to search for him, but with a time   limit? Say... two hours per week, not more?"

"I tend to not trust you when it's about me. You've always been overprotective. Will two hours per week keep me sane?"

"Yes, it will teach you to control this urge you have to obsess about the puzzle piece you're missing."

"Can I do four?"

"Huh?"

"Hours. Since you tend to be overprotective and all that," she said, tilting her head to the side in a flirting gesture.

"No. Not more than two hours per week. Please promise me. Go back to doing what you loved to do, put your heart in each client you're working. If your mind is elsewhere, your work will suffer."

"This client's fine, it's Brian's client anyway, not mine. I can afford to do it. I'm just support, not that important or essential anyway."

"Would you be comfortable repeating that statement to Brian?"

She blushed and pursed her lips. *Damn.*

"Umm... No."

"Why do you let yourself think that? We're all risking our lives when we go undercover. Our support is critical, and you know that. You should know that better than anyone. We're all counting on one another, and we're all counting on you. When you're primary on a case, we don't cut corners on your support, or allow ourselves to become preoccupied by something else."

"All right," she admitted. "I'll give you that. But if I limit this to only two hours, the only question is what would I do for fun?"

He let out a long, pained sigh.

"That's your choice too. I could be here with you every day, if you'd only let me. We could spend our lives together."

"No. We've discussed this. As long as we work together, we can't have that type of relationship. Weekends and vacations, and only if we go out of town. That's it, and I'm not budging."

His blue eyes didn't hide his sadness very well.

"You know we talked about it," she continued in a softer voice, "you know why I can't. It would be risky for us both, for the entire team. We can't, and you know that. Even if Tom doesn't mind, I do."

"Then let's get going," he said, trying to put some cheer in his voice and mostly failing.

She took a quick shower, changed, and got ready for their weekend trip at his cabin up in the mountains near Alpine. He grabbed her bag, opened the door for her, and loaded the bag in the trunk of his black Mercedes G-Class.

Alex turned on her heels and headed back into the house.

"Be right there, I forgot something," she said, as she closed the door behind her.

She went straight for the blue bedroom. She pulled the window curtains shut, turned on the powerful track lights, and took several pictures of her crazy wall with her phone. Satisfied, she turned off the lights, pulled the curtain that concealed the corkboard shut, and locked the main door on her way out. *Two hours, four hours, whatever, but who's counting?*

"I'm ready," she said, smiling, and hopped in the car. "Let's go."

President Piotr Abramovich, the most powerful man in Russia, felt nothing, if not powerless, that morning, irritated by his prime minister's continued inability to name a new defense minister.

Arkady Dolinski, the chair of his government, just couldn't get it right. He had suggested a few names, but none of those generals had what it took to drive Abramovich's military vision. They were weak, comfortable with their set ways and their overflowing vodka guts. None of them was the crusader Abramovich was looking for.

He missed Dimitrov, his former minister of defense, his old friend Mishka. Abramovich paced his Kremlin office slowly, remembering the last time he'd seen him. Hearing that a critical intelligence operation had failed, Dimitrov had collapsed of a heart attack right there, on that rug, breaking the Bohemian crystal coffee table on his way down. He didn't die that day, though. He recovered, but Abramovich had no other choice but to announce his retirement to the entire world.

Almost five months later, the defense minister seat on Russia's government was still empty. Dimitrov's shoes were hard to fill. Abramovich still remembered the days when they had worked together in the First Chief Directorate of the KGB, in Foreign Operations. It was the two of them and Myatlev, all three united by their ambition, their willingness to pay all costs only to win, advance, and lead, and their pledge to have one another's backs, regardless of circumstances.

Unlike Myatlev, Abramovich's early life hadn't benefitted from having a father as a high-ranking KGB officer. His parents had been blue-collar workers in a system that squeezed them dry and spat them out, sick and forgotten. After a life-long struggle, working twelve-hour days in noisy, toxic manufacturing plants, followed by standing in long lines to buy the bare necessities of food and supplies, his parents didn't even live long enough to make it to retirement. His mother had died of bone cancer, her screams of pain waking up their entire neighborhood for weeks. His father had a stroke before he reached age fifty, leaving young Piotr to figure out how to survive on his own.

He had sworn to himself he'd never follow in their footsteps. Not him. Let the rest of the Russians sweat their lives away in god-forsaken factories. That life was not good enough for him. He was going to be different. He was going to have it all.

He had to claw his way into the system and hadn't hesitated in doing so. He'd started at the ground level, at eighteen, fresh out of high school with no other place to go that would have been in alignment with his ambitions. He joined the KGB's Seventh Directorate as an entry-level surveillance agent, locked in windowless rooms and listening all day to the conversations that key party leaders had in their secretly bugged homes.

Most Russians knew there was no such thing as a private conversation in the apparent privacy of one's home. The KGB bugged private residences without hesitation, especially those belonging to men and women holding ranks of power in the Communist Party of the Soviet Union. Even though they suspected their homes could be under surveillance, the occasional slipup still happened, and Abramovich was there to hear it, record it, and use it. A political joke told by a visiting relative, a snide or bitter comment, or just the stating of a simple fact, such as the absence of heating on a cold winter day, could be easily taken out of context, manipulated, and turned into a life-ending report.

Abramovich figured out that once he filed his reports, most of the people in question were never heard from again. Inspired by the newly gained awareness of his secret power, he started building a strategy.

His boss was easy to manipulate and quite indifferent, but his boss's boss, a man named Konev, was a hardheaded, old-school idiot who disliked him and was never going to let him advance. Abramovich spread the seeds of doubt regarding Konev's allegiances, and then offered to the right people to bug Konev's home and spend a couple of weeks recording his conversations.

A few days later, carefully edited tapes played back, in front of a shocked audience, the voice of unsuspecting Konev responding to his wife's comment about the scarcity of meat in their meals with a phrase expressing angrily that the situation had gone on long enough, was intolerable, and he was going to do something about that. Only Abramovich knew that Konev had said that phrase in the context of his ten year old getting bad marks in school. Abramovich had learned how to cut tape, edit, adjust the sound levels to make it smooth, and recopy the edited pieces onto a brand new tape. He had also learned how to dispose of the fragments, how to destroy magnetic tape without leaving a trace of evidence behind.

Last he had heard, Konev was being shipped to Perm-36, a forced labor camp administered by the GULAG. The GULAG, just as dreaded as it was notorious, was an acronym for the Russian Main Administration of Corrective

Labor Camps and Labor Settlements; in short, the forced labor camps management.

Konev never resurfaced; few people who entered the GULAG's camps ever did. But Konev was not the only one Abramovich had sent to Perm-36; he was just the first.

In recognition for his exemplary work in the identification and capture of an enemy of the people, Abramovich was offered the chance to enter the Dzerzhinsky Higher School of the KGB. He took the opportunity enthusiastically and started on the path to become a career KGB officer. He was only twenty-two.

At Dzerzhinsky he met both Myatlev and Dimitrov, just as young and ambitious as he was, and their early friendship evolved into a mutually benefitting long-term alliance, forged to help one another propel their careers. They grew to rely on one another, even trust one another to some extent. People like them knew better than to fully trust anyone.

Then Abramovich started ascending to power. His reputation for ruthlessness and his deep knowledge about how to destroy lives parted the crowds in front of him; nothing and no one stopped him on his way up. No one who wanted to stay alive or see his or her family again dared oppose unrelenting Abramovich.

After graduation, he had the choice of service, and he chose to lead a small division within the Fifth Chief Directorate reporting to Lavrentiy Beria, later known to have been responsible for the political abuse of psychiatry in the USSR. Fascinated by the incredible power he'd have in that role, he didn't go for the coveted Foreign Intelligence unit in the First Chief Directorate. Although foreign intelligence was his next goal, he wanted to learn new ways to control opponents, to extract information, and to incarcerate indefinitely without anyone questioning the validity of his decisions. What better place to do all that than the psychiatric unit?

Anyone who was a dissident, who said anything or did anything that contradicted the communist dogma, could happen to have a nervous breakdown. Sluggish schizophrenia was a popular diagnosis at that time. Any such diagnosis required admission for treatment in a special psychiatric ward, bitterly yet unofficially known as *psikhushka*, a Russian term for what would freely translate as the loony cage. These psychiatric wards were nothing more than psychiatric detention centers, where unwanted dissidents were chemically brainwashed into long-term, quiet obedience, and forgotten there until they drew their last breaths.

Of course, any dissident could have a public nervous breakdown if the right drugs were administered, with or without their knowledge. Abramovich learned a lot about drugs, manipulation with drugs, and information extraction under the influence of drugs. Thus, he became an even more successful, feared, and unstoppable career KGB officer.

He gave punitive psychiatry almost two years of his life. Then he moved on to Foreign Intelligence, where his newly acquired pharmacology knowledge enabled him to get above average results in the extraction of information from both willing and unwilling participants. Seven successful years later, he left Foreign Intelligence, having yet again a choice of careers in front of him. He chose the Second Chief Directorate, dedicating himself to learning the ropes of internal political control. He was thirty-five and a major general, the youngest ever to hold that rank, multiple decorations adorning the uniform he wore with immense pride.

The path opened for Abramovich's political ascension. He was a general during Gorbachev's tenure at the Kremlin, and watched in horror how that reckless traitor was dismantling the USSR and selling the parts. Right when he was so close to holding supreme power in his country, the USSR was disappearing right in front of his powerless eyes.

There was no way he could fight Gorbachev and stop his damned glasnost. He tried and failed on multiple occasions. Gorbachev was fiercely pro-West; he strongly believed in all that transparency and reform bullshit that was going to ruin Russia and bring it to its knees. They were all at the mercy of Western puppeteers who had made fools out of Gorbachev and all his followers.

When the KGB dismantled, he was forty years old and more decided than ever to take the Kremlin one day and restore his country's lost greatness. It took some effort. He had to adapt to a changing political landscape, new entrants in the game, and new political structures emerging all around him. Ultimately, people feared the same things, whether in communism or democracy, and he knew how to master those fears.

The Kremlin was his now and had been for a few years. He was almost midway through his third term as president, proving again that he could achieve the impossible. He had started his path to reconstruct Russia's fallen greatness. The urgency of his vision kept him up at night, counting the years he had left before he'd win the supreme game of his career.

Few people embraced or even understood his vision, and his tolerance for them was wearing thin. He hadn't grown any more patient with the passing of years; he often felt he was running a desperate race against time, the world, against everyone.

Abramovich slowed his pacing enough to grab a quick shot of vodka from the readily available bottle of Stolichnaya waiting on ice near his new coffee table. Grabbing ice cubes with his fingers he let them drop in a glass, and covered them with the clear liquid. He took a large gulp, letting out air in a satisfied, audible expression of satisfaction, typical for Russian career drinkers. Then he went to his desk and pressed a button.

"Da, gospodin prezident?"

"Get Dolinski in here."

Minutes later, after a quick knock on the door, his prime minister entered.

"Dolinski, tell me you have a defense minister."

Dolinski kept his head lowered, eyes fixated on the floor.

"Gospodin prezident, I have a couple of names you might want to consider."

"Like whom?"

"General Sokol would be a good fit. He's old guard, a hardliner, combative."

"He's a hundred years old, for fuck's sake, Dolinski, what the hell? I need someone who's going to *live* long enough to make things happen. Someone who can still think of war, want a war, start a war."

"Then General Chaplinski would be great. He's only sixty years old, very determined, a great leader."

"Do you think Chaplinski shares my vision? In his heart? Or just does it lip service? Is he a communist or United Russia?"

United Russia had become the leading political party after the fall of communism. It was non-ideological in nature, a party uniting all the politically disoriented survivors of almost a century of communism. But as a member and former leader of United Russia, Abramovich knew that anyone could function under the colors of United Russia and have their own hidden agendas.

"He's United Russia. Did you want a communist for defense minister? How would the world see that?"

"Screw the world, Dolinski, I don't care about what they see and don't see. This is about making Russia great again, not about impressing the damn West. The West can go to hell, and if I can help make that happen, I will. Stop trying to kiss the West's ass, Dolinski. Do you still have the balls to do your job? Or has it castrated you already, left you impotent?"

Abramovich's voice had reached thunderous levels, his anger taking over. He gulped the remaining vodka and slammed the empty glass on his desk.

"N–no, sir," an intimidated Dolinski managed to utter.

"I'm surrounded by impotents." Abramovich continued to pontificate from the bottom of his lungs. "No one has the guts to help me get back what's ours, what has always been ours. Where are the great men of Russia? Where are the fearless leaders of tomorrow, our brave generals? Doesn't anyone have what it takes to get me results? To think and plan great things? Who's been handling defense since Dimitrov retired, and what have they accomplished?"

"Umm... I worked with Generals Chaplinski and Sokol to keep things in motion until we name a new defense minister."

"Is that what you think this country needs? Keeping things in motion?"

"We continued to execute the plan set by Minister Dimitrov before he retired. The readiness for engagement, the incursions outside the national territories, even Division Seven."

"How's our readiness?" Abramovich's tone dropped to almost normal levels.

"It's going according to plan. We've restored to 100 percent readiness all our missile sites, nuclear submarines, and military jets. We've conducted exercises and assessed the readiness levels of our ground forces. We've taken an updated inventory of our arsenals and started research and production on every item we still need. We estimate that by midsummer we will have all our arsenals replenished as per the former minister's plan."

Abramovich started pacing again, slowly, pensively.

"Get me more," he said after a few seconds. "Get me more than what the plan called for. Revise the plan and bring it to me for review. I know START limits our arsenal counts, but I want to have bigger nukes, new planes, more powerful nuclear submarines. Double the fleet of Borei submarines, get rid of all the junk. And authorize more funds for nuclear research. Put all of that in your plan."

"Umm... how about funding? We're running out of funding for defense. With the sanctions, it's been hard."

"Screw the sanctions. Take from somewhere else. Social security, education, health, I don't care. Raise some taxes. Just make it happen."

"Yes, gospodin prezident."

Abramovich dismissed Dolinski with a wave of his hand, and Dolinski disappeared, closing the door quietly behind him.

Dolinski might be able to pull it off, but he still needed a good defense minister. No, he needed a great one.

The day held several firsts for Henri. Her first time at the White House. Her first time going anywhere with Director Seiden. Her first time in the same room with the president. She hoped she'd rise to the occasion and make Seiden proud.

"We should get started shortly," Seiden said, "we're his first agenda item. That always helps."

She nodded, not sure what to say. Seiden read right through her self-imposed calm.

"You'll do fine. Just remember what we discussed. Keep it short and clear, no speculation. Short phrases, minimum words, keep it simple. And it's OK to say that you'll have an answer in a few days if you're not sure about something."

"Uh-huh, yes, sir," she confirmed.

"This is a briefing, not a brainstorming session. Only confirmed facts and finalized analyses, got it?"

"Yes, sir."

"You can take your seats in the conference room now," a staffer said, and showed them the way. "Would you like anything to drink? Coffee, tea, water?"

"Thank you, we're good," Seiden replied for both of them.

An assistant took a seat at the remote part of the table, getting ready to take notes.

President Krassner entered, followed closely by two of his advisors.

Brief introductions identified General Foster, the president's military advisor, a tall, proud man in uniform, with his chest covered in decorations, and Norbert Purvis, the national security advisor, who looked more like a businessman than a politician.

"Good morning, everyone," Krassner said, "let's hear it."

Going straight to the point, Doug Krassner was exactly how Henri thought he'd be, after seeing him on television on numerous occasions. Krassner had the reputation to be a smart, open-minded, and gutsy leader, willing to go a little differently about things and break some molds if that meant progress.

"Mr. President," Seiden greeted him with deference, "thank you for seeing us on such short notice."

"What's on your mind, director?"

"This, sir," Seiden said, pushing slightly forward Henri's report, bound nicely in report covers bearing the CIA insignia in gold emboss.

"I flipped through some pages," Krassner said, "makes for a very interesting read. So... we've entered Cold War two-dot-oh, huh? Great way to start my presidency." Krassner smiled, an open smile not in the least bitter.

"Two-dot-oh, sir?" Seiden asked.

"My technology advisor said the new Cold War will involve technology way more than we'd anticipated. He came up with Cold War 2.0 instead of Cold War II, and it stuck."

Everyone chuckled lightly.

Krassner cleared his throat quietly. "OK, let's get started. What do you think this means?" He pointed at the report.

"War, sir," Seiden replied. "Maybe not now, not this year, but definitely going toward war. Crimea might have been the trigger for a chain of events leading to global conflagration."

"Can Russia go to war with the entire Western world? NATO is a powerful alliance."

"My analyst suggested that we shouldn't think of Russia in the traditional way, as planning to go to war directly and amassing thousands of tanks and troops in a direct, open invasion. Marino and her team think this war will be different, based on the profile they've built for President Abramovich and his actions to date."

Krassner turned slightly to face Henri.

"What do you think these military actions are about?"

"Sir, I think these incursions are testing our response times, our response procedures, and our response strength. Overall, they're testing our response, or wearing out our vigilance while testing our response."

Seiden looked away briefly to hide his irritation. The incursions analysis was not completely finalized. Yet she was venturing a non-substantiated hypothesis, the exact opposite of what they had discussed on their way in. Well aware of that, Henri swallowed hard and mentally prepared to walk on thin ice. Whatever the risk for her career, Krassner needed to know the facts ASAP. It was an acceptable risk, if she were to be proven wrong. Much better than taking the risk of informing Krassner a few days too late.

"What for?" Krassner asked.

"Nothing good, that's for sure," she blurted. Without turning her head, she caught Seiden flashing an angry glance toward her.

"That's an understatement," Krassner commented. "Can you venture some guesses?"

"Umm... sure. I think they could be testing our response to figure out where and how to conduct a first strike. That's one theory. Another theory is that they could be conducting these territorial displays of aggression to distract us, while they're looking to launch ballistic missiles. The missiles scenario is covered in my report. In addition, a third scenario is that they could be doing these close-call incursions in the hope that someone on our side gets nervous and engages by accident. Although, in all fairness, I don't see them caring too much about who started it, or who's to blame. Abramovich is beyond that. He just wants vengeance for the Crimea sanctions and the public humiliation they brought him."

"If you were to choose one scenario, which one do you think is the most plausible?"

She hesitated a little before answering, wondering, as many other people had wondered lately, how sure she was. Very.

"I'd have to say scenario two, sir. I'd have to go with the nuclear-strike scenario."

Silence fell thick, lingering for a few seconds that seemed like hours. Krassner opened the report and briefly browsed through it, making a quick note on one of the pages.

Then he looked up at Henri again.

"What do you think of my technology advisor's opinion, with respect to the new cold war? Do you think he has a point?"

She hesitated, not sure whether the question was directed at her or at Seiden.

"Can you venture a guess which technologies would be more interesting to acquire or develop to consolidate our offensive and defensive positions?"

Krassner was looking straight at her, and so was Seiden, who nodded discreetly.

"Mr. President, I don't have this analysis completed. I can look into this issue and prepare a report in a matter of days."

"You're an analyst, right? Then analyze, speculate with us. Let's hear what you think."

Krassner wasn't going to give her any room to maneuver out of the situation. She might as well use the opportunity to tell him what she thought. Henri took a deep breath before speaking, reminding herself to slow her machine-gun verbalization to an easier-to-follow delivery rhythm.

"Mr. President, I think technology should be a much higher focus for the US military. *Should have been* would be the right way to put it. We need to allow innovation to penetrate our weapons systems, aircraft, communications, everything technology.

"The backbone of our Air Force is based on thirty- to forty-year-old concepts. The fifth-generation jets are coming into service way too slow. So slowly, they're already somewhat out-of-date by the time they become operational. We fly the same planes as we did thirty years ago. Maybe they're not thirty years old, but their concepts are. Yet most of us can't stomach having a car older than eight years."

"Enough," Seiden whispered into her ear, barely audible. She clammed up promptly.

"Not at all, let her continue," Krassner said.

She cleared her throat, suddenly constricted by seeing how stiff the president's military advisor seemed. His pursed lips, flanked by two deep ridges formed around his mouth by an expression of offended consternation, were conveying a clear message. Drilling, unforgiving eyes focused on hers with an intensity she hadn't encountered too often. She decided to lay off the fighter jets for a while.

"We put satellites into orbit at roughly five to seven times the cost that other countries spend to do the same thing. Private entrepreneurs can figure out how to build rockets and move cargo into space cheaper and faster than NASA."

She paused for a few seconds, waiting to see if they wanted her to continue. Krassner made an inviting gesture with his hand.

"Did you know that European countries are significantly more advanced in their search for clean energy? They are decades ahead of us. The list can continue, but the bottom line is that our traditional resistance to change has cost us dearly in terms of progress. The weapons we build are clunky, obsolete and carry huge price tags. They're not efficient; they don't make use of modern technologies, light materials, process innovation (like three-dimensional printing), or materials innovation, such as carbon fiber molding. The Chinese have already 3D-printed an apartment building and are manufacturing light jets made from carbon fiber: light, maneuverable, and fuel-efficient. Yet we build the same clunky rust buckets designed in the fifties, so I would say yes, your advisor was definitely right. Technology will definitely play a role in future war strategy, from more perspectives than just cyber warfare. By the way, I think we're actually doing fairly well in cyber warfare. At least, courtesy of the NSA, we seem to be better prepared in that area."

"Please continue," Krassner said. "What would you do?"

"Well, we did make some progress in the past decades, not much, but we've made some. Unmanned flight, stealth technologies, computing power, all these new technologies gave us immense strategic advantages. We just need to continue on this path. For each area, we should drive innovation before we spend trillions more ineffectively on antiquated technology. I'd also focus on revamping NORAD and our antimissile defense; it might come in handy sooner than we'd like. We also need to observe more, to find out what's out there, to, well," she chuckled slightly, thinking of paraphrasing a known movie title, "to spy hard. For many years, we've been focused on GWOT and forgot all our other enemies. Global war on terror must continue, but we need to redeploy in other areas." Seeing Seiden's consternated look, she added quickly, "In my humble opinion."

Krassner smiled.

"Thank you for your candor and original thoughts; they'll keep us busy for a while." He turned slightly and looked toward Seiden. "Director Seiden, as soon as the intrusions analysis is complete, I want it on my desk. Let's talk strategic response immediately; get it set up."

Krassner walked briskly out of the conference room, followed closely by his two advisors and his assistant. Seiden and Henri left immediately after them, heading for the parking garage.

Alone with Seiden in the car, she allowed herself to take a deep breath.

"Sir, am I fired?"

"Not sure yet," Seiden replied without a trace of humor in his voice. "This wasn't like any other presidential briefing I have attended, that's for sure. Put some numbers together to substantiate your theories on those Russian incursions. Write your report, do the most thorough work you're capable of. Ideally, do that before presenting to me, to anyone, especially the president. But in this case, keep me posted as you go, tell me what you find, as soon as you find it."

"Are you concerned I might be wrong in my theories?"

"No... I'm afraid you might be right."

Vitaliy Myatlev enjoyed the crisp winter air and the fading sunshine on his home's terrace. Bundled up in a long astrakhan fur coat and matching hat, he sat on the lounge chair smoking his cigar and drinking vodka, impervious to the frigid air.

He loved the feeling that the terrace gave him. Offering a great vantage point, he could see in all directions for miles, while enjoying privacy and peace when lounging on the imported patio furniture. It was this terrace that had tipped the scale and made him fork out almost seven-hundred-thousand dollars for the villa. The colonial-style, two-story, white mansion had six bedrooms, four baths, a sauna, and a Jacuzzi suite, and the fantastic terrace spread out over almost two-thousand square feet.

His staff took great care of the terrace. The snow was removed promptly as soon as it fell, the patio furniture cleaned and dried, and gas patio heaters imported from America had been installed in the appropriate spots. That was where Myatlev liked to sit and think about the important things in his life.

He felt comfortable there, whether night or day. He felt on top of the world, unperturbed, untouchable, superior, and that sat very well with his ambitious nature. One of the richest men alive, Myatlev was a true Russian oligarch with global interests in banking, gas, oil, and whatever else he could think of.

A former foreign intelligence KGB officer, and now a talented businessman, Myatlev knew how to seize opportunity and put it to work, and he had done that aggressively since the day Russia had started to turn from communism to capitalism. Self-made and uncompromising, he had the innate talent to spot favorable circumstances or events and to construct the fastest, most profitable, business enterprises exploiting such circumstances.

Decisive, fast, unscrupulous, and ferociously ambitious, Myatlev was never satisfied. He forged ahead in quick bursts, building enterprise after enterprise and launching initiative after initiative, amassing wealth at a stunning rate.

Yet not everything was perfect in his world. Unaccustomed to defeat, Myatlev still ground his teeth, thinking of the recent failure he had suffered. His plan had been perfect, majestic. The execution had been spot on, carefully monitored by him personally, step after carefully planned step. It should have never failed, yet it did, and the unknown reasons behind that failure kept him up at night. That ill-fated failure could still get him killed.

That's why Myatlev appreciated a place where he could unwind, put his thoughts in order, and prepare for new challenges, new opportunities. His Kiev villa offered that perfect spot, unique among all his other properties. He was never going to sell the villa.

He signaled his bodyguard, Ivan, for some more vodka. Ivan topped his glass promptly, adding several ice cubes to it. He took a sip, inhaled the harsh alcohol vapors, and took another sip.

His cell phone came to life and caused Myatlev to frown. He took it out of his pocket and, seeing the name on the display, his frown deepened as he cussed under his breath before picking up.

"Gospodin prezident, what a pleasure!" Myatlev managed to sound sincere.

"Vitya, yes, it's Petya; you recognized me!" Russian president Piotr Abramovich sounded glad to hear him, almost cheerful, which could prove even more dangerous than the alternative.

They exchanged pleasantries for several minutes in typical Russian fashion when old friends catch up. They recounted their recent holiday meals and guest lists, recommended new exotic foods to each other, and gossiped about mutual acquaintances. Then Abramovich switched gears abruptly and got to the point.

"Vitya, I want you to come visit with me. We need to talk."

Abramovich sounded very determined. Myatlev felt his blood freeze in his veins.

"It will be my pleasure, Petya," he managed, "just give me a few days to wrap things up here. I'm in the middle of something big, you know."

"Ha ha, aren't you always," Abramovich laughed. "All right, but don't make it too long. I need to see you."

Myatlev ended the call with trembling hands. He had been a fool to think that if he moved to Ukraine he could escape Abramovich. He had failed his mission, and Abramovich was not a forgiving man. His epic defeat had caught up with him. There was nowhere on Earth where he could hide from the fallout.

He gulped the remaining vodka in his glass and decided to go inside. He needed to come up with a plan.

Holding the door open for him, Ivan asked, "Are you OK, boss? You look pale."

Vernon Blackburn rarely left his office at 5.00PM sharp. He felt uncomfortable busting through the gates among the masses of blue-collar, younger employees. Most engineers rarely went home on time. He felt almost embarrassed making his way through security at the exit and waiting in line after several exempt employees, but today he just had to get out of that office. He couldn't breathe in there... He'd tried to open the window, dropped the thermostat setting to 68 degrees, but nothing helped. He had to get out.

As he climbed behind the wheel of his Jeep Grand Cherokee he took a deep breath, the first deep breath he'd been able to take in more than an hour. He was ready to go home.

He started the slow commute, lined up behind several other cars crawling out of the parking structure in the five o'clock rush. A few minutes later, he picked up speed, driving eastbound on Virginia Beach Boulevard. Then he approached the stoplight at the corner of Virginia Beach and 460. If he took a right turn, that would lead him to I-264 then I-464, on the road to his home in Chesapeake. A left turn would take him to his favorite bar on Lafayette, the 1700 Somewhere. Nope, he was going to go home this time, he promised himself. He preselected for the right turn and set the blinker on, waiting for the light to turn green and letting his mind wander.

The car behind his Jeep honked twice, startling him. The light had turned green and cars were zooming past him. On an impulse, without any thought or concern for the fast-moving cars coming from behind, he cut all lanes and made a left turn, pedal to the metal, among screeching tires and a concert of angry honks. Once he made it out of the intersection he slowed down, resuming his normal, calm driving demeanor and rubbing his forehead furiously. All right, just one drink, just one, he promised himself again. Maybe this promise he could keep.

His watering hole of choice was a bar aptly named 1700 Somewhere. The owner, retired Navy, had rebranded to military time one of the world's most famous excuses for a drink. This time it was 1700 right here where he was, and he needed no excuse. The blue light of the bar's neon sign looked inviting in the darkening dusk.

He parked his Jeep on the side of the building and went straight inside.

Vernon was a regular; the bar was almost empty, and the bartender didn't wait for any order. He filled a glass promptly with double bourbon on the rocks and placed it on a napkin in front of him.

Vernon liked this familiarity, this sense of belonging that comes from being a regular in a place, any place. It almost felt like home in a twisted kind of way for the mentally weary, exhausted man in search of a break between work and family.

He held the glass with both hands, playing with it and making the ice cubes clink in the liquid as he swirled the glass gently. He cherished this moment, the furtive moment when he still had a drink in front of him, still having something to look forward to before resuming the dullness of his daily existence.

He looked at the familiar walls, decorated with identical clocks showing the time in various places of the Earth, labeled neatly as if the bar were some kind of special operations room at the CIA.

The walls wore the patina of time gracefully. Still showing traces of the era when smoking was permitted indoors, those walls were a living memory of the times when people were allowed to gratify their senses with more than just alcohol.

He almost didn't notice the woman taking a seat to his left at the bar. He felt her scent first, a fine, expensive hint of French perfume. He decided it was French, but he wasn't really sure. That's what French perfumes smelled like in his mind: discreet, classy, and almost arousing.

Vernon turned to look at the woman, making eye contact with her for a split second. She wasn't the typical barhopper looking for action. She was neatly dressed in a tight skirt and silk blouse, and her high-heeled shoes looked expensive.

She didn't shy away from the eye contact; he did. But before looking away he had noticed the beginning of an inviting smile on the woman's perfectly glossy lips.

She touched his arm gently to get his attention.

"Hi," she said, almost whispering. "I'm Michelle."

He turned to look at her, surprised. In the rare occasions he had started conversations with women in bars, he had initiated them, not the other way around.

He was relatively attractive, in his early forties, wearing his six feet even quite well and enjoying the artistic looks given by his brown hair, almost at shoulder length, and a neatly trimmed beard. Most people took him for an artist, actor, or musician rather than an engineer, a laser electro-optics engineer no less, holding a PhD in laser applications.

Vernon enjoyed his bohemian appearance a lot and cultivated it carefully, ever since that day in junior college when Samantha, a long-legged dazzling blond two years his senior, had invited him to take a hike because, according to her, nerds never got laid. He let his hair grow that fateful, abstinent summer, combing it back and growing a beard that gave him an early air of maturity. Samantha acknowledged the improvement the following fall by becoming the second notch in his belt, standing proof that artists got laid a lot, even if nerds didn't. After all, his looks got him all the action, not his student ID card.

"Vernon," he replied, turning toward the stranger. They shook hands. "What can I get you?"

"Whatever you're having," she murmured, smiling and touching his arm again.

He gestured the bartender who executed promptly, placing new drinks in front of them.

They clinked their glasses and laughed quietly, in an unspoken greeting.

She looked at his left hand holding his glass.

"I see you're married," she probed, pointing at his wedding band.

"Yes, I am," Vernon said.

"Will your wife be joining you later?"

He almost groaned loudly. He didn't need any of this shit.

"Listen," he said in a rigid tone of voice, "I'm not exactly asking you what you're going back home to, all right? I'm actually not asking you anything whatsoever."

"Fair enough," she replied unfazed, touching his thigh. She squeezed it gently, a couple of inches above his knee, in an unmistakable invite.

He looked her straight in the eyes, searching for a confirmation. She didn't blink, didn't avert her eyes. He waved at the bartender, gave him a twenty to pay for the drinks, and grabbed Michelle's hand. She followed him without hesitation as he took her behind his SUV, parked on the darkest side of the parking lot. He slammed Michelle against the wall, hidden from view by the Jeep, and searched her eyes again. She smiled.

He kissed her passionately, almost angrily, holding her with one arm and gently caressing her breast, almost in contradiction with the strength of his kisses. She replied, searching for his belt buckle with probing fingers. He pulled her skirt up and lifted her on his hips, pushing her against the wall, and she responded, clasping her hands behind his neck to hold on. Then he ripped her panties and penetrated her with an urgency he hadn't expected to feel for a complete stranger.

A few minutes later, Vernon set her down and zipped up his pants. He avoided her eyes, focusing on his boots instead.

"I'm sorry…" he mumbled. "You probably deserve much better than this."

"Vernon," she said, reaching out to touch his face.

He turned and left, ignoring her call. He hopped in his Jeep and drove away, managing to avoid any eye contact with Michelle.

"Damn fool," he admonished himself bitterly as he took the highway to Chesapeake to go home.

Vitaliy Myatlev sat in front of his computer, in the comfort of his home office housed in the Kiev villa. Almost two weeks had passed since Piotr Abramovich had called and invited him for a visit to the Kremlin. Almost two weeks of anguish, of sleepless nights, and careful planning.

Abramovich was famous for throwing people in the depths of Siberia for lesser shortcomings. Myatlev knew he couldn't hide forever in his Kiev fortress, and there was nowhere else he could go. Abramovich had already run out of patience and had called him again, reminding him in a firmer tone of voice of his standing invitation. He had continued to sound friendly on the phone, but that friendliness could change on a dime. The Russian president was notoriously unpredictable and easily offended.

Myatlev had spent the past weeks moving assets, waiting for bank transfers to complete, organizing his vast operations to be led from outside Russia, and preparing for the worst-case scenario. He hoped Abramovich hadn't learned of his activities, but Myatlev was no fool. Abramovich's internal state security, the all-feared FSB, was everywhere, and even Myatlev's Kiev residence was not as secure as he liked to believe.

Myatlev had a long history of facing terrible odds fearlessly and coming out of dire situations unscathed. The KGB in his earlier career, followed by his years of service as an intelligence officer, had taught him how to sense danger and prepare for it. Then he had applied all he had learned in the emerging post-glasnost capitalist economy, building his fortune. Business had proven to be just as treacherous to navigate as foreign intelligence had been. That's why he always had a back-door exit built into his plans. He always prepared for the worst-case scenarios, and he always survived.

This time he wasn't so sure. He was missing critical information. What if Abramovich had his home in Moscow under surveillance, waiting for him to show up? The FSB could arrest him the moment he'd walk through that door. What if the FSB had already raided the place, opening his safe and turning his secrets into incriminating evidence, enough to put him away for the rest of his life? There was only one way to find out.

"Ivan?" Myatlev called his bodyguard and assistant, who came promptly.

"Boss?"

"I need you to help me with something." He paused, thinking what amount of information would be safe to share with Ivan at this point. The less he knew, the better off he'd be.

"Yes, sir," Ivan acknowledged.

"I need you to go to the house in Moscow and bring me some documents."

"Yes, sir."

"I'm going to trust you with some very critical information, Ivan, I hope you will not disappoint me."

"*Nyet*, Vitaliy Kirillovich, you can count on me," he replied, addressing his boss with the utmost deference, by his given name and patronymic

"I will give you the combination to my safe and trust you to bring everything in it to me, right away."

"Your safe, boss?" Ivan looked confused, almost scared. The man, an ex-Spetsnaz, who didn't hesitate to kill with his bare hands, seemed flustered at the thought of opening his boss's safe.

"Yes, Ivan, I trust you," Myatlev said. "Am I wrong to trust you?"

"N–no, sir, nyet."

Myatlev stopped for a second, thinking of the best way to do this. If he was right in his worst fears, Ivan was never to be heard from again. He hesitated a little, thinking whether to send Ivan on his personal jet, the Citation X. If worst came to worst the twenty-million dollar plane would be gone, confiscated by the FSB immediately after its wheels touched down on Russian soil. On the other hand, if he sent Ivan on a commercial flight he could be caught leaving the country with his documents, and those were enough to compromise him and start a shit storm, even if one hadn't already started yet. Ivan's life and the plane were the risk he had to take to ensure he could return safely to Moscow.

"I'm going to send you on my plane, and you can leave as soon as possible."

"Thank you, boss, consider it done."

"Bring me everything you find in my safe. Don't read anything, don't open anything, just grab it all, and bring it to me, understood?"

"Yes, sir. I will leave now."

Myatlev told Ivan how to access the safe and gave him the code, making him repeat the information. He tapped his empty glass with his index finger, and Ivan replenished his Stolichnaya dutifully before leaving the room.

He leaned back in his chair, feeling some relief. Soon he would know. But he wasn't safe here either, not entirely, although he was in a different country. Ukraine had been an independent country for many years, but the Russian president had armies of separatists operating within the Ukrainian border, a border that was becoming more irrelevant, especially after Crimea.

"Who am I kidding?" he muttered between two rounds of cursing that would have made career sailors jealous.

He got up from his desk and went to the safe in the corner of the room. He opened it and took all the papers out, sorting through them. A small pile went back into the safe. A larger pile accompanied him to the terrace, where Myatlev personally held each piece of paper as it burned, ashes blown by the wind staining the spotless white of the fresh-fallen snow.

Jeremy Weber sat in front of the TV, pretending to watch the Orioles clenched in a death match against the LA Dodgers. His mind wasn't in the game though; every minute or so he checked the time on his watch, wondering when his son would come home.

Michael, his sixteen-year-old son, had been pretty good about respecting the rules for being out on a school night. Never after eight; that was the rule. Two long hours after that 8.00PM had come and gone, Jeremy was trying to remain calm and think positive. He could be making out with some girl and forgot the time. He could be hanging out with friends and didn't care to come home.

Jeremy found it hard to think positive though. In his experience as an FBI agent, he had noticed that all family member accounts in cases of missing persons, homicides, kidnappings, or other tragedies started with the simple statement "he didn't come home last night." In this case, he was the family, the only family his son had.

He checked the time once more, then speed-dialed his son's cell. Again, it went straight to voicemail. He stood up, grabbed the untouched glass of scotch from the coffee table, and poured it in the sink. Then he grabbed his work laptop and powered it up.

He watched the Data Integration and Visualization System login screen load. His special-agent status gave him unrestricted access to the most powerful search tools available to the FBI. The DIVS compiled and cross-referenced data from the most used databases, allowing him a single-point access for any search.

He set the parameters of the search, but DIVS returned zero results. Michael wasn't in the system, but that didn't necessarily mean he was OK. It was time for some legwork, time to hit the streets.

He put his weapon holster on, checked the ammo in his gun, then put on a down jacket and packed its pockets with two spare clips for his Sig.

Noises came from the hallway as he opened his front door. Two uniformed officers were dragging his son out of the elevator, kicking and screaming. He stepped back and allowed them to enter, speechless. His son, his Michael, was high as a kite, his glazed-over eyes throwing fiery glares while drool was dripping out of the corners of his contorted mouth.

"Hey, Weber," one of the uniforms said, a guy looking vaguely familiar, "thought I'd do you a solid and bring him here instead of lockup."

"Yeah, yeah, much appreciated," Jeremy managed to say, shaking the officer's hand.

"Will you be OK from here?"

"Yeah, sure, I'll handle it."

Jeremy closed the door behind the two officers and turned to look at his son.

"Michael—"

"I hate you," his son yelled, then pounced and hit him in the chest with both fists. "I hate everything about you!"

Jeremy held his son tight against his chest, ignoring the punches and the muffled screams.

"I wish you were dead, you hear me? Dead! Why aren't *you* one of those feds who get killed on duty, huh?"

"It's OK, son, calm down, it's OK. It's the drugs. What did you—"

"Ha! I know! 'Cause only the good guys die... Assholes like you stay here fo'ever, makin' my life hell!"

"Tell me what you took, Michael."

He screamed from the top of his lungs, an unnatural sound resembling the shriek of a dying animal.

"Ev'ything! Ev'ything I could get my hands on, that's wha' I took!"

He was starting to slur, and that made Jeremy worry. He looked at his pupils again, dilated to the size of his green irises, glossy and fixated. They looked like they were made of glass, unnatural. He could feel his son's rapid heartbeat get even faster and saw sweat beads form on his forehead.

"We need to get you some help," Jeremy said, putting Michael gently on the sofa.

"We need you to die!" Michael wiped the drool of his mouth with his sleeve. "Should have been you who died, not Mom!"

He stopped, frozen in place, the pain hitting him in the gut. Almost seven years after his wife's death, the pain felt just as real and intense as if it were yesterday. Maybe his son was right. He had thought the same thing many times, but he couldn't dwell on it now. There wasn't any time.

He pulled out his phone and flipped through some contacts, finding the one he needed. It was almost midnight, but the man was a doctor; he'd understand.

The conversation took less than a minute. Jeremy sat on the sofa, next to his son, now curled up in the fetal position and breathing heavily.

"Listen, Michael, you need medical attention. There's an ambulance on its way that will take you to a rehab cen—"

"Go to fuckin' hell, and never come back!"

Maybe I'm already there, Jeremy thought bitterly.

"You'll stay there until you recover and I gain the confidence you'll never do this to yourself again. I'll come visit."

"Fuck yourself…" Michael mumbled, exhausted, his face buried in the sofa pillow.

It was almost 2.00AM when the ambulance finally left, taking Michael to the ER for stabilization, then to rehab. The EMS crew members sounded reassuring, saying they didn't think the episode would lead to any permanent brain damage.

Jeremy watched the ambulance turn the corner and disappear. Then he curled up on the sofa and sobbed, long, breathless sobs stifled in the pillow that still carried his son's scent. After a few moments, he slowly rose. Grabbing his keys, he headed out the door to the hospital. It was going to be a long night.

Major Evgheni Aleksandrovich Smolin hung up his office phone and started arranging his tie, getting ready to meet with his boss. The meeting was unscheduled; Colonel Markov had just called to invite him over for a quick chat.

Smolin straightened his tie and buttoned his uniform jacket, watching his reflection in the window overlooking Yasenevo District. He loved the elevated view of the district and, as he had climbed through the ranks of the Foreign Intelligence Service of the Russian Federation or SVR, his view had improved through the years, serving as a constant reminder of where he'd been and where he wanted to be. At forty-eight, he was just as ambitious as he'd been at twenty-three.

His career as an intelligence officer had started with a serious roadblock. Just when young Smolin was graduating from the university with a four-year degree in economics, recently turned twenty-three and dreaming of nothing else but to join the KGB, things were changing dramatically in Russia and the KGB was being dismantled. Smolin still recalled how he had learned the news on the radio and had rushed to Lubyanka Square, pleading with every man or woman exiting the building that day.

"Please help me," he had said to every KGB officer leaving the agency's headquarters that cold November morning in 1991, "I always wanted to join the KGB, could you please tell me where to go?"

"Go home, kid, it's over," some people answered. Others just ignored him.

He somehow managed to go against the flow and enter the building. He found the personnel office and asked for employment application forms. The personnel officer laughed in his face.

"Haven't you seen the news on TV? KGB is being dismantled, it's over. Done. Finished. Go home."

"Yeah, I know, but somebody will still have to do this work, right? A country can't function without security services, without intelligence officers. Dismantling or not, I want to apply for a job here."

The personnel officer stared at him as if he was some sort of a nut case. Smolin stood his ground.

"Please, sir, I've always wanted to work in intelligence. Please help me."

"All right, whatever; you're going to be Russia's own James Bond, I can see that," he said, offering him the employment forms bearing the KGB logo. "Fill these out, and if there's any recruiting happening in the next months I'll keep you in mind."

He went home happy and hopeful that day and didn't budge from the phone, waiting for the interview call. No call came for many weeks, and he soon lost hope. Every couple of weeks or so he'd try to reach that personnel officer, but he couldn't get him on the phone. He even went back to Lubyanka Square a few times, but he wasn't allowed inside the building.

Then one day the call finally came, taking him by surprise. A few weeks later, he entered formal training as an intelligence officer, after having persuaded the hiring manager that he could recruit anyone to do anything. He had made a powerful impression on his future leaders, his self-confidence and commitment opening the door for him to start in Directorate S—Illegal Intelligence.

His first assignment was to recruit a foreign national traveling on a short business trip. His mark was British, a corporate employee working in the research department for one of the major digital imaging companies in the West. She was scheduled to be in Moscow for twelve days, attending a series of conferences. By the sixth day she was turned, spending her nights in bed with Evgheni Smolin and her days gathering useful information that helped him promote his career. For years to come she had continued to send him passionate love letters and valuable information in the field of digital imaging, from medical applications to imaging data compression, satellite-image processing and mapping, encryption algorithms, and high-volume data storage solutions. She traveled to Moscow to see Smolin every few months or so, couriering the intel herself and making his job and his advancement really easy. Smolin did his part, keeping their flame alive, and his source of intel motivated and satisfied.

A tall, well-built man with blond hair and charming blue eyes, Smolin was a talented actor who could play any part. He could tell any lie without blinking and be very convincing at it. He was a natural.

His favorite story, the one he used on numerous traveling foreigners with access to useful intel, was that he had to get some valuable intelligence back to his bosses or suffer unspeakable cruelties at their hands. Either he brought good quality information, or he risked dying in some god-forsaken corner of Siberia, freezing to death in a nameless labor camp, just like his father had died. Nope, glasnost and perestroika hadn't changed the core issues of Russia, he was telling his marks. The same people held the power and influence, and Siberia was still there, waiting for him to fail.

They all fell for it, mostly women, but also a few men. They all worked hard to help the young, desperate, and sexy Russian who had no other choice. Only no element of his story was true. His father hadn't died, at least not yet, anyway. He hadn't even traveled outside of Moscow, not even once. A low-level mechanical engineer who worked in a machinery factory, the senior Smolin had failed to instill in his son the willingness to put in a hard day's work. Evgheni Smolin wanted to be in the elite, to see the world, to live adventurously.

His fame in the SVR was consolidated the day he received a commendation for a very successful operation on foreign soil. His boss, a little intoxicated at the time, had said about Smolin that, unlike the rest of the men in that room who thought with their dicks, Smolin fucked with his brain. A few weeks later, jokes about him were heard all over the building:

Why doesn't Smolin ever wear condoms? So his dick can ask questions when he fucks.

Why doesn't Smolin ever get blowjobs? Because his women need to keep on talking.

He was famous. He loved it.

A couple of successful recruiting missions in Germany, where his physical appearance and natural talent for foreign languages made him pass for a native, brought him recognition and advancement in the ranks of Directorate S. He enlisted the services of numerous Russian emigrants who were living in Germany, and those recruits stayed productive and in contact, although Smolin's methods were not always direct and honest, or charming. Some, he had to threaten. A few, he had to kill: stupid idealists who believed that if they made it to the West they were free of their obligations toward Mother Russia.

He knocked on his boss's door and entered, then stood at attention.

"Sit," Markov invited him. "Have you ever heard of Division Seven?"

"No, sir."

"Seven is an ultra-secret intelligence division, reporting directly to the minister of defense. Only the best of the best from the SVR, GRU, and FSB are invited to join Division Seven. Its mission is top secret, above my level."

"Sir?"

"You are being promoted, major. You have been selected for an urgent mission and you'll be joining Division Seven. You'll report tomorrow morning to the ministry of defense. Congratulations."

Smolin stood and saluted his soon-to-be former boss.

"Maxim Sergeyevich, it's been a privilege."

"Good luck. Make us proud!"

Smolin closed the door gently behind him as he left Markov's office. Then he allowed himself to smile, a wide smile filled with excitement.

Sylvia Copperwaite wore a pink halter dress, very little jewelry, and her blond hair tied in a simple ponytail. Her green eyes were focused intently and her forehead showed lines of strain as she evaluated her hand. Two kings, a jack, a ten, and a six. She could have used better luck.

She checked the other players briefly. The skinny guy at her left had a satisfied hint of a smile in his eyes. He had something. The swine across the table, the overweight, sweaty asshole who had made lecherous comments the entire evening looked worried. The guy in the blue shirt at her right showed nothing; he was impassible, apparently not even paying attention. Blue Shirt was dangerous.

She checked the diminishing pile of chips in front of her and took a leap of faith.

"Three, please," she asked the dealer, holding on to the kings and ditching everything else.

"Two," Blue Shirt asked.

"I'm good," said the skinny guy at her left. He was served, as they say in poker, which meant his hand had been strong from the start.

"Give me a slice of that," the swine said pointing at her, "and two great cards."

Sylvia flashed an angry glare across the table. She could always leave, but she wanted to play a couple more hands, that's all.

The dealer ignored the first part of the swine's request and delivered the two cards.

"I'm out," Blue Shirt said and folded.

"I'm in," declared Skinny, and threw a few chips in the pile.

Sylvia hesitated. Skinny Guy hadn't asked for cards, which in many cases meant he had a flush or full house. She checked her new cards. Another king and two nines. It was worth a shot, but she was gonna try to play it safe. She added a few chips and said, "Call."

A minute later the swine raked in the entire pot, brought to him by a full house aces high. He smiled at her and asked, "Would you care for some of this back, honey? There are a few ways I can think of."

"Yeah, like a good hand," she snapped.

"If you're into hand jobs, I'll take it," the swine commented.

"Your last warning," Blue Shirt said, "we're here to play cards, not insult each other. I will call the manager on you. We don't have to put up with your shit."

Sylvia blushed. Why hasn't she stood up for herself? Why hasn't she stood up, period? She could just leave, instead of sitting here, an easy target for the slimy worm across the table, and losing money on top of it all. *One more hand,* she decided, *then I'll go.*

The problem was she needed a big win. She'd had a streak of losing hands lately, emptying her bank accounts, maxing out her credit cards, and leaving her stranded. She needed a big win to make it to the next paycheck. The next paycheck, seven days away, was going to bring her some relief, but until then she was screwed. She had a good job and made a six-figure income as an electromechanical engineer, but her luck at cards needed serious improvement. She held a PhD in computational modeling, but couldn't model herself out of spiraling gambling debt.

Her next hand held a nice surprise, three aces, a seven, and a deuce. She asked for two cards, and got another ace. She went all in, not paying attention anymore to her opponents' tells. This was her last chance. Minutes later, she was cleaned out, losing in favor of a straight flush drawn by the swine.

She stood up, a little dazed, and made for the exit. The swine grabbed her hand as she walked pass him.

"Let me help you out of your bind, you beautiful thing," he said, licking his revolting lips. "I have a lot of money to spend. Let me make your day."

She yanked her hand from his grip and walked out of the casino, tears welling in her eyes. She approached her car and leaned against the hood, trying to regain balance, as her sobs grew louder and a wave of nausea hit her, causing her to convulse and vomit near the front left wheel.

She didn't feel sick because she was drunk. It was because for a split second she had considered taking the swine's offer for another chance to sit at that green table, play a few more hands, and maybe win it all back. She needed help.

Myatlev had three of his bodyguards lined up in his home office. Ivan, who'd just returned from Moscow the night before, stood half a step closer to Myatlev than the other two, reflecting his status in Myatlev's personal security detail.

"All right, Ivan, here's what we're going to do. I'll meet with President Abramovich in the next few days. I'll call his office and get an appointment. But we have to be prepared for anything."

"Sir?" Ivan seemed confused.

"Our friend Abramovich has a reputation for impulsiveness and for destroying people. You'll have to protect me, Ivan."

"Inside the Kremlin? *Bozhe moi...* "

The other two bodyguards shifted their weight from one foot to another, probably feeling uneasy at the thought of entering the Kremlin with guns in their hands.

Myatlev looked Ivan in his eyes. "Yes, inside the Kremlin."

"But... How?"

"You'll form three teams of four men each, all Spetsnaz, all strong and gutsy, in full tactical gear, armed with silenced MP5s. Pay them well, and then pay them some more. You, three others, and I will take the limo, the armored Bentley. The other two teams will take the G-Wagens."

"But how do we enter the Kremlin armed like that?"

"You won't. If you do, it will look like we're there to overthrow Abramovich."

"Huh?"

"You won't enter the Kremlin unless it's strictly necessary."

"I... I don't think I understand, Vitaliy Kirillovich."

"I'll be wearing that," Myatlev said, pointing at a new Breitling watch still sitting in its opened box. The yellow packaging resembled more of a toolkit than a watch case, and had Breitling Emergency Night Mission II branded on the lid and on the black shock-absorbing interior lining. The Breitling was a serious downgrade from Myatlev's half-a-million dollar Patek Philippe, but it came with serious advantages.

"And you'll be carrying this," Myatlev continued, handing Ivan a small device. "This watch has an emergency beacon built in. If I get in trouble, I'll press the button and you and your Spetsnaz will barge in and get me."

"And I'll see it on this?" Ivan gestured at the locator.

"Yes, yes. If I press the button, you'll see where I am. It works by satellite, just like GPS."

"Oh, good."

"But you have to move fast, Ivan. The moment you see the beacon, you storm the Kremlin, understood?"

"Y–yes."

"You'll be waiting outside, the Bentley in front of the entrance, and the G-Wagens around the corner, and wait for my signal. Are we clear?"

"Y–yes," Ivan replied, still hesitant.

"What's the problem?" Myatlev asked, impatiently. After all, it wasn't so damn hard.

"Are you saying you want us to shoot our way inside the Kremlin to get you out?"

"In case the beacon goes off, yes. Bring lots of ammo. Do you have a problem with that?"

"No, Vitaliy Kirillovich. Just making sure that's what you want. You can count on me."

"Good. You have seven days to get everything ready. Then we go to Moscow."

The sun had set and twilight had faded away, leaving a moonless night in its place. Yet the window curtains pulled shut didn't let a single hint of light be seen from outside, despite multiple powerful light bulbs flooding the blue room with a blinding light.

The corkboard covered in images, Post-it notes, and pushpins tied together with colored yarn hadn't changed much in the past few weeks, yet Alex studied it carefully, processing again every bit of information as if it was the first time she'd seen it.

Curled up in her armchair, legs folded underneath her and leaning against one of the armrests, she went over every milestone in her timeline, looking for anything she might have missed. Nothing new... nothing, whatsoever.

But there was a troublesome article in the newspaper she had just flipped through, a short entry about a near-miss incident involving a Russian military aircraft and a Canadian vessel in the Black Sea. Nothing had really happened, but Alex vaguely recalled a few of these incidents occurring in recent weeks, maybe even months.

She made a mental note to research it a little and see if anything out of the ordinary came to the surface, but it would all be speculation even if it did. There was no visible connection between any recent Russian military activity and the terrorist plot The Agency had just folded. None whatsoever... she was just reaching.

Her cell phone rang, almost startling her. She smiled, seeing the caller ID, then accepted the phone's prompt to encrypt the call. Ever since she'd started working on her last case, she'd been using cell-phone encryption software on every call, ensuring that her private conversations remained private.

"Sam!" she answered cheerfully, glad to hear from him.

"How are you, kiddo?"

"Great, just great," she answered excitedly. "I was just thinking of you. Were your ears burning?"

"Nah... just wanted to check on you, see how you are."

She paused for half a minute, not sure what to say.

"Well, I've been thinking," she started, "maybe there's a correlation between our case and these Russian military incidents?"

"Ah... Your mind still goes there, huh?"

"Yup," she confessed in a sheepish voice.

"Crazy wall and all that?"

"Yup."

He let out a long sigh.

"We might never catch him, kiddo, you know that, right? We discussed it."

"Yeah, but—"

"The *yeah buts* are not gonna cut it, you know. We talked about this. I've spent my entire life chasing spies and terrorists, and I haven't caught all of them, only some. The vast majority," he clarified further with pride, "yet not all of them."

"But you know what I mean, right? You've felt this; you've done this too, right?"

"What? Obsessing about some anonymous face that eluded me for years? Yes, and I almost lost my mind because of that. That's why I want you to be smarter than I was." He grinned, and she heard the smile in his voice.

"So, if you've done it too, how come you expect me to not wanna do the same? How can I let go? Who's gonna catch this guy?"

"Listen, kiddo, if anyone's gonna catch this guy, it's gonna be you, I promise you that much. But if you wanna have a real shot to catch this son of a bitch you have to let your mind be free of obsession, of bias and frustration. You have to be cold and factual, and see facts and data only where facts and data exist, not where you want them to exist."

"What do you mean by that?"

"There's no visible real, logical correlation between the Election Day plot and the Russian military incidents we've been reading about lately, yet you thought there might be one. Is that your gut talking? Or is that wishful thinking? Only you can answer this question. Only after you have become completely level headed and rational about this case. You need to stop caring about it from an emotional perspective, and only care about the intel—the facts, whatever the facts might tell you."

"Yeah, but that data might tell me we're never gonna find out who he is," she protested angrily.

"That might be true. But imagining correlations where there aren't any is not gonna help either."

She swallowed hard. "Right... What should I do then?"

"Just keep in mind that it's not over yet, but don't let it ruin your life. Be ready; get ready. Watch your back. Be aware of your surroundings. See if anyone is following you. Spend time at the firing range with Louie until you're better than he is."

"Ha! That's never gonna happen!"

"Are you sure? 'Cause I'm not!"

She fell silent for a minute, taking in his advice.

"I miss you, Sam. I miss your training, your friendship, your advice. I miss the life, the buzz of the action. I can totally see how someone can become addicted to this life."

"Of course you do," he laughed. "You're a natural born spy; it's in your DNA. Are you working on a case now?"

"Yeah, I'm support on Brian's new case," she said, letting a tad of disappointment color the inflexions in her voice.

"Is it an interesting case?" Sam probed.

"Yeah, they all are... to some extent."

They both burst into laughter at the same time.

"Not nearly as interesting as our last case, Sam, not even close. Just the typical, run-of-the-mill case."

"Just be patient, that's all. This country has many powerful, motivated enemies. Their interests will flush your Mr. X out from whatever hole he's been hiding in, and you'll be right there to nail him. Just hang tight, and I promise you he's out there and you'll get him one day."

"I'll hold you to that, OK?"

"Deal!"

Minutes after they'd hung up she still stared into the cell phone screen that displayed the end message of an encrypted phone call. Just a few months earlier, she hadn't even known she could encrypt calls on her cell. Now she didn't conceive of making or taking a call without encrypting it.

Things did evolve, and did change. With these changes, always came a change in perspective. That's what she needed, a change in perspective.

Quentin Hadden read his latest email, clenching his teeth. His boss wanted to see him. Not good. Lately, their relationship had turned from bad to worse, his conflicts with the idiot in charge—as he liked to think of Bob McLeod—evolving from technical disputes into full-blown arguments followed by sit-downs and feedback sessions eagerly delivered by the idiot with arrogance and condescendence.

He decided to face the music now rather than let the thought of it torment him for much longer. He walked briskly down the hall and entered McLeod's office after a quick tap on the door.

"You wanted to see me?" Quentin prompted.

"Yes. Sit down, please."

McLeod took his time shuffling papers, making Quentin feel how insignificant he was. Quentin didn't matter... he could wait. What an asshole.

"I called you because of the installations project on the *Lloyd*. Your team has fallen behind schedule. Again."

McLeod liked to underline the points he was making with movements of his hand, almost like an orchestra conductor, increasing the perceived arrogance of his demeanor. The man was insufferable.

"Bob, we encountered issues with the installation, and I filed the documentation with you two weeks ago. You knew about that... we discussed it."

McLeod leaned back in his chair.

"I am tired, you know, tired of how I can't get the message through to you. Not now, not ever. All I want you to do is own your issues, so we can work with them and make you and your team better professionals."

"But, Bob—"

"You have filed the paperwork. I heard you the first time. You've covered your ass with paper. Do you think that's what I care about? Do you think that's what *you* should care about? We have a client who's not able to deploy his vessel on time because of us, and we have a contract with the Navy that specifies penalties for all delays."

"Bob, listen, please. The readiness assessment for the *Lloyd* was altogether wrong. The weapons control system was incompatible with this installation.

I filed the findings, the change order, and the amended schedule with you and the client immediately after we discovered the discrepancy. It's really not my fault. What was I supposed to do?"

"I'm gonna tell you again, although I can't really figure out why I keep explaining. Quentin, you're a smart engineer, talented, bright, yet you decide to oppose the company's direction and mine with every opportunity. Your mind is hermetically closed, watertight even. Every piece of feedback I share, you take personally and decide to fight the change instead of embracing it. How am I supposed to work with you if you won't accept any feedback? If you won't make the tiniest effort to change, and if you consider your judgment to be above everyone else's? This is a collaborative environment, we work as a team, and we care about our clients' deliverables, not about the paper trail."

Quentin felt the blood boil in his veins and made a supreme effort of will to not punch the idiot. Wrapping his stupidity in corporate lingo, McLeod was too much of a coward to ever stand up to someone and say he was wrong. That was, of course, if that someone was a higher up or a client. With him, and others on McLeod's team, he showed no restraint, demeaning the value of their work with every opportunity he caught. *Small steps*, Quentin encouraged himself, *small steps.*

"Bob, please tell me how you would have wanted this situation handled. What would you have done if you found the weapons controller onboard the *Lloyd* to be incompatible with the new weapons system?"

"It wouldn't be the first time we've done this, but fine. I would have explored the possibility of installing middleware instead of replacing the entire controller. I would have presented the client with alternatives. One was the alternative you took, a new weapons controller, very expensive and a hefty delay. I would have added the middleware alternative, much cheaper, minimum delay, and a recommendation to schedule the controller replacement at a later date."

"You do realize the middleware option would have sent the *Lloyd* out to sea with an unreliable weapons configuration, right?"

"You're missing the point, again. The point is to present the client with options and recommendations, and make it their decision, not yours."

"But the client is not technically qualified to make this decision, we are!"

"Yet it's their vessel and their money!"

Both men had stood up from their chairs, their postures matching their escalated frustration with each other. A few moments of loaded silence ensued, each of them throwing angry glares at the other.

McLeod broke eye contact and sat back down.

"I'm done explaining, Quentin. If you don't see the value in what I just said, there's no point. Not now, not ever. You're dismissed."

Dumbfounded at finding himself thrown out of his boss's office like a misbehaving five year old, Quentin left the room, summoning whatever shred of dignity he could find. The moment he reached the privacy of his own office and slammed the door shut, he clenched his fists and started pacing the office angrily, mumbling curses at every step.

"What an asshole, can't believe the nerve on that guy. Who the *fuck* does he think he is?"

He felt the blood rise to his head, the pounding of his own heartbeats deafening his ears and clouding his vision. Recognizing the signs of a high blood pressure attack, he tried to calm himself down, while reaching for his pills.

"This idiot's gonna give me a stroke, while he's gonna live like all bastards do, until he's a hundred years old." He settled down at his desk and took his throbbing head in his hands. "God, I need a way out of this... can't take another day!"

The thought of leaving infused a little hope in his weary mind, then that hope faded away. "Who am I kidding?" he mumbled, "where the hell would I go?"

It hurt his ego badly to find himself so vulnerable, so defeated. He was better than that.

Quentin had been born in rural Virginia and started his early life as an isolated, lonely kid. Other kids rejected him, although he wanted to engage and play with them, to belong to their group. Soon he had learned to reject them too and be comfortable in his loneliness. Aloneness, he would call it, the state of being alone but without any of the negative connotations of loneliness, of missing the presence of others.

Naturally, he hated his first seven or eight years of school, years that forced the solitary boy to be involved in activities all day long. He deeply missed his aloneness and was bored beyond his wildest dreams. That was the perfect recipe for trouble, and little Quentin got into more than his share of that. Whatever school bully had the poor inspiration to pick on him would be punished well beyond the size of the offense. Quentin's defense was always valid in the fact that he never started those fights. Yet he finished them each time, angrily, drawing blood mercilessly, making sure everyone got the message and left him alone.

He spent his alone time reading, absorbing a variety of books at an incredible pace. A school advisor who had the opportunity to notice Quentin's behavior conducted a few tests, and then advised his parents that he didn't belong there. She recommended that they move Quentin to a school for the gifted and enroll him in an accelerated study program, one that would challenge the young boy's well-endowed brain. His parents did that, despite the fact that they had to uproot their comfortable rural life and move to the city, get new jobs, and adapt to an entirely different lifestyle. They struggled, but Quentin flourished.

He loved his new school and finished one-and-a-half years ahead of schedule. Then he had his choice of colleges and soon held a master of science degree in electrical engineering, with honors.

College life hadn't changed his demeanor all that much though. He remained isolated, focused on his work, and a bit awkward around people. He understood many things quite well. Complex mathematical models, complicated technology, futuristic concepts were easy for him to grasp; people, not so much. Finding himself aware of his limitations, he continued to study and explore science rather than relationships.

His physical proximity to the plethora of military contractors in the area offered the new graduate a career path in weapons systems. He embraced it happily and soon held several unpublished patents that bore a numeric code instead of an intelligible title.

He'd been relatively happy in his career, as happy as someone like him could be if forced to be around people for eight hours a day. He'd made a name for himself in the industry, and his achievements were numerous and well recognized. Well, that had been true for the best part of his career, until the arrogant, political, and idiotic Bob McLeod had joined the organization as technical director and Quentin's boss.

The man had no vision and not much technical ability either, despite MIT degrees and solid credentials. Although he scored above average, he wasn't nearly as intelligent as Quentin was, but had the talent to be political and gain advantage despite his technical limitations. In Quentin's opinion, it wasn't the paper that made the man; it was the work, the ideas, the solutions. But that was just Quentin's point of view; the rest of the world believed McLeod was better, because of his highly skilled political acumen.

There was instant and sizeable incompatibility between the two men, who didn't see eye to eye on anything of any importance. Quentin's relatively satisfying career had turned to crap overnight, forcing him to consider new avenues.

But where would he go? He was forty-seven years old and not at all eager to start fresh somewhere else, having to prove himself again after having given Walcott twelve years of his life, the peak of his career.

He felt trapped, a victim, and deeply hated that feeling. The independent, resilient, and creative Quentin couldn't settle for being some idiot's bitch for a living; the thought only brought anger to his heart and the need for more blood pressure medication. It was putting his life at risk. He had to do something about it.

Myatlev saw the familiar structure appear against the gloomy sky after the driver had turned left off Tverskaya Street and onto Mokhovaia. The Kremlin. The name brought yet another shiver to Myatlev's spine.

"We're here," he said. "Are we ready?"

"*Da*, Vitaliy Kirillovich, we're ready," Ivan answered promptly, checking his holstered weapon.

Myatlev checked his new watch again, just to make sure it was still there. The Breitling had a beacon function, an emergency feature he could activate if things were to go badly during his meeting with President Abramovich.

Everything was set. Ivan looked confident and ready. The three ex-Spetsnaz mercenaries, armed to the teeth and keeping their finger on the MP5 triggers, looked apt and fearless. The two Mercedes G-Wagens following closely behind them held four more ex-Spetsnaz each, all ready to storm into the Kremlin and rescue Myatlev, if that beacon went active.

The Bentley drove through the Kremlin wall portal and pulled in front of the presidential quarters entrance, greeted by two guards. Myatlev was expected. The limo's heavily tinted windows hid Myatlev's personal escort really well, and Ivan took additional precautions when he opened the door for his boss. Instead of holding the door open while stepping aside to make room for Myatlev to climb out of the Bentley, he stood right between the open car door and the guards, blocking their line of sight to the mercenaries inside the limo. It was unusual, but no one seemed to notice.

Myatlev approached the Kremlin entrance walking calmly, projecting the confidence and power expected for someone of his status. He didn't feel that confident, but there was no turning back. Soon enough he would know to which side his luck had turned. Wherever President Abramovich was involved, that was always hard to guess.

"*Dobroye utro*, Gospodin Myatlev," the Kremlin guards greeted him.

He waved his hand and nodded slightly, passing them by on his way in. A uniformed aide escorted him directly to Abramovich's office, where he was allowed to enter immediately.

"Vitya," Abramovich greeted him cheerfully, "so good to finally see you!"

Abramovich approached him with his arms wide open and offered a strong hug followed by the three traditional welcome kisses on the cheeks.

"Petya, good to see you too! You look better than ever. You have to tell me what you do to stay so young," Myatlev offered.

"Ahh... just this," Abramovich responded, pouring vodka in two glasses and handing one to Myatlev. "Drink with me. *Vashe zdorovye!*"

"*Vashe zdorovye! Ura!*"

They downed their vodkas in one gulp, and Abramovich refilled their glasses.

"You took long enough to come see me, Vitya. It made me wonder if you still value our friendship," Abramovich said bluntly.

Myatlev swallowed hard, his right hand touching the Breitling instinctively.

"I am very sorry, Piotr Ivanovich, work got the best of me. You blink, and a month's gone by. Business has been challenging lately. I hope you can find it in your heart to forgive me. I remain now and always your loyal friend; count on me!" Myatlev raised his glass in an unspoken toast, and Abramovich met him halfway. They clinked their glasses loudly, gulped the second shot, then slammed the empty glasses on the table with a satisfied laugh.

"Ha!" Abramovich said, "I hope I can count on you, Vitya, because I want you to be my new defense minister. What do you say?"

Myatlev's mind went into high gear. He'd thought of every possible scenario and had prepared for all, except this. He needed to buy himself some time. He put his right hand over his heart and said, "What an honor, Piotr Ivanovich, what an honor! But why choose me? I have failed you."

"Next time you won't fail," Abramovich said. "Your plan had greatness, a strategic ability I need in my new defense minister. So you failed once, you learned from it, you won't fail next time, da?"

"I appreciate your vote of confidence, Piotr Ivanovich, and I promise you I will make you proud. You have my utmost commitment to your cause, our cause."

"Great, that's what I wanted to hear. I need you to take us where we need to be, I need you to show us how we become great again, how we put the West in its place and make the bastards sorry they ever disrespected us the way they did."

Myatlev listened quietly, encouraging Abramovich with supporting nods.

"My predecessors were weak," Abramovich continued, "tame dogs licking the West's hand and showing no pride, no spine, no guts. Lame men have stood in this office, bringing shame to it, and humiliation to Mother Russia. No wonder the West thinks it can kick us around as if we're tail-wagging bitches. How disgraceful... They thought they could leash us? It's time we take our greatness back!"

"Ura!" Myatlev responded with a shout of victory, gulping down his third shot and hoping he'd be able to stay sober enough to survive this conversation. Abramovich was a resilient, long-haul drinker.

"We need change, my friend, at the hands of a feral businessman like you," Abramovich continued. "You are a man who can't tolerate to lose and who'd do anything to win. A man who has the balls to win this war."

What war? Myatlev thought. Russia wasn't at war with any country as far as he knew. Unless Abramovich was thinking of the war he was planning to start, against his lifelong enemy, the West, the United States first of all.

"Look at the state of our Armies," Abramovich continued. "The same old weapons, the same old people, the despicable result of decades of impotence and dereliction."

"You want to focus on research, build new technologies?" Myatlev prompted. "Or do you agree the time has passed and it's too late to do that now?"

"It *is* too late," Abramovich agreed. "What do you say we do?"

Myatlev paced a little, pensively, weighing his options before answering.

"How's Dimitrov? Is he better?"

"Yes, he's recovered almost completely," Abramovich answered, frowning at the change in topic.

"I tried to call him a couple of times, there was no answer. That got me worried."

"He's at his home at the Caspian Sea, resting. Why do you ask?"

"He was a great defense minister for you, Petya."

Abramovich nodded, a hint of regret clouding his eyes.

"He'd make a great defense minister for you again," Myatlev continued. "Just think about it. It would be the three of us together again, just like old times."

"So you're saying no to my offer?"

"I'm saying you wouldn't be using me for what I'm good at, Petya. I'm no good stuck in political meetings all day long. I am good in executing stealth strategies, at making people do things for us, at throwing money and power behind whatever you want done. But the true strategist is Dimitrov; it was always him. I am a business strategist, yes, but you need a military strategist, and that's Dimitrov. He's got balls, he's got brains, he's got ambition like no one else in your government, and he's cunning, devious. He's perfect."

Abramovich rubbed his hands together, thinking.

"I always liked Dimitrov, you know that. But I personally announced his resignation to the entire world, just a few months ago."

"And since when do you give a crap about the world, Petya?"

Abramovich turned toward Myatlev angrily, but before he could speak, a smile took over his face.

"Fuck them! Yeah! Let's drink to that! You solved my problem, Petya!"

Abramovich poured another round, larger than the first few.

"Remember that bringing the old KGB back as the covert Division Seven was his idea, right?"

"Yes, and that was a great idea. A secret service hidden inside a secret service, who would have thought of that?"

"And with Dimitrov leading it, we'll acquire everything we need to be ready, ahead of everyone else. To Dimitrov's comeback!" Myatlev answered and drank his vodka.

"To his comeback!" Abramovich cheered.

"This brings back memories," Myatlev started, slurring a little. "Do you remember that time when we went hiking in the mountains, the three of us, and ran out of booze money?"

"When?"

"Ahh... we were still in school, at Dzerzhinsky, remember?"

"Yeah, I do. I don't remember what we did though."

"We drank too much one night, and we didn't have any money left. We were poor back then; those were bad times. But Dimitrov thought of something. He went into this pub, flashed his KGB ID, and told the pub owner that he had information that enemies of the people were congregating at his pub. Then he came out of there with a serene smile on his face, followed by that pub owner carrying a case of vodka."

"I remember now," Abramovich said, laughing hard, tears flowing on his red cheeks.

"The poor shmuck even brought it to the car, shitting his pants while at it. Oh my God... "

They both laughed at relived memories for a little while longer, then Myatlev resumed a more serious tone of voice.

"We are where we are today because of Dimitrov, Petya. He's got that genius strategist mind. He's what you need to win this war."

"Do you think he'll accept? He had a heart attack right here, in this office."

"I'm sure he will, Petya. He won't be able to resist the thought of the three of us working together again."

Vernon took another bite, absent-mindedly playing with his food. His wife was sharing some work story at the dinner table, but he couldn't focus, couldn't follow what she was saying. His mind wandered a lot lately, escaping reality.

Two weeks had passed since he had met Michelle at his favorite bar, the 1700 Somewhere. He'd regretted the encounter immediately; that type of affair got people, careers, and marriages destroyed. Yet he'd gone back twice looking for her. No one had seen her since. Then he started avoiding the one bar where he felt like home, or even better. And that hurt. It felt like he'd lost his best friend somehow. A ridiculous thought, but that's how he felt.

"Really?" His wife stood abruptly, pushing the chair back and slamming down her fork. "Have you been hearing anything I've said? Do I even matter to you anymore?"

"Madi," he pleaded in a pacifying tone, "I'm sorry, baby, I'm just tired, that's all. My mind wanders when I'm tired."

"So how exactly am I supposed to reach you? Book a goddamn appointment during business hours?"

She sometimes got irrationally angry, her bottled-up frustrations clouding her judgment and making her see everything in darker colors than they really were. Her eyes were throwing menacing glares, and her beautiful face reflected her internal anguish. Vernon braced himself for a long argument. Their fights were usually long and painful exercises in diplomacy and self-control. But he loved his wife. Deep down he desperately wanted to make her happy, yet he was doing stupid things like that Michelle encounter.

"Baby, you can talk to me now, I promise I'll pay attention." He pushed his plate away and focused on her. "Tell me what's on your mind."

"You're what's on my mind, Vern. You. You bring your work home a lot, and not in a good way. You're down all the time, depressed, sour. Living with you is like driving through this endless dark tunnel. I want to feel alive. Is that too much to ask?"

"No... It's just that I'm stressed out with work, baby, I can't shake it off."

"Well, you better figure out a way, Vern. You have a permanent frown on your forehead. I don't even exist anymore; you don't even see me. You come home stinking of some bar or another, and you don't even make eye contact with me."

"Oh, come on, can't be that bad," he attempted, aware that he was starting to get angry too.

"Can't be that bad, huh? When's the last time we went out? Did you even notice it's been months? What's happening to you, to us? We deserve to have some fun, to live a little."

"It's just the work, baby, nothing more, I swear."

"Go easy with the swearing. Don't think I don't smell the stink of bar whores on you. I let it slide a couple of times, thinking it's a phase and you'll come out of it, but I don't know anymore. I don't know *you* anymore."

He felt a wave of anger rise, triggered by guilt and shame. She didn't deserve this... Yet he was pushed to the limit, backed against the wall.

"So I'm to blame for trying to make a living? Is that what you're saying?" He stood and started to pace the room. My work is not that easy. It's stressing me out. What am I supposed to do?

"Leave your work in the goddamn office, that's what I do. I work, too, but I don't get drunk every other day to forget about it."

"Madi, you don't get it. You don't get how hard what I do is. It's not your fault, but I can't... I can't extricate myself. I keep replaying things in my mind. Conversations, arguments, theories."

"Well, you better try. You better figure it out. You're a PhD for crying out loud. You're smart, think of something. If I can come home with a smile on my face every day, give you a hug, treat you like you exist and live here, why can't you? Do you think I'm not stressed out? Do you think my boss isn't an asshole? Do you think I have it super easy at work? Everybody's got crap going on in their lives, but some people are smart and decide to leave the crap at work. It's a decision you need to make; it's that simple."

He stood by the window, looking outside at the faint city lights in the moonless night. That's what they were, faint flickering lights in an endless pitch black night. What made it worse was that she was right.

"I wanna feel alive, Vern," she continued, her voice turning from angry to pleading. "I want to go out with you, dance, have some fun. I want you to buy me flowers and make love to me. Do you even know how long it's been?"

He felt another pang of anger.

"All you can think of is yourself, Madi. Jeez... it's unbelievable," he fired back. "It's always about you and what you want! When's the last time you cared about what I want?"

"How about today, when I asked you what you wanted for dinner, and I fixed you precisely that! Or when I opened the door and let you come in, after drinking who knows where with who knows whom! You take it all for granted, don't you? Well, I'm not your damn servant!"

"But that's not what I need... " he said, letting his anger subside. "I couldn't care less if you fed me tuna from the can. I need to be able to unwind at home just as I do at the bar, where no one judges me."

"Ahh... you're such an idiot, Vern, I just can't believe it! Those people let you drink in peace 'cause they don't give a crap about you, that's why. I care about you and I'm trying to help you. But you have to make a commitment to change. You need to bring your clipboard and start taking notes with what needs to happen to help our marriage survive. I have a whole damn list!"

"Oh, I am sure you do!" Vern yelled. "There's no limit to your selfishness!"

He regretted the words the moment they came out. He saw Madison's eyes open wide in dismay.

"Baby . . ." He reached out, trying to hold her hand.

"Don't touch me!" She turned and started for the garage. "This is your final warning, mister, your wake-up call."

She slammed the garage door behind her. He rushed to catch up with her.

"Where are you going?"

"None of your goddamn business, not until you get your shit together."

She started the car engine and left, screeching her tires against the pavement. Vernon stood there, speechless, unable to move, watching her brake lights disappear in the darkness. He couldn't lose her. *Oh, God, no...*

Myatlev had to admit Abramovich moved fast when he really wanted something. Only a day after he had suggested to Abramovich that they bring Dimitrov back as defense minister, Myatlev had already been set up in a new office in the Ministry of Defense, on the top floor, right next to Dimitrov's old quarters.

The Ministry of Defense was only minutes away from the Kremlin, at the center of Moscow. It was housed in a massive building as only communists could build; a gray, dull palace housing thousands of offices, a monument to communist bureaucracy.

Yet his new office was decorated to his modern, cosmopolitan taste, down to his favorite art pieces, cigar brands, and perfectly chilled bottle of Stolichnaya. His new assistant was young, very pretty, probably SVR, and judging by her smile, instructed to go to any length to fulfill his wishes. Yes, when he wanted, President Abramovich had class.

Dimitrov was already on his way in from the Caspian. He had boarded a flight immediately after accepting the reinstatement with enthusiasm. Abramovich wanted both of them to join him for a late lunch, to catch up and discuss new plans. New plans for his war... that was all he cared about.

Myatlev didn't want to waste time waiting around for Dimitrov's arrival. He had requested the files for all the top resources who Division Seven had enrolled, planning to interview them personally, one by one.

He looked at the first file, the most recent addition to Division Seven, a highly decorated intelligence officer by the name of Evgheni Aleksandrovich Smolin. He had built a reputation that he'd do anything to get the mission done, employing a variety of unusual methods in his tradecraft. Interesting.

A few minutes later, Smolin entered Myatlev's office, saluting by the book, with a hint of almost imperceptible hesitation as he recognized Myatlev.

"You asked to see me, sir?"

"Take a seat, Smolin."

"Sir."

"Have you recruited foreign assets before, Smolin?"

"Yes, sir, for years."

"What do you like most about it?"

"Sir?" Smolin frowned, trying to understand the meaning of the question.

"A man with your results must like what he does," Myatlev clarified, tapping his fingers on Smolin's personnel file. "So, again, what do you like the most about what you do?"

"Umm... The sense of power it gives me," Smolin said after hesitating a little.

"Excellent," Myatlev answered, reaching for a cigar and offering one to Smolin. "Almost like playing God, right?"

"Yes, sir." Smolin ventured a faint smile.

He accepted the cigar with a nod and both men focused on lighting up for a while, savoring the thick smoke.

"How do you recruit, Smolin?" Myatlev resumed the interview.

"I offer the assets something they need. Money, solutions to their problems, umm... sex," he said, unable to refrain a quick smile.

"Yes, I've heard that about you," Myatlev laughed. "If it works, that's fine by me."

"Good to know, sir."

"All right, Smolin, here's what I want you to do. I want you to open your mind from working a localized asset into thinking wide nets, redundancies, and backups for every single source."

"Sir?"

"Everyone is gettable, Smolin, everyone. If they don't have a problem that we can fix in return for their intelligence, then let's create one for them! It's cheaper than paying for the intel anyway. I want you to organize the largest network of assets anyone has ever had, and extract every bit of intel you can get."

"Intel on what, sir?"

"On everything," Myatlev answered with a wicked smile. "We don't know what we don't know. Who knows what's out there? Let's put our ears to the ground and get everything we can."

"How are we going to go through so much information?"

"I'll organize a center for information processing; I'll set it up on this end. You just get me the information; we'll filter and analyze here, in Moscow. Then we'll figure out what we need to pursue."

"Sir, that's highly unusual for an intelligence operation, I mean that with all due respect."

"I know it is... but soon you'll see the value of my plan," Myatlev said, amused that Smolin challenged him. That meant he had a brain *and* a spine, both very useful assets for a foreign intelligence leader.

"Sir, if we're not after a certain target in our intelligence efforts, then are we targeting a specific geographical area?"

"Yes," Myatlev answered, "of course. The United States."

"I am to build a network of assets in the entire United States, sir?"

"Precisely. Is this too large an operation for you to handle, Smolin?"

"No, sir, just making sure I understand the task correctly. There are almost a million Russian immigrants in the US. I have a good place to start."

"Excellent. Anything else?"

"Umm... If I may, I was surprised to see you, a famously wealthy businessman, having an office here, and being involved in intelligence work, sir."

"So you think that if I'm rich, my duties to Mother Russia suddenly cease to exist? I have taken an oath," Myatlev said. "That oath goes with me to my grave."

"Yes, sir, thank you. That is inspiring."

"I started in intelligence, just like you, and I never stopped using the skills I have acquired. I used them in business just as much as I did in the early days of my intelligence career. And you're right, Smolin, it's all about the power, and what we can do with it for our country. So go out there, cast a wide net for us. Find ways in; establish an asset array. Grab that power for Mother Russia," Myatlev ended his speech closing his fist in the air.

Judging by the inspired, almost fanatical look in Smolin's eyes, Myatlev knew he'd chosen well. Smolin was going to do a great job. And yes, he was still good at this; he could still motivate people to go to their death if needed. He still had it in him.

Quentin let his briefcase drop to the floor as soon as he stepped inside his home. Closing the door behind him, he kicked off his shoes and started taking off his work clothes, in a hurry to separate himself from the awful day he'd had in the office.

He lived alone. He had gone through life without feeling the need for a family, and without being tempted to commit to one. There had been relationships in his life, but he managed to keep them at arm's length somehow, breaking a few hearts in the process. That was why no one waited for him to come home from work, but he didn't miss that.

He skipped his traditional routine involving a shower followed by a TV dinner, and poured himself a large bourbon instead. He went straight to his home office and powered up his laptop.

He took a big gulp of the distilled spirits, enjoying the sensation it left behind as it went down. It burned his throat, then warmed his stomach, and from there, seeped relaxation in his weary muscles. He massaged his high, prominent forehead, trying to dissipate the early signs of a headache, then opened his Web browser and clicked on one of his favorite links stored among the navigation bar favorites.

The browser immediately opened a site aptly named Rat Olympics, bearing the tag line, "A Cyber Café for the White-Collar Working Wounded." He logged in and immediately received a welcome message accompanied by a familiar chime.

Welcome, DespeRatt—the system acknowledged him.

Several other users were logged in the chat room, and Quentin typed his first message without having someone specific in mind. Most users there were regulars, familiar with one another.

DespeRatt: I'm having a terrible few days... hope it ends soon.

Another user quickly responded.

LostGirl: What's going on?

DespeRatt: My free spirit is dying under the pressures of idiocy. Can't stand it   anymore

... I caught myself trying to figure out what he wants instead of doing what's right.

LostGirl: It can happen... it's normal to cave under pressure at some point, we all do. Cut yourself some slack.

DespeRatt: I'm turning conflict-adverse... a coward! I can't stand it anymore! WTF am I gonna do?

JustAnnonymous: Move on, man, don't cling to hell, or hell'll cling to ya'.

LostGirl: Yup, that's right. Leaving your hell will seem like the best thing that's ever happened to you.

DespeRatt: What—and start over from scratch? Having to prove myself every day, not knowing whose ass to kiss? How's that better?

JustAnnonymous: How many years have you been there?

DespeRatt: Almost thirteen.

JustAnnonymous: That's your problem. You've become codependent, forgotten how to fight, how to get out there and hunt. Wake up!

DespeRatt: Shit...

JustAnnonymous: I'm willing to bet you don't even have an updated résumé.

DespeRatt: Okay, I'll give you that, you win. I can update the damn résumé, but starting over and not being sure who's who at the new place, etc.?

LostGirl: Stop lying to yourself... don't you have to prove yourself every day now, to an adverse manager no less? Do you know whose ass to kiss now? I seriously doubt it, 'cause if you did, you wouldn't be in this bind.

DespeRatt: Point taken. Arghhh... LostGirl, you have no mercy.

LostGirl: Oh, but I do... I'm trying to set you free, dear Ratt.

DespeRatt: True. Thank you for your brutal yet kind help.

LostGirl: Repeat after me: fuck these bastards!

DespeRatt: Yeah, fuck these bastards.

He raised his glass toward an invisible LostGirl and drank down the remnants of his bourbon.

JustAnnonymous: Hear, hear!

DespeRatt: Gotta go now, guys, got a résumé to write. SYT

LostGirl: See you tomorrow, Ratt, and may your résumé writing be inspired.

Quentin closed the Rat Olympics browser window and opened a Google search page instead. He approached his task with the seriousness he engaged when working on a weapons systems project. Thorough, well documented, well researched, all calculations verified twice, and all steps written down for future reference.

He retrieved several sample defense engineer résumés off the Internet and looked through them. Things had changed dramatically in the past twelve years or so. His current résumé was well below expectations; it was a complete write-off.

He right-clicked on his desktop, created a new Word document, and renamed it QuentinHaddenResume.docx. Then he started typing.

She'd had a moment of inspiration while in the client's office, working with Brian on his new case, and couldn't wait to see if it made sense in front of her crazy wall. When she arrived home, she went straight to the blue bedroom, not even bothering to get rid of her high-heeled shoes, and pulled open the curtain hiding the corkboard timeline.

She'd been stuck in this long, boring planning session at the client's firm, where her role was to observe who might have had a different agenda. While sitting and observing, her mind started speculating on how people gain access to positions of power. What makes them get it, what makes them seek it? What makes others want to be their followers? *We all want the same things,* she responded to her own thoughts. *We want achievement, financial stability, security for our families, and a sense of purpose.*

So, then, what the hell could the mysterious Mr. X promised his followers? His followers had been some of the wealthiest men on Earth, natural born leaders, not followers. So how does one enroll the support of such moguls? What would they still want to achieve that they hadn't already?

The answer was simple: a sense of purpose. The men who had it all had followed Mr. X, or V—if that piece of intel about his name would ever prove to be accurate—to gain or satisfy a sense of purpose.

Her initial thinking might have been wrong. She'd always assumed the common denominator had been the Islamic connection of all conspirators, which canned them as typical Islamist militant terrorists. But that didn't tie into Russia's beliefs, interests, or agendas at all. And V was definitely Russian; several sources had confirmed it. That's why she couldn't find V. He wasn't about Islamism, or typical Muslim terrorism. He was about something else, something they all had in common, Muslims or not. Something she hadn't thought of yet.

She stood in front of her crazy wall, eyes fixated on the Post-it note marked X. Her cell phone rang, startling her. Still thinking of Mr. X, she accepted the encrypted call.

"Hello," she answered.

"Hey, Alex, it's Brian. Did you send it?"

"Umm... send what?" she asked without thinking.

"Oh... you forgot," Brian responded, his disappointment discernible in his voice. "You were going to send me the email activity logs for the product and R&D teams."

Oh, shit, she mouthed quietly as she heard Brian's explanation.

"Oh, that," she said, trying to fix it. "No, I haven't forgotten. I'm on it as we speak. I thought you meant something else. You'll have it in just a few, Brian."

She ended the call with an irritated hand gesture and rushed to her laptop, swearing colorfully as she trotted in a hurry to make up some of the lost time. She hated to disappoint her team; yet lately it seemed that was all she was capable of doing.

Her old case was killing her, driving her crazy. She needed to close that chapter once and for all. She needed to catch the bastard.

John Baxter, Navy liaison and VP Navy Programs, entered the conference room wearing a smile that didn't fool anyone. Tall and slim, with thinning, buzz-cut, gray hair, and a very straight back, Baxter emanated corporate efficiency. His charcoal suit, white shirt, and burgundy tie brought the final touches to his professional demeanor; the man was all business.

He looked around the conference room, nodding greetings to the five people present, then checked his agenda briefly.

"Good, we're all here. Let's get started."

Baxter cleared his throat quietly, then continued, "Welcome to Project Z1005LC1, everyone. You have been invited to participate in this TOP SECRET project based on your skills, expertise, and record of achievement. Congratulations!"

Most of Baxter's audience nodded a silent thank you. Some even smiled a little.

Baxter continued his introduction.

"The project's scope is the evaluation, readiness, and installation of the first laser cannon onboard a stealth destroyer, the USS *Fletcher*. The *Fletcher* is a Zumwalt-class destroyer, as some of you may know, hull number DDG1005."

Baxter paused for a few seconds, waiting for questions that didn't come.

"Let's introduce the team and define roles and accountabilities," he stated. "You probably all know Bob McLeod, technical director, Navy Installation Projects. He will be the project manager for Z1005LC1. Most of you have worked with him before. Some of you report to him. Bob has excellent experience in prototype assessment and installation; that experience will come in handy on this project."

Bob McLeod nodded slightly, thanking Baxter for his appreciative words.

"Sylvia Copperwaite," Baxter continued, making an introductory hand gesture toward the only woman in the room, "will be in charge of the mobile platform installation. She's a highly accomplished electromechanical engineer, and holds a PhD in computational modeling for mobile-platforms installations. She's also an expert in mobile remote-sensing technology. Both her areas of expertise will prove useful for this particular project. Welcome,

Sylvia."

"Thank you, John," she replied.

"Faisal Kundi," Baxter continued the introductions, pointing toward a dark-haired man with an intense look in his eyes, "is the embedded software engineer who's going to make sure the laser cannon can actually be fired and can hit the target."

Faisal nodded silently, the expression on his face remaining concentrated, intense, serious.

"Quentin Hadden," Baxter moved on, "is our weapons systems expert. He will be in charge of deploying controls and running tests. He has some exposure to the laser cannon from its research and prototype testing days."

Quentin's frown didn't disappear as he acknowledged Baxter's comments.

"Finally, Vernon Blackburn," Baxter said, "brings to the project team a PhD in laser applications. He will be our laser optics expert. The cannon's ability to fire a shot is under his purview. He is also familiar with laser weapons systems, or LaWS. He was part of the original R&D team, so he can probably answer more questions about the laser cannon than I can."

Vernon smiled shyly.

"Any questions so far?" Baxter asked.

No one offered.

"All right, then. Deployment starts on Monday. Please use the rest of today to wrap up or park your remaining active items. Please make sure your attention will be undivided while you work on this project. The *Fletcher* is ready for your visit; her location is in the documentation in front of you. Captain Anthony Meecham will make himself available to you at all times."

Baxter gave them a few seconds to process the information, then continued.

"Pay attention, think sharp, make notes of everything you see that will help us deploy laser weapons systematically without any hiccups. Part of the project's list of deliverables is writing the first draft of the laser cannon installation manual." He straightened his tie a little, then said, "Good luck to all of you. Make me proud!"

Back in his own office, Bob McLeod closed the office door gently and immediately leaned against it, staring at the ceiling and letting out a long sigh.

"Son of a bitch . . ." he whispered.

He loosened his tie a little, not leaving the support offered by the door. It was unbelievable... He couldn't wrap his head around the fact that no matter what he did, he never got promoted.

He had joined Walcott eight years before, as technical director for Navy installations, and he was still technical director for the same Navy installations. He had a top-notch record of accomplishments, yet it was always people like Baxter who were the vice presidents, while he was being forgotten in the director role. What did Baxter have that he didn't?

Project after project after project, they were all the same routine. Yes, bring in the invaluable Bob McLeod to do the work for us, spend his days on and off ships of all sorts, moored all over the place. This way, he can enjoy the cold, humidity, and oblivion, as far from corporate headquarters as possible for yet another year or so, while people like Baxter become senior vice presidents, climbing the ladder on the fruits of his labor. How did Baxter even become a VP? He seemed to have had that role for a while... Was he *born* a damn VP?

No matter how hard Bob tried, he couldn't figure out why he was repeatedly assigned on projects as lead, but never promoted. His career had been at a standstill since the day he entered the corporate headquarters of Walcott Global Technologies, a thick, impenetrable glass ceiling keeping him from advancing. Even his applauded patents didn't make much of a difference; for the most impressive one he had received a ten-thousand dollar bonus, then nothing. No mention of it again. And he knew for sure that patent was worth many millions for his employer.

If things didn't change, if a miracle didn't happen soon, he would probably end up retiring as technical director, having effectively killed his career by waiting on these people to recognize his value and promote him. He still had a good twenty years until retirement, but at this pace, yeah, he'd still be a technical director at that point.

Bob McLeod was one of the best electrical engineers in the country. He'd graduated from MIT, second in his class. Then he had decided to pursue a career in defense technologies. He felt his work should have meaning, help a great cause. And for what? Probably any of the Silicon Valley mediocrities, carrying bachelor degrees from dubious Midwestern online universities, made twice his pay, and climbed the corporate ladder every two years so that he wouldn't go work for the competition. Huh! How infuriating.

He had been lured by the glamour of a worthy cause, by the thought of doing his job in the service of his country, but he felt he was taken advantage of. Simply p ut, he had bet his career on the wrong horse.

Major Evgheni Aleksandrovich Smolin was a visiting officer on FSB territory; yet he was treated with the utmost respect and deference. The FSB had been nothing but cooperating, especially since rumors had started surfacing that he'd been assigned to work on a special project with the recently reappointed Defense Minister Dimitrov.

The rumors took only a few days to transcend the invisible border between the Defense Ministry and the FSB, despite their rivalry and physical distance. People talked. With the rumors, of course, in Smolin's case came the jokes. The latest one was, Why was Smolin promoted to work with Dimitrov? Because his penis enlargement surgery was very successful.

The jokes and the rumors that he used to love before made him a bit uncomfortable now, considering his career had ascended to the point where he wanted to be taken more seriously. He could be a lieutenant colonel in a few months; the damned jokes had to stop. He had been offered the opportunity of a lifetime, to lead his own network of agents on foreign soil. On American soil. This was his time to shine, and he would stop at nothing to get the job done. Mr. Myatlev had been clear; one's allegiance and duty toward Mother Russia never ends. Mr. Myatlev believed he had what it took to become a national hero; Smolin wasn't going to let him down; not on his life.

Smolin took the elevator down to the interrogation level. He checked the file he was carrying briefly; the detainee was waiting in Interrogation Room 9.

He walked the semi-dark corridor looking for the assigned interrogation room. Distant wails were tearing the silence of the tomb-like floor. It reeked of chlorine and human excrement, a nasty side effect of extracting information forcefully from people. In there, the interrogators had life-and-death authority over the detainees. If a detainee happened to die during the interrogation, the paperwork the interrogator had to file was simpler than an application for a new parking permit. Human life had no value on this floor; only information mattered.

He opened the door and walked in. The detainee, a young girl, looked at him with fearful eyes. She'd been crying; her face was all swollen and smeared with makeup and tears. Good; she was ready. It shouldn't take that long.

Without saying a word, Smolin went to the video camera installed in one of the corners and unplugged the connectors. The girl gasped.

"Good," Smolin said in a low voice, almost whispering. "It's just the two of us now."

He reached out to touch her face. She squirmed and whimpered, but couldn't withdraw too far because of the chain tying her handcuffs to the table.

He touched her cheek, softly, smiling, watching intently how her pupils dilated with fear. Then he grazed the back of his hand against her breast. She whimpered some more, tears flowing freely from her eyes.

"Nyet," she begged, "please, no."

"Hmm... " Smolin responded, feigning offense. "All right, then, let's get down to business if that's what you want."

She blubbered something unintelligible.

"Let's look at your file."

He took his time going through the pages, quite numerous for a nineteen year old. He took his time, using time against her, fueling her anxiety. Smolin's interrogation technique had gained expertise over time, making him one of the most effective interrogators in the intelligence service. He knew how to extract information even from unwilling, non-participative, and unaware targets, people who would later swear they weren't interrogated.

"Interesting... " he mumbled, loud enough for her to hear him, but ignoring her.

A long, agonizing wail tore the silence from the hall, followed promptly by the girl's gasps and quiet whimpers, while she fidgeted pointlessly in her chair.

"Don't worry," Smolin said without looking at her, "we won't get there unless we really have to. It's messy... I don't like it. People... well, people can't control their bodily functions very well when they reach that level of pain, and that is disgusting. I'd rather avoid that if possible."

He looked at her and liked what he saw. She was pale, her mouth half opened, letting out quick bursts of air in a shallow, rapid breathing, and her eyes were dilated with fear to the point where he couldn't discern the color of her irises.

"Valentina Davydova, yes?" Smolin asked.

"Yes," she whimpered.

"Says here you were an orphan, living in the streets after fleeing your foster home. What happened to your parents?"

She sniffled a little and cleared her throat.

"Social orphan," she managed.

"Huh?"

"I was a social orphan. That's what they call it when your own mother kicks you out in the street."

"What did you do?"

"She was a mean drunk. I didn't do anything but refuse to give her new boyfriend a blow job, that's all."

Smolin turned a page in the file. "You were... umm... twelve then, right?"

"Yes," she confirmed, looking at her hands and sniffling a little. "They picked me up from the streets and put me in an orphanage."

"Says here within a year or so you ran away and weren't heard from again until last year. Why did you run?"

"Have you seen an orphanage?"

"No... can't say that I have, no," Smolin answered, letting a faint smile flutter on his lips.

He already knew enough about what made his detainee tick. She was strong-willed and had a sense of right and wrong, of pride, and strong self-preservation. She wanted to have a good life. She wasn't going to sit idle and let people, no matter who they were, ruin her life or play games with her. Smolin knew everything he needed to make her comply, because he knew exactly how he could break her.

"Tell me about the missing years," Smolin continued, tapping his index finger on her file. "What did you do? Where did you live?"

She hesitated before answering, searching his eyes, as if to weigh how much truth she needed to put in her answer.

"In the streets, mainly. Lived off people's trash, here and there a kind person would give me money or something to eat."

"You panhandled? Begged for money at street corners?"

Moscow had hordes of street-corner beggars, polluting the city streets with a constant reminder of the country's descent into poverty and stringent social issues.

"Yes, I did. Cleaned windshields too."

"Prostituted yourself?"

A split-second hesitation before she answered, "No."

"What else? Where did you end up living?"

"Nowhere, just the streets, that's all. I couldn't get a place until last year."

Smolin stood and walked toward her side of the table, then leaned against the table in front of her. He reached out and grabbed her chin gently, forcing her to look him in the eye. She shivered, her whole body trembling uncontrollably.

"It's not gonna work like this, you know," Smolin said firmly. "I can protect you from the pain and misery detainees endure within these walls only if you don't insult my intelligence by lying to me about obvious things."

"Umm... I'm sorry, I don't un–understand," she whimpered, stuttering and shaking.

"You were arrested for cyber crimes, for one of the most advanced hack attacks ever performed on an American retail chain. The Americans have a reward on your head."

He stopped talking, looking intently at her as she averted her eyes.

"Don't tell me you learned how to do that by washing windshields and panhandling at street corners."

She sighed, a shivered sigh mixed with an almost inaudible whimper, almost like a stifled sob. Another wail of agonizing pain resonated through the walls from a neighboring interrogation room and she reacted again, gasping and trying to crouch in her chair.

"This," Smolin gestured in the direction the wails came from, "this doesn't have to happen to you."

She looked up at him, a glimmer of hope appearing in her eyes.

"I don't care about the Americans you stole from... They have enough. I don't care about their reward either. I'm not going to turn you in to them; I don't work for them. But I do need you to help me with the work I do for our country."

He stopped talking, waiting for her reaction.

"Y–yes," she said, nodding.

"Let's start again, then. Where did you live all those years?"

She sniffled and wiped her nose against her sleeve.

"In the streets at first," she said, her voice gaining a little more strength and confidence than before. "Then I met a group of young computer geeks who squatted in various places, unfinished buildings, low-security office buildings empty at night, and so on. We'd ride the subways at day and squat in some office building at night, grabbing laptops people left behind and cracking their encryptions to gain access to the net."

"How old were they? Your friends?"

"I was the youngest, but not by far. The oldest was twenty-two, and he got us our first real home."

"How did that happen?"

She looked sideways, afraid to say more and incriminate herself and her friends.

Smolin grabbed her chin again, forcing her to look up.

"Listen, we're past that, all right? We already have you for cyber crimes, and there's really no viable alternative for you other than to cooperate with me. If not, there's little chance you'll ever leave this room alive." His voice stayed friendly, like someone giving advice. He stood and started walking slowly, stopping behind her. He grabbed a strand of her long brown hair and she almost jumped out of her skin. He ran his fingers through it and let it go.

"You see," he continued, "being here is not what I do for a living, but I do need someone like you to work for me. If we can't come to an agreement, I'll leave you in the capable hands of the Cyber Unit interrogator and be on my way. Considering we haven't heard a sound in a few minutes, I am thinking he's become available. He must be done with the other detainee."

"I can work for you, just tell me what you need," she said quickly, sniffling and breathing heavily.

"First, you tell me what I need to know. How did your group get the place you lived in?"

"We... we grabbed credit card lists from many places, retail chains, cell phone operators, hospitals. We took their client lists with everything they had, addresses, payment info, full names, etc."

"And then?"

"Then we started ordering stuff on eBay, direct from China, stuff that sold really well here for cash. Electronics and jewelry, mostly."

"How did the payments go through? The shipping address is supposed to match the credit card billing address, not an address in a different country. That's basic fraud prevention."

"It could be different from the billing address, but yes, we did use the billing address as shipping address, but then sent a private message to the seller to instruct him to ship the goods here."

"And he didn't think that was a fraudulent transaction?"

"Why did you think we were ordering only from China? The sellers don't care... they make the sale and move on to the next customer. Then we sold the goods here, for cash, when they arrived."

"Then what?"

"Then we started having real cash, enough to get us homes and a real life; no more street corners and squatting."

"How did you get caught?"

"I–I don't know. I was very careful... I only handled transactions from unregistered equipment, different locations every time, someone else's laptop, and a new credit card for each transaction, extracted from various databases." A tear started making its way down her cheek. "Someone must have rolled on me... can't think of any other way."

Smolin stood, and she crouched again. He walked aimlessly around the table a couple of times as she watched him intently, then sat back down.

"Here's what I need you to do for me. I will give you a list of IP addresses, and for those IPs, I need you to build me a Web crawler that identifies all Internet activity for the people associated with those IPs."

"That's... that's major programming, not something I can slap together in a few minutes."

"Will you do it?"

"Does it look like I have much of a choice?" Valentina asked with a bitter, resigned smile.

"No, you don't; I'm glad you figured that out. Now tell me what you need to get the job done."

"I need processing power and serious Internet bandwidth. I can write it down for you," she offered, "but before that I need to find out more about what you need done. What are those IPs about? Whose are they?"

"Various organizations that interest me."

"And whom do you want to track?"

"Any people associated with those organizations: vendors, employees, clients, partners, etc."

"That could mean a lot of people," she said, warning him. "A lot of processing power, and a lot of data for you to sift through when it starts coming in. People do a lot of shit online these days."

"And I want to know all about it," Smolin confirmed.

"Suit yourself. Anything in particular you're looking for?"

"N–no," he replied, a little hesitant.

"Look, I'm stuck here at your mercy. I can't spill your secrets, but I might help you better if you tell me exactly what you need. Then maybe, I am hoping, you can let me go?"

"We're not there yet," Smolin replied dryly, "you'll have to earn that freedom. I want you to look for any activity that signals an edge we could have against individuals. Are they cheating on their spouses? I want to know. Have they stolen anything? I want to know. Do they have an unpaid parking ticket? I want to know."

"Got it, I think," she replied.

"How soon can you get it done?"

"I'll need two to three days after I have all the equipment, and I need a place to stay if I can't go home."

"No, you can't go home, but I'll place you under supervised house arrest at a safe house of ours. And you only discuss this assignment with me, is that understood?"

"Yes."

"Then we're done here. See? It wasn't that bad," Smolin said, leaving Interrogation Room 9.

He reached the ground floor and headed for the exit.

An aide caught up with him and asked, "Will you need anything else, Major Smolin?"

"Yes. Keep me posted as soon as the American State Department offers a reward for one of our hackers. Make that a standing order. Apparently it knows better than we do who's our top cyber talent."

Alex came out of the shower wrapped in a huge towel and headed for the living room. She turned on the TV, then walked toward the bedroom to get her hair dryer. Absentminded, she almost missed the announcement on the news, yet somehow the familiar name caught her attention.

"... Minister Dimitrov's reinstatement comes as a surprise to the international community. Analysts had initially believed that his departure from Russia's Ministry of Defense last November had been a disguised ousting, considering Dimitrov's moderation and President Abramovich's belligerence," the TV announcer stated.

"What?" Alex exclaimed, rushing toward the coffee table and grabbing the remote. She was able to rewind the newscast and watch it all from the beginning, word for word.

She sat on the couch, not minding the dripping water from her soaked hair. What did that mean? She'd always thought that Abramovich had removed Dimitrov, or maybe even imprisoned or killed him, for having failed the most daring mission in the history of black ops.

How was Dimitrov's reinstatement going to play out? What did it mean to the already tensioned relations between Russia and the United States? What value did it bring to Abramovich's plans? What did it mean for her chances to find X?

She went into the blue bedroom and grabbed a new Post-it note. She wrote Dimitrov's name on it in green marker and hesitated a little before placing it on the corkboard. Where did it belong? Definitely at the top somewhere... She made her decision and placed the Post-it right next to the one marked "X."

Evgheni Aleksandrovich Smolin wasn't stressed at all, lining up for immigration documents control at Toronto Pearson International. He was good at his job and he knew it. His documents were all in order, prepared by one of the best support teams in the world. He wore the typical business travel attire for an eastern European: brown slacks; a sport jacket; and a white shirt, top button undone; all a little wrinkled. His blond, silvered beard and hair completed the image of a middle-aged business traveler, a little tired from too much time spent on a commercial jet.

Happy to deplane after the long flight from Zurich, he stretched his legs and walked in place, waiting his turn.

"Good evening," he greeted the passport control officer as he approached the desk. The Canadian greeted him back with a nod and a professional smile and took his passport.

"Mr. Rudnitsky?" the officer probed.

"Yes," Smolin answered.

"What is the purpose of your visit?"

"Mostly business, but some pleasure too, I hope," Smolin answered unperturbed.

The officer scanned his visa under a reader.

"How is that?" the officer asked.

"I am here for a series of business meetings during the next couple of weeks. But I hope to make it to the CN Tower and see Niagara Falls," Smolin answered with the candid smile of a naïve tourist.

"When are you planning to go back?"

"At the end of two weeks, on the twenty-second."

"Are you flying back to Russia?" the officer questioned, looking him in the eye.

"No, back to Zurich, I'm afraid."

"Why is that? You are Russian, right?"

"Yes, but my employer has business offices in Zurich, and that's where I spend most of my time lately. Far from home, too far." Smolin put just enough sadness in his tone to sound natural.

The officer typed something in his computer, scanned the passport again, then stamped it with a loud bang.

"Welcome to Canada, Mr. Rudnitsky; enjoy your stay," he said, handing him his passport and customs declaration form.

"Thank you," Smolin replied, and walked briskly in the direction indicated by large signs marked "Ground Transportation."

He didn't go straight to ground transportation. First, he went through customs and then entered the first men's room he could find. He fidgeted with his luggage until the last remaining traveler left, then placed the "slippery when wet" sign outside in front of the door, and locked it from the inside.

He shaved his beard quickly and changed his clothes. The slacks, jacket, and shirt were replaced by worn-out jeans and a canary yellow T-shirt, marked "Le Tour De France." He packed everything carefully, and extracted a new set of documents from the double bottom of his suitcase. As a finishing touch, he put on a baseball cap and Ray-Ban Aviator sunglasses before leaving the lavatory.

A few minutes later, a courteous car rental employee greeted him at the VIP counter.

"Welcome to Enterprise, Mr. Duncan, we have your car ready for you."

Smolin smiled. With a little bit of luck and a few cups of Tim Hortons coffee, before breakfast he could be in Norfolk. He was ready.

Quentin's day had been once again remarkably annoying, irritating, and endless. The minutes had dragged by slowly, making the day seem eternal.

He wasn't feeling all that great. His hands were shaking a little, very unusual for him. A migraine had clouded his brain for the better part of the day, and now was impairing his vision, making it blurry, unfocused. He stopped a little to analyze what was going on with his body, why it was betraying him. Then he realized he was deeply upset; he'd gone way past the typical workday irritation with the idiotic boss and with everyone else who wouldn't let him be. He was upset to the point where his entire being struggled to compensate and failed miserably.

He went for the bourbon bottle and filled a glass with almost double his usual serving, then fired up his personal laptop and logged in to the Rat Olympics chat room; maybe talking about it would make it better. Maybe hearing how other people struggled just as badly would make him feel less battered.

DespeRatt: Hey guys . . .

LostGirl: Hey stranger, it's been a while. ☺ I was thinking maybe you got another job and forgot all about us.

DespeRatt: I wish. ☹ No, I'm still there, and today it's been worse than usual.

LostGirl: Why? What happened? Someone gave you shit?

DespeRatt: Sadly, that's almost the norm, but no. They gave me a free lunch!

Slave19: And why is that bad? What am I missing?

DespeRatt: Ah... where do I even start... I need a break from them to survive my day. Today they gave some of us a mandatory working lunch, which to me it means they squeezed another hour of work out of me for $10.50, the price of that salad. Huh... if they even paid that much for it. I could barely hold it together the whole time.

LostGirl: Some folks like it, you know. I don't think anyone wanted to offend you or anything.

DespeRatt: I know they didn't want to offend me, but they did want to get more work out of me for free, and that's hard to swallow.

LostGirl: You sound like an hourly employee. Aren't you salaried?

Quentin rubbed his hand through his hair. Today it was hard to find sympathetic ears even here, where he'd always found kindred spirits.

DespeRatt: I am salaried, but this is nonsense, IMHO. Time is time, for everyone, salaried or not. Every hour is a tiny little sliver of our lives that they rob us of. So what if I'm salaried? I shouldn't want to have a life, or need rest— a damn break, like I am entitled to? I have to go nonstop, like some nightmarish automaton, for eight, nine hours in a row without needing a break? Yes, LostGirl, I am salaried, but so the fuck what?'

LostGirl: I am sorry, dear Ratt, I really am. Didn't mean to upset you even more. I totally see your point.

DespeRatt: I apologize too. I know you mean well, you always have.

Slave19: Even with cars you have to stop the engine when refueling, right?

DespeRatt: Right. Didn't think of that, but yeah, absolutely.

Slave19: Because they could blow up otherwise. ☺

DespeRatt: Very true. This is precisely what happened to me today.

LostGirl: Are you in management? Are you able to influence these decisions?

DespeRatt: No, and no. I'm an engineer, LostGirl. I never wanted to be in management, still don't. I... I'm not really a people person. Ideally, I wanna be left the hell alone to do my work. A good workday is a day in which I interact with people remotely, not face to face. Oh well... nobody's perfect, right?

LostGirl: Are you socially anxious?

DespeRatt: I guess you could say I am, although I'd call it much more comfortable alone. Plus my work doesn't get interrupted by others every minute or so.

Slave19: I know an exercise that can help wipe that frown off your face. Let's plan revenge.

LostGirl: ☺

DespeRatt: Huh?

Slave19: Just virtually, of course. If you had all the power in the world, what would you do with the offenders at your job?

Quentin caught himself smiling, the first time in countless hours.

DespeRatt: Ahh... let me think. The asshole with the working lunch—I'd prevent him from having a non-working lunch for at least a month. But he might like that. Huh... What would you suggest?

Slave19: How about having him serve lunch to people as a career? Wouldn't he look just great as a waiter in some cheap diner?

DespeRatt: Totally. You're so much better at this than I am. Let's continue; my migraine started going away.

Slave19: Glad to hear. Who else is on your shit list?

DespeRatt: My boss, of course. The biggest idiot who ever walked on this planet with an MIT degree. Entitlement meets arrogance but fails to meet any superior brain function with this guy.

Slave19: Thinking... Arrogant, you say?

DespeRatt: And then some.

Slave19: How about street vendor, selling hot dogs right in front of your corporate office?

LostGirl: ROFL.

DespeRatt: Gotta give it to you, you have talent! If I'll even be in a position to think of real revenge, I'll know who to ask.

Slave19: You will. Life circumstances change every day. Soon, your time will come. Just hang in there.

DespeRatt: I will. Thanks, you guys, you're awesome.

Quentin closed his laptop and leaned back in his chair, letting out a long sigh. Yeah, this was fun, and helped him forget the miseries of the day, but it was definitely not progress. His résumé still needed a little tweaking, and that's where he should have spent his time instead.

He rubbed his forehead for a minute; his migraine was returning with a vengeance.

Under the cafeteria's flickering fluorescent lights, Jeremy Weber waited for the coffee machine to finish brewing his second fix of the day, then headed back to his office.

"Hey, Weber, SAC Taylor was looking for you," one of the operational support technicians said, passing him in the hallway.

"When?" Jeremy asked?

"Just now," the tech replied and disappeared behind a door marked Special Investigations.

Jeremy left the coffee cup on his desk and walked right out, heading for his boss's office.

Special Agent in Charge Taylor was a procedural investigator, more focused on the procedure manual than on following his gut. Jeremy rarely interacted with Taylor; both of them liked it that way. Jeremy's way of thinking, of following leads and uncovering information, was more in line with what one saw in old detective movies than in the standing FBI procedures, despite his almost twenty years with the bureau. All that mattered to Jeremy was the truth and catching the bad guys as fast as possible. He routinely followed his gut and forgot to file the paperwork. That's why Taylor wasn't his biggest fan.

He knocked on Taylor's open door.

"You wanted to see me, sir?"

"Come in, get the door," Taylor replied, pointing at one of the chairs in front of his desk.

Jeremy closed the door behind him, then sat on the indicated chair.

"Before we start," Taylor said, "please note this is the final verbal warning you'll get from me. If I have to repeat today's spiel ever again, it will be in writing and it will go on your permanent record. Am I making myself clear?"

"Crystal, sir," Jeremy replied, clenching his jaws. He felt his palms starting to sweat.

Taylor opened a file and started reading from his handwritten notes.

"You have interrogated a minor without a legal guardian present. You have used borderline excessive force during the interrogation of the Mortimer kidnapping suspect, and he wasn't even the right suspect to begin with. He's filed a lawsuit. All this, in the last month. Oh, here's a real gem. You drove off and left your partner at Starbucks, where he was buying you both breakfast, and didn't return to pick him up."

"I'd just received a tip from one of my informants in the Wilson case. I thought human trafficking takes precedence over donuts, sir."

"Don't be a smartass with me, Weber. Your partner wasted half his day, waiting for you, covering for you, then taking a goddamn cab to get back to the office. Now he's filed a request for reassignment."

"Oh, I see... " Jeremy whispered.

"Yeah... how many times have we been on this path, Weber? How many partners? No one wants to work with you, and I understand why. You don't care about your partners. They believe you don't have their back, and they don't trust you!"

Taylor ended his tirade forcefully, slamming the folder on the desk, and his open palm on top of it. Jeremy almost flinched, but remained quiet. There was no point in arguing.

"You're not a cowboy, Special Agent Weber," Taylor said after a minute or so, "You're not some Midwestern small-town sheriff who thinks he is the law and nothing else matters. You are a federal agent. And it's about goddamn time you start behaving like one." Taylor paused, waiting for Weber to respond.

"Yes, sir."

"People smarter than you have written our procedures manuals. Follow them at all times. If in doubt, don't break protocol; just follow the manual, without any exceptions. And learn how to be a team player. There's no way I'm gonna allow you to work without a partner; it's in the manual for many reasons. So find one who'll work with you and do whatever it takes to stay in his or her good graces, because one more reassignment request from one of your partners and it goes on your record. Is that understood?"

"Yes, sir," Jeremy answered. "If I may—"

"You may not! Dismissed!"

Jeremy left Taylor's office and headed back to his own. Yeah... he'd have to change a few things. He promised himself he wasn't gonna go through another one of Taylor's rants, no matter what he had to do, and whose ass he had to kiss.

He sat down at his desk and took his weary head in his hands. It was amazing how all the things that seemed right to do in the heat of the moment ended up biting him in the ass.

He'd given the bureau the best twenty years of his life and he loved his job. He didn't just think of himself though, he thought of his son; he needed to consider his family. He wasn't going to throw everything down the drain for some gut feeling in some stupid case, or anything. Going forward, he was gonna follow procedure at all times; he had to. He'd promised himself that many times before, but this time he really meant it.

Smithfield represented the best rural Virginia had to offer for someone like Evgheni Aleksandrovich Smolin. Quiet neighborhoods with houses sitting on large lots, far enough from one another to present numerous advantages from a privacy perspective. Scarce law enforcement presence, their services not needed much in one of Virginia's safest neighborhoods. A small community of close-knit families, where a visiting family member from abroad would be instantly adopted and incorporated in the community, not many questions asked.

That was Smolin's cover. He had arrived in the small town as the father of Olga Novachenko, visiting from Russia, there to stay a couple of months then go back home. He'd arrived ten days before, and people on the street already knew him and greeted him. It was perfect for his needs.

No matter how peaceful Smithfield was, Smolin wasn't there to relax. He constantly worked on his laptop, installed in the home's living room, from behind window treatments that maintained his privacy and kept all curious neighbors in the dark.

Smolin was comparing two long lists of IPs, closely reviewing each entry, and marking on the second list whenever a corresponding IP was associated with a name of interest from the first list. The first list was quite simple, only holding corporate names, their IPs, and their physical locations—their headquarters address in most cases. The second list was significantly more complex. It had primary IPs on each row, most of them matching entries in the first list, then a secondary IP associated with a user name, password, website, even credit card information for some entries. From studying both lists, Smolin got the information he was looking for: the people identified on the second list and their Web browsing habits were employees of the companies of interest found on the first.

Smolin put his headset on and made a Skype call to his aide back in Moscow. It rang a few times before being answered, maybe because in Moscow it was well after 1.00AM.

"Yes, sir," his aide answered the call, recognizing his Skype ID.

"Anton, get me Valentina Davydova on the line. She's staying at the Sosnovaya safe house."

"Umm... they moved her back to the detainment center two days ago, sir."

"*Chto za hui*, Anton, what the hell? So she can get raped and killed by some idiot in there and leave us hanging? She's an asset, Anton, what the hell were you thinking?"

"Sir, if I may, no one asked me. I just found out last night. They needed the house for something else."

"Who?"

"Major Vorodin from FSB."

"He'll be first in line to serve soup at the detention center, tomorrow and for the rest of his insignificant life. You wake him up and tell him that, Anton, you hear me?"

"Umm... yes, sir," Anton answered hesitantly.

"Now get Davydova on the phone and then move her back to the safe house immediately. Call me when you have her."

Less than an hour later, an incoming Skype call broke the silence in the quiet Smithfield residence. Smolin connected with video.

She'd been roughed up. Her left eye was swollen shut, her jaw was almost black and distended on the left side, and her hair hung in dirty strands sticking to her bruised face. Her left hand was wrapped in dirty gauze and hung limp. She'd developed the demeanor of someone who's constantly expecting to be assaulted or killed: jumpy, averting eye contact, trying to look small.

Considering how badly he needed her to cooperate, that roughing up might have been for the best after all. Good thing they didn't kill her, the stupid morons.

"Y–yes?" she said insecurely on the Skype call.

"Valentina, good morning," Smolin said.

She squinted into the camera, trying to recognize the man in the blurry, choppy video transmission.

"Ahh... g–good morning, sir," she managed to articulate.

"This shouldn't have happened. You'll be going back to the safe house immediately, right now," Smolin said.

A tear started rolling from her swollen eye. She didn't say anything.

"I need you to do something for me," Smolin said. She nodded, and he continued, "I received your first reports a few days ago and they were excellent work. Just what I needed. But I need more, and I need you to get me the physical addresses for some of those users. And I'll need some kind of alert system to call me, or something, whenever one of these users is online. I'll send you the list of the ones who interest me."

"I–I don't have a computer," she whimpered. "They took everything away from the house when they took me. I lost the program I wrote for you. They took it. It was on that computer."

"*Tvoyu mat!* You'll have everything back," he said, feeling anger raise a wave of bile in his throat. "Anton!"

"Sir?"

"Take her to a hospital first; see that she's taken care of. Then take her to the house and have the dimwits who took my stuff bring it all back tonight. All of it! Then draft reports for every one of them and file them on their personnel records. Tell them to pray this doesn't delay my op, 'cause if it does, I will kill every one of them with my own bare hands."

He hung up the Skype call without waiting for any confirmation from Anton, and started pacing the room angrily. Those ignorant, reckless idiots could have ruined it all.

Normally, Fridays made him feel great, exhilarated almost. Just the thought of not seeing them for two whole days, of not going there two whole days. Quentin smiled bitterly at the thought that he probably wasn't all that different from the vast amount of workers in the world. All the Friday jokes he'd heard over the years, all the expressions, all the "Happy Friday" wishes, all hinted to the same reality: most people just hated going to work every day, and they did that out of necessity.

So why couldn't he just accept that fact as one of life's many crappy realities, and stop being so miserable? He wasn't the only one; he got that. Yet he couldn't find his balance.

He paced the living room slowly, ignoring the muted TV and delaying the moment he'd have to turn on the lights. He loved the soft light of dusk; it brought peace and the promise of a restful night.

He looked out the window at the evening sky. There were just a few scattered clouds, and the reddish hues of a great sunset. A beautiful end to another miserable day. Watching that amazing sunset, he wished he could just reset his brain, make it turn silent and stop obsessing over every word that had been said, every email, document, or schematic involving work. But no matter how hard he tried to stop the madness, his brain carried on internally and silently all the arguments he wished he could have had with Bob McIdiot, his infuriatingly irrational boss.

Quentin wished he had the power to walk out of that building for good, slamming the door in the bastard's face on his way out. He fantasized for a minute or two how that would feel. It would feel great for a second, and then what? Unemployed, without a fat bank account, without a serious job prospect, who knows how long it would take him to get back on his feet? Maybe in a few days he'd end up regretting his sudden departure, regardless of how great it would feel for those few moments. Nope, he couldn't do that... His exit strategy needed some well-conceived tactics, like finding a new job first.

Reaching that decision, he tried to relax, to idle his overactive brain. But the darn thing had a mind of its own and went instantly back into obsessing over arguments he could have made with his boss, things he could have said but didn't.

He weighed his options for a little while, then decided to find a friend online and talk about it. It always helped.

He logged on to Rat Olympics and smiled recognizing some familiar names present in the chat room.

DespeRatt: Happy Friday, folks. ☺

LostGirl: 2U2, dear Ratt. ☺

Slave19: How have you been, my man?

DespeRatt: Ahh... don't even ask. ☹ Just another day in paradise.

LostGirl: What's on your mind? What happened?

DespeRatt: Nothing out of the ordinary. Same shit, different day. But today I can't turn my brain off for some reason.

LostGirl: Why? What's going on in there?

DespeRatt: Just thoughts... What I should have said and done instead of what I actually said and did. How it would feel when I'd finally be able to resign and get the hell out of there to never see them again. What my idiot boss meant when he said this and that... Pure insanity!

LostGirl: Sounds like anxiety to me... racing thoughts and all that. Are you suffering from anxiety?

DespeRatt: N–no, I don't think so. If they leave me alone for one day or so, it completely disappears. So I guess the answer is no.

LostGirl: Sounds like you may be heading in that direction anyway, you know. That's how it starts. Welcome to the club, my friend. Soon we'll be exchanging our experiences with anti-anxiety meds instead of having our regular bitching sessions. ☺

DespeRatt: Oh, I hope not! I just need to get my ass in gear and get that new job you're recommending, LostGirl. That's what I need to do.

LostGirl: Go for it!

Slave19: Why is it worse for you today?

DespeRatt: I'm agitated, but also very angry. You see, this is *my* time, this Friday afternoon, my time off away from work. And what do I do with it? Obsess over work, over my idiot boss. I obsess and waste my free time on them. And that makes me incredibly mad... I could smash stuff right now. And I can't turn this stupid brain off, no matter what I try. And don't tell me about meditation, 'cause then I'll really start smashing stuff.

Slave19: LOL, no I won't, don't worry. I was wondering what's making it worse today out of all days. Is it because it's Friday? Or did something happen today?

DespeRatt: I think it's because it's Friday, but you're right, something did happen. Today it felt personal, my argument with him. Usually, it's just technical... we argue over specs, blueprints, solution design, that kind of crap. Today it was more personal. He picked at the way I do things, my interactions with people, that kind of stuff. Oh God... how I hate this shit and what it does to my brain!

LostGirl: Ahh... screw him! Just imagine him sitting on the toilet and running out of TP or something.

DespeRatt: LOL, that might actually work, thanks much for that visual!

Slave19: Hey, what are you planning to have for dinner?

DespeRatt: Haven't thought about that yet... I'll order some pizza, I guess.

Slave19: Here's the deal: if you tell me where you order it from in the next half hour, I'll cover your tab.

DespeRatt: Whoa... are you stalking me or something? Sorry... paranoid here, but creeps are everywhere.

Slave19: ☺ nah... no stalking, you're not that pretty. I didn't ask for your home address or your name, just the location where you order your pizza. Put a code name on the order, say... My Free Dinner.

DespeRatt: Sounds reasonable enough... all right, you're on! With my many thanks!

Slave19: Cool! Where do you order from?

DespeRatt: From Pie in the Sky, it's close to where I live.

LostGirl: How about me? ☺ I'm just as hungry, pissed at life, and anxious as the Ratt is.

Slave19: How about this: I'll buy you dinner next Friday—same deal.

LostGirl: You're on! Thanks!

DespeRatt: I just placed the order, thanks again! You must be making some really nice coin, treating strangers like this. How can I repay you?

Slave19: No need. Just be happy, do what's right for you, and enjoy your pie. And pay it forward someday, help someone in need.

DespeRatt: That I can do.

Slave19: Just called in and covered it—enjoy. Gotta sign off now, have an excellent weekend everyone!

LostGirl: See you next week, 19!

Quentin closed the lid on his laptop and leaned back in his chair. His anxiety gone, he decided to sacrifice the entire weekend to his newly fueled desire to find a new job. He had a résumé to finish, references to organize, a job search to conduct, and several recruiters to contact. All that considered, he should be done before Monday.

He couldn't hope for immediate results, but it was definitely better that sitting idle, obsessing over an idiotic boss who wasn't gonna turn any smarter, revenge fantasies that were never gonna come true, and a new job that wasn't gonna just materialize by itself.

Zane Pemberton was always first on the flight deck, and always mad at his wingman, who made a habit of being late. Not by a whole lot, not enough to get them in trouble with the commander. Just by a minute or two, enough to fuel Zane's irritation and get them both a preflight jogging session to avoid getting canned.

Zane paced the empty briefing room, watching the antiquated wall clock's hand move, second after second. Voodoo was pushing it this time, that reckless asshole. Zane had left his helmet— printed with his call sign, Zombie, in gold lettering over colorful flames—on a table nearby, so he could repeatedly slam his right fist into his open left palm.

"He's doing it again?" the controller asked with mischievous eyes barely showing from behind one of the largest cups of coffee known to man.

"Yup," Zombie replied grumpily.

"What is it this time? His zipper won't close, or something? Did he get stuck with his dick hanging out?"

Zombie chuckled. "Nah... just a combat dump taking too long, I guess."

Just as Voodoo trotted in, making more noise than an elephant and not even bothering to apologize, the speakers above their heads crackled and came alive.

"Scramble! Scramble! Cub One, Cub Two, cleared for takeoff. Cub Three, Cub Four, line up on the ready. Incoming bogeys approaching ADIZ, no transponder, possible hostile, not a drill. Vector 115, inbound from Russian mainland. NORAD tracking. Move to intercept. Scramble! Scramble!"

"Ahh... screw it!" Zombie snapped. "This time we'll get busted. We should acknowledge from the damn cockpit, engines roaring."

"Then what are you waiting for?" Voodoo asked, already ahead of Zombie, trotting hastily on the flight deck toward his plane.

Before running out to catch up with him, Zombie caught a glimpse of the controller laughing out loud.

"Glad to provide entertainment," Zombie muttered, running as fast as he could toward his Raptor, his suit and helmet clattering like a truckload of loosely packaged household items.

Zombie climbed up, hopped in the Raptor, and connected his helmet just in time to hear Voodoo's communication with Control, calm, professional, not even panting.

"Grizzly One, this is Cub Two, ready for takeoff."

"Grizzly, this is Cub One, ready for takeoff," Zombie added, painfully aware his voice gave him up. He was still panting from the run, and very annoyed with being late again, compliments of Voodoo.

Zombie needed method in his day; he was calculated and rigorous in nature and liked well-planned, well-executed things. Voodoo was a risk taker, always cutting it close, always one step behind in planning, but two steps ahead when results were measured, driving Zombie crazy. Zombie did everything by the book and always ended up second. His wingman, on the other hand, had adrenaline instead of blood coursing through his veins, and everything he touched, everything he did, ended up on the merit board. Well, annoying or not, Voodoo was his wingman, and that meant something, including that Zombie would never leave Voodoo behind—not in the briefing room, on the flight deck, or in the air.

They took off in tight formation, throttle to the max. Zombie enjoyed the soaring of the F22 Raptor's takeoff maneuver more than any other part of flying those jets. It made him feel all-powerful and unstoppable and fueled his spirit every time.

"Grizzly One, we're airborne," Zombie called in. "Moving to intercept bogey. I have bogey on radar, vector 265 to intercept."

"Cub One, Cub Two, this is Grizzly. Unidentified aircraft unresponsive. Attempt redirect."

"Grizzly, Cub Two. I have four bogeys onscreen, repeat four bogeys."

"Grizzly, Cub One. Confirm four bogeys."

"Cub Three, Cub Four, cleared for takeoff. Move to intercept bogeys."

"Excellent, that's more like it," Zombie added. "I love a fair fight."

"Zombie, Voodoo, put eyes on that bogey and confirm, stat!" The commander's voice thundered in his helmet.

"Yes, sir!"

"I have bogey at 500 miles and closing fast. I have the sun in my eyes; the bastards knew when to come calling."

"Grizzly, Cub One. I have six bogeys on screen, six bogeys. This could be a major Charlie Foxtrot," Zombie said, a little tension seeping in his voice. "Motherfuckers," he muttered to himself.

"Copy that, Cub One. Ready, Cub Five, Six, and Seven aircraft. Ready tanker. Hang tight, help's on the way." Grizzly's voice remained unperturbed; their commander had stones the size of tanks.

"Here they are, dead ahead," Voodoo yelled.

"Where? Goddamned sun's in my eyes!" Zombie blinked a few times, then said, "I see them! I see them! I'll break left, go check them out."

He turned and slowed a little, preparing to observe the incoming aircraft.

"I see two Backfires, and two Fulcrums," Zombie said, identifying the aircraft by NATO's designated reporting names. *Backfire* stood for the Russian Tupolev TU-22M supersonic, variable-sweep wing, strategic long-range bomber, and missile platform, able to fly almost 4,000 miles without refueling. The Backfires were capable of launching long-range nuclear missiles that could reach San Francisco from right where they were. *Fulcrum* stood for the dreaded, highly maneuverable MiG 29. The MiG could fly Mach 2.25, but had a very limited range.

"Two more bogeys farther out," Zombie added, "I'm guessing refuelers. Driving by to put eyes on them," he said, pushing ahead.

A few seconds later, he had eyes on the tankers and was able to confirm.

"I have two Candids here, two Candids," he said, then started maneuvering to return near Voodoo.

Candid was NATO's designated reporting name for Ilyushin-Il76 strategic airlifter and airborne refueling tanker. The Candid could also serve as an airborne command center.

A familiar alert started beeping.

"I have missile lock on me," Zombie said, "Grizzly One, advise!"

He checked the radar, then turned to look behind him and saw one of the MiGs approaching fast, while the alarm continued to make the beeping sound that all pilots dreaded the most. He felt sweat beads form on his forehead and at the roots of his hair.

"Cub One, do not engage unless fired on. Acknowledge!"

"Acknowledged," Zombie said. It was standard protocol. Rules of engagement stipulated that under no circumstances was an American pilot allowed to open fire, if not fired on first.

He understood the value of the rule; it was meant to avoid starting a war. But it also meant he could become the first victim in that future war, even if his country wasn't the one that started it.

Sweat pooled and formed a drop that started rolling down his nose. He took his oxygen mask off and wiped it with a quick swipe of his sleeve. "Damn, if I'm gonna die here today," he muttered.

Every time he got up in the air, he knew he was risking his life. Yet situations like these were prone to end in disaster. Nerves taut and decisions made in split seconds as they flew through the air at Mach 2 were bound to cause disaster at some point. He just hoped it wasn't going to be today.

He started evasive maneuvers, and Voodoo caught up with him shortly.

"Eagle, Lance, how far behind are you?" Voodoo asked.

"Under two minutes," Lance answered. "Hang in there, guys."

"In two minutes World War III could be over," Zombie commented.

The beeping persisted, and the second MiG was on their tail, as they swerved and turned through the air, trying to keep their distance from the relentless MiGs.

"They've got missile lock on me," Voodoo said. "Readying ECM."

"Where the hell are those Backfires?" Zombie asked. "Breaking left and low to follow the Backfires."

He turned abruptly, the MiG on his tail. Voodoo came right after him, with his own MiG in tow.

"The bastards are keeping us busy here, while their Backfires have other plans. They're under sixty seconds from being within missile range distance from Seattle."

"Cub One, Cub Two, keep your eyes on those Backfires. Cub Three and Four, how much longer?"

"Sixty seconds," Eagle said.

"I wanna lock a missile on a MiG, partner," Zombie said.

"Godspeed," Voodoo replied. "But they're behind us, and we're targeted."

"Watch this and learn," Zombie added cryptically.

He suddenly and abruptly reduced his air speed and pulled up at the same time, executing the flying equivalent of slamming on the brakes, lifting his Raptor in the air like a cobra. The MiG flew right under him continuing its original flight path. Then Zombie dropped back to the same altitude with the MiG and cranked up his speed again, falling right on the MiG's six. He locked guidance on the MiG and yelled, "Yeah, baby, and that's the way it's done!"

"Yeah! Tables are turning!" Voodoo cheered.

They had the Backfire bombers in their sights now, and Voodoo locked a missile on one of them, while continuing to fly an evasive pattern, listening to the obnoxious alarm noises from his missile lock warning system.

They were deep into the Alaskan ADIZ, the air defense identification zone, when unexpectedly the two bombers broke formation and separated their flight paths. One of them turned southeast, while the other remained on course, heading straight for the Aleutian Islands.

"Uh-oh," Voodoo said.

"Grizzly, this is Cub One. Backfire One changing course, new vector 135 to San Francisco. Backfire Two staying the course, vector 115. Advise."

"Split up and keep eyes on those bombers. Cubs Three and Four should reach you in fifteen seconds."

They waved and gave each other a thumbs-up, then they split. With their attention refocused on the bombers, the MiGs took advantage and repositioned to reacquire and target them. They flew evasively while remaining near their assigned Backfires.

A few endless seconds later, Lance's voice came to life in the speakers.

"Cub One, I have you in my sight."

"Cub Two, I have eyes on you," Eagle added.

"This is Grizzly. Thirty seconds more and you'll have Five, Six, and Seven. Do not let those bombers proceed on their paths, do you copy?"

"Loud and clear, Grizzly," Zombie said, his fingers tensing on the stick.

"Crystal," Voodoo added.

Zombie pushed his throttle and flew above the bomber, then fell in front of it and turned around, getting in its path in a zigzag pattern. The MiG was still on his tail, his alarm was still beeping, but Lance had missile lock on the MiG, and he had his on the Backfire. As soon as the remaining three Cubs approached the area, the bomber turned widely, changing its vector to 310 degrees.

"Grizzly, Backfire One is bugging out."

"Backfire Two is bugging out, new vector 355."

"Bravo Zulu, all call signs. Clean up the area and come home."

While Grizzly spoke, they could hear background cheering coming from the people in ground control operations.

"Copy that, Grizzly," Zombie said, "taking the garbage out and then coming home for dinner."

The doorbell made Quentin jump from his armchair, rubbing his palms together in excited anticipation. His free pizza was here.

He opened the door, took the box, and tipped the delivery boy generously. The boy smiled widely and left with a spring in his step.

He took the pizza box with both hands, almost subconsciously noticing it wasn't as hot as he'd expected it to be. He set it on the table, grabbed a plate and a napkin, and turned on the TV. Then he lifted the lid to get a slice, but froze mid-gesture, speechless, his jaw dropped.

Several hundred-dollar bill packets, all used currency, lay neatly arranged in the pizza box. Judging by the label on one of the packets, there were eighty-thousand dollars in total. A disposable cell phone was in there too, and a folded sheet of paper, which Quentin grabbed with trembling hands.

It read, "If you wanted a change in your life, well, this is opportunity knocking. I'm offering you a way out of your desperate rat race. Call the number stored in this phone's memory to talk."

His knees felt weak and he sat down at the table, unable to take his eyes off the disposable phone. What did that mean—a way out of the rat race?

He knew he had to call... there was no other option. People don't just send eighty grand and expect nothing in return. He played with the idea of calling the cops for a few seconds, then quickly discarded it. *That would really make me deserve my rat race, now, wouldn't it?*

With ice-cold, sweaty fingers, he grabbed the cell phone and retrieved the stored number. He stared at the displayed number for a few seconds, then took a deep breath and pressed the *Call* button.

Alex pulled in the visitor parking lot and looked at the familiar building. This was where it had all started, just a couple of years before. She remembered her job interview with Tom Isaac, The Agency's owner; she remembered how scared, self-conscious, and insecure she felt at first, and how exhilarated she was when she had accepted the unusual job offer, without worrying about any of the risks.

She had always considered herself very lucky to land her dream job. Although, in retrospect, knowing what she knew of how The Agency operated, she wasn't that sure it was luck that made it happen. Tom had fielded her direct questions by saying she had been selected, but never offered a word more.

She was grateful for his confidence, for the opportunity to work with a fantastic team of smart, powerful, and knowledgeable business people. She had a lot to learn from them and she enjoyed it. She was happy she didn't have to deal with boredom at work; after all, she had to infiltrate a new organization every few months or so, and start a brand new investigation.

Alex was a little worried on that particular day, considering Tom had summoned her to the office. They typically met at his home, where Alex had become a part of the family, welcome any time without announcing herself ahead. Her conscience was bothering her a little too, because she had been unable to focus lately. Tom might have sensed that. Who was she kidding... for sure he had sensed that, otherwise he'd make a very poor observer of people's behavior, and that was impossible, considering his company's line of work and record of success.

She braced herself for the meeting, and a wave of sadness came upon her as she walked through the doors. She hated disappointing Tom, or any other member of the team, yet that had been the norm in the past few weeks.

She reached Tom's office and tapped quietly on the door.

"Alex, come in," Tom said, getting up from his massive leather chair to greet her. "It's good to see you! You've been a stranger lately!"

"Good to see you too, Tom, and yes, I have. And I've missed you, all of you," she said, averting her eyes.

She turned her back and poured herself a cup of coffee from Tom's machine, then sat down, sipping it slowly, and inhaling the French Vanilla aroma. All good reasons to avert her eyes some more.

"So, why the absence? What's on your mind?"

"Nothing much, really, just tired, I guess," she replied, continuing to avoid his scrutinizing glance.

At sixty-three, Tom Isaac was the father figure in her life: friend, mentor, boss, and a shoulder to cry on when she needed one. He was an amazing man. Very bright and profound, extremely perceptive with people and a keen investigator, yet someone so independent and so motivated by his own beliefs that he had chosen to start a private investigations firm that exclusively handled corporate clients, a unique and challenging business. It was very hard to lie to him.

"You're doing it again," Tom said in a kind voice.

"What?" she asked.

"Remember your job interview? You're giving me the bullshit dance, Alex." He smiled encouragingly, then continued, "Is it this office? You've only done this twice since I've known you, and both times it happened here, in this office," he clarified humorously. "It must be the office, I believe."

Scratch that, Alex thought. No, it was impossible to lie to him.

"Busted," she laughed sheepishly. "Yeah... I *was* giving you the bullshit dance. But I won't anymore."

"Wanna try again?"

"Yeah... It's my last case, that's all. Still keeps me up at night."

"But we closed that case," Tom argued. "Why is it still bothering you?"

"Everyone, including you," she said, gesturing with her hand, a little irritation seeping in her voice, "says we closed the case successfully. But did we? We didn't catch the leader; we don't even know who he is, other than he's Russian. All we have is a piece of very thin intel that his name might start with the letter V. We caught the rest of the terrorists, but this guy... This guy drives me crazy. He has to exist somewhere, leave a trace somewhere."

Tom leaned forward in his chair, with a look of concern on his face.

"Alex, one of the most difficult things we have to face in our jobs is letting go. It's not risking our lives, it's not being held at gunpoint, it's not even being arrested or shot. It's exactly what you're going through now, letting go."

"Has it happened to you too?" she asked, looking him in the eye for the first time since she'd arrived in his office.

"More than once," he admitted.

"How did you manage to let go?"

"I had to pull myself out of it, because I was screwing up my new client engagements, just like you are screwing up yours now. An unfocused mind can be deadly in our line of work, to you, to all of us."

She blushed instantly, feeling her cheeks burn and tears coming to her eyes.

"I am sorry, so sorry, Tom, I hope you know that," she whispered.

"I know you are, but this isn't the point." He paused a little, letting his words sink in. "This," he continued, pointing at her, "is not the girl I hired. The girl I hired had gumption and drive. There was no stopping her and no messing with her. She always got the job done, effectively, courageously, and intelligently. She cared about her clients to the point of self-sacrifice. While you, you are spaced out half the time, mulling over an unsolvable problem."

"If I only had a lead, I would instantly turn back into that girl," Alex said timidly.

"And what if you don't? What if you'll never get that lead? Is this it? You're gonna throw your career and life away for a Russian ghost, whose name potentially starts with V?"

She couldn't bring herself to answer. He was right. Well, Tom was always right, that made him who he was.

"How did you let go? Tell me what I should do, please," she pleaded.

"First of all," he stated, counting on his fingers, "you have to decide to let go, with all your being, all your willpower. Until you do that, you won't find peace in letting go. Mind over matter, remember?"

"Yes," she whispered, her eyes fixated on the carpet's gray and blue pattern.

"Then you act on your decision," Tom continued, "you do the things you have to do to close that case for good."

"Like what?"

"Burn your crazy wall. Get rid of that corkboard and everything that's on it, and turn that spare bedroom into a movie screening room, or something. Turn it into something you like, something that makes you happy, and let some sunshine in."

She looked at him with piercing eyes, while her faced transformed from the earlier embarrassment and sadness into sheer anger.

"You've never been in that room, Tom. How did you know about it?"

Tom cleared his throat, obviously uncomfortable. "Steve... well, Steve talked to me about it."

"He did, now, didn't he?" Her voice was low, threatening.

"You have to understand, Alex, we all care about you and we want you to be healthy, get on with your life."

"So that makes it all right to talk about me behind my back?" she snapped, standing up so abruptly that her chair tipped over. She didn't even notice it, as she started pacing the room like a caged animal. "What, Mr. Shrink now thinks I lost it and has turned me into you? Is that how it works?"

"You should know me better than this," Tom said in a hurt voice, "you should know *us* better than this."

Maybe she should... She stopped her pacing and looked out the window, focusing intently on a distant palm tree, glimmering in the sunlight as if it were made of tinfoil.

She took a deep breath, trying to calm herself. This was her boss she was yelling at, and she loved her job; she definitely wanted to keep it. She needed to act as such.

"Tom," she said, turning toward him apologetically, "I am very sorry for my outburst. I–I felt betrayed, that's all. Steve and I have a relationship, and I thought... well, I never thought he'd do this to me."

"I understand," he said, "but it just confirmed what I was saying. You've distanced yourself mentally to the point where you feel the need to protect yourself from us. You feel the need to hide what's on your mind. What happened to that trust we had to work so hard to earn from you? Is it all gone?"

It had been a challenge for her to learn to trust The Agency's team. Her teenage years and early adulthood had been riddled with hardship and heartbreak stemming from her parents' spiraling descent into discontent with each other, verbal violence, and psychological abuse. She had left her parents behind as soon as she had turned eighteen, but she continued to remain wary, almost suspicious of people.

"I guess I'm falling back into old patters of behavior," she admitted. "You have a point, Tom, and I'll work hard on letting go, I promise. Thank you for continuing to believe in me."

"I'll never stop believing in you, Alex, that's a promise. But you have to do your part and come back to us. Please try," he said, standing up to see her out.

Her heart melted a little hearing his words. She welcomed his hug and inhaled the familiar scent of aftershave mixed with cigar smoke. She took in the feeling of safety and comfort for a second, then replied, "I will. It's a promise."

Only half of the ground level in Walcott's multilevel parking structure was open to the employees and visitors. The rest was blocked off for the company-owned fleet, for their parking spots, in addition to light maintenance, car wash, and detailing. It had a built-in automated car-wash station and a fully equipped detailing station, staffed by the fleet manager and two helpers.

Walcott Global owned several vehicles. A few black SUVs waited, readily available for traveling executives in need of transportation. The limo was used for company events and to impress visiting clients and government officials. Finally, a black Mercedes Sprinter functioned as a shuttle, hauling personnel and delegates to and from airports, conferences, and events, and Naval Station Norfolk—one of Walcott's employees' most frequent destinations.

Walcott Global's revenue had topped seven-billion dollars the prior year, most of it coming from the Navy. One of the top government contractors for engineering consulting services, Walcott was the US government's top resource in weapons and communications research and deployment, focused almost entirely on mobile platforms. That made the US Navy and the US Air Force its biggest clients. With the growing tensions in the world and a rejuvenated interest in scaling up arsenals and new technologies, Walcott was buzzing with activity.

That activity buzz reverberated all the way to the ground floor of the parking structure, where the Sprinter had to be detailed quite often. Terry, the fleet manager, handled that task personally whenever he had the time; the Sprinter had to look impeccably clean and ready to transport official delegations without notice.

The Sprinter accommodated fifteen passengers, and its luxurious, custom leather seats were organized like those on a commuter jet: two adjoining on one side, with a single one on the opposite side, while the end row had four seats without any space in between.

Terry's first job when detailing the Sprinter was to check for any forgotten or dropped items, before bringing in the vacuum cleaner. He moved swiftly from seat to seat, sliding his gloved hand between the seats and the side panels of the vehicle, normally taking less than five minutes to finish the search. It was routine.

That morning however, he never made it past the third row. A sheet of paper had fallen between the edge of the single seat on the third row and its corresponding side panel, only a small corner of it visible.

Terry grabbed the visible corner gently with his gloved hand, careful not to tear the paper. There was enough room between the seat and the panel; the paper came out easily, without any tearing. There was nothing written on it. Terry flipped it on its other side and froze.

It was the cover page of a technical documentation file, but that wasn't the most disturbing thing about it. The fact that it was marked TOP SECRET wasn't either.

The most disturbing fact was that the TOP SECRET mark was in black and white, a clear proof that the document was an unauthorized photocopy of a TOP SECRET document. All legitimate copies of classified documents had to bear a stamp in original ink, with the copy date and authorization code.

The header read, "Walcott Global." The document was titled, "Evaluation Memorandum: Compatibility and Readiness Assessment for the Installation of Laser Cannon Technology Onboard Zumwalt Class Destroyers."

They had a leak.

He has a passion for weather. He loved observing changing weather patterns, having his forecast down to each passing cloud and wind gust. The digital weather station on his wall was the first thing he checked in the morning of each day, religiously. The information displayed on it stated that it was going to be a nice day, with partly cloudy skies, barometric pressure was going to hold steady, and temperatures reasonable for the season.

Adrenaline had kept him awake for the best part of the night; excitement and anticipation for what that day was going to bring turned more and more intense as he approached the drop time. His first drop... his first step on a path from which there was no coming back. And yet, despite the adrenaline rushing blood through his veins, the moment he entered his office, his usual obsession with weather took over and he spent a good five minutes analyzing the data on the digital weather station.

He had time though, plenty of time to prepare. His plan was relatively simple, and he was already halfway through with it. First, he had gained access to the documents. To do that, he had waited patiently for the first day when legitimate business reasons called for him to access the highly restricted document storage area named CDR—Centralized Document Repository. Each employee had to have a project number associated with each visit, and the CDR's staff entered that information in a computer, together with the files accessed or removed. Any discrepancy between retrieved files and active projects triggered an immediate alarm; doors would go on lockdown, and no one would be allowed to leave the CDR level until cleared by internal security. The place was airtight, with procedures and systems worthy of the secrecy of the content they protected.

That's why he had to wait a while, but the day before he was able to access the CDR and remove the three files that interested him. He could only borrow them for a few hours, not more. The second step was to make copies of the files—unauthorized copies, of course. That, in itself, had proven to be a bit of a challenge, but he had had a few days to find a way to work around that challenge while waiting for CDR access.

The challenge was the copier. The building's new copiers were modern pieces of equipment that needed his personal code before doing anything, and stored all copied material in their memory, time-stamped, where the Internal Security department could access anything at will during random checks. There was no way he could use one of those machines. But he had found another copy machine, a forgotten piece of junk from the 1980s, still in service in the basement mailroom. It still worked; albeit not perfectly, leaving a narrow vertical black line on each page and moving very slowly, but it didn't need access codes to work, and it didn't store any activity logs or images of copied documents.

Accessing the copier in the mailroom was another challenge; he started the copy job during the mailroom clerk's lunch break and had to stay late the night before to finish the nerve-racking job on the slowest copier ever invented. Every paper rustle, every footstep on the hallway resonated in his mind louder than cannon fire, causing his heart to skip a beat and his blood to rush to his head. And that piece of junk took two minutes to copy each page... how did people ever get any work done with equipment like that? The job had taken so long to finish that he ran out of time to return the files to the CDR the same day; internal security procedures rendered it inaccessible after 7.00PM.

Then he had a panic attack... the adventures of the day had probably been the most that he could handle. He wasn't experienced at this game... not yet, anyway. It was well after 7.00PM when he had finished; he was still in possession of the original files, and he just couldn't bring himself to walk out with the copies in his briefcase. He was too scared, too jumpy, too exhausted.

The next step required him to get the copied documents outside the building and take them home, where he could take pictures and save them on a digital memory card. He had thought of bringing a camera inside the building, but every morning he had to walk through metal detectors to get in, while his briefcase was being X-rayed. No way could he pull that off. Personal phones were kept in lockers at the main entrance during the day, and the corporate phone's camera was a bad idea for obvious reasons.

He had decided to put it off for a day, and that had been a good decision. He knew exactly what he had to do. He wanted to organize the copies before the day's madness would start and he risked people interrupting him or barging unannounced in his office. He also needed to return the originals to the CDR. Then, at the end of the day he'd leave with the rest of the crowd at about 5.00PM or so, and walk right out of the building with the copied files hidden in the lining of his briefcase. Easy peasy.

He started organizing the copied documents in order, by file number, making sure every page was there. As he reached the bottom of the copied papers pile, he froze... He was missing one copied page, the cover page from one of the files.

His own heartbeat deafened him, pumping hard in his chest as he tried desperately to breathe, to control the onset of another panic attack. Where could he have left it? He was sure he had copied every single page.

He rushed downstairs to the mailroom; luckily, no one was there. He went straight for the copier and almost tore it apart looking for the missing page. Maybe it got stuck in the copier somewhere, like a paper jam? Nothing there, nothing on the small table he had used, or behind it, where it could have fallen.

He looked everywhere in his own office; opened every drawer, checked every piece of furniture, every file folder he had on his desk. Nada. Exhausted, his knees weak from excess adrenaline, he let himself drop in his chair.

He tried to retrace his steps on the day before, but couldn't focus. He had been in and out of the office, but everything was a blur. The entire day he had been painfully aware of each surveillance camera in the building and had to jump through hoops to avoid them.

He remembered he had to go to Norfolk Harbor with the project team for a few hours after lunch, but he was positive he had left the documents carefully hidden under his area rug at the time. He couldn't remember when he took them from there, or where else he went; his memory was failing under the wave of brainwashing adrenaline.

Maybe he simply hadn't copied that page... errors can happen, he thought. He must have just skipped it by mistake. Steadying himself, he grabbed the original of the missing page and ventured to the mailroom again. The slower-than-molasses copier finished the one page copy job just as the mailroom clerk came in with the day's mail delivery, giving him a start.

"Can I help you, sir?"

"Y–yes," he said, holding the manila folder with the original and its copy as if he were about to hand it to the clerk, "can we ship something overnight to our New Zealand office? What's the procedure?"

He hoped the clerk would not pick up on the strong smell of copier toner, activated by heat in the antiquated copy process, or notice how badly his hands were shaking.

"You need it interoffice, sir?"

"Yes," he confirmed.

"You'd need an IE9D form filled, signed, stamped, and attached to the document package, together with your auth code."

"All right, I'll get that started."

He left the mailroom briskly but couldn't bring himself to breathe until he was alone in the elevator.

He had a few more hours until the drop... he was going to make it with plenty of time to spare.

"Just show me exactly where you found it," Mason Armstrong encouraged Terry, following him inside the Sprinter with some difficulty.

Armstrong, the chief of internal security for Walcott Global, had a painful, bothersome limp in his left leg, an unwanted memento of his days in the US Secret Service. He had been in the service of President Bill Clinton, a president so peaceful that few people still remembered the 1994 assassination attempt that took place at the White House. Armstrong did, however, because one of the bullets fired on that day by the attacker's semiautomatic weapon had shattered his femur, leaving him crippled and desk-ridden since he was thirty-one.

Despite several rounds of reconstructive surgery, Mason never walked straight again, and every time he put his weight on that leg it was a painful reminder of what a single fateful moment can take from one's life. None of that pain showed on his face though. Completely bald and clean-shaven, with features that appeared carved in stone, immobile, and free of any emotion, Armstrong was perfectly suited for the high-stress job he had. He remained calm under any circumstance, an invaluable skill he picked up during his training with the Secret Service, a skill that had proven useful many times.

As head of security for Walcott Global, he was responsible for every aspect of security, from the protection of the company's physical facilities, to the safety of its employees, and the safeguarding of all information. Armstrong combined his calm, thoughtful mental process with a procedural, structured approach to all events and situations. He had earned the trust and respect of his employer for the smooth, efficient, and discreet handling of all matters security, regardless of how delicate.

Armstrong watched as Terry demonstrated where he had found the document, using a blank sheet of paper snatched from Armstrong's printer.

"When's the last time you detailed the van?" Armstrong asked, jotting down notes.

"Yesterday morning, sir."

"How many times has it left the garage since then?"

"Five times, sir. One outbound, two airport pickups, and two roundtrips with our teams."

"Get me the lists of all people who touched or used the van since the last time you detailed it. You keep logs, Terry?"

"Yes, sir. I'll get you everything you need."

Armstrong stepped out of the van slowly, holding on tight to the handrail on the door.

"Onboard cameras would have been nice to have now, right, sir?" Terry ventured.

"Yes, definitely," Armstrong confirmed with a frown.

Armstrong had been an advocate for video surveillance in all company vehicles, but with no success. Walcott's CEO had resisted the thought, stating that it would insult their guests and visiting officials with such a blatant manifestation of distrust, shown as early as an airport pickup—their first contact with Walcott Global. Maybe the current situation would get him to reconsider.

"Did you touch the document with your hand at any time, Terry?"

"No, sir, I wear gloves when I work on the vehicles."

"Good, good," Armstrong said, giving Terry an encouraging pat on the shoulder before he turned away and walked toward the main building.

A few minutes later, he closed the office door and immediately pulled out his cell phone, using voice recognition for his command.

"Call Sam Russell, encrypted," he said.

"Calling Sam Russell, mobile, encryption active," the smart phone's robotic voice answered.

Two short rings later, a familiar voice picked up.

"Mason, hey, good to hear from you," Sam said.

Armstrong stifled a sigh before responding.

"Well, maybe not so good... Sam, I need your help. How fast can you get here?"

He closed the door behind him and leaned against it for a minute. It felt good to be home after such an emotionally draining day. He closed his eyes and let out a deep breath, loosening his tie. He'd made it home in one piece, documents included. He could make the drop now, and that was going to be easy.

He went straight for the dining room table, where he placed his briefcase carefully on the shiny surface. He pulled the curtains shut, making sure their edges overlapped to ensure perfect privacy, and only afterward he turned on the lights.

He opened the briefcase and carefully tugged at the bottom lining, separating it from the edge on one side. He gently pulled the file folder from underneath the lining, and then he stuck the lining back under the edges with his fingernail.

Photographing was next. He took an older digital camera, one that didn't connect to anything via any technology, Internet, or Bluetooth; one that didn't have a GPS built in. It was a simpler model, one of the first to use an SD card. He opened the file folder and started photographing the pages one by one, in the right order.

As he worked, his hands steadied and his heart rate dropped to more normal levels; he was getting used to the idea of what he was doing; he was getting more comfortable walking on the path of no return. He had no regrets... he was actually happy he was going to even the score with his employer... the bastards deserved what was coming to them, and more. That feeling of accomplishment, of setting things right overcame all his fear—fear of getting caught, of spending the rest of his days serving a life sentence for treason, fear of death.

He paused after each file, verifying his work on the camera's tiny screen. All three documents were going to make his handler very happy. Not bad for his first drop: the capabilities assessment for Zumwalt-class destroyers, the evaluation memorandum regarding the compatibility and readiness status for laser cannon installation onboard the USS *Fletcher*, and the performance and capabilities assessment for the laser cannon. Yep, not bad at all. Well, actually too good. Why give him everything in one drop? He could make more money if he delivered the valuable goods one gem at a time.

He chose the evaluation memorandum for the drop, and brought an extra SD card to store the other two files.

When he finished photographing the last page of the memorandum, he verified the images on the camera; they were all there. He removed the SD card from the camera, then packed it neatly in a small Ziploc bag.

He took the documents and camera out of sight, hiding them in a kitchen drawer. He made a quick call to his favorite messenger service, FastLite, asking them to pick up a package.

Taking a new canister of three Dunlop tennis balls, he carefully opened it, making sure the clear wrapper stayed as intact as possible. Using a box cutter, he cut the tape sealing the cap on the clear plastic wrapper, and took two of the balls out. He carefully made a small incision in one of the balls, slicing along the gum line for about an inch. Then he slid the packet containing the SD card in its Ziploc bag inside the tennis ball. He verified carefully; the cut wasn't visible at all, hidden in the green fuzz at the edge of the gum line. Satisfied, he put the ball on top of the remaining one in the canister, then topped it with the third ball and sealed the package with a fresh piece of tape.

He finished everything moments before the messenger rang his doorbell. He opened the door promptly.

"Got a package, sir?" A kid, no more than sixteen years old, wearing a FastLite tee and cap, stood in his doorway, still mounted on his bike, leaning sideways on one foot.

"Yeah, just this," he said, showing the boy the set of tennis balls. "It's my kid's birthday; I need these to get to him tonight. It's not far... Can you do it?"

"Sure... that's what we do," the boy answered, a bit confused by the question.

"Great, just give me a second, let me wrap this real quick."

He took gift-wrapping paper from one of the drawers and packed the tennis balls quickly, slapping some tape at the ends so it stayed wrapped. He handed it to the boy, together with two twenty-dollar bills.

"No card?" the boy asked.

"Huh?"

"It's his birthday... no card?"

"N–no," he said, caught off guard. "I called him earlier." *Shit...* he thought. *That's really sloppy work, damn it.*

"Ok, I'll go, if that's it," the boy said, filling out a small form and handing it over. He started looking for change, but the sender stopped him.

"Nah... keep it!"

"Thank you, sir!"

He closed and locked the door carefully, and put the chain on. He had one more thing left to do before calling the job done. He had to destroy the documents.

He pulled the file folder from the drawer and took it in the garage. He grabbed a bucket and filled it halfway with hot water, tore the papers in a few pieces, then submerged them in the water, one by one. The water dissolved the bonding agent that held the cellulose fibers together, and the paper quickly turned mushy. He helped the process stirring the contents of the bucket with a long screwdriver, and, within minutes, the paper was mashed up in small little bits, the writing on it gone, liquefied by the hot water.

He carried the bucket to the bathroom and flushed its content down the toilet. He put the bucket back in the garage where it came from, and looked around to see if everything looked in order.

Finally, he did the one thing he'd been waiting for the whole day. He poured himself a double shot of whiskey neat, and gulped it with a couple of antianxiety pills.

"I need to get better at this," he heard himself saying. "Way better."

Alex curled up on her couch in the semi-darkness of her living room. The dusk projected long shadows on the walls, but she didn't turn on the lights or close her curtains. She welcomed the nightfall in her home to match the gloom in her heart.

She'd kept the word given to herself and slept on her resolution, avoiding any rash decisions. A full day of anguish and pain had passed since she had her eye-opening conversation with Tom. Despite her sleeping on it, the decision remained the same. She had to regain control of her life and clean up her own mess. The decision felt right rationally; it was the logical thing to do, but broke her heart.

A rebel tear rolled on her cheek. She wiped it with the back of her hand, just as the doorbell rang.

"Yeah, come right in," she said, not moving.

Steve walked through the door, a frown of concern replacing the smile on his face as soon as he took in the details of what he was seeing. He reached for the light switch on the wall, but she stopped him.

"Leave it off," she said.

"All right," he said in a pacifying tone. "You left your door unlocked again, and we—"

"Save it," she cut him off bluntly. "Take a seat somewhere; this isn't gonna take long."

He seemed to turn pale, but she couldn't be sure; it was quite dark in the room. He sat in the armchair across from her and remained silent, waiting.

She let the silence match the darkness for a while, thick, bothersome. When she spoke, her voice was broken and quiet, whispers hiding sobs that were pressing to come out.

"We have to part ways, Steve. We're over."

He jumped on his feet and came toward her. She raised her palm outward, stopping him.

"Don't. Please. It's hard enough as it is."

"Then why do it, Alex? What's wrong?"

"It was a mistake to mix our work with a relationship, an idiotic rookie mistake. We both knew better," she articulated with difficulty. "We both knew there was no way this could end well, despite how we feel."

"What happened?" Steve asked in a soft voice.

"You betrayed me, that's what happened."

The surprise on his face was genuine.

"What you see in my house," she clarified, "when you come visit, is private. It's mine and only mine. My secrets, that I chose to share with you, were mine and only mine, yet you chose to share them with others without my permission."

"But it's Tom we're talking about," Steve said, gently. "Tom only wants what's best for you, and so do I. We're all worried."

"I need to be in control of my life, Steve," she said, wiping another tear with the back of her hand. "Tom is also my boss, you're forgetting that. You jeopardized my job, my existence."

"Tom would never fire you—"

"It's not about that, and yes, given enough reason, he would," she interrupted. "He's not running a daycare; he's got a business to run. Maybe I'm too new at this, or maybe I don't feel so confident anymore. In any case, I need to regain full control of my life." She paused for a few seconds, closing her eyes. "And that means letting you go," she whispered.

"Alex, I'm sorry, I promise I'll ne—"

"It's too late, Steve, I'm sorry. I fell in love with you and I made excuses; I rationalized how we're not gonna be a cliché; not us, 'cause we're so much better than everyone else is. We're not gonna fall into the traps of doomed office relationships, not us. But we did, we did exactly that."

His head hung, and he clasped his hands together, in an unspoken plea. She stifled another sob.

"After yesterday, I could never trust you again, not like before, and my heart would ache for that kind of trust, for that loss. I would have to lie to you, hide from you. It would slowly ruin our relationship, putting us through more pain than either of us can handle."

He looked at her silently, unable to say a word, the sadness in his blue eyes speaking in his place.

"I'm sorry, Steve, I really am." She wiped another tear with her sleeve, then said in an agonizing voice, "Please, go now."

He approached her slowly and took her hand, holding it gently. She didn't turn to look at him; she just continued to stare into the thickening darkness.

"There's one thing that neither Tom nor I were going to tell you, but I think you should hear it anyway. This obsession you have with your elusive Russian terrorist, your stubbornness to accept that the case is closed, is who you are: dedicated, persistent, driven. The fact that saving a few lives and catching a few terrorists just isn't good enough for you, well, that's what makes you who you are. That's what makes you great, what makes you special. That's what makes you so damn good at what you do. But that's also what could destroy you. And we just couldn't sit idle and let it happen... we're here for you. I'm here for you... always."

He placed a gentle kiss on her hand, then let it go. She still didn't look at him; she couldn't.

He turned away and walked out, closing the door behind him silently, after releasing the auto lock on her deadbolt.

She heard his car start and pull away from her driveway. Soon thereafter came a deafening silence, the time for her to mourn her loss.

Jeremy Weber knocked three times on the doorframe before stepping in his boss's office.

"You wanted to see me, sir?" Jeremy asked.

"Yes. Sit down."

He sat where instructed, and waited for SAC Taylor to speak.

"I'm putting you on the Walcott case," Taylor said, pushing a file folder across the desk.

"Me, sir?" Weber blurted, then bit his lip. Stupid remarks like that cost people their careers.

"Yes, and I'm doubting my own sanity as we speak," Taylor replied coldly. "There's no better choice... believe me, I tried. I had assigned Porter and Sinisky on it yesterday, but their car got rammed by an eighteen-wheeler. They'll both be out of commission for weeks." Taylor stopped for a second, drilling Jeremy with his intense gaze. "You're it. Don't screw this up. One moment of embarrassment from you while you're on this case and you're history."

Jeremy didn't reply; diplomatically he diverted Taylor's attention to the work at hand.

"What's the scoop?"

"Walcott's got an info leak, state secrets, major damage," Taylor replied. "The rest is in the file. Read it. Carefully."

"Yes, sir. Umm... I don't have a partner assigned yet," Jeremy said hesitantly. "I'm perfectly fine without one, sir, but—"

"But I'm not," Taylor cut him off. "Just get me preliminary findings and come back to report. I'll assign you a partner."

Jeremy stood and grabbed the file from Taylor's desk.

"Understood," he said, turning to leave.

"Weber?"

"Sir?"

"This could be a major clusterfuck... Huge government contractor, massive political influence, and the leak is scary as hell—their latest weapons technology, no less. Tread lightly, be thorough, but get the facts ASAP. Follow the damn procedure, got it?"

"Yes, sir, got it. You can count on me," Jeremy added, and immediately regretted it.

"Well, that's precisely it, Weber, I can't. Can't count on you, now can I?"

Jeremy hesitated, inclined to make additional promises to his reluctant boss, but decided to keep quiet instead.

"Sir," he said in lieu of a farewell, then stepped out of Taylor's office.

He didn't even stop by his office; he went straight for the parking garage. He wanted to get as much work done as possible, before getting who-knows-who for a partner to slow him down or drive him crazy.

Henri Marino checked her reflection in the stainless steel doors and repressed a sigh. She looked professional, of course, yet not really in line with what she had in mind for herself. The loose ponytail keeping her long brown hair in check looked sloppy and hasty, like she'd tied that up in a hurry. Well, in fact, that was the truth. She had to admit it, remembering how she had finished dressing in her building's elevator that morning.

She checked the time again; just a few more minutes before Director Seiden would see her. She put down the brief she had prepared for the director, afraid her sweaty palms would leave marks on the elegant cover bearing the CIA logo in gold foil emboss.

Now she had two idle hands and nothing to do, while waiting, pacing, checking the time once more.

"You can take a seat," Seiden's assistant said, visibly irritated by her restlessness.

She was tempted to oblige for a split second, then declined with a shy smile. "I'll be fine, thank you."

For the next few minutes, she tried to stay true to her commitment to never crack her knuckles again. She'd read somewhere it was a bad habit, not necessarily causing arthritis or anything, but annoying the hell out of everyone present.

"You can go in now," Seiden's assistant said.

She headed straight to the director's door, then turned on her heels and grabbed the report she'd forgotten.

She knocked twice, then entered the director's office. Seiden had loosened his tie and rolled up his sleeves, but the perma-frown on his forehead looked deeper than usual, ridging canyons above his bushy eyebrows.

"Henri," he greeted her and pointed to a chair in front of his desk.

"Sir," she croaked, then cleared her throat. "Good morning," she added, to demonstrate she could still use her vocal chords.

"So?" Seiden asked, keeping his hand extended toward her. "Are you gonna let me read it?"

"Umm... sure," she said, handing him the brief, painfully aware she was blushing.

Director Seiden took the brief and started reviewing it, flipping through pages at a constant pace, for what seemed like endless minutes. Finally, he spoke.

"OK, never mind this," he said, putting it on the table and placing his hand on it. "What do you think?"

"Well, it's in there," she started talking, then stopped abruptly. *Of course, it's in there, you ninny,* she thought. *He knows that. He just wants to have a conversation with his senior analyst.*

"Since my last report, the count of incidents climbed to sixty-two total," she finally heard herself say, in a relatively confident voice.

"Since when?"

"I've gone back eighteen months, but their frequency has increased over time."

"What do you mean?"

"There were only seven incidents in the first six months I looked at. Then in the following six months, the count jumped to nineteen. And the most recent six months had forty-three incidents, more unevenly distributed from a geographical perspective, and more aggressive each month."

"Any geographical prevalence?"

"N–no, not really, not overall, anyway. While the incidents remain relatively evenly distributed on the map over the entire eighteen months, the past six months showed more North American occurrences, and their severity has increased on average."

"How do you measure that?" Seiden asked.

"I classified all incidents in one of three categories. They can be near-routine incidents, such as flight intercepts, interference with normal civilian operations, or incursions into our Air Defense Identification Zone. Then they could be serious incidents with escalation risk, such as the Russian aircraft that approached the Danish island of Bornholm in what appeared to be an attack, then broke off at the last minute. Finally, they could be high-risk incidents, such as the Russian submarine incursion into Swedish territorial waters, or the Alaska missile lock incident last month."

"And how do they break out by severity, the incident counts?"

She opened the brief to make sure her memory didn't fail her at the wrong moment.

"Umm... there were fourteen high-risk incidents, twenty-one serious with escalation risk, and twenty-seven near-routine incidents." She pushed the brief over the desk, so the director could read the numbers from the table.

He looked at the page for a few seconds, then deepened his frown.

"But that's not it, sir," she added, pulling the brief from under his hand.

"*This* is what's more interesting," she said, flipping a couple of pages and showing Seiden an image of the world map with colorful pins on it. "I've colored the oldest incidents blue, the six-to-twelve months old in purple, and the most recent ones in red. What do you see?"

Seiden looked at her for a second, surprised by her unusual question. She wanted to kick herself... it was unprofessional, rude even to question a high-ranking executive as if he was a child.

Before she could figure out if she should apologize or just fix her blunder, he answered.

"Yes, that is interesting. The red dots are mostly near our borders, with just a couple elsewhere, just enough to keep things confusing. So what are you saying?"

"I am saying things are definitely escalating. The same worrisome distribution remains true from the incident severity point of view, where we see the high-risk incidents clustering more and more near our borders, near NORAD space."

Seiden remained silent for a minute, staring pensively at the colorful map that spelled trouble.

"We need to inform USNORTHCOM about this. Let's talk threat scenarios," he said, rubbing his forehead forcefully.

"In my previous report, I was listing three possible threat scenarios. The most plausible at first sight is that they're testing our response. The second one is that they're keeping the world busy while they're preparing a nuclear strike and the commencement of World War III. Finally, the third, and least plausible considering President Abramovich's psychology, is that they're provoking us, our allies, so we end up being the ones who push one button or another and start World War III."

"Why do you think the third scenario is not that plausible?" Seiden asked.

"Abramovich, well, he's a pure sociopath on a mission of revenge over Crimea and what he perceives as a colossal offense brought to Russia by the West, by America. This particular psychology is incompatible with caring what the world has to say about who started the war. He wouldn't care... he doesn't." Henri stopped for a few seconds, collecting her thoughts, to make sure she wasn't omitting anything. "He is actively working to restore Russia to its pre-glasnost position of power," she continued. "But I don't think that his strategy is contradicting either of the first two scenarios."

Seiden took a sip from a bottle of sparkling water, then took his time to screw the cap back on.

"If you were to pick one of these scenarios to prepare response strategies for, which one would you choose?" Seiden asked, suddenly looking at her with focused, intent eyes. "Do you maintain your former assessment, does the nuclear scenario still seem more plausible to you?"

"Y–yes," she responded, not blinking under the director's scrutinizing gaze, just letting a split moment of hesitation show.

"Why hesitate? What's on your mind?"

"Well, sir, you might think I'm crazy," she blurted out, "but even the nuclear scenario seems too clean, too easy for Abramovich at this time."

"Too easy? How the hell can nuclear war be too easy?" Seiden said, letting his voice reflect his frustration. He stood and started pacing the room.

A little flustered by his unusually emotional response, Henri tried to formulate an answer that could make sense to other people, not just in her own mind.

"You assigned a task force under my command, sir," she explained. "I've engaged the team in several areas. I had an analyst focus on Russian uranium ore extraction and potential arsenal build-ups. Another one was tasked to monitor Russian ICBM sites and any related activities. The field operative you deployed came back with preliminary findings into the research facility being built near Moscow—it's gonna be a huge data processing center, storing massive amounts of data and a basement full of computing capabilities, 350,000 square feet. Finally, I had a senior analyst look into the military training, simulation exercises, and readiness."

"And?" Seiden asked impatiently.

"Well, their activities sort of line up, more like they line up with two different strategies. One," she held up one finger, "they are most definitely getting ready to engage data in a new, unprecedented way. That could mean cyber warfare or increased foreign intelligence activities. Two," Henri's second finger went up, "if they're looking at more traditional warfare, including nuclear, they are definitely getting ready, but not in a massive way."

"What are you trying to say, Henri?" Seiden made a visible effort to calm down and took a seat back in his leather chair.

"We need to get back to Abramovich's psychology and state of mind to understand this," Henri said almost apologetically. He nodded, and she continued, "OK, we've established Abramovich is a pure narcissistic sociopath who will stop at nothing. Correct?"

Seiden nodded again.

"But what does that mean? What does it feel like to be Abramovich and to have the world tell you what you can and cannot do and insult you all over the news channels for Crimea, for the ethics of your policy, and so on?"

Seiden silently encouraged her to continue, intrigued by her approach to the point where his frown almost disappeared.

"He's in pain, sir, that's what that means," she said, gesturing with her hands to underline the simplicity of this fact. "He's in immense, excruciating psychological pain, and has been ever since Crimea. He's lost so much because of what the world thought of his actions in Crimea—cash flow, the respect of other world leaders, the intoxicating devotion of his oligarchs. He's hurting so badly he can't think of anything else but how to make us all pay for it, painfully, slowly, indefinitely, and beyond repair. From his perspective, we are torturing him and he's dying to get even and then some. In his mind, he's screaming, *How could you do this to me?*"

"What are you trying to tell me, Henri?" Seiden asked again, his voice only slightly stronger than a whisper.

She hesitated a little, then said, "Dropping a few nukes on us would be too easy in his mind. We'd just retaliate; millions would die on both sides of this war. He needs much more than that... he needs us helpless at his mercy, begging for his help. This is the only scenario that would heal Abramovich's pain and restore his blemished image of greatness, as he perceives it."

"What would do that?" Seiden asked quietly.

"I don't know... not yet."

"So all this is just a hunch?" Seiden's irritation was seeping back in his voice.

"No, sir, this is the result of my analysis. I still think the Russians are preparing for some kind of a nuclear attack. I just don't think it will be anything like a traditional war. I'm not seeing them pick an American city or a military target and just strike. It would be too clean, too easy and painless by his standards. I strongly believe they're trying to keep us busy while they're prepping some terrorist-type incursion in our space, with a nuclear threat on the agenda."

Seiden loosened his tie a little more, while his deep frown reappeared.

"Find out what that is, Henri, find out now. Get all your people on it, and get more people if you need them." Seiden stood and looked outside at the sunlit cityscape. "This incredible scenario of yours makes sense; it fits. We need to brief the president."

After shaking Mason's hand warmly, Sam Russell sat quietly for a few seconds, and Mason didn't disrupt the silence either.

Sam absorbed the visual details in Mason's office. The office had stayed the same, unchanged, over the entire time he'd been consulting for Mason. It had barren walls, no artwork, no plants, and no décor whatsoever. It was a practical, cold, impersonal, almost monastic space, furnished with efficiency in mind.

He looked at Mason and had to repress a smile. They must look really funny, the two of them. Both had shaved heads, wrinkled foreheads, and had preserved their athletic builds. Both were wounded warriors of a bygone era. Sam's CIA days were just fond memories now, and so were Mason's Secret Service days. Oh well. . . time does fly. Yet both of them still had a lot of fight in them, still had a lot to offer.

They went back a long way, the two of them. Sam always chuckled when he remembered how the two of them had met. Sam had been invited to the White House Correspondents' Dinner in reward for forging one of the most enduring alliances between the CIA and MOSSAD. The alliance between the two agencies, initially based on the friendship between two intelligence field agents, had evolved beyond Sam's wildest dreams when his old MOSSAD friend took the reins of the Israeli government as prime minister. That course of events had brought him the invitation to attend the correspondents' dinner.

Sam had never been a guest at the White House before and was a little uneasy about the whole thing, not really knowing anyone there, not sure where he could and couldn't go. No wonder he took the wrong turn at some point and entered the wrong men's room, one that was not open for guest access. Oblivious to his error, he had proceeded to the nearest urinal, pressed by an urgent need to relieve the pressure on his bladder.

In that very personal moment, he had felt a firm hand on his shoulder. A Secret Service agent escorted him out, barely giving him the time to zip his pants, and pointed him in the direction of the guest men's room. That agent was Mason Armstrong, and, over the years, their unusual encounter led to a strong friendship. After Sam had retired from the CIA, Mason had extended him a consulting contract with Walcott, engaging him whenever the business needs required it.

Sam decided to open the conversation.

"This can't be easy, Mason; how are you holding up?" Sam asked.

"I'm fine, it's not me I'm worried about. It's everything else. Our CEO and SecNav want this entire issue contained and the case closed ASAP."

Mason stretched his left leg to the side of his desk.

"That's tight," Sam said. "In all the years we've been working together I haven't seen such an ugly one. What does SecNav say?"

"He's livid, and that was to be expected. He calls me three times a day, and I'm sure he's calling the directors of the FBI and NCIS just as often. It's our best weapons technology, so new we haven't even deployed it on our fleet yet, and it could have been compromised already. He's pressing us for a sitrep within forty-eight hours, and twenty-four are already gone."

"What does the FBI say, or NCIS?" Sam asked quietly.

Mason rubbed his forehead for a few seconds before answering.

"You're not gonna believe this, Sam. The federal agents deployed on this case were involved in a traffic collision with a tractor-trailer, and now they're both in the hospital, fighting for their lives. They're deploying someone else now."

"Coincidence? Or not?" Sam probed.

"I think it's too early to be anything else but a coincidence. But we've lost a day, nevertheless. And a day can make or break a case like this, you know that."

Sam nodded, regretting he couldn't light up in that office. Smoking cleared his mind, and somehow increased his perceptive skills. He'd just have to wait.

"Let's go through the facts, Mason. Let's see what we've got."

Mason picked up a document enclosed in a transparent envelope, and pushed it toward Sam.

"Our fleet guy found this when he detailed the corporate van."

Sam whistled in amazement. "Unauthorized copy, huh?"

Mason nodded, while his eyebrows came together in a frown.

"You know," Sam said, "there's no logical reason to assume that this document was the entire breach. You know that, right?"

Mason nodded again.

"Most likely they copied the entire file, and only lost the first page, the cover page," Sam continued.

"The entire file, or more files," Mason added grimly.

"Yes, there could be more."

Sam examined the document through the transparent envelope in detail. "How or where the hell did they make the copy?"

"IT is looking into the usage logs for all the copiers in the building, and cross-referencing those logs with all authorized copies that were made in the past two weeks. We have an internal team on that. But it will take a while. We have seventy-eight copiers and forty-three fax machines, all digital and requiring access codes."

"OK. Let's change direction, then. Who used the van, do we know? Any video?"

"No, no video, but we do know who used the van between the previous detailing and the moment the document was found."

"OK, let's work that list," Sam said, scribbling on a piece of paper. "Go," he invited Mason.

"There was one senior executive returning from a business trip, it was an airport pickup," Mason said, looking at his notes.

"I think we could safely eliminate any inbound pickups, don't you agree? Anyone stealing secrets from Walcott wouldn't bring them inside the company once they were out, right?"

"Right... yes," Mason confirmed. "It makes sense. Then that eliminates the delegation from South Korea, also an airport pickup."

"Yes, scratch them off the list too. Who else?"

"I'm sure we can eliminate the CEO's wife going on a shopping trip to France, don't you agree?" Mason asked.

"Well, maybe not entirely."

"The van picked her up at her house, not here. And she doesn't have any access, obviously."

"It was just a courtesy pickup and drop off? Then yes, she's off the list too. I'm guessing you're happy about that one, aren't you?" Sam smiled.

Mason looked in Sam's eyes and relaxed a little. "You have no idea," he confirmed, a faint smile showing on his list for a split second.

"OK, then, who's left?"

"Two engineering teams. They both left Walcott to go to two different engagements on a Navy vessel in Norfolk Harbor and their return trips. But that's not all."

"Oh?" Sam said.

"Both teams were deployed to work on the USS *Fletcher*. And the technology that was leaked is being installed on the *Fletcher*. That makes these people our most likely suspects."

"I see. How big were the teams?"

"One was five people, one was six," Mason said, after consulting his notes briefly.

"Any disgruntled employees on those teams, any motive, any issues we know about?"

"No, none whatsoever. That's the first thing I checked."

"All of them have clearance? What levels?"

"Yes, all were top secret clearance; very few Walcott employees are not cleared at that level."

"Have you interviewed them?"

"Not yet. The feds made it very clear we're not to engage the eleven employees in any way. They want to handle it themselves, have the first stab at it."

Sam frowned a little, thinking. "Then why am I here, Mason? How can I help? You seem to have it all covered really well."

"To some extent, Sam, to some extent. Yes, the feds are on it, and NCIS is partnering with them all the way, but they represent larger interests than Walcott Global. No one is looking after Walcott's reputation during this investigation, and we need to have someone to represent and safeguard our interests. Not at the expense of, or against national security, of course, but just be there, keep us informed with potential pitfalls or media disasters." He paused for a second, collecting his thoughts. "If we lose the Navy as a client, we are done, out of government business permanently. We can't afford any screw-ups. You do understand what I'm trying to say?"

"Perfectly," Sam confirmed, deep in thought.

That was one tall order. It wasn't that obvious how to get someone to tag-team with not one, but two law enforcement agencies conducting a counterintelligence investigation, on what could easily prove to be the biggest espionage scandal in recent history.

"Wow," Sam said quietly, "you do know how to make life interesting, Mason. This isn't going to be easy, you know."

"I know," Mason replied, looking at Sam with a serious, intense gaze.

Sam thought for another minute or so, regretting he had earlier declined the invitation to get a cup of coffee.

"I might have a solution for you," he said. "*Might* being the operative word here."

"I'm all ears," Mason replied calmly.

"There's a private investigations firm called The Agency, have you ever heard of it?"

"No, never," Mason replied.

"I didn't think so. Their experts specialize in corporate covert investigations. They infiltrate organizations and conduct their analyses from within, discreetly, no one being the wiser. Then they report their findings to the company owners or leaders and disappear, just as naturally and inconspicuously as they had appeared. They might consider taking your case."

"Interesting," Mason said, a trace of optimism coloring his voice. "Are they government contractors? Will there be a conflict of interest?"

"No, they're not," Sam replied, unable to repress a chuckle. "The owner, Tom Isaac, would never even consider becoming a government contractor. He loves being a free, unregimented spirit."

"Then they probably don't hold the clearance to even hear my case," Mason said, all optimism disappearing from his voice.

"One of them does, Alex Hoffmann is her name."

"How come?"

"Well, not sure if I should share this with you, but here it is. She handled the NanoLance drone case."

"By herself?" Mason reacted.

The NanoLance drone incident was a well-known subject in government circles, where just months before a congressional hearing had taken place to examine the facts leading to several incidents involving military drones. Some of those incidents had been responsible for a substantial loss of lives, both in the United States and abroad, in combat zones.

"Not entirely, but she was the lead in the investigation, the only Agency executive deployed inside NanoLance. She's not your average investigator, you know. She's a CalTech computer science major with an IQ that's thirty points or so north of genius level. She took a director of technology job with NanoLance to get inside, and no one was the wiser. That's how she does it."

Mason whistled appreciatively and scratched the back of his head, thinking.

"Now that you mentioned it," Sam continued, "there might be a second Agency employee with top-secret clearance. His name is Louie Bailey; he's a computer expert of sorts. He used to work for NanoLance, so he must have been cleared."

Mason thought for a minute, then said, "I'm not sure what they could do for me, but if this is your best bet, Sam, why not? Let's give it a shot and see how it goes. I'll have to clear it with the boss, but I'm sure he'll be OK with it. Go ahead, set it up."

Sam looked at Mason for a second, to see if he was sure about that. Satisfied, he pulled out his cell phone and retrieved a number from memory.

A familiar voice picked up almost immediately, expressing loudly a string of complaints sprinkled with expletives.

"Yeah, kiddo, I know it's 6.00AM in California, but how would you like to hop on a plane and come work on a case with me?"

He put the phone back in his pocket and smiled. "She's on her way."

Mason Armstrong's office seemed small and crowded with so many visitors, yet they all crammed in there instead of moving to a conference room.

Jeremy Weber came in last, seven minutes tardy for the unexpected early morning meeting that had been announced late the night before. Surprised to see such a large audience, Jeremy closed the door behind him and studied everyone's face, not recognizing anyone other than Mason.

He had to stand; Mason's two other visitors had taken the only two visitor chairs available, while Mason took his own, behind his desk.

Jeremy shoved his hands deep into his jacket pockets and frowned. This investigation was turning into a corporate circus.

"Come on in, Agent Weber," Mason greeted him. "Thank you for taking the time to come in this morning."

He nodded a silent greeting to all those present.

"What is this about?" Jeremy asked, cutting to the chase.

"Agent Weber, please allow me to introduce Sam Russell."

The two men shook hands.

"Sam is a security consultant with Walcott Global. He is former CIA, and he's helping us handle this investigation on behalf of Walcott," Mason continued. "Alex Hoffmann works with Sam. She will also be involved on behalf of Walcott Global."

Jeremy shook Alex's hand and was a little surprised to see the woman shook his hand firmly and openly, the type of handshake he'd expect from a man.

"A pleasure to meet you," she said.

"Agent Weber," Mason said, "Walcott Global would really appreciate it if you'd partner up with our consultants during the investigation. They both bring a lot of value and can assist the FBI and NCIS teams. Considering the time pressures and the sensitivity surrounding this issue, Walcott believes that a joint task force should conduct the investigation. Our CEO is ready to make the necessary calls to your director, if need be."

"Mr. Armstrong," Jeremy replied, "are you suggesting we bring into our investigation civilian contractors? Uncleared civilians, no less?"

"They're not just any civilians," Mason said in an appeasing tone. "Sam Russell is ex-CIA, and Ms. Hoffmann holds a top-secret clearance and a portfolio of achievement in covert investigative work inside government contractor organizations. I hope you'll reconsider."

Jeremy struggled to contain his irritation. SAC Taylor was gonna have his ass on rye with mayo if he let this happen. There wasn't an excuse in hell he could find to justify this. And why should he? There was no valid reason for that. He didn't need to trail on some retiree and some chick during the entire time, just to make Walcott's fat cat happy. They're gonna call the director? So be it... at least this time he was gonna follow procedure.

"I'm sorry," Jeremy said, "This is simply not going to happen. We have procedures to follow, and this is a high-profile case, where we can't risk making any mistakes. I hope you'll understand," he ended, as politely as he could, getting ready to leave.

"Again," Mason insisted, "we are willing to make all necessary phone calls to get the approvals to make this happen. Just let us know who to call."

"We have procedures for a reason," Jeremy said, almost entertained to hear himself making the case for procedures, him of all people. He continued, "There's simply no way this can happen. Plus, in all fairness, and pardon my blunt honesty, I don't see the value in this partnership. It would slow us down and risk compromising the outcome of the investigation. If you feel the need to make those phone calls, please do. Have a good day."

He turned away and grabbed the doorknob, getting ready to leave.

"She worked the NanoLance case," Mason threw out. "Ms. Hoffmann did."

Really? Jeremy thought. That was maybe worth spending a few more minutes, but he still wasn't gonna change his mind.

He let go of the doorknob and turned toward his host, registering the sudden blush in Hoffmann's face and the frown on Sam Russell's.

"All right," Jeremy said, "how exactly do you see us partnering on this, Ms. Hoffmann?"

"It's Alex," she replied. "I can bring a different angle to the investigation; gather information without hard handing it, without any visible authority. Your kind of authority scares people into silence, Agent Weber. I bypass that."

"Pfft . . ." he scoffed. "Ms. Hoffmann, do you even know what's at stake here?" Jeremy asked, feeling a little embarrassed to hear how assaholic his voice sounded.

"No, can't say that I know any of the details yet. I just arrived late last night."

"Let me tell you exactly what this is about. We have developed a new weapon, the laser cannon. It's the biggest breakthrough in weapons technology this country has seen in decades. It can be installed on any military vehicle, air, sea, or land, from destroyers to MRAPs to drones, since you're so goddamn familiar with them. Why is it such a big breakthrough? Because that cannon can blow anything out of the water or out of the sky with precision and for under a buck a shot! Yes, you heard me," he emphasized, registering her reaction, "less than one dollar per shot. And someone just stole that technology and gave it, or is planning to give it to our enemies. Now, can you please explain to me exactly how you think you can bring value to our investigation?"

She didn't seem intimidated; she looked annoyed. She cocked her head defiantly, and her lips curled up just a little, in the most irritating hint of a smile he'd ever seen. When she spoke, her voice was calm and cold, factual.

"Well, maybe you're right and I can't assist in this case. But don't get me wrong. That's only because you're one of the most stubborn, head-up-your-ass, sorry excuses for an agent I've ever met. I can't work with someone who's so closed-minded. We wouldn't be able to communicate; we don't coexist on the same planet."

She stood abruptly and walked toward Sam, and quickly leaned down and kissed him on the top of his clean-shaven, shiny head.

"Sorry, Sam," she whispered, then turned around and left, closing the door gently behind her.

Jeremy stood speechless, watching her leave without being able to articulate an answer. He saw Mason covering his face with both his palms.

"You idiot!" Sam said. "You just blew your only chance to infiltrate that group of people. If the feds want to go undercover on this, it will take you weeks to prep."

Jeremy looked at Sam. "Are you kidding me? You've got to be kidding me, right?"

"I wish I was," Sam said, shaking his head in disbelief. "If you're thinking of investigating this with guns blazing, locking each one of your eleven suspects in a room with a polygraph and hoping you'll find who-done-it, well, think again."

"Why?" Jeremy asked and instantly regretted it.

"Because the moment the word gets out there that we're looking at this, whoever's done it will run for the hills, expedite whatever delivery he had planned, and take as much intel with him as he can carry. Your only shot is to somehow start the interrogations and polygraphs with the traitor first, before anyone else. You keep forgetting you *must* contain the information leak *and* identify the uplink—find the handler, not just catch the traitor. And you're running against the clock, you need to infiltrate that group today. How do you like your odds now?"

Jeremy didn't reply; he processed Sam's point of view, trying to poke holes in it and couldn't find any.

Damn it, he thought. *Who the hell are these people?*

Sylvia Copperwaite watched in a blur how the man sitting across from her raked the entire pot over the green velvet to his side of the poker table. His satisfied, wide grin was disgusting, showing discolored teeth, crooked, most likely about to fall from their rotted gums. A lifelong of poor hygiene, of smoking cheap crap, and drinking moonshine can do that to almost anyone.

She shuddered, thinking how different she was, how she didn't belong with that crowd, yet there she was, again. She looked around the table, at the four   strangers   around   her. Horrible... this couldn't be her reality, just couldn't be true.

The truck driver at her left was about to deal.

"Ante?" he called out.

"Huh? N–no," she said, after looking at her chips for a second. "I'll sit this one out."

"Hey, if you're at the table, you gotta play, lady," the man across said. "In, or out," he said, pointing his thumb over his shoulder in a gesture inviting her to take a hike.

She only had two blue chips left, twenty dollars; that was all. She'd come in at 8.00PM or so with seven-hundred dollars, and now she was down to twenty bucks. She felt tears burning her eyes.

Where did it all go? Where and when had she lost her mojo? She used to win, and win big. She used to be able to read her opponents so clearly that she could almost tell every card they held, with accuracy, in cold blood. She knew who was bluffing and who had a strong hand. She used to know when to bet and when to fold. God... One night she'd won thirty-two large ones at a game, bought a new Volvo the next morning. But that was all gone... including that car. She'd sold it a year later, to pay off debts that piled up quickly once Lady Luck had decided to be a bitch and hung her out to dry. She drove a beat-up Honda now, bought from a curbsider for less than two grand.

"Hey, lady," the man across barked, "either ante up, or take a hike, you hear me?"

She got up clumsily, arranging her skirt that clung stubbornly to her sweaty legs, and dropped her purse. Her belongings scattered on the floor— her lipstick, cell phone, car keys, her wallet. The man at her right obliged, reaching out under the table to help pick up her belongings.

"Ah, don't bother, buddy, that wallet's empty," the brute across laughed, "I just cleaned that baby to the bone." He continued to laugh, a coarse, disgusting laughter that made the other three men look away with embarrassment.

"Don't mind him, miss," the man helping her said, "he's just your garden-variety asshole."

She heard everyone talk like in a dream. Unable to articulate an answer, any answer, she stood quietly, her mouth slightly open, her brain unable to process her reality. They all seemed far, distant somehow, in an alternate plane of existence. Her eyes couldn't focus; everything around her was a blur, a cacophony of sounds and images that didn't make sense.

The man across whistled sharply and repeated the gesture with his thumb, inviting her again to get lost. She grabbed the two remaining chips and moved away from the table, heading for the cashier.

As she walked away, she regained a little more of her connection with reality, and she suddenly realized what was wrong. She was too desperate, that's why she couldn't win anymore. Back when she used to rake in all the chips on the table, she was cool about it, did it for fun, and didn't really care. Now her back was against the wall, all her credit cards maxed out, and the line of credit exceeded and past due. That's why, she realized, that's why she felt forced to bet on a losing pair of stupid nines, when the smart thing would have been to fold and wait for a better deal to come. It's written in the mathematical rules that govern chaos; the better hand will come eventually. All she needed to do was pace herself, so that her money would last the needed time she had to wait for the winning hand to show up. Huh... that simple. You can't win at poker if you're desperate or in a hurry.

She turned and went for the ATM instead, and put in her debit card as soon as the line of gamblers in front of her cleared up. She entered her pin and saw the option to withdraw cash was grayed out. She checked her balance; it showed $-2,482.27, and available funds $17.73. Even her overdraft protection was maxed out.

One by one, she tried all her credit cards, under the judgmental, impatient, sympathetic, or annoyed looks of customers waiting in line to use the ATM.

Nothing; no stars aligned to give her access to the little cash she needed to win again, now that she knew what she needed to do to get back in the graces of Lady Luck. Nada... she was cleaned out, with one more week left until payday.

Stifling a sob, she went straight for the cashier's desk and actually made it, exchanged her two remaining chips for a twenty-dollar bill. She needed to eat until next Friday.

In the silence and bleakness of her apartment, she sat on the side of her bed, nurturing the few remaining drops of liquor she'd been able to squeeze from the bottom of some empty bottles. Her tears had run dry, getting the emotion out of the way so that her brain could take over and think rationally. She was an engineer; the years of discipline, deductive reasoning, and use of logic finally engaged in the process of identifying what her problem really was and figuring out how to fix it.

In the silent darkness of her bedroom she whispered, "Hi, my name is Sylvia, and I'm an addict."

The doorbell startled Alex a little; it was almost midnight. She thought it must be one of the guys, with something so urgent and confidential that it couldn't be handled over the phone.

She smiled, remembering how she had sneaked in to slide a piece of paper under Tom's door one night, and scared the crap out of both of them when she'd stumbled upon him smoking his cigar on the patio, in complete darkness. Yup, emergencies like that can happen.

She paused the TV, put on a bathrobe, and opened the door widely, without checking the peephole. She was expecting a friend, but the man standing in her doorway wasn't one of her Agency colleagues.

"You!" she exclaimed, perplexed. "What the hell are you doing here?"

"Well, believe it or not, I've come to apologize," Jeremy Weber said, "and to ask you to come back to Norfolk."

She mumbled some oaths and, after thinking for a few seconds, reluctantly got out of the way.

"Come in," she said eventually, "take a seat. Need anything? Water? Beer?"

"Beer would be nice," he said, sitting down on her couch, uneasy. "It's been a long flight."

She brought cold Stella Artois for both of them, took an armchair, and folded her legs under her.

"So," she said, "let's hear it. What could have possibly been so serious to make you hop on a plane and waste a whole day in flight when you're supposed to be chasing spies in Norfolk?"

She was making him uncomfortable, irritating him, and she was doing it on purpose. He was clasping his hands together, and obviously refraining from being his usual douche-bag self that she remembered clearly from earlier in the morning. She almost chuckled; she wasn't gonna make it any easier for the jerk.

"Walcott considers... well, actually they believe very strongly you should be involved in this investigation."

"Huh... do they now?" she replied pensively.

"They believe it so strongly that my director was persuaded before I even got back to the office this morning. We have his approval. We'll set you up as an FBI contractor, have you take the polygraph needed to gain full access to this case, and we're ready. We should be ready in twenty-four hours."

"Wait a second," she snapped, "I haven't exactly said yes, now have I?"

The smug asshole! That was his version of an apology? Where did the feds find these people?

"You don't really have a choice, Ms. Hoffmann," he replied serenely, a crooked smile showing on his lips.

"Yeah? And how's that?" She stood and started pacing angrily, her bathrobe fluttering around her like a fuzzy superhero cape. She didn't care if he saw her jammies; she just wanted the asshole out of her house, pronto.

"I've done some research on you, to find out why exactly you're so damn critical for Walcott's investigation."

"And?" Alex asked impatiently, tapping her bare foot on the carpet, her clenched fists stuck firmly in her pockets.

He leaned back, looked her straight in the eye, and said, "I know what case you've just worked on."

She felt a rush of blood to her head and the fist of adrenaline hit her bowel. *Fuck!*

"I don't know what you're talking about," she managed to articulate, sounding calm and plausible.

"Oh, yes, you do. I'm talking about the twenty-something laws you and your team broke just by knowing about that threat and not calling us in. I'm talking about the elections case. I'd say this fact limits your options somehow, wouldn't you agree? It should definitely improve your attitude for starters," he scoffed.

She weighed her options quickly, then replied dryly, "Well, if you know that much, Agent Weber, then you probably must already know that the last asshole who sat where you're sitting right now ended up dead, and my only problem with it was that I had to replace my favorite couch."

He laughed, stood up and approached her with his extended hand. "It's Jeremy."

"Huh?" she reacted.

"You can call me Jeremy."

Alex looked at him for a second, thinking. He obviously wasn't there to arrest her for her work on the elections case, and she *was* interested in this challenge. Her gut was telling her that by working with Walcott she could come closer to identifying V, her elusive Russian mastermind, the mystery man taking the front and central spot on her crazy wall. That gut feeling, that thin wisp of hope was worth putting up with Agent Weber. Maybe there was room for some decent collaboration between the two of them. Maybe.

She shook his hand and replied reluctantly, "Alex."

"Shall we start again?" Jeremy asked insidiously.

She grabbed her Stella and gulped down half the bottle, then sat back in her armchair.

"Tell me again, why do they need me? Or why do *they* think they need me?"

"Here's the long story, short. Two teams of engineers used the corporate van between detailings. On Tuesday, the fleet manager found an illegally copied document in the van. One of these eleven people dropped it by accident, but that means someone made an illegal copy of a file containing critical state secrets, the laser cannon technology I was talking about this morning."

"And?" she asked. "I still don't follow why me."

"You can infiltrate technical teams, that's what you do, right?"

"Right... That's what I do. So what's your plan of action?"

She reached over to the coffee table and grabbed her laptop.

"What are you doing?"

"Booking us flights. Never mind me, what's your plan?"

"Get you acquainted with the case, get you credentialized first, then we proceed from there."

"Polygraph, huh?" Alex asked, thoughtful and a little concerned.

"Yup," he said.

"Mandatory?"

"Gotta do it."

"Then you better make sure they don't ask me the wrong questions," she said.

"What do you mean?"

"About the case I've never worked on," she said and winked, "the elections case."

"I think that can be arranged," he replied coolly. "What else would you need?"

"I need reading materials about the laser cannon. I can't hope to infiltrate those teams without having the slightest idea of what that is and how it works. And I'll need Walcott's procedure manual, or someone who'll walk me through everything I need to know about making copies, gaining access to documents, that kind of stuff. I think Mason Armstrong can take care of that."

"What else?" Jeremy asked, taking notes.

"I need you to work with me and run background checks, people's profiles. I need access to their files, work histories, financials, all that. Just routine for you."

"You got it. How are we doing on flights?"

"Like hell," she replied, frowning and slamming the laptop shut. "With these options we won't make it to Norfolk before 10.00PM. Let me make a call."

"It's 2.00AM!" he exclaimed.

"He won't mind... I hope."

She dialed a number from her cell's memory, and the call was answered immediately.

"Brian? Sorry to bother... I need your help badly. I need to bail out on your case, and I need to borrow your jet."

She paused for a minute, listening to Brian's answer, and watching with amusement how Jeremy's jaw dropped. Then she thanked Brian and closed the call.

"Who are you, people?" Jeremy asked.

Vitaliy Myatlev and Defense Minister Dimitrov lit their cigars, waiting impatiently for the aide to finish his work. The two of them stood by the open window overlooking Moscow's cityscape under a rare and wonderful blue sky.

The young aide set up a tray of hors d'oeuvres on the small coffee table. Small saltine crackers in a silver bowl. Beluga caviar in another bowl, this one sitting on a bed of ice. Pate de foie gras on a crystal tray, set on bite-sized pieces of toast. An unopened bottle of vodka, Myatlev's favorite brand, Stolichnaya, ready to serve in an ice bucket.

"Will there be anything else, sir?" the aide asked. Myatlev just waved him away and the young man disappeared.

"What are we celebrating, Vitya?"

"How can you ask that?" Myatlev responded, feigning offense. "Only the first successful recruitment in our new network of agents. And what a first!"

"Smolin's asset?"

"Da," Myatlev replied, engulfed in thick cigar smoke. "Smolin said the first set of documents is impressive."

"Tell me already, I'm growing older by the minute," Dimitrov said humorously.

"Smolin's asset confirmed that the Americans have the laser cannon weapon ready to deploy."

"Fuck it... Petya's going to be mad, so mad. He'll say we were asleep at the wheel again. You know how much he hates any news that anyone's ahead in anything."

"Smolin's source is very close to the project; he'll give us more intel. Then we'll know more."

Dimitrov reached for the bottle and poured vodka in two glasses, then threw some ice cubes in them. He handed one to Myatlev and raised his in a joyless cheer.

"Ura," he said, then gulped the liquid.

"Ura," Myatlev said in unison, then continued, "You keep forgetting something, Mishka. You keep forgetting we should celebrate.

"Hard for me to think of celebrating, when the news is so bad."

"Yes, but think of the big picture," Myatlev insisted. "You, more than anyone else in this government, should be able to see the big picture. We have a new network in place. We have new handlers in the field, recruiting and getting us results. We have intel, good intel, and we'll have better intel soon. And we have channels that we've tested now and we know they work. We're back in business, Mishka, like in the old days."

"Good," Dimitrov cheered up a little, "I can drink to that!"

Myatlev quickly obliged and refilled their glasses with generous amounts of vodka.

"It only took Smolin a couple of weeks to hook his first asset, just a couple of weeks. Do you know how rare this kind of talent is? Even for us?"

Dimitrov nodded appreciatively.

"And I have found more like him. We can deploy all the good ones, to consolidate our network of assets."

"What are you going after, Vitya?"

"Big data, Mishka, I am going after big data."

Dimitrov rubbed his forehead thoughtfully.

"Do you want to hear me say I'm too old for this game? I won't say it. Maybe I'm too old for your methods, but not for the game."

"We're both old fucks, Mishka, don't kid yourself. But we can still get it up, we can get the job done like never before. That's why we have hordes of young people in our organizations, da?"

Both men laughed hard, clicked their glasses, and drank their vodka.

Myatlev invited Dimitrov to approach the coffee table and try an appetizer.

"Now tell me," Dimitrov asked, "what's with this big data you're talking about?"

"There isn't anything you can't find out when you're willing to grab data in a massive way. The Americans are joining all their databases now, associating what people do with where they work and what they spend money on. Such incredible power."

"And you want us to do the same?"

"Umm... yes, but in a different way. I want us to create backup plans to our backup plans, to grab any amount of intel there's to be had out there."

"On what?" Dimitrov asked, his eyebrows at an angle, conveying his confusion.

Myatlev stuck two of his right-hand fingers in the caviar and licked them, letting out a groan of satisfaction.

"On anything," Myatlev replied. "Even if we don't know on what, they will."

Dimitrov swallowed a cracker dipped in Beluga, then said, "Now I am convinced you lost it. You're not making any sense, my friend. I think the stress of life and of working with Abramovich has caused you some permanent brain damage," he ended, half-jokingly, patting Myatlev on his shoulder.

"Nah... nothing like that," Myatlev reassured him between bites of pate de foie gras washed down with another sip of vodka, "nothing like this, you'll see. I'll explain."

"Huh... I'm curious to hear it," Dimitrov said, then sat in a large leather armchair, stretching his legs, unbuttoning his jacket, and choosing a cigar.

"Just imagine we deploy a hundred assets, managed by ten handlers, on the American East Coast. We don't know what to look for, but *they* don't know that. So the handlers simply tell them to bring valuable information—the latest research, new technologies, and so on. We grab all that, we decrypt it, we study it."

"Nah... that is ridiculous, Vitya."

"I agree, some of the intel will be unusable crap, but some of it will be good. Good enough to let us know at least what's out there worth looking for. Then we target our intelligence-gathering efforts, once we know what they're doing."

"So, you're saying . . ."

"I'm saying Russia hasn't conducted any decent intelligence work in the past two decades, Mishka, no offense intended. The Chinese are ahead of us in intelligence work, Mishka, the fucking Chinese! We have a huge gap. We don't know who the players are any more and what they're doing. This laser cannon thing caught us by complete surprise. And it was a pure shot in the dark."

"Don't tell me we don't have lasers . . ." Dimitrov said, a hint of irritation coloring his voice.

"We do, but ours can't be installed on battleships. First, we never thought of that, then second, we seem to be unable to make them smaller than a house."

"Crap . . ." Dimitrov took another drag from his cigar and blew the smoke out in small circles toward the open window.

"You see my point? The laser cannon intel was a shot in the dark. Smolin had no idea he had to ask for it. He just put the bait out for the asset, and the asset delivered one big motherfucking surprise."

"How did he even find this asset?"

"He started from a list of interesting companies, from information that's publicly available on the Internet. Now you see?"

"What?"

"What we could do with this type of approach, if we go after data and intelligence in a big way."

Dimitrov nodded almost imperceptibly, then whistled quietly in admiration.

"You're not crazy, my dear friend, not at all. Your diabolical genius still inhabits your attic," Dimitrov said, tapping his own head with his finger. "But how are you planning to work through that massive amount of data?"

Myatlev smiled cryptically.

"How's the construction going at your new military data center?"

"Almost done. They're scheduled to bring in the equip—oh, no," he stopped mid-sentence, "oh no, the Army needs that center, Vitya."

"So you'll build another one, Mishka, what's the big deal? We need that center to build the biggest intelligence and security center in the world—the ISC. Ours. Just think what we can do with all that computing power."

"We need that center, Vitya, for satellite operations, for military research, for new weapons."

"And it will do all that, indirectly. Well, maybe not satellite operations, but everything else I think we can do."

Dimitrov scratched his head, a doubtful look shading his eyes and wrinkling his forehead.

Myatlev didn't let him think it for too long; he put a glass filled with vodka on ice in his hand, and toasted enthusiastically,

"To the ISC, ura! To Operation Leapfrog!" Myatlev cheered, baring his teeth in a wide smile filled with contagious confidence.

"To the ISC, to Leapfrog, *na zdorovie!*" Dimitrov replied, a little hesitant at first, then wholeheartedly.

The two men drank, then sighed loudly in the typical manner Russians express satisfaction when drinking to their hearts' desire.

"How are you going to pay for this intelligence gathering, Vitya? It will cost a fortune. Intel is expensive, especially in America. People won't betray their country for five bucks. You'll need billions for such a bold plan."

"I'm not going to spend a lot of money," he said and winked. "I'm going to spend fear. And a little money too, but mostly fear. Just a little bit of carrot for our future assets, but mostly stick."

Dimitrov looked him in the eye, surprised.

"That's the value of big data," Myatlev replied, but Dimitrov's gaze remained puzzled.

Myatlev smiled a little arrogantly and whispered, "Trust me, everyone can be turned, everyone is gettable."

The four of them huddled closely together around Mason's desk, a desk covered in paper and file folders unlike the typical organized workspace Mason liked to keep. Alex pushed the stack of files away from her a little, making room for the steaming cup of coffee she had brought in. Sam sat quietly, watching her get ready with a faint smile on his lips.

"Thank you for accommodating us this morning," Alex said, "we appreciate it."

"You're welcome. It's the least I can do," Mason replied. "Wouldn't a conference room work better, considering the size of my office?"

"For now, I think we're good," Jeremy replied.

"Great, let's get started," she said.

"I'll start," Jeremy said, "by giving you your temporary FBI credentials," he said, handing Alex a badge. "Welcome to the FBI."

"Thank you," she replied, studying it on both sides. "I understand contractor, but why temporary?"

"You haven't passed your polygraph yet. You're scheduled for tomorrow morning; that was the earliest I could arrange."

"All right," she replied with a little hesitation and a frown. Sam smiled encouragingly, and she nodded an unspoken *thank you* to him.

"This credential clears you to gain access to all information regarding this case," Jeremy continued, "so if you have questions, now's the time to ask them."

"I have plenty," she said. "Mason, can you please walk me through the procedure one needs to follow to make a photocopy of a document—any document—inside Walcott corporate offices?"

Mason ran his hand over his shiny, clean-shaven scalp and thought for a second before answering.

"The protocol differs significantly between any document and a TOP SECRET file," he said.

"Let's focus on the TOP SECRET files, then," Alex asked.

"Let's start with gaining access to TOP SECRET files. One can only do that if one has access to the CDR, our Centralized Documents Repository. Even if someone has clearance to enter the CDR, they can only access or remove files they are cleared to work on. We have an internal system that keeps track of everyone's projects, tasks, and workloads, and matches those with document inventory numbers. With me so far?" Mason asked.

"Yes," Alex replied, while Sam and Jeremy nodded.

"So it's safe to assume that our leak had access to the repository, otherwise he couldn't have gained access to the source document in the first place," Mason continued.

"Does this CDR keep track of who accessed what documents? Is there a log?" Jeremy asked.

"Yes, absolutely," Mason confirmed. "We have checked the CDR logs for anyone accessing the file in question and there are several names. Sixteen to be exact, who have gained access to that file in the past two weeks."

"Did you cross-reference those names with the van travelers?" Alex said.

"Yes, just did that this morning, and I think we caught a break," Mason said, "our first break since this whole mess started. There wasn't a single name on the first team, the team of six engineers who used the van in the morning, who had accessed any laser cannon documents. That team worked on ballistic systems, not on the laser weapons. That tells me we're down to one team, the five engineers who used the van right after lunch."

"Yes, that is a safe assumption to make and one big break," Alex said smiling, visibly relieved. "I was having serious concerns about my ability to infiltrate two teams."

"How about sharing?" Jeremy asked. "Can you pull a file, for example, and share the use of it with me, since we're colleagues on the same floor?"

"N–no," Mason replied. "Technically, no. It's against procedure and there isn't a single reason why someone would risk that type of breach just to save a colleague a trip to the CDR."

"All right, I think I got it," Alex said cheerfully, taking another sip of coffee. "Let's talk copier procedures next. Who gets to copy documents and how's that controlled?"

"A few years ago we replaced all our copiers with modern equipment that only works if you enter your personal code," Mason started to explain.

"All copiers?" Jeremy probed, looking up from his notepad where he was jotting notes.

"Yes, all of them. It was a company-wide measure we took to increase the control over the duplication of our secret documents. Before we rolled out the coded copiers, documents were copied freely, sometimes even recklessly, and the risk of leaks was significant. So we controlled the risk with the coded copiers, or at least we thought we did," Mason summarized, a trace of frustration showing on his immobile face.

"How about faxes?" Alex probed.

"We don't have traditional faxes anymore, haven't had them in the building since 2006. These coded copiers handle everything: copying, scanning, faxing—both inbound and outbound."

"Do you keep a log of users and what they do with the copy machines?" Jeremy wanted to know.

"Yes, there's a procedure everyone must follow to duplicate or scan any restricted document. Before copying, any restricted document duplication request must be entered in a database, complete with document name, restriction class, number of pages, and reason for duplication. Then an approval is issued. This approval is a numeric code. Then the user goes to the copier and enters his personal access code to unlock the copier, followed by the approval code. Only then, can the user actually copy the document. Once the copy job is finished, the code is invalidated."

"Are your copiers integrated on your network? Do they communicate with the database of approvals?" Alex asked.

"Yes, precisely so," Mason confirmed.

"I'm assuming all documents, faxed or copied, are stored in the machine's memory?"

"Yes, they are. We have a special document security team who pulls random copy and fax jobs and checks the restrictions, access codes, everything."

"What if someone wants to copy an unrestricted document?" Alex asked.

"Then they only use their personal code."

"So what keeps the user from copying restricted documents without approvals?" she probed on.

"We have several layers of security to ensure that doesn't happen. First, the copiers have an OCR system—that's optical character recognition—that scans each page searching for the classification stamps," Mason replied.

"Classification stamps, as in TOP SECRET?" Alex asked.

"Yes," Mason replied. "If the OCR recognizes a classification mark in the absence of an approval code, it will stop the machine and page systems security with the personal access code of the offender who started the copier in the first place."

"Hmm . . ." Alex muttered, at a loss for questions. "So, there's really no way anyone could have copied the damned thing, is there?"

Mason frowned a little, surprised by her choice of words. He was probably not used to anyone swearing in his office. He seemed so proper, so perfect, Alex thought. They all did—all the employees she had encountered, all of them seemed perfectly contained, procedural, almost robotic in their restraint and perfection. Hotheaded and many times slipping an oath here and there, especially when frustrated, she wished she could be more like them. *But only on the outside*, she thought. *I'd suffocate if I had to live like this, think like this, act like this all the time. Brrr...* She almost shuddered. *I wonder if there's something brewing under these perfect images of professionalism.*

"No, there's not," he said quietly.

"Huh?"

"Just responding to your comment," Mason said politely, "there's no way that document could have been copied without us knowing about it."

"And yet it was," Sam said his first words that morning. "How else could that have happened?"

Silence took over the small office; no one had an answer to that.

"Before we attempt to answer that million-dollar question, here's another one, much easier," Alex said. "When the fleet manager found the document, everyone knew instantly it wasn't an authorized copy. How did they all know that?"

"Oh, that's simple," Mason replied. "When the copier duplicates a restricted document under an approval code, it automatically prints the word 'copy' faded in the background of the document—a watermark—and the approval code at the bottom of each page. So if we see a document that has a classification in black and white, without being marked as an approved, registered copy, we know immediately that stamp was run through a copier without proper authorization. That's how we knew."

"Ingenious," she said. "Pretty thorough and very secure, I'll give you that."

"Then what scenarios make sense for unauthorized copies? How could someone copy a file in this building?" Sam asked.

"No one enters the premises with any cameras or personal phones. We have lockers on the main floor where employees have to leave their personal gadgets during the day. Then they are screened, just like in an airport. Nothing makes it in."

"Maybe you have a hacker in your midst, someone who could have overridden the copier's configuration; that's one scenario," Alex offered. "I'll ask Louie how hard that would be."

Sam nodded. "That's a good idea," he confirmed.

"Who's Louie?" Jeremy asked.

"He works with me, at The Agency," Alex replied. "I'll also ask him if it could have been done remotely."

"I've also tasked a security team to inspect every office, closet, restroom, and conference room in this building," Mason said.

"Looking for what?" Alex said.

"Not sure, some forgotten piece of equipment, maybe. I might be overreaching, but it's a big building," Mason said apologetically, seeing the reaction on their faces. "We have more than 6,000 employees; we have a lot of offices."

"That could spook your spook, pardon the pun," she said.

"True," Mason agreed. "I'll instruct them to go easy and be careful."

"No," Alex said abruptly. "Ask them to wear insignia and protective wear with your pest control vendor's markings, and leave some spider traps here and there."

Jeremy chuckled. "Sneaky," he said.

"Pest control people are just like the leaf-blower man; they're sacred. No one ever questions them. Ever," she smiled. "We all hate bugs more than we fear anything else."

"I'll do that," Mason said, after a little hesitation.

Alex stood and stretched a little, relieving some of the tension she'd been accumulating in her muscles. She didn't have much to go on for now; she had to get near the team that used the van. One of the members of that team was the leak, regardless how he managed to copy the file. She felt a wave of anxiety mixed with excitement, the type of excitement one feels before running a race. She needed to catch this mole fast; there was a lot at stake, and she was running against the clock. She might already be too late.

"Jeremy," she said, "I'm turning this over to you. Let's talk people. What, or who do we have?"

"We have a few things," Jeremy said. "Before we proceed, let me clarify something. Team One, let's call it that, the team of six who used the van in the morning, you're saying they should be off the hook, 'cause they didn't have access to the documents?"

"Yes, that is correct," Mason replied.

"Every one of these eleven people are under round-the-clock surveillance. I feel inclined to play it safe and keep these six people under surveillance for a little while longer. Just to be thorough. I can think of a few scenarios in which one of them could be involved even without having direct access to the document. Any objections?"

"None," Mason said.

"But you're saying you want to infiltrate Team Two first?" Jeremy turned toward Alex.

"Yes, can't do both at the same time and I want to start with the most likely ones."

"Makes sense," Jeremy confirmed. He took some of the folders stacked in front of him and pushed them aside, then focused on the remaining five folders. "These are our guys—well, four guys and one gal."

Alex pulled her tablet and got ready to take notes.

"I've run full background on all of them. Financials, credit cards, and phone records will take a little longer 'cause we need to wait for the warrants to come in, and then execute them."

"OK, shoot," Alex said impatiently. Everything took forever with the government.

"All right, the first one is Robert McLeod, forty-two years old. He's the team lead for this project. He's Walcott's technical director for Navy systems. Single. He's an electrical engineering graduate from MIT, finished second in his   class.   He   specializes   in   electronics, and . . ." Jeremy hesitated, flipping through the pages of his file, "yes, has been with Walcott for eight years. This is his picture," he added, pushing the file toward Alex.

"I'll need their pics sent to my phone," she said.

"I'll arrange that to be done," Jeremy said.

"Ahh... don't bother," she replied, taking a quick picture of Bob McLeod's personnel headshot with her phone.

"Or that can work too," Jeremy said, almost laughing. "OK, what else do we know about him, Mason? What makes Bob McLeod tick?"

"It's really hard to say, Agent Weber. As I was saying, we have thousands of employees; I don't have this kind of information readily available for any of them. But I will talk to human resources, see what they have."

"Please do. Move on, then?"

"Yes," Alex replied.

"Quentin Hadden, forty-seven, weapons systems engineer. Masters of science in electrical engineering, cum laude. Nothing much else in here. Single. Been with the company for twelve years.

Alex snapped another picture, then gestured for Jeremy to move on to the next suspect.

"Sylvia Copperwaite, thirty-three. She's the youngest of this elite crowd. She's an electromechanical engineer and holds a PhD in computational modeling for mobile platform installations and use of remote-sensing technologies—wow, that was a mouthful. At that age, very impressive, I'd say. Single, attractive."

Alex snapped another picture, then said, "It's amazing how you didn't mention the attractiveness factor about the two men."

Sam chuckled.

"Touché," Jeremy responded. "OK, next one is... Faisal Kundi."

"Whoa . . ." Sam interjected. "They have a Middle Eastern on the team?

Where from?"

"I can assure you all Walcott employees undergo thorough background checks in addition to the clearance investigation they have to pass," Mason offered, sounding almost defensive.

"OK, so... Faisal Kundi, twenty-nine," Jeremy continued, "he's an embedded software engineer, whatever that means."

"I can explain," Alex offered.

"Umm... maybe later," Jeremy replied. "Faisal is a Muslim. He was born in Pakistan, and emigrated at age three with his family. Married, two children. American citizen, of course, otherwise he wouldn't have had any clearance."

Jeremy stopped talking, waiting for any comments. No one said anything. *Could it be that easy?* Alex thought. It could, but that shouldn't cloud their judgment. Shouldn't cloud hers, anyway. She needed to remain cool-headed and not jump to any conclusions. She suddenly realized she felt sorry for how hard life must be for Faisal Kundi, if people instantly suspected him of treason by just hearing his name.

She snapped her picture, then said, "Next!"

"The last one is Vernon Blackburn, forty-four. Married, no children. He's a... here comes another mouthful, a laser electro-optics engineer, with a PhD in laser applications."

Alex took her last picture, then asked, "Is this it? Is this all we have?"

"Afraid so," Jeremy replied.

"Let me see what I can get from human resources," Mason offered.

"What are you planning to do, kiddo?" Sam asked.

"Well, tomorrow I have the f—" she stopped abruptly, refraining from dropping an f-bomb in front of the composed and ultra-professional Mason Armstrong. "I have the polygraph test," she continued, "without which I can't enter the premises beyond this point, or board the vessels, right?"

"That is correct," Mason confirmed.

"Any exceptions we could pull off?"

"No, I'm afraid not," Mason replied.

"OK, just thought I'd ask. We'll work on my cover story and run that by you, Mason. Then, assuming everything goes well and I pass, Friday I can deploy with this team."

"Sounds good," Sam said. "You'll pass the test, don't worry. We'll work on that later today."

Mason's surprised gaze moved from Sam to Alex and back. Neither of them flinched.

"Until then, Jeremy, I'll need as much background info as you can get me for all five suspects. I can't go in like this, with nothing but their names, and expect to pull it off."

"Understood. What will you do in the meantime?"

"Who, me? I need to prepare, to be able to sustain a conversation with these people. I guess I'll have to learn a little about... what was it?" Alex consulted her notes briefly. "Yeah, electro-optics, laser technologies, embedded software, remote sensing, and all that kind of fun stuff. I have forty-eight hours. Wish me luck!"

Alex lounged on Sam's deck furniture, engulfed in how beautiful the rural Virginia landscape could be on a May evening. The sun was getting ready to set, a pleasant heat still lingered in the air, carrying the smells of spring blooms. Cottonwood, insects, and birds randomly passed through the sweet sunset light, occasionally disrupting the perfect stillness of sound and air. Sam's deck and yard backed toward a farm's countless acres, spread on mild sloping hills and green pastures. It was a peaceful, scented paradise.

"Sam," she called, "your view here is worth more than your house!"

"I agree," he said with a chuckle. His voice sounded distant coming from the kitchen, where he was fixing them both some coffee. "Be right with you."

He came through the screen door carrying steaming cups of cappuccino.

"Yum," Alex said, grabbing one of the cups with both her hands and inhaling the aroma.

"Glad you like it," Sam said. "On the rare occasion when I have guests here I like to show off my new cappuccino maker."

"Sam, you are the king of caffeinated delights," Alex remarked after tasting her brew.

She sensed she wore a milk-foam mustache, which made her look childish, and licked it quickly. That brought back memories that had been locked away for years, memories of a time when she had been a happy, worry-free little girl growing up with hot-cocoa whiskers and laughter on her face. *Life changes fast on you*, she thought. *It can take you by surprise and throw you on a different continent.* How those times have gone!

"What's on your mind, kiddo?" Sam asked. "You're frowning at the cappuccino and that can't be good."

"Ah... it's just the polygraph, Sam. Scares me to death."

"All right, let's attack that beast," he said, fidgeting a little to find a more comfortable position on the wicker armchair. "First of all, remember, you have nothing to lose."

"But, if I fail the test, I won't be able to work this case," she protested. "I do have access to the case documents now, but I won't be able to roam the building freely, or board the damn ship."

"True, but in the grand scheme of things that doesn't mean much. You just go home, and work on another case, that's all. Don't work yourself up for nothing."

"Huh . . ." she replied thoughtfully. "But maybe it's not nothing, you know. Maybe the cases are related somehow."

"Which cases? This one and the elections case?"

"Yup. That's what I'm hoping. I'm hoping for another lead. I'm hoping somehow this time we'll be able to find who V is."

"Fair enough; that thought has crossed my mind. But it's way too early for that. How do you even know it's the Russians behind this, not the Chinese?"

Alex thought for a second and grunted angrily at herself. She'd jumped to conclusions again. Somehow, despite that logic, the idea felt right.

"Just my gut, I guess."

"OK, then, let's prep you for tomorrow," Sam said, putting his empty cappuccino cup on the side table. "Ready?"

"As I'll ever be," Alex replied smiling, to hide the tight knot she felt in her stomach. "What should I expect?"

"You'll be taken in a small room with no windows, a couple of chairs, and a table on which the polygraph is installed. Some rooms might have the old-style one-way mirror, but all rooms have video cameras installed to record the interview."

"What kind of sensors will they use?"

"They normally measure heart rate, blood pressure, breathing, and perspiration. Perspiration is measured through sensors attached to your fingers. Breathing is measured with two sensor bands fitted around your chest, and blood pressure and heart rate with a blood pressure cuff on your arm."

"Fantastic," she commented gloomily. "What kind of questions will they ask?"

"To start, they'll ask baseline questions, such as your name and place of birth, and then they usually ask if you're planning to lie during the test."

"Huh," she snorted, "that depends on the questions they're gonna ask, right?"

"Wrong, kiddo. Plan to tell the truth. They'll ask trick questions, like if you've ever smoked pot, or other self-incriminating crap like that. Just admit it. Even if you did and cop to it, it's not a disqualifier. They wanna see you're willing to tell the truth."

She stared at him with eyes opened wide in disbelief.

"What if they ask... well, things no one should know about?" She involuntarily crossed her arms and immediately uncrossed them, painfully aware of the body language clues she was giving out. How the hell was she gonna pass the stupid polygraph if she couldn't control her body language here, in the safety of Sam's backyard?

"Like what?"

"Like... if I've ever killed someone?"

"Just say yes."

They fell silent for a minute. Sam allowed her to process that information before moving on, and she was grateful for that minute of reprieve. She suddenly felt a wave of panic taking over her rational brain. *Oh God... this could go wrong in so many ways,* she thought.

"Sam," she whispered, "I don't know if I can pull this off. I'm... I'm afraid."

"Everyone is, kiddo," he replied in a soft, parental voice. "I've been doing this all my life, and I've yet to meet someone who's not afraid to take the poly. But you just deal away with the fear, that's all."

Her shoulders hunched, and she clasped and unclasped her hands nervously. "How?"

Sam laughed. "You're asking *me* how? After everything I've seen you handle? Oh, no, kiddo, ask yourself that, 'cause you've got all it takes to pull this off like an ace. I'm just a retired old spy, that's who I am. I'm yesterday's news, kiddo. You're tomorrow's."

She couldn't refrain from smiling. She loved how Sam cheered her up and instilled self-confidence in her every time she was in a bind. She suddenly wished they had enough time to share some of his war stories; he must have a few worth telling.

She'd met Sam just over a year before, when he had brought The Agency a new and troublesome case. He was a wartime friend of Tom's; they went way back. Now sixty-one, Sam was a retired CIA agent, enjoying his free time fishing in the waters of his backyard lake and grilling catfish whenever he'd get lucky. That's what Sam wanted everyone to believe his current life was all about. However, soon after they met, the two of them had become comrades in arms, chasing terrorists together in exotic destinations. It was a case they should have never worked on, but did anyway.

Sam had identified in her the passion for covert work going beyond the corporate realm. He'd told her many times she was secret-agent material and offered to open the CIA doors for her. Yet she'd stayed true to Tom Isaac and his Agency, jokingly saying that Tom paid way better than the government, but secretly enjoying the family she'd found in Tom and his crew. With Tom, she felt she belonged. She didn't want to trade that and turn into some faceless, bar-coded agent who no one gave a crap about in an agency as massive as the CIA was. And she did like the bigger paycheck too; it had considerable appeal. There was nothing wrong with having a little wealth and security for a change. She enjoyed the sense of safety that having money brought to her life.

Yet there was something about spies and secret-agent work that lit her imagination and injected her with a deeper sense of purpose. She couldn't name what that was, and rarely spent any time thinking about it. She just reacted, like she'd done just a few days before, dropping everything else and rushing to the East Coast to catch a spy.

She smiled crookedly, secretly entertained by thoughts about how her career had evolved.

"What?" Sam asked, crinkling his nose, amused.

"Bond. Alex Bond," she mock introduced herself, and then burst into laughter.

"What? You married James Bond?" Sam laughed with her.

"No, that's not what I meant," she said feigning offense and throwing a pillow at him.

"Then your real name should suffice, kiddo. You're it. You just need to trust yourself a little, that's all."

She stopped laughing abruptly, her face turned suddenly serious, almost grim. "All right, let's work this. How else do I prepare?"

Sam handed her a red, stick deodorant, Old Spice, with a strong minty flavor.

She looked at him, eyebrows raised in surprise.

"Of course I shower and use deodorant. Sam, what are you trying to tell me?"

"Relax, kiddo, you don't stink," he said and winked, reading her mind. "You'll apply this on your hands before leaving the house to go to the test. This one, not any other brand, because this one is a perspiration inhibitor."

She was confused... How was that going to help with the test?

"They'll attach sensors to your fingers to measure perspiration. Even if they wipe your fingers with alcohol before starting the test, if you apply this deodorant before leaving the house, it will have time to enter your pores and partially inhibit perspiration for a few hours."

"Huh... interesting, got it. What else?"

"What's your stress food? What do you eat when you're sad, worried, or PMS-ing?"

She blushed slightly. "Chocolate chip ice cream, with whip cream and chocolate syrup on top."

"Eat that before leaving for the test. It will release serotonin and calm you down. You'll mellow out and be less likely to spike your heart rate and blood pressure under stress."

"I see. That's easy," she replied with a nervous smile. "What else?"

"No coffee tomorrow, none, understood?"

"Yes, no coffee."

He thought for a little while, then added, "Maybe you can take a beta blocker in the morning, to relieve anxiety."

"Where would I find that?"

"I'll share mine. How's your blood pressure, normally?"

"Perfect, about 130 or so."

"OK, you can take one beta blocker, not more. And drink chamomile tea tonight."

"Ugh... Got it. What else?"

"Can you dissociate easily?"

"What do you mean?"

"It's like daydreaming. You just did it minutes ago, when you were miles away thinking of something."

"Oh, that... yes, I guess I can," she replied.

"That's the biggest secret of passing the poly; focus on something else, miles away, so intensely that you can barely hear the questions and you reply to them like in a dream. You think you can do that?"

"I–I hope so," she said hesitantly. "What else?"

"That's it, that's all I have. Sleep well tonight, then go in there tomorrow and knock it out of the park, kiddo."

"I'll try. Tea, no coffee, ice cream, beta blocker, deodorant, dissociate, I think I've got it. Thanks, Sam, thanks much!"

She gave Sam a hug, said goodnight, and went out to climb behind the wheel of her rental car. Easier said than done, the entire polygraph thing. Regardless of all the advice and paraphernalia, she could still screw this up royally, and lose her only shot at a lead to catch her Russian ghost.

Olga and Nikolai, Smolin's cover daughter and son-in-law, had left the dining room immediately after finishing dinner and cleaning up the table. They were still uncomfortable in his presence and kept quiet almost all the time.

Smolin understood how he intimidated them; having a high-ranking SVR officer stationed in their home while on a covert mission in the United States was a dangerous position for them to be in. However, they had been nothing but supportive and dedicated since he'd arrived, proud and eager to serve Mother Russia the best they possibly could.

Well-trained by the SVR, prior to their arrival on a visa lottery green card, the Novachenkos proved to be unexpected assets for Smolin. He had to recognize the wisdom of the case manager who had recommended them and their residence for Smolin's base of operations.

Alone with his laptop, Smolin logged into his webmail server and started drafting a new message. He no longer used Gmail or Yahoo; not since he'd learned the NSA swept those servers systematically, and that the major technology players of the Silicon Valley had signed secret alliances with the NSA, participating directly in security actions alongside the American government. Bastards...

He had moved to a smaller, private server that managed domains for sale, and, under one of those domains, he had set up a webmail account. Well, it hadn't really been his idea. Valentina Davydova had taught him to bypass the monster servers and go with the smaller, inconspicuous email servers, more likely to be omitted from the systematic security sweeps the NSA conducted.

Smolin typed his email message. The subject line read, "Happy Birthday To You!" and the message body contained a few lines of text.

Dear Mother,

I have arrived home and started preparing your party. I've invited a few guests, not too many, but I can invite more if you'd like. I've also picked a couple of gifts for you that I hope you will enjoy.

More to come soon. Happy birthday!

Love,
Your devoted son,
Zhenya

When he finished typing, Smolin read the message again and smiled. He was happy with his idea. The message read like a plain birthday email greeting; yet he was clearly telling his boss, Vitaliy Myatlev, that he had deployed his first few assets and already had valuable pieces of information to send home.

Satisfied, he closed the message without sending it, saving it into the drafts folder of his webmail application. Sending it would mean the message would have to go through the NSA's screening, and why risk it? Even if the message seemed inconspicuous, it was better if he didn't send it at all.

Instead, he had set up a communications system before departing from Russia. He had shared his username and password for that email account with Myatlev. Soon, Myatlev or one of his people would log in using a proxy server and read the message saved in the drafts folder of the webmail application, then delete the draft or edit it to reply. No email message would ever cross the NSA-guarded servers, because, technically, no information would leave the American-based servers heading toward Russia.

Wasn't technology great? Too bad he couldn't use the same method to transmit the actual intelligence; the risk was too big with large amounts of data, schematics, or images that could trigger the interest of who-knows-what network engineer to sneak a peek. Even encrypted photos ran the same risk. The NSA was aware of the practice to embed information into the background of banal photos, and they screened every server, every photo-sharing application, everything. He had to find another way to send the intel home, and he had to move fast. The stuff he was sitting on could do miracles for Russia's aged military technology. Maybe he could ask Mother how she'd like her gifts sent to her; maybe she had an idea.

He reopened the webmail drafts folder and adjusted his message, then saved the unsent message, closed everything, and went to bed.

Her cell phone chimed, startling her from agitated, restless sleep. She'd been on pins and needles, waiting for the polygraph test result, not very confident she was able to pass, not sure of the consequences of some of the answers she had given.

She picked it up with a groan and checked the new text message responsible for the familiar chime sound.

"Poly passed," the message read. "Meet the team tomorrow 9.00AM at Naval Station Norfolk—Pier 7, USS *Fletcher*—Jeremy."

"Yes!" Alex gave an excited yelp, jumped out of bed, and started dancing around the room. "Yes!"

Alex had no problem whatsoever locating the USS *Fletcher*. Her hull was distinctively different, standing out from a distance. She quickly found parking, right across from Pier 7, then trotted toward the vessel, curious to explore.

She'd read about it during the past couple of days, thirstily absorbing every bit of information she could, and hoping she'd be able to retain something. Some of it read like a foreign language, filled with concepts she didn't understand and had to look up.

Mason had given her credentials to join the team as an engagement consultant, her official cover job being liaison between the project team and the US Navy. Not all projects needed an engagement consultant, but some did, and Mason felt this was the most inconspicuous manner she could join the team with her limited knowledge of naval warfare and laser systems, and limited time to prepare.

She waited eagerly for Walcott's van to appear and drop off the project team at the pier, so she could finally board the Fletcher with them. She checked every minute or so, but then turned her head back to study the ship's elegant hull.

There had been controversy about that stealth-hull design, and, apparently, the jury was still out whether its seaworthiness exceeded that of an Arleigh-Burke class vessel, the backbone of US Navy's destroyer fleet. The *Fletcher* was a Zumwalt-class destroyer, capable of sending more than a hundred guided missiles toward their targets before having to return and rearm. Its hull was what they called a tumblehome design, narrowing up from the water level and giving her a unique silhouette.

That was part of her stealth design; more stealth features were built in, like its inverted bow, designed to cut through the waves and generate minimal wake. The deckhouse was integrated into the hull design, making the *Fletcher* appear smooth in its narrowing toward the top and presenting minimal visible detail into its technical and weapons equipment. The power and propulsion systems were also integrated, none of that equipment visible above sea level. If she were to compare the *Fletcher* with any other type of vessel she'd seen, it would have to be a submarine. Yes, the Fletcher looked just like a submarine, more than 600 feet long, floating proudly on the surface. Amazing.

"And I'll need you to help me with that, Quentin," a female voice disrupted Alex's study of the *Fletcher*.

There they were, passing her by, the Walcott team of five engineers, unmistakable; they all wore color-coded hard hats with Walcott's logo on them. She caught a glimpse of the Sprinter leaving the dock and she hurried to catch up with the project team.

"Excuse me," she said, and they stopped and turned toward her. "Are you guys the Walcott project team for the laser cannon installation?"

"And you are... ?" the man Alex knew from photos to be Bob McLeod asked.

She extended her hand and gave Bob a firm handshake.

"Alex Hoffmann, engagement consultant for the Navy. I'm supposed to tag along with you guys, help you out with whatever you need, and document and observe the installation, to give our PR something to work from," she spouted at machine-gun speed. "You do realize they want to make a big deal out of this launch, right?"

"Yeah, we do; we were wondering when you'd come. Sylvia Copperwaite, mobile installations," the woman introduced herself. She was charming and delicate in person, features that her human resources file failed to convey. She also had a haggard, almost ashen look, covered for the most part with carefully applied makeup, but revealed here and there, especially around her tired, sad eyes.

"Bob McLeod, PM," the first man introduced himself, a dutiful smile fluttering on his lips for exactly one second, quickly replaced by a look of irritation, complete with clenched jaws and tense muscles she could see knotting under the skin of his cheeks.

"Faisal Kundi, embedded software." Faisal shook her hand politely, a little hesitant. Alex noticed about him a shyness, almost fear of scrutiny. Faisal averted his eyes immediately after introducing himself, and stared at the blue waters instead.

"Vernon Blackburn, lasers, but you can call me Vern." This one studied her at large; there wasn't a shred of shyness in this guy, as he was measuring her from head to toe. *Whoa, buddy, we just met,* she thought, feeling how he was undressing her with his eyes. He was an attractive man, his shoulder-length hair giving him an artistic, rebellious air. The way he studied her, his smile and body language, was a powerful, heady mix. *Mr. sex-bomb with a PhD,* she thought, almost chuckling. She refrained from that and returned a gigawatt smile instead, almost flirting. Sylvia rolled her eyes discreetly; she'd probably seen hordes of naïve women fly like moths into Vernon's perma-flame.

She turned toward the last man and extended her hand.

"Quentin Hadden, weapons." Quentin also averted his eyes and shied away from the physical contact of the handshake, making it as superficial and as quick as possible.

"All right, let's get this show on the road," Bob McLeod called them to order. "We're on a very tight schedule."

They boarded the *Fletcher*. Alex's head was on a swivel, taking in all the details.

"Welcome aboard," a uniformed man greeted them, "I'm Captain Anthony Meecham," the man said.

Alex shook his hand enthusiastically, and said, "You must be proud of your command, captain."

The man gave a wide smile, showing two rows of perfectly aligned, white teeth. "I sure am, ma'am." Based on his record, he was a highly decorated sailor, although he didn't seem a day older than thirty-two. None of those ribbons hung on his chest though; he was wearing a Navy working uniform.

"Call me Alex, please."

"Ma'am," he replied unperturbed, as if acknowledging the order, yet making it clear he was going to maintain his professional distance.

"You act like you've never done this before," McLeod said, causing her an instant adrenaline rush.

Damn...

"You're right, I haven't," Alex replied, deciding to go with the least amount of lying necessary. "You're very observant, Bob. I just got this assignment; they were short on staff and gave me the opportunity to leave my desk and come out here, meet all of you in person and visit the *Fletcher*, get some hands-on experience. I am thrilled to be able to do that; it will help me a lot in my work."

McLeod shrugged and went away, probably to start working. Most of the team had scattered the moment they set foot on the ship. They knew their way around, and they had a team of sailors and shipyard workers waiting for them.

"Then maybe you'd like a tour?" Captain Meecham asked.

"I would love it!"

Meecham turned and started walking quickly, after making an inviting gesture with his hand. She rushed behind him, trying to keep up.

"The easiest way to go down these stairs is to descend facing them, like this," he demonstrated, leading the way below deck. She followed.

"The *Fletcher* is a stealth, guided-missile, destroyer," Meecham explained, "or at least it was until now. The installation of the LaWS will enhance the ship's capabilities, and might even drive the addition of a new battleship type in our nomenclature."

He stopped and turned toward her, showing her into a large room that resembled an office more than the inside of a battleship.

"This is our operations center," Meecham continued his presentation. "This is the only class of battleships that features the total ship computing environment. Any operator can control any of the ship's systems from any of these stations." Meecham pointed toward one of the computer desks, each featuring three monitors.

Alex looked around the massive room.

On one of the walls, above the operations center, were three main LCD screens displaying radar and navigation information. Alex counted at least twelve of those computer workstations, some staffed, some deserted. At one of the manned stations, an operator was showing something to Faisal Kundi.

She had a million questions, but didn't want to flaunt her ignorance and raise any red flags. She proceeded cautiously.

"What else is unique to the Zumwalt-class destroyer?" Alex asked.

Meecham smiled proudly and said, "Almost everything. Nearly all systems are integrated; for example, we have an integrated power system, generating electricity for the ship's propulsion, weapons, and electronics. The propulsion is all electric, quiet, and it can do thirty knots and still power up everything else. Our engines are Rolls-Royce gas turbines driving generators."

"This is unusual, right?"

"It's innovative, new, and has only been deployed on this class of destroyers so far. We call it the all-electric ship. And here's another unique feature—the integrated undersea warfare system," he said, pointing at a specific area on the ship's blueprint displayed on a monitor. "It's an automated system of two sonar arrays, offering early detection for any underwater threats, such as mines, torpedoes, or submarines."

"How about weapons?"

"Our missile launchers are vertical, buried in the hull along the sides; that's a key feature to maintain our stealth capabilities. Above deck we have two 155mm guns that can shoot self-propelled, in-flight guided ordnance, with a range of eighty-three nautical miles."

"Sea targets?" Alex asked.

"Sea, land, and air," Meecham replied with parental pride.

"How about the new laser cannon? Where are they installing it?" Alex looked at her notes.

"That location was quite the controversy with the Walcott engineering team members. Originally, they wanted to remove one of the 155mm guns, to make room for the cannon. Then someone figured out that because the cannon doesn't weigh much and doesn't recoil, it could be installed on top of the helo hangar. After they did a few studies to confirm that the radar cross section or the aerodynamics of the ship would not be impacted by that choice of installation, it got approved."

He turned and started walking briskly, and she followed, curious to see the cannon's future location.

They entered the helo hangar from inside the deckhouse; it was deserted and marked with signage to alert that construction was in progress. Noises of hammers hitting metal, and the distinctive sound made by welding torches was coming from outside.

"We needed to reinforce the structure to support the cannon installation. The entire deckhouse, including the hangar, has a composite structure, to make it light and reduce radar signature. Now that reinforcement is complete; they've started the actual installation work. Let's see," he said, carefully exiting the hangar, trying to avoid tripping on loose cabling, scattered tools, and equipment crates.

Alex saw Sylvia discussing energetically with Bob over a blueprint, their heads close together; from a distance, they seemed to be having an argument, some sort of a technical disagreement.

Quentin was working on a mobile weapons control interface, a device that looked like a rugged laptop. As for Vern, the sex-bomb with a PhD, he was nowhere in sight.

"Do you have women serving on the *Fletcher*?" she asked innocently.

"Yes, we do. Out of our complement of 140, there are 27 women, mostly in computer operations."

Probably that's where Vernon Blackburn was, looking for his next adventure at sea. Alex turned her attention back to Captain Meecham, who stood silently, waiting to be of service.

"How will the laser cannon work? Why is it so special?"

"It will reside in a cupola, whose components will retract allowing the cannon to become exposed and have line of fire with the target. You can see the components of that cupola over there," he said, pointing at two white quarter-sphere assembly elements. "The cannon brings a sizeable advantage to our weapons array, because of its precision, which is unprecedented, and its low cost to operate. It also brings a humanitarian aspect to our military engagements. With the laser, we can target the propulsion or the weapons systems of an enemy vessel, and cause zero or almost zero casualties. We don't need to sink ships to disable them; not with the laser cannon."

"How precise are we talking?" Alex asked. "You mentioned your 155mm guns have in-flight guidance, right? That makes them fairly precise, I'd guess."

"With the laser cannon we can blow up a can of Coke from the hull of a vessel from 500 yards and leave the vessel intact, that's how precise it can be. We can take a drone out from the air at 250 yards, where few people even see it. Actually, if everything goes well with this installation, on Memorial Day, we'll host a ceremony and demonstrate the cannon to SecNav and SecDef."

"You mentioned cost as being one of the advantages?"

"Yes, and a major one. An in-flight guided 155mm shell is almost $50,000, and a Tomahawk missile will set you back $1.41 million. Even if you choose to use 'dumb' 155mm shells, unguided ones, they go up to $1,000 each, and the cost stacks up fast due to the loss in accuracy and effectiveness. So, you see how the laser cannon brings an advantage at roughly $1 per shot, right?"

"Yes," she said, absorbing everything and putting it into the perspective of her mission. "Thank you, Captain Meecham, I think I'm good from here," she said.

"You're welcome," he replied. "Please let me know if you have any other questions. You haven't worked on Navy ships before, have you?"

"N–no, just got the assignment, but thank you for the tour, it was very informative," she replied without skipping a beat. "You have a fantastic ship, captain."

He smiled and then quickly disappeared.

She turned her attention toward the Walcott team and started approaching Sylvia and Bob, who were still engulfed in their dispute. She decided to spend a little more time watching them from a distance, and stopped near the hangar door. In the meantime, Vern had made his appearance and was working intently on his laptop, installed on a makeshift table.

She heard a faint noise to her left and caught a glimpse of a young sailor sneaking carefully through a bulkhead. He looked left, then right, carefully making sure no one saw him.

"Hi," she said, surprising him.

He looked down, averting her eyes. He was young, maybe not even twenty years old, and had tousled red hair and the freckled complexion that typically accompanies that hair color. He looked scared, almost as if someone was chasing him, or was about to.

"It's OK," she said, "I'm a civilian consultant. Out to smoke?"

He nodded sheepishly, blushing copiously, and throwing guilty glances left and right.

"I don't really care, you know," she continued, "go ahead and smoke if you want. It'll be our little secret."

The sailor nodded and mumbled something that sounded like "thanks," then disappeared through the same bulkhead he'd appeared from.

Huh... she thought. He's quite stressed out for someone who just wanted to smoke. I wonder what the deal is with him.

...Chapter 49: An Order
...Friday, May 20, 10:13AM EDT (UTC-4:00 hours)
...Federal Bureau of Investigation—Norfolk Division
...Norfolk, Virginia

"Sir, with all due respect, she's a civilian!" Jeremy's voice escalated to the point where SAC Taylor frowned and felt the need to stand up, to assert his position.

"Weber, this is an order, not a debate. If SecNav and the director think she's good enough to work this case, she's in. Need I remind you no one here wants to work with you? I have no other partner to give you, and sure as hell you're not working this case alone, in your typical cowboy style."

"Yes, sir," Jeremy replied.

"Let's see how you make it work with Hoffmann. I better not hear from the director on this issue, do you understand me?"

"Yes, sir, perfectly," he said, and turned to leave.

"And Weber." Taylor called.

"Sir?"

"Don't fuck this up."

The modified Kalashnikov rifle made for an interesting choice of tabletop lamp, fitted with a black lampshade. It was unexpected and attention grabbing to see such a weapon displayed so casually. The unusual décor features gave the restaurant its unique personality: sassy, vibrant, screaming high-end cuisine and ridiculous prices. A hangout place for Moscow's socialites and top politicians, Bon's black walls, curtains, and accessories contrasted strongly with the white, starched Damascus tablecloths.

The typical lunch hour buzzed with guests, whose reservations had been made at least two days in advance to get a table. That Monday was different though; the restaurant was eerily quiet, and only two men occupied a table. Vitaliy Myatlev and his friend and lunch guest, Mikhail Dimitrov, minister of defense of the Russian Federation.

There were four other men in the restaurant, all standing guard at the doors, carrying automatic weapons. They were Myatlev's personal guards, all ex-Spetsnaz. As for the servers, they moved almost unseen and unheard, catering to their guests' connoisseur tastes and healthy appetites as discreetly as they could.

A waiter brought hors d'oeuvres on a set of black plates combined with tiny white bowls, all placed on a sterling silver serving tray. Then he opened a chilled bottle of Stolichnaya, filled their glasses, and withdrew quietly, leaving the two men to talk business.

"Ura!" Myatlev raised his glass, holding it up until Dimitrov clinked his own against it.

"Ura!"

They drank and set down the glasses noisily, a signal for the waiter to approach and refill them.

"It's good to be out of the office, Vitya, great idea you had to take us out for lunch," Dimitrov said, taking a piece of fried calamari and savoring it. "I have so many questions for you, after we talked last time. This plan of yours, the mass intelligence gathering, that made me think . . ."

"Yes, Mishka?"

"And the more I think, the more questions I have." Dimitrov paused a little, delved into a miniature shrimp salad, and chewed with his mouth open.

"What do you want to know?"

"Look, between the two of us we can build a strong plan to rebuild the power of Russia to what it used to be. No doubt about that. Petya believes in us; I believe in us even more. But something I still don't get, and that is how will you know what intelligence to gather? How are you thinking you can manage and process all that information?"

"If we apply enough pressure on our sources, they will tell us what we need to be looking for, even if we don't know it yet," Vitya said, starting to work on his appetizer, a tiny stack of blini, small crepes layered with smoked salmon and doused in a light, savory mayonnaise.

"You told me that last time we spoke, but still I don't get it. What exactly are you planning to do? We need to get ready to go to war, Vitya. We can't continue to sit on our asses and look impotent."

"We are going to war, Mishka. We are at war as we speak. I call it our total war and it started already. There are no innocent bystanders in my strategy, and no one is safe from it. Our handlers will apply the necessary coercion on a variety of sources. Some will deliver; some will fail, or get caught, and will be the casualties of this first stage of total war. But they will be an acceptable loss, Mishka, even if these losses will hit the Russian diaspora living in the United States."

"You're targeting the diaspora?" Dimitrov's eyebrows ruffled, brought together by a deep frown.

"No, but they are the keystones in my plan. They will be the first level of field assets, resources we can use in our deployment of Division Seven agents in the field. You see, given what we're trying to do and how fast we need to compensate for twenty years of nonexistent military progress, I need to go big, Mishka. I need to go big and fast."

"I understand, but how will it all come together?"

"Our handlers will recruit assets without a clear agenda in the first phase, leaving it to the assets to fight to prove their value. We cannot do that with incentives without spending billions; we talked about that. That's why we need to bring more stick than carrot. We can achieve this level of engagement only if we use fear as our currency, and we coerce them into fighting on our side. Then we harness all the bits and pieces of information they will bring, and we will see clusters appear, signaling what we should target."

"What clusters?" Dimitrov asked, while his eyebrows still furrowed.

"In the massive amount of data we are going to harvest, multiple sources of information will bring pieces of intel around certain items of interest. I've assigned a few of my brightest people to study big data analysis models and come back with plan scenarios. If we cast a wide enough net, we will start seeing clusters of value in certain areas, especially if the assets feel pressured or highly motivated to prove their own value."

"But the diaspora might not necessarily have access to such valuable intel," Dimitrov objected.

"Agreed. The diaspora is just the entry point and the support layer for our handlers. We will use the American big data banks and their own patterns of behavior to identify who are the most easy to turn individuals. The Americans have huge databases, but not very secure; nothing that our cyber assets can't get into."

"And then?" Dimitrov asked, still unconvinced, while the waiter discreetly removed the appetizer tray and served them hot borscht in small, black bowls.

"Then, when we have clusters formed and identified, we will know what to hunt for, and we'll send in assets dedicated to certain targets. Let me give you an example of what I mean," Myatlev said, seeing the unconvinced look linger on Dimitrov's face. "The laser cannon, did we even know it existed until a week ago?"

"N–no," Dimitrov replied, visibly uncertain of where Myatlev was going with that.

"Exactly," he confirmed. "We didn't know it existed before we sent in our best handler, Smolin, to enroll some assets and see what he could get. He enrolled an asset who brought the laser cannon news to us. Now we know exactly what we need, what to ask for. Smolin has a clear direction on what information he needs to target. He knows we need the plans for the cannon, the list of scheduled installations, everything there is to know about the cannon, about the same laser cannon we didn't know existed last week."

"Bozhe moi, I get it, Vitya, you are a genius!"

"Now you see? We'll continue doing this on a large scale, unofficially declaring our total war, and more such nuggets of information will come our way. Anyone can be an asset for us."

"Why do you call this a total war? We're not firing a single bullet."

"There will be losses of all kinds, even from the ranks of the diaspora. We will apply pressure on many people, and not everyone will survive without being caught, killed, tortured, and so on. But we can't afford to care, Mishka, we just can't. Not when we have twenty years of stagnation and obsolescence to make up for... not when we have to go to war and win!"

"Na zdorovie!" Dimitrov raised his glass and cheered, then gulped down another shot.

"Na zdorovie!" Myatlev followed suit happily.

"How many handlers do you have? How many can you send in the field?"

"I've sent our best so far, Smolin. I have others that I'm preparing to send. I found another gem, a captain by the name of Anatoly Karp. That one can turn Jesus Christ into a spy, Mishka. Given enough time, that one can turn you!"

Both men burst into laughter.

"But you only have a few, Vitya, how are you going big with just a few handlers? Abramovich doesn't have the patience to wait for you to build your ranks." Dimitrov's cheerfulness was gone, replaced by a look of worry brought by the thought of the irascible and bellicose Russian president, eager to start his vengeance war as soon as possible.

"I am building an intelligence infrastructure, Mishka, just like we had in the old days. The handlers are leading the deployment, then the diaspora operates as a second level. Some of them are still willing to fight and give their lives for Russia, even if they're now American citizens. And for those who won't, well, the handlers can find ways to be persuasive. I've chosen handlers who don't take no for an answer, and who won't stop until they get the job done."

"You're the businessman, Vitya, this is right up your alley. Just be careful, because that's what you said last time, that your plan can't fail, and it did."

Vitya ran his hand over his forehead and against his buzz-cut graying hair.

"I still don't know what went wrong with that one," he said quietly, after a few seconds of silence. "It should have never happened. I thought of everything. It was almost like I had an enemy out there, someone so decided to foil my plan that it almost felt personal. Someone who could see through the complexities of what I'd laid out to perfection on a global scale. Did you know they're all dead? All the players? Apparently unrelated accidents of all sorts, but I'm no idiot, Mishka, they all died within less than a week," he said, unaware he was wringing his hands almost convulsively, in a rare display of frustration and resentment. "If someone's cleaning up, why am I still here?"

"I didn't know they're all dead," Dimitrov replied quietly. "No one told me."

"You were sick, Mishka, fighting for your life. I didn't need to burden you with my nightmares. You have no idea how many nights I've spent awake in bed thinking of what could have gone wrong, and I can't think of anything." He rubbed his head again, then continued, suddenly refreshed and in control of his emotions, "But I promise you, this time we'll get the job done."

"Good," a thoughtful, almost gloomy Dimitrov replied. "You focus on getting us the intel, while I work on getting the military ready for our war. They're unprepared, untrained, sloppy. The commanders have grown lazy and fat, while their livers are giving up on them, dying of cirrhosis. Just like you found your handlers, I have to find my future generals." He stopped talking for a while, sipping a few spoons of borscht. "We're thinking a nuclear strike might be possible, preemptive, or defensive, but these men aren't ready for any of that. Not yet, anyway."

"Can you talk to Abramovich?" Myatlev asked, halfheartedly. The Russian president wasn't open to such suggestions, nor was he willing to listen to the voices of reason.

"You know there's no way I can get Abramovich to give us some more time. Any day now he could wake up one morning and decide he wants to push the button, and we better be fucking ready when he does, otherwise we're finished... screwed to the bone."

They both reflected quietly on that perspective for a while, eating absently, engulfed in their own troublesome thoughts. Then Myatlev changed direction.

"I love the idea of rebuilding Russia, Mishka, but I don't like the idea of war that much. War can be bad for business, you know."

Both men savored their food for a minute, then Dimitrov answered, "It doesn't have to be. War creates a lot of need, and maybe you can help your country with that."

Myatlev's face lit up a little.

"Maybe it's time to diversify my business portfolio. What do you anticipate the military will need?"

"Many things; I'll make a list. Guns. Helicopters. Ammunition. New tanks, new ships, new weapons technology. Manufacturing the technology you're going to steal for us with your new network of spies. Not to say that in the event of a nuclear strike, we have almost nothing, no protective equipment, limited countermeasures, and nearly no contingencies. The same goes for biological and chemical warfare; we might even go that route. Who knows what Abramovich decides to do . . ."

"Just send me your list and quantities, and let me know if you have a preference as to where these items should be manufactured. Whatever you need done, you'll have done. You can count on me."

"I am. And I hope you won't forget your friends, when war brings its windfall your way."

Myatlev filled their glasses with vodka to the brim.

"To a war that's good for business, ura!" he cheered and downed his glass.

"To old friends and a new Russia, ura!" Dimitrov replied cheerfully.

The waiter gave them a few seconds to finish their round of drinks, then cleaned away the empty borscht bowls and brought in their steaks.

Alex struggled to open Mason's office door. A steaming, tall cup of coffee and her laptop bag kept both her hands occupied. Jeremy hopped off his chair and helped her get in.

"Thanks!" she said, smiling briefly in his direction. "Good morning." She put her coffee cup down on Mason's desk and the bag on the floor, next to the only open seat in the room.

"Good morning, Ms. Hoffmann," Mason greeted her, briefly standing as a courtesy then sitting back down in his massive leather chair.

"Please, call me Alex," she encouraged him.

"What do you have?" Jeremy asked. "What can you tell us?"

"I've spent two full days with the team. Friday we spent the entire day working on the *Fletcher*, yesterday we were there only half a day, then I joined them for a meeting here, in the seventh floor conference room. It was a project review, very helpful for my study."

Mason watched her intently, waiting for her to cut to the chase.

"And?" Jeremy said. "Do you have anything we can use?"

"I think so, but you're not going to like it." She looked first at Jeremy, then at Mason, and continued. "Almost all seem to be likely candidates for this leak of information. The only one who seems the least likely to be our traitor is Faisal Kundi."

"Oh, for Christ's sake . . ." Jeremy said, leaning back in his chair and pushing away from the table, failing to hide his frustration. "That's just great... the one who made the most sense, the foreign-born national, the Muslim; are you saying he's clean? How sure are you? And based on what?" Jeremy's voice escalated with every rapid-fire question he threw out there.

"I only had two days," Alex started to explain apologetically, but then regained her self-confidence. "I know what I'm talking about. All the others are preoccupied by something else. When they think no one's watching them, their body language shows they're concerned, worried, and fidgety."

"Has any of them said anything?" Mason asked.

"No, nothing that would definitively put them at the top of the suspect list."

"This gives us nothing," Jeremy said with a grunt. "How are we better than last week? Why did we even go through all this trouble to get you aboard that ship?"

"Why don't you tell me what the almighty FBI was able to do in these couple of days? Did you get their phone records, backgrounds, banking info? How's that coming up?"

Jeremy cleared his throat and frowned before responding, visibly annoyed.

"We have some background, not everything. Warrants are still pending to get their finances and phone records; the judge turned us down. He said group probable cause doesn't apply to individuals. Our DA is appealing it, playing the trump card of national security."

"So you got a bigger nothing than I did," Alex chuckled bitterly. "How about we drop the attitude and start cooperating?" Alex offered.

"Meaning?" Jeremy asked, irritation still seeping in his voice.

"Run me through the background you have on all these people, and let's take it from there. We might be able to get some progress made today after all."

Mason silently watched the dialogue, but his almost perfectly immobile face started to show signs of concern. For a man like him, a man used to taking charge and getting things done, being almost powerless was not acceptable.

"I've pulled the work records for all five," Mason said, "and I've interviewed in detail all their current and former supervisors."

"How sure are you they're gonna keep quiet about these discussions?" Alex asked, frowning slightly. "The word could get out there from former supervisors just as well."

"I don't think that's a possibility. I'd say that's a low risk. We have to have something to go on with," Mason replied.

"True," Alex said. "Let's paint a picture of each one; let's combine the background information you have, Jeremy, with their personnel files and supervisor interview notes. That will give us a better idea of who these people are. By the way, before we start, is it possible that one of the seamen on the USS *Fletcher* used the van?"

"No, I am positive about that," Mason replied. "Why do you ask?"

"I ran into a very anxious, apprehensive young man on the ship. Well... maybe it was nothing," she dismissed it, ignoring the feeling of uneasiness that still tugged at her gut when she remembered the boy's red hair and freckled face.

"I have something too," Mason said. "Our pest control found a godforsaken copier forgotten in the basement mailroom. I have no idea how that was missed. It's very old; must have been there since before the 1990s.

I've instructed them to remove it ASAP."

"No!" Alex blurted. "That would draw our spy's attention. Ask them to just disable it, make sure it doesn't work anymore, and dust it for prints if they can do it discreetly, after everyone else has gone home. We don't want to get anyone's attention. A piece of junk like that could break anytime; no one will be the wiser."

"Consider it done," Mason said.

"On second thought," she said, fluttering a mischievous smile on her lips, "scratch that. Wouldn't it be nice if they fitted it with a camera and watch who's using it instead? We might hook us the traitor faster that way."

"I will get on it," Mason said, with a hint of a smile.

"OK, then. Let's start with the one I thought was our prime suspect, Faisal Kundi. Graduated from Columbia with a master's of science in computer engineering," Jeremy read from his file, then flipped through some pages. "Immigrated to the United States at age three. He did well in school, even better in college. He had very few friends, and he didn't participate in any team sports. Umm... that's about all we have for now. He lives in a townhouse, and his wife is a homemaker."

"He is highly appreciated by his supervisor," Mason said, "who finds him reliable and calm under stress. He is talented and creative. He is quiet and not engaging much with the rest of his coworkers, he's not the water-cooler kind of guy." Mason closed the file he was reading from and set it on the table. "That's all we have that's relevant on Faisal."

Alex thought for a second, then asked, "What kind of car does he drive?"

"I can access the DMV database, just give me a second," Jeremy replied, pulling his tablet and logging in. "A two-year-old Toyota Corolla."

"Any recent foreign travel?" she asked.

"No," Jeremy replied, after taking a minute to check Homeland Security's database.

"OK," she replied thoughtfully. "It matches what I saw; a quiet, relatively withdrawn individual, who does his work, keeps socialization to a minimum, and is very calm, almost relaxed. He might be clean after all."

"I find it hard to swallow," Jeremy objected. "His background is Muslim, a foreign national, it fits."

"You can't hold people accountable for the place they were born," Alex protested.

"No, I can't, and I won't," Jeremy replied. "But I can use statistical information to profile a suspect; that's my job. Statistically there's a strong correlation between this type of background and anti-American interests. That's all I'm saying."

"I have to agree, to some extent at least," Mason intervened. "Even here at Walcott, bringing a foreign-born national on staff is frowned on, and a Middle Easterner fares worse. But we recruited Faisal straight out of school, at the end of his master's program. We chose him."

"That was how long ago?" Jeremy asked. "Seven years? Many things can change in seven years, especially the allegiances of a Muslim. Statistically, we have a better chance of finding that Kundi is the spy."

"And, of course, to every such rule there are exceptions," Alex pushed back. "Let's try to keep an open mind this time, and move on to... who's next?"

Jeremy groaned and opened the next file.

"Sylvia Copperwaite, thirty-three, PhD in computational modeling," Jeremy replied. "She was quite popular in school, partied a lot. She studied at Duke. Divorced five years ago, no boyfriend that anyone knows about. No travel, and . . ." Jeremy switched focus from his paper files to his tablet, "drives a 1998 Honda Accord. Huh... No recent foreign travel, outside of a trip to Cancun last year."

"1998 Accord, you said?" Alex asked. "That jalopy is a pretty dismal set of wheels for a six-figure income."

"Agree," Mason said. "Her supervisor said she's very talented, yet sometimes she lacks focus. She can fall behind on projects if not closely supervised, which is a bit of a concern for someone in her role. On rare occasions, she snapped at coworkers, slamming them for minor issues, then immediately apologizing. She's behaving like she's under a lot of stress."

"That aligns with my observations," Alex added. "She looks pale and distraught, camouflaged somewhat by makeup, but below the chin and jawline the pallor of her skin showed clearly. Her state of mind seemed to vacillate between deep sadness and all-consuming worry. In short, judging by everything we have so far, she's distraught and broke. Not necessarily the makings of a spy, but you never know. I think we need to understand what's going on in her life before ruling her out."

"Got it," Jeremy said. "Next we have Robert McLeod, the project leader. MIT grad with honors, played football on his school's team, he was a quarterback. Popular with girls back then, enough to be noted in his file. On his school record there was a mention of a cheerleader who got pregnant. McLeod persuaded her to get an abortion, then the girl had a nervous breakdown and he never wanted to have anything to do with her again. He's extremely intelligent and quite arrogant. He's ambitious and competitive. He drives a Mercedes S-Class, and travels every year to Europe on vacation. He's single and doesn't enjoy long-term relationships."

"Mercedes? How new?" Mason asked. "That could be a factor."

"A year old," Jeremy replied. "But before that he had another Mercedes, and before that, another. It's more of a lifestyle choice than a red flag, I would say."

"I didn't like this guy," Alex said. "He's an arrogant ass. His attitude burns like acid. He seems to be engulfed in a cloud of constantly frustrated superiority, as if someone had done him wrong somehow, and that someone is everyone. This man is angry at the entire world. It could be him. We need financials, more data to confirm."

"His boss said that he was passed over for promotion a number of times for precisely this reason—his arrogance and superiority, which is not conducive to good team cohesion," Mason reported. "They've also said he tends to be very harsh on his subordinates, to the point where there were concerns with potential lawsuits from psychologically abused employees. Several people transferred out of his team, and two quit, leaving detailed information about his abrasive style in their exit interviews. On the bright side though, he holds several patents of significant value," he added.

"Makes you wonder why he is leading a team instead of being a researcher," Alex said.

"Apparently he wants to grow into leadership; his boss was concerned with completely demotivating him by taking his team away, considering McLeod's potential for invention."

"So they sacrifice some people knowingly, just so this guy can invent more stuff?" Jeremy said, shaking his head in disbelief.

"That *stuff* is what keeps this country safe, Agent Weber," Mason replied coldly. "That stuff can make a difference during wartime, a difference we can't afford to lose. It might not be an ideal situation, I agree, but managing talent of this man's caliber is not an easy job. Inventors, scientists, men like McLeod are desperately needed, and they're not only scarce, but also very fragile. We all have our battles, Agent Weber, so before you pass judgment on Walcott Global's management practices, I'd like to remind you what's at stake."

Jeremy's face reddened.

"Here's an interesting fact for you, Jeremy," Alex said, trying to defuse the tension in the air, "Quentin Hadden reports to Bob McLeod."

"Let's look at him next," Jeremy said, opening a new file. "Masters, electrical engineering, another Ivy League, this one went to Cornell's College of Engineering on a scholarship. He's one of those people who can read extremely fast. Very comfortable alone, there was note from his school counselor in his file, stating that he shows signs of sociophobia, and recommended several actions to rehabilitate and integrate him. A later note stated that everything they tried had failed; that the boy just didn't want to be around people. A couple of items on his record showed that he responded with extreme aggression toward bullies, but he never started the fights, just defended himself. What else... drives a three-year-old Acura MDX and doesn't travel," Jeremy ended his briefing and closed Quentin's file.

"I don't have much," Mason said, "considering he reports to Bob McLeod. I couldn't ask him. We do have on his record that he complained twice to Human Resources that McLeod is being unreasonable and abusive."

"Yeah, we already know he was right on that one," Jeremy commented.

"And he's also one of our top inventors," Mason added. "He holds several patents under his name, a couple of which are highly valuable and strategic, and have been filed under a code instead of the description, to protect the secrecy of the invention."

"I didn't know that was even possible," Alex said. "Again, it matches what I observed in the past few days. Quentin is withdrawn, keeps to himself, he barely said a word. When he does speak, he averts his eyes and wants the interaction to be over soon. And you know what else I'm thinking?"

"What?" Jeremy asked, while Mason looked at her with curiosity.

"I think it must be awful for a man like Quentin to put up with a Bob McLeod in a position of power, especially thinking how Quentin dealt with his bullies in school. I'm thinking our Mr. Quentin Hadden is a time bomb, waiting to explode."

"I agree," Mason said. "After we finish this investigation I will make sure Human Resources becomes aware of what's going on."

"The last one is Vernon Blackburn," Jeremy said. "Another PhD, married, no kids, and quite the playboy."

Alex chuckled.

"What's the matter?" Jeremy asked.

"That's an understatement," she replied. "The man is constantly hunting, flirting, scouting, spreading his pheromones. I feel sorry for his wife."

"Our people found out their marriage is in trouble. His wife walked out on him recently, and he's been trying to get her back."

"That's not exactly what he was doing last Friday on the ship," Alex replied caustically, "and he wasn't working much, either."

"He also likes a drink or two after work. He drives a Jeep Grand Cherokee. No recent foreign travel. Did you notice anything else noteworthy?"

"No," Alex replied. "Just philandering and jumpiness. He did seem very jumpy, but quick to recover and start flirting with just about any female who could fog a mirror."

"I have feedback from two supervisors, his current and former. Both very happy with his performance, although both had to talk to him about office flirting. No one has complained about him though; apparently women appreciate his attention; he has a certain... charm," Mason ended his briefing, a little uncomfortable.

"That it?" Alex asked. "That's all we have so far?"

"Yes," Jeremy replied. "As soon as the warrants come in, we'll get financials, phone records, and data records. Oh, and forgot to say, we have all five under surveillance, round the clock, since we took over last week."

"Any movement?" Mason asked.

"Not yet, but one of them will move soon. They always do."

"Until then?" Alex pressed on.

"We'll keep digging," Jeremy said.

"I'm afraid the documents might have already been transferred. What if we're too late by the time the warrants come in? We need to stop the info leak before it leaves the country."

"Thanks for stating the obvious, Ms. Hoffmann, very valuable input," Jeremy said, frustration getting the best of him.

"We know that, Ms. Hoffmann," Mason intervened. "We're all painfully aware of the consequences and the loss we will incur if that document leaves the country. Yet there's only so much we can do. We have to wait for the warrants."

"Ahh... the hell with it," she snapped. "We need that info now. We need to find out who changed their behavior lately, even a tiny little bit. No one bought a new car yet, but what else changed in their lives?"

"What are you saying?" Jeremy asked.

"What would you do if you recently got into some cash, the type you can't deposit in your bank account?"

"I... I'd start using it, I guess."

"On what?" she insisted.

"On everything... groceries, gas, restaurants."

"And how would we see that?"

"I'd stop using my credit cards, that's how," Jeremy said, a crooked smile tugging at his lips. "But we don't have the financials yet."

"Like I said, the hell with it," she whispered. "Just do me a favor; pretend you're not hearing this, OK? Both of you, please," she added, turning toward Mason. He nodded silently, surprised and intrigued.

"And since you're *not* hearing this, you might as well pretend you're not hearing all the details of this call, so we save some time." She pulled her cell and dialed a number using her cell's encryption, and then switched it in hands-free mode.

A man quickly picked up.

"Hey, boss,"

"Hey, Lou, what's up?"

"How's the East Coast treating you?"

"Jury's still out on that one, Lou," she replied, unable to contain a smile. "Hey, I need help, pronto."

"Shoot," he said.

"I need financials, phone, and car GPS tracking, credit card activity, data usage for five individuals; I'll send you their names. They're all local here, in Norfolk. I need all that ASAP, but run them through your pattern recognition software first, and tell me what changes happened recently."

She caught Jeremy's jaw dropping, and she made an effort to refrain from smiling. Mason listened just as impassible as usual, only a flicker in his eyes showing his keen interest in her approach.

"How far back?" Louie asked.

"Go six months."

"You got it."

"How long, Lou?"

"It's probably gonna take me a couple of hours, maybe more."

"ASAP, Lou, please. It's burning, this one."

"You got it."

The call disconnected, leaving the room engulfed in silence.

Jeremy spoke first, perplexed.

"Two questions for you, Ms. Hoffmann. Do the laws of these United States mean absolutely nothing to you? Do you often break the law blatantly in front of law enforcement, just to see what you can get away with? Do you expect me to break every rule in the book and look the other way? Do you realize what you've done?"

"Yes, saved us time, precious time that we can't afford to waste. And you said two questions, but you asked four."

Mason looked at her approvingly, although she struggled to figure out how that was expressed. His face looked just the same as usual, and so did his eyes, yet there was that flicker in them.

"That was only my first question," he growled.

"Then what's the second?"

"Who are you people?"

Smolin wiped his mouth with a napkin and put it down on the table, next to his empty plate.

"Thank you, it was good," he said.

"*Spasiba*," Olga thanked him and started to clean the table. She put all the dishes and empty glasses away, then cleaned the tablecloth of breadcrumbs using a small brush and a miniature dustpan. When she finished her work, she nodded briefly and disappeared, leaving the two men alone.

"Good, now let's talk some business." Smolin poured himself a cup of coffee from the machine. "Nikolai, I need you to travel to Moscow in a few days," he said. "I need you to take something there."

"How big?"

"Not big at all, but very important. I have important information in my possession that needs to be taken to Moscow and personally delivered to the Division Seven leader. You've heard of Division Seven, yes? You'll have the opportunity to meet him face to face."

Nikolai turned a little pale and clasped his hands tightly, visibly uncomfortable.

"Will I stay long?"

"No. A couple of days at the most."

"What if... what if I get caught?" Nikolai muttered, staring at his clasped, white-knuckled hands.

"You won't get caught, Nikolai," Smolin said. "We've been working on an intel transport system that is 100 percent guaranteed to work. It's never been used before; they'll never see it coming."

"Yes, sir," Nikolai answered faintly. "I hope so. What kind of system is it? What will we use?"

"We'll use the latest in biotechnology."

"OK, let's deal with the elephant in this car, Jeremy," Alex said, "what have I done to piss you off?"

He hesitated before answering. His face read like an open book for Alex. Frustration, uneasiness, and a little sadness.

"It's not you," he eventually answered. "I–I've had a rough patch lately. I've changed partners quite a bit lately, and it's impacting my work."

"Let me see if I can translate what you said in plain English... no one wants to work with you, and you're in trouble with your boss because of that?"

"Whoa... you are direct," he said.

She looked straight at him, inquisitively.

"Yes," he admitted. "Something like that."

"I was wondering why you were on your own, you know. Feds normally roam in pairs," she said, smiling. "What happened?"

"I'm impatient, I guess, and don't care much for procedure, if it's in the way of catching the bad guy sooner," he said, relaxing a little.

"We have that in common, you know," she chuckled.

"Yeah, no kidding."

"He's on the move," Alex said in a brisk tone. "He's going into the picnic area."

They had been stuck on a stakeout, watching Quentin Hadden's every move. Just hours earlier, Louie had brought the results of an in-depth pattern analysis for the five suspects on their list. His analysis included credit card charges, bank account transactions, phone and data records, the whole shebang.

He'd spent significant time digging into Sylvia Copperwaite's background. Typically, a gambler carrying a significant amount of debt fit the profile, but she was clean. She'd been living on the edge for more than a year, and she never did anything wrong, not even a speeding ticket. She was clean as a whistle. The only unusual phone call she'd made in the past months had been in the past week, and it was a call to an addiction help center. She was getting help.

Everyone else's financial transactions and phone usage had stayed unchanged, following the usual patterns seen in the past six months, except one.

Quentin Hadden had stopped using his credit card almost completely, and no cash withdrawals were made out of his bank accounts. There wasn't any other discrepancy in Hadden's patterns of behavior, which was strange. He wasn't making or receiving any different calls than the usual. Of course, he might have purchased a burn phone, for which they had no records whatsoever. However, he hadn't been traveling, eating out, or buying any large ticket items since surveillance had started. That was it, the only shred of discrepancy they had was the fact that the man had stopped using his credit cards for anything other than gas and online shopping. He either had an influx of cash to burn, or he somehow stopped needing food and toilet paper.

They had no better lead to go with, so Alex and Jeremy had decided to stake him out, one of the first points they had agreed on since they had met. Hadden had taken the day off, raising another red flag, and for some reason had been sitting for a few hours in his car, reading, right there in the Botanical Gardens parking lot.

Spending countless hours locked in the car with a grumpy fed had been a bit of a pain in the backside for Alex, that was for sure. But Hadden was finally on the move, leaving his parked car behind and heading toward the picnic area.

Alex hopped out of the car and put on shades and a baseball cap. Jeremy followed suit, then they locked arms and walked slowly and casually down the alley, just a few yards behind their target.

Hadden approached the picnic tables, where several people sat. There was a family with three children at one of the tables, packing their cooler and food containers and getting ready to leave. They were noisy and gregarious, but he didn't pay any attention to them and didn't stop there; he continued walking down the alley.

Several tables farther, two older men were playing backgammon, completely absorbed in their game and letting out sounds of frustration or exhilaration to go with the rolls of their dice. Hadden slowed down, as if captivated by the game, and stopped, watching the players.

"Who's winning?" Hadden asked.

"I am," one of the men replied.

"The hell you are," the other one said. "Not as long as I have breath in me."

Hadden smiled and patted the first man on his shoulder, leaning into him and discreetly sliding a small envelope in the man's jacket pocket.

Alex and Jeremy almost missed that.

"That's it, that was the drop, we got it," Jeremy said.

"No, we don't," Alex replied, grabbing him in a side hug and taking what appeared to be a selfie, but in fact snapping a quick and somewhat distant image of the man at the backgammon table.

"Let's go," Jeremy said impatiently, "Hadden's leaving."

"So let him," Alex said calmly, "we know where to find him. We have a bigger problem, in case you haven't noticed."

"Yeah, and I'm arresting the bigger problem now," Jeremy said, reaching in his pocket for his cell to call the backup unit stationed at the park entrance.

"No, you're not," she said, forcing his hand away from his pocket.

"Jesus, woman, what the hell is wrong with you?" Jeremy snapped.

"Don't you wanna know where this lead takes us? If you book him now, I'm sure he'll clam up and you got nothing else."

"There isn't a single case in the FBI's procedure manual where we let spies go free when we catch them red-handed. What if we lose him? Then what?"

"Give me a minute, will you please?" Alex replied unperturbed, and sent the picture via encrypted text message, with just two letters typed under it, "ID."

Hadden had disappeared around the corner, headed most likely for his car, and the two of them took a bench under an old oak tree, with a direct line of sight to the backgammon game that still continued. She sensed the frustration in Jeremy, who could have easily closed the case as a win and make amends for his lack of partner retention, but she didn't care. She still fostered some hope that this case might somehow be related to her mystery man, the Russian ghost with the initial V.

A chime coming from Alex's mobile got their attention a few minutes later. A new text message read, "Major Evgheni Smolin, Russian Foreign Intelligence (SVR), entered via Toronto Pearson as Rudnitsky inbound from Zurich. Then crossed as Duncan, Canadian passport, at Niagara Falls on April 9. Current address, Smithfield Virginia, Novachenko residence."

"There, see?" Alex said, exhilarated to see the suspect was, indeed, Russian. "Now let's set up surveillance to find out who else is invited to this party."

"There he is," Jeremy said, pointing at Hadden's Acura, following the gentle curves of Norview Avenue, headed for the highway. "Let's pull him over."

She grunted, still angry that Jeremy insisted on picking up Hadden himself, and he let the two surveillance teams follow Smolin. Smolin is who she cared about; Smolin could potentially hold information about her mystery man, while Hadden was yesterday's news.

Jeremy flipped a switch on the console of his Dodge Charger and the blue lights embedded in his radiator mask turned on, accompanied by the siren. Alex couldn't stifle a smile.

"I've always wanted to do this," she said.

The Acura slowed down and came to a stop.

"Stay here," Jeremy said and got out of the car. Alex obeyed him for about ten seconds, then jumped out of the car and followed him.

Quentin had handed Jeremy his driver's license.

"Step out of your vehicle, sir, we need to perform a sobriety test," Jeremy said, acting just like an off-duty highway patrolman.

The moment Hadden got out of his car that changed. Jeremy grabbed him and turned him around, forcing him face down against his car's hood, and cuffing his hands behind his back.

"Quentin Hadden, you are under arrest for espionage and treason. You have the right to remain silent—"

"Hey, I know you," Hadden said, looking at Alex.

"Yes, you know me," Alex replied dryly. "That doesn't change a thing."

Jeremy helped Hadden get in the back seat of the Charger.

"I will need an attorney," Hadden said.

Jeremy burst into laughter. "What? You think we caught you robbing a convenience store and you still have rights? Where you're going there are no lawyers, and you have no rights and no privileges. The sooner you get that into your head, the better off you'll be."

Hadden remained quiet for the duration of the short trip to FBI headquarters. Upon arrival, Jeremy booked him and had someone put him in an interrogation room.

Alex trotted behind him and followed quietly everything he did.

"Jeremy, I want to sit in on the interrogation. I wanna ask him some questions, my way."

"No, absolutely not."

"Please," she insisted, "it's really important to me. I think I can get to him. I read in his file he has a lot of frustrations with his employer. I can use that, I've experienced it myself and I can create rapport with him. Please, let me try."

"No, Alex, I'm sorry, I can't. We can't allow contractors to sit in interrogations; it's against the procedure."

"And since when do you give a damn about procedure?" Alex asked in a raised voice, letting frustration get to her.

"Since I have a son to think of," he blurted out before thinking.

"Oh," she said quietly, backing down. "I understand."

Jeremy rubbed the back of his neck, exasperated. "Look, you can sit in the observation room and watch."

"OK," she replied. "But, Jeremy?" Alex called as he was walking toward the interrogation room.

"Yeah?"

"He's too calm, and that's a bad sign. Be careful."

He stood there for a second, unsure what to say, then went into the room and closed the door behind him. Alex entered the adjacent room.

She saw Jeremy take a seat across the table from a calm, composed, and somewhat sad Hadden.

"One question for you, Quentin. Why?"

Hadden looked Jeremy in the eye with a faint smile on his lips and stayed silent.

"Why betray your country? Why sell state secrets, our latest technology? Why?"

Jeremy leaned forward in his chair, reducing the distance between the two. Hadden wasn't fazed by it. Minutes of silence went by, uninterrupted.

"They deserved it," Hadden finally spoke. "And more."

"Who?"

"The swine at Walcott. The corporate fat cats who can't find it in their hearts to give us a damn lunch break without squeezing more work out of us. The assholes who treat us like disposable objects, like doormats."

Hadden's voice escalated with every phrase, as emotion took over his rational brain.

"I have to put up with an arrogant idiot like McLeod every day, and what options do I have? I couldn't transfer, they didn't approve it. I can't stop working, 'cause, you see, everything is a perfect slave game. The system lets you have just enough to become vulnerable, enough to have something to lose, but never enough to be free. You just can't get ahead in this life. Everything is pointless, not worth it."

"Why not leave Walcott, get another job?" Jeremy probed gently when he caught a second.

"And exchange swine for swine but lose my tenure benefits too? Have you worked a single minute in a for-profit organization? Or have you just indulged in the relaxed pace and job security of government employ?"

"I'm not important right now, Quentin; let's focus on you."

Alex cringed and bit her lip. Hadden will see that as rejection and withdraw. But she definitely didn't expect what followed next.

"Who am I kidding?" Hadden was saying, wearing a bitter, crooked smile and letting more sadness seep into his eyes, his voice. "No one ever gives a crap. Well, neither do I, not anymore. I'm done."

He looked Jeremy in the eyes as he cracked something in his teeth, then started convulsing almost immediately.

Alex rushed in the room, just in time to catch Hadden taking his last breath, loaded with the distinctive smell of cyanide. There was nothing she could do.

"Oh, boy . . ." she said quietly, looking at Hadden's distorted features.

"I–I didn't see that one coming," Jeremy said, looking a little lost.

"He was too calm, Jeremy," she replied. "He had reached his decision; it was just a matter of time before he was gonna do it."

"We got nothing out of him we didn't already know, goddamn it," Jeremy said angrily, his face reddened with anger and the suffocating feeling of powerlessness he must have felt.

"Yeah, but we still have Smolin out there," Alex said encouragingly, touching Jeremy's hunched shoulder. "There's still something to go on with, so let's get to work."

Alex was still uncomfortable entering the FBI headquarters as one of their own. Every time she swiped her badge, she expected to hear the beep and see the red light turn on, yet it turned green and let her proceed through the gate just as it was supposed to.

She took the elevator and headed to Jeremy's office.

"Good morning," she said cheerfully, tapping on the open door.

"Hi," he replied. He had dark circles under his eyes and looked very tired.

"Sleepless night?" Alex asked.

"I lost a suspect in my custody, what did you expect?"

She sat on a chair in front on his desk and said, "Let's focus on the next suspect, the one who's still alive and can still cause this country a ton of damage. Don't you agree?"

"Yeah... We need to find out how the hell they're moving the intel, and if they've sent it yet." He scratched his head for a little while, then his hand moved lower, scratching the stubs growing anarchically on his unshaven face. "What's that gut of yours telling you, can we still contain this leak?"

"In all fairness we don't even know the size of the leak, what was leaked, and since when. Apparently, judging by Hadden's credit card usage history, this leak is fairly new, and we have to assume they didn't have much time to work through a ton of documents. However," she continued, letting a deep frown cloud her forehead, "it doesn't help to be dealing with someone so extremely motivated and extremely smart at the same time. That man could have *invented* a new copier, just to get this job done. What a shame... "

"Yeah. Let's see," Jeremy said, consulting his notes. "We know for sure one document was leaked, but we have zero information about anything else. Did Mason say anything today?"

"Nope, nothing. Speaking of Mason and Walcott, you know what I find very strange?" Alex asked.

"What?"

"The fact that they were overprotective with McLeod to keep the invention faucet open, but they didn't feel the same about Hadden, who also had critical patents with them. I wonder why. It was almost like Hadden was right when he said he felt he was disposable."

"We'll ask Mason to look into it. Not sure it's relevant though."

"Maybe not, but I'm still curious."

"Yeah... Hey, how come you knew Hadden was gonna kill himself? I didn't," Jeremy asked.

"I didn't know it, Jeremy, or I would have told you. I sensed that something was wrong on a deep level with that guy, that's why I wanted to interrogate him myself."

"Ahh... crap," Jeremy said, swiveling his chair and looking out the window, as to avoid the mistake he'd made.

"But there's no guarantee this wouldn't have happened to me too, all right? Then you would have been in a world of trouble, with a suspect death during an unapproved interrogation. I don't blame you, so why do you blame you?"

Jeremy crossed his arms and frowned, keeping his eyes averted. "Yeah . . ." he said.

"Tell me about your son," Alex asked, reading a lot in the single word he had spoken.

"He's... he's in rehab right now," he replied.

"Drugs?"

"Yeah . . ."

"He'll be all right," Alex encouraged him. "I'm sure about that. Let's focus on our Russian now."

"You didn't really answer my question, how did you know something was off with Hadden?"

"I read a lot," she said, then remembered something and added, "oh, and I used to date one hell of a corporate psychologist," she laughed, just a hint of sadness in her eyes.

"OK, let's go," he invited her, leading the way. "We've set up a centralized surveillance lab for Smolin and the rest of the players. We've pulled surveillance out for the remaining four."

"Do you think that's smart?" Alex asked.

"Why? What are you saying?"

"Nah... nothing. Just my gut, that's all."

"I'm listening this time, spill," Jeremy said, stopping his trek toward the surveillance lab and looking at her intently.

"I'm just saying we don't really have it yet. We don't have the envelope Hadden gave Smolin. We don't have any information, we only have the fact that Hadden didn't dispute the treason charge, that's all."

"And that's not enough because?"

"Yeah, I guess you're right, pull them. I'm just... overly sensitive when it comes to Russian spies, that's all."

"Because of your other case?"

"Yup," she confirmed.

"Will you ever tell me what happened on that one?"

"Maybe," she smiled. "Maybe after we close this one."

They entered the surveillance lab. Several analysts were working on workstations placed closely together.

"Alex, please meet NCIS Special Agent Moore," he said, as a man approached them. The man smiled widely and had an open, welcoming demeanor, and an almost elastic gait, typical for sailors.

"Alex Hoffmann," she said, shaking Agent Moore's hand. "A pleasure. But... NCIS?"

"Whenever the Navy is involved, we come in. Your spy was on our ship, Ms. Hoffmann," Moore said, continuing to smile. "We're Navy's counterintel."

"Alex, please," she said.

"Gabriel," Agent Moore replied.

"We're pleased to have Moore with us," Jeremy said. "Our agencies pooled resources to work faster to get more done."

"Walk me through what you have here," Alex said.

"We've deployed surveillance on Smolin from almost all angles. Here," Gabriel said, pointing at one of the desks loaded with several computer monitors, "we have all feeds from street cameras around his residence. We've pulled in traffic cams, ATMs, security cams. Over there we have the feeds coming in from his phone's GPS and the GPS tracker we placed on his car last night."

"All warrants are in?" Jeremy asked.

"Yes, they moved really fast this time," Gabriel confirmed. "We have phone records, insignificant. Bank records for Smolin and the Novachenkos, also nothing remarkable. We bugged the house early this morning, when everyone left. We have video and audio in every room. And there," he showed them another desk, this one with four monitors. "we have cloned phone-activity trackers. Smolin was using a burn phone."

"And you cloned that?" Alex asked. "How the hell did you pull that off?"

Gabriel's smile widened. "We have a technology now that allows our agent to clone a target's phone just by walking next to them or past them for a second. That's all it takes. When our agent walked past Smolin at the park exit last night, the system picked up two signatures, so now we have two cloned phones for Smolin, and one for each Novachenko."

"Impressive. Data too? Or just voice?"

"Everything. Text, apps, voice, email, Internet. And we're tracking all data and Internet usage inside the Novachenko residence. They can't make any move without us knowing about it."

"What the hell?" she mumbled, awoken from a dream-filled, agitated sleep.

She listened for a minute, not sure the noise she'd heard was real or a dream. Then she heard it again, this time loud and clear, three knocks on her hotel room door. She jumped out of bed and looked through the peephole, then unlocked the door, turning on the light.

"You again? Or is this some sick déjà vu moment?" she said, inviting Jeremy in. "You already know what my jammies look like."

"Yeah. Sorry about that. We got a problem, a big one."

She turned on another lamp and sat at the small desk. "What's up?"

"Smolin has a backup asset in play. We have another leak."

She frowned and wiped her eyes, chasing the remnants of sleep away.

"How did you find out?"

"He's using a webmail service to communicate with home base, without even sending email, just by saving message drafts. He referred to 'still planning to go shopping for the real big salami,' or sausage, or something like that."

"Or something like what?"

"Like... dick," he spilled it out after hesitating, a little embarrassed. Alex didn't seem to mind.

"What was the original phrase he used?"

He checked his notes, then struggled pronouncing, "*Bolshoy khuy kolbasy.*"

"Yup, they're talking about the cannon all right," she said thoughtfully. "When irritated by objects, things, or even people, Russians compare them with male genitalia. Just like we'd say about someone 'he's a dick,' or 'that dick, George.' Our laser cannon must irritate the hell out of them. So what do the analysts think?"

"They're thinking he's targeting the plans for the laser cannon this time, not only the compatibility and installation. They're saying that Smolin's plan has escalated."

"Any idea who this backup asset is?"

"None whatsoever. It could be one of Walcott's people, or anyone on the ship for that matter. We're running background checks and surveillance on everyone, effective immediately. But it could still not be enough, that's what I'm afraid of."

Two teams watched the Novachenko residence, waiting for Smolin to make a move. About noon, he left the house, unwrapping a sandwich as he stepped down the five concrete steps in front of his door.

Smolin stretched a little, apparently enjoying the warm sun. Then he started walking casually, continuing to unwrap his food.

He took one bite and chewed it, letting disappointment show on his face.

"That must taste like shit," one of the agents in the stakeout car commented with a chuckle.

"He, he, Russian cuisine, what would you expect?" his partner replied, and they both laughed.

Smolin wrapped his sandwich, continuing to look disgusted, and disposed of it in the nearest trash can. Then he continued his walk, followed at a safe distance by the two surveillance teams.

Minutes later, a street bum started going through the Dumpster where Smolin had thrown his sandwich. He retrieved it carefully, studied it for a few seconds, then placed it in his pocket and vanished, unseen.

Mason's office at Walcott was crowded again, contrasting with the deserted corporate office building on a Sunday morning. Jeremy, Sam, and Alex were all standing, leaning against the walls of his small office.

"Thanks for coming in on a Sunday, Mason, we appreciate it," Alex said.

"Sure, no problem," Mason said, seeming a little surprised. "We're in this 24/7 until we're done."

"Here's where we are," Alex said. "We have identified a Russian, most likely a handler, by the name of Smolin. He's Russian intelligence, a major. He's here under the cover of a visiting parent with a family of Russian-born American citizens, the Novachenkos. This man is key."

"Why don't we arrest him? How sure are we?" Mason asked.

"Very sure. Before he killed himself, Hadden handed Smolin an envelope. We assume some intel was in there."

"Did we recover it?" Mason asked.

"No, we didn't," Jeremy replied. "We wanted to continue to investigate this leak, and it gave us results. Now we know it's a bigger operation, bigger than just Hadden."

"But you could have contained it!" Mason almost yelled. "You saw that happen and you didn't arrest them? Why?"

"Because we thought—" Alex started, but was immediately interrupted by Jeremy.

"Allow me," he said, and she nodded. "Interrogations in these cases are risky, as we've seen with Hadden, and statistically speaking highly unreliable. Our best bet to contain *the entire leak* is to let Smolin proceed under extremely tight surveillance."

A few moments of silence ensued, while Mason was processing the information.

"All right," he said. "What's our game plan? How do we minimize the exposure and contain the intel?"

"I've worked intelligence for thirty years, Mason," Sam intervened, "you know that. I've worked countless assets, and they all did the same thing. They trickled down the intel, looking to squeeze more money or more favor out of each document. No one comes to a handler and drops everything he knows or he has on one date. Not unless they wanted to defect, and that is obviously not the case here."

"Then what do you think our exposure is, Sam?" Mason asked. "Can it still be salvaged?"

"I'm thinking some of the intel might have leaked all the way to Moscow, but I'm guessing it was the preliminary intel; the bait, as we called it out in the field. But this is too new to have gone too far, that's what my gut's telling me."

"Ms. Hoffmann, are you in agreement with this strategy?" Mason asked.

"Wholeheartedly. We need to stay on Smolin like ticks on a dog, and he'll lead us to the other assets."

"What about leak containment?" Mason probed.

"It's highly unlikely he'll be able to drop a dime on the street without several agents seeing that. We're confident no information will change hands without us knowing about it. I am positive the leak is contained."

"Good," Mason said with a long sigh. "Then one thing remains on today's agenda. Tomorrow's Memorial Day ceremony and inaugural demonstration of the laser cannon onboard the USS *Fletcher*. Are we canceling that? Do we have reasons to be concerned for anyone's safety? Let me remind you it's a highly anticipated event. It has been publicized everywhere, and canceling it will put a big blemish on the Navy's reputation, not to mention SecNav's."

"These are paper spies we're dealing with," Jeremy said. "I am confident everything will be all right tomorrow. We don't have any information about any threat to the USS *Fletcher*. Neither do NCIS or Homeland. All quiet."

"Ms. Hoffmann?" Mason asked.

She nodded in response, a little preoccupied.

"Then we're good," Mason replied. "See you all tomorrow at the ceremony."

They left the office and headed for their cars, Alex still preoccupied and tense.

"Something tugging at your gut there, kiddo?" Sam asked her, patting her on the shoulder.

She thought for a second of Smolin's loathing message. *Bolshoy khuy kolbasy...* The message reeked of hate, hate against the weapon itself, against the object. Or maybe she didn't really grasp the Russian culture, and she was overthinking the issue.

"Nah... it's nothing," she said, and forced herself to smile.

The colors were flying high on the USS *Fletcher*, and she was dressed up for the ceremony, with red, white, and blue garlands all around.

The guests were starting to arrive and traffic was jammed in front of Pier 7. Guests walked from the parking area across from the pier, where their limos would drop them off, and then lined up for the security screening before boarding the vessel.

The laser cannon demonstration of accuracy had attracted an elite attendance; admirals and NATO secretaries-general came in great numbers, attracted by the novelty of a weapon that promised to change the balance of power at sea, on land, and in the air.

Security was very tight for a Memorial Day ceremony. There were millimeter wave scanners and X-ray machines on loan from the TSA, installed overnight. Everyone had to go through the screening, no exceptions. When he arrived, the SecNav frowned a little at the unprecedented security measures, but then proceeded through the scanners with a smile, under the flashes of the cameras.

Media was present in hordes, attracted by the select attendee list of the event, and by the novelty and buzz about the new weapon scheduled for demonstration a little later in the day. A couple of news helicopters circled in the air like vultures, from a respectable distance imposed by restrictions and the promise of a laser cannon demo, waiting to catch a snippet of sensation, and causing an irritating, omnipresent background noise.

The helipad at the stern of the *Fletcher* had been set up for the ceremony. Rows of folding chairs were laid out in a semicircular pattern, facing toward the laser cannon dome at the right and toward the open sea at the left. A lectern was erected on a small platform; SecNav, SecDef, and Captain Meecham would give their addresses from there.

Alex took in all the details, together with the crisp smell of salty air in the morning sun. It was a beautiful day for such a ceremony. She waited patiently in line to be screened, then boarded the *Fletcher* and started looking around for familiar faces. Sam, Mason, and Jeremy were attending the event, and, of course, Special Agent Moore of NCIS was planning to be aboard, with a team of naval counterintelligence agents.

"There you are," she heard Jeremy say.

"Hey," she replied, focused on a familiar silhouette, a young man with fire-red hair, wearing a full-dress white uniform.

"What's the matter?" Jeremy asked.

The red-haired man turned and locked eyes for a second with Alex, then bolted through a bulkhead.

"Something's wrong," she said, "really wrong."

"But what? We've screened everyone who came aboard."

"Maybe the problem was aboard to begin with," she replied. "Help me track down that guy," she said

"You got it," Jeremy said, then dialed Moore to brief him.

"Suspect is young, maybe twenty, has bright red hair and freckles, wears whites," she heard him say as she disappeared though the same bulkhead, just when several NCIS agents were entering the deckhouse from all directions.

She caught up with the young man in the cafeteria, where she found him sitting inconspicuously at a table, with a half-empty coffee cup in front of him.

Smart, she thought, jumpy, but smart.

She sat at his table, across from him.

"May I?"

There was no answer, other than the young man turned a sickly shade of freckled pale.

"We just want to talk to you, that's all," she said, smiling as gently as she could.

"I've got nothing to talk to you about," the sailor answered, then looked away, averting his eyes from her intense scrutiny.

"What are you afraid of?" she pressed on. "What's wrong?"

He turned paler and tightened his lips, as if forcing himself to clam up. Then all of a sudden he sprang up from his seat and bolted, heading for the exit. Alex jumped off her chair and lunged, grabbing his right sleeve with all her strength. Then she came right behind him and kicked the back of his knee with a Krav Maga move, bringing him to his knees. Then she pushed her foot between his shoulder blades, forcing him flat on his stomach, face on the deck.

"I'll take it from here," a man said, flashing an NCIS badge. "What's he done?"

The agent pulled the sailor up from the floor, now handcuffed with flex cuffs.

"Umm... not sure," she said, a little embarrassed. "Not sure yet."

"What? We can't just grab people and handcuff them because a civilian is not sure. Pardon me, ma'am, even if my boss asked me to extend all support, this is all wrong."

He started to uncuff the sailor, but Alex stopped him.

"No!" she said. "Something's wrong, you got that right. Search his quarters, please. And tell me his name."

"His name is Mike Simionov," the agent said. "Petty officer third class."

Mike, my ass, she thought. *I bet he was born Mikhail. A Russian... What a coincidence.*

Jeremy entered the cafeteria, followed closely by Gabriel Moore.

"I'll handle it from here, take him downstairs," Moore told the other agent. "What's going on?"

"His behavior was off, both times I've seen him. This is the man I was asking about on Tuesday, in Mason's office, Jeremy. This is him. He's definitely hiding something."

"We'll talk to him," Moore said.

"While you pull the information out of him, let's address the potential issues by order of urgency. Jeremy, can you call in explosive-sniffing dogs?"

"Yeah... I can, but it will take a while for them to get here. Aren't we jumping the gun from a scared sailor to explosives?"

"Look," she said, checking the time. "The demo is scheduled to start in twenty-three minutes or so. And it's not just another sailor. He's a sailor with a Russian last name. And Smolin's message about the sausage reeked of hate— hate against an object, that one," she ended pointing her finger at the laser cannon cupola, installed on top of the helo hangar.

"How sure are you?" Jeremy asked quietly, running his hand through his hair.

"Make the call, Jeremy, make the call now. Then I'll explain."

"I'm all ears," Moore said. "Do you realize we have admirals, SecNav, SecDef, and NATO aboard this ship today?"

Captain Meecham entered the cafeteria and stood silently, listening as Jeremy called the K9 unit in and Alex explained her point of view.

"That's precisely it, Gabriel. I guarantee you will find explosives around the cannon. It's in close proximity to all the visiting officials, and the plan has grandeur in it, has a greatness I've encountered before. Can you imagine the effect of taking out the elite Navy leadership under hundreds of cameras ready to roll? If the cannon blows up during a demo, everyone will think it just blew up, and that we're just a bunch of incompetents who can't fire a weapon safely. The effects of this attack would ripple for decades."

"What do you want to do?" Moore asked. "Evacuate?"

"It would make sense to evacuate," she agreed. "Captain?"

"For a civilian's hunch? Agent Moore, we have nothing but speculation to support this theory, nothing else! I'd love to have a career in the Navy after today's ceremony, if possible."

"Then delay the demo a little," Alex pleaded. "Buy me some time before we start the demo. Can you at least do that?"

"Yes, I guess we can, although it will be embarrassing," Meecham agreed reluctantly. "I'll think of a way."

"Was the start time of the demo announced anywhere?" Alex asked.

"Yes, in the event program. It was distributed to everyone," Meecham said.

"Great... just great," she groaned. "Listen, the device, if I'm right, might be on a timer, rigged to go off at the time the demo was scheduled to start, in about seven minutes or so. What do you have in mind for a delay?"

"My officers will sing a few Navy songs, and no one's ever refused coffee and cookies," he replied.

"All right, let's get it done," she encouraged him, and thanked him with a thumbs-up.

She climbed up the stairs from the mess hall, and almost tripped and fell over a German Shepherd on a six-foot leash, dragging his handler in tow.

"Where do you wanna start?" Jeremy asked.

"Helo hangar," she replied.

The dog led them through a bulkhead into the helo hangar, from where they could see everyone in attendance seated and listening to a choir of officers singing the all-time Navy favorite, "Anchors Aweigh."

Then the Shepherd stopped and stared up, his tail wagging rapidly, at the ceiling structure of the helo hangar, recently reinforced to support the dome and the laser cannon installation. They followed the direction the dog was looking and there it was, hidden between the structure's beams, a C4 block the size of a brick and a timing mechanism.

"Oh, shit . . ." Alex said, "how much time left? Can't see from here."

"1:18," Jeremy said.

"Evacuate?" Moore asked.

"No time," Jeremy said. "Close the hangar doors and give me some light."

He climbed on a barrel and reached the device. The digital timer was counting down, less than thirty seconds left.

He took a deep breath and steadied his hands. He studied the device a little, calmly, like he had all the time in the world. They were in luck apparently, no failsafe, just a detonating pin stuck in the plastic explosive and hooked up to a timing device.

He held his breath and went for the pin, grabbing it gently as the timer showed seven seconds left.

He started pulling it out, and cleared it from the plastic brick, then removed the timer and stopped it. The red, ominous digits displayed 0:02.

"Whew," Alex said, "great job, Jer."

"Is this the only one?" Moore asked grimly.

"Officer Rambo thinks so," the K9 officer replied. "But we'll walk the entire ship just to make sure."

Alex chuckled, hearing the dog's name. How appropriate.

"Now what?" Jeremy asked, wiping the sweat off his forehead with his sleeve.

"We should evacuate," Moore said. "Per procedure, I have to evacuate the ship and bring the bomb squad in. We have a block of C4 in the ceiling, for Christ's sake," he insisted, seeing the resistance in Alex's determined eyes.

"I say we stay, carry on with our demo as scheduled. Well, maybe not as scheduled," she joked, pointing vaguely in the direction of the choir now going through their third hit song. She opened the hangar door a little, letting some air and sunshine in, but making sure no one outside could see the NCIS agents removing the C4 brick from the ceiling.

"Is that safe?"

"Without a detonator, C4 is pretty safe to handle, so I'd say yes," Jeremy asked.

"Then let's continue," she insisted.

"No way," Gabriel replied. I'll have to inform SecNav about this. Good thing he's right there," he said, pointing him out.

Captain Meecham locked eyes with her from a distance, and she made a rolling gesture with her hand, encouraging him to carry on with the choir performance.

Gabriel started toward the helipad, but she grabbed his sleeve and said, "Listen to me, please."

He gave her a fiery look, then dropped his intense gaze to where she was holding on to his sleeve. She let that go instantly and mumbled an apology. Then she continued, "Look at them, at all that media. News crews, helos, camera flashes."

"And?" Gabriel asked impatiently.

"Do you want the world to see the elite of our naval defense running for their lives, screaming, pushing one another around to get out of here faster, scattering like a bunch of scared cats? Because that's what's gonna happen, no matter how you try to manage this. I, for one, won't give anyone this satisfaction. I, for one, am staying."

Silence fell between them for a few seconds. She turned and kneeled next to the German Shepherd, taking his head in her hands and rubbing him behind his ears.

"Rambo, how sure are you, buddy?"

"He's pretty sure," the dog's handler replied.

She turned back toward Jeremy and Gabriel, and asked, "Then? What's it gonna be? Anyone keeping me company on the USS *Fletcher* to see the demonstration of our best weapon yet?"

"Yes," Gabriel Moore said. "I'll stay. Let's do this."

"You?" she asked Jeremy

"Me? I wasn't going anywhere," he smiled.

"All right, then, let's laser blow something up," she said with the excited smile of a child who's going to try a new toy.

She signaled Captain Meecham, who immediately turned toward the choir and signaled them.

They ended "The Banner of the Sea" before the second chorus and switched to the familiar notes of the national anthem.

Everyone stood, turned toward the flag, and placed their hands on their hearts, as the choir sang the anthem.

And then, silently, the white dome opened and the laser cannon became exposed, coming into firing position, as a drone was launched from the bow deck. The drone flew out to sea, then turned and approached the USS *Fletcher* from the northwest, coming in fast, barely visible against the clear sky. The cannon discharged a quiet laser ray into it, turning it instantly into a ball of fire, under hundreds of cameras rolling and snapping images of the best weapon yet.

A roar of applause covered the choir and the constant roar of helicopter rotors coming from above.

"Anyone care for a cup of coffee?" Alex asked.

There was almost no activity on the quiet little street, with most of the neighborhood folks out to school, work, or about their business. They approached Smolin's address and slowed to a stop under the pine tree that cast a thick shadow over the house.

The house had an elevated first level. Five steps led to a small front porch that expanded across the entire front. An Appalachian rocking chair and a dying potted plant were the only objects on that porch. A hedge grew five feet tall and was thick, well-maintained, and neatly trimmed. It surrounded the house and stopped at the edge of the narrow path that led to the steps, then turned to follow it all the way to the porch. That hedge provided some privacy.

They checked the neighborhood, looking down the street, in the rearview mirror, scrutinizing the windows of the neighboring houses, then they parked a few houses down the street. They'd driven in Alex's rental, less noticeable than Jeremy's Dodge Charger. Even that decision had been a cause for a bitter argument.

"Let's go," Jeremy said, a little nervous.

"Thanks for doing this," Alex said, and hopped out of the car.

"Yeah . . ." Jeremy replied with his usual tone and one-word answer that could mean anything. "It's one thing to execute a warrant and another to sneak in like this. It's not like we don't have a warrant."

"We still don't know enough about this man, and something tells me he's not going to be extra forthcoming in an interrogation. With his rank in the SVR, he's probably trained to resist more torture than we're even willing to put him through." She sighed, watching Jeremy open the door carefully using a lock-picking toolkit, then hooking up a code-breaking device to the alarm system. "Maybe... maybe we can learn more about his network, his people back home." *And about V*, she completed her phrase in her mind, but decided not to share it.

A minute later, the alarm system beeped and the LED turned green.

They snuck in and closed the door behind them.

"I'll take the kitchen," she offered.

She went ahead to search the kitchen and little there caught her attention. It was clean, neatly organized, taken care of. The windows had white sheers, and the cupboards had been refaced recently.

She opened the dishwasher; empty. She checked under the sink and pulled out the trashcan. It was lined with a new white plastic liner, but it smelled a little of burned paper. She lifted the liner and saw the burn marks on the trashcan's metallic surface. She put everything back how she found it and moved to the cupboards.

Nothing was out of the ordinary; pots, pans, plates, cups, all boringly normal, except one place, the two shelves above the fridge. In there she saw a small stack of Petri dishes, seven in total. *Huh... that was strange.* There wasn't a single explanation she could think of to justify those Petri dishes.

She opened the fridge next, and saw an assortment of deli meats, cheese, and vodka. A few sandwiches already packed in tinfoil took half the middle shelf, next to an olive jar and a small pot of borscht. She opened one sandwich: ham and cheese. Again, nothing out of the ordinary.

She closed the fridge just when the radio crackled to life.

"One, this is two, come in."

She picked up her radio. "Go for one."

"One, you have traffic inbound. Will have eyes on you in two minutes."

She groaned and cussed under her breath. "Copy that."

Jeremy came downstairs right after he heard the radioed message.

"Found anything?" she asked.

"Nothing much, just a crisscross paper shredder. You?"

"Petri dishes. And someone really cares about this guy, they're packing lunch for him. Let's go."

"One, traffic has eyes on front door," the radio crackled again.

"Copy," Jeremy replied.

She had already opened the door, looking carefully to spot any movement. She saw Smolin coming down the street.

"Shit," she muttered, then grabbed Jeremy's sleeve. "Arm the alarm and keep your head down. The hedge will cover us."

Jeremy pulled the door gently behind him as he exited the house, while Alex crouched on the porch. He locked the door just when Smolin's hat started to be visible in the distance, above the hedge line.

Without saying a word, she pushed Jeremy hard toward the hedge on the opposite side, and he went through it with a thump, landing behind it. She had nowhere to go, it was too late; Smolin was looking straight at her, as she sat crouched in an unnatural position on his front porch.

"Can I help you?" he asked, his Russian accent thick and unmistakable.

"Yes, please," she whimpered. "I twisted my ankle right there, in that pothole," she said, pointing at a small indentation in the asphalt. "My cell's battery is gone; can you please help me call a cab to take me home?"

She extended her leg as to show him, but Smolin frowned, unconvinced.

Barely audible, she discerned the faint beep of the alarm system arming itself. She almost sighed with relief.

"If it's too much trouble, I'll go away," she said, feigning an attempt to stand up.

"Wait here," Smolin said, then tried the handle on his door. Alex held her breath for a second, feeling the sweat break at the roots of her hair, but the door was locked. Smolin entered the house, disarmed the alarm, then brought outside a cordless phone.

Anatoly Karp paced the room slowly, carrying himself tall and proud, with his hands clasped behind his back, measuring up his audience. The improvised training room was packed to the brim with people of all ages, taking every available seat, some standing.

What a spoiled bunch they were, all of them! Every one of these men and women had left their country behind and decided it wasn't good enough, because they wanted a bigger car or more money. How disgusting! Like whores they were, all of them, selling themselves to whoever had the deepest pockets.

But even whores served a purpose; so could these people. After all, they owed their abandoned country a debt of service and of loyalty, words most of these fat pigs didn't even know the meaning of.

His mouth filled with phlegm mixed with bile, coming up his throat, stimulated by the wave of disgust he was feeling. He turned his head slightly toward the wall and sent out a spitball that landed a few feet away.

He felt better after sending that projectile, cleaner. Karp was an unusual, memorable man, not blond or sandy-haired like most of his compatriots. His hair was raven black, and his eyes matched a shiny, almost bluish shade of color. His square jaw and strong features showed character and determination, and the premature lines on his face were a testimony to the sacrifices he had made in the service of his country.

"You're here today," Karp finally spoke, "because your country needs you. Russia needs you."

The hundred or so attendees started murmuring, turning to one another to exchange whispered comments.

"I do not care," Karp continued undisturbed, raising his voice slightly, "that you are now American citizens. I do not care that you have renounced your loyalty to Russia when you swore your allegiance to America. You have taken an oath of lifelong loyalty to this institution, the SVR, and that's the only one that matters. Your debt of honor to your motherland hasn't been paid and will be owed until the day you draw your last breath. All of you," he continued dramatically, making an all-encompassing gesture with his hand.

The murmurs in the audience stopped abruptly, and the silence became deafening.

"You are integrated in the American society. You have American-born children. You have jobs, nice cars, and expensive houses. And now you have a mission. It is *not* optional."

He let the silence dwell over the crowd for another minute or so, while he studied them. They had come in walking proud and feeling superior, thinking they had it all if their wallets held blue passports and gold credit cards. Now they were showing some respect, like they were supposed to in the presence of an SVR officer.

"You, all of you here, will be the first line of offense and support in our new intelligence network. You are now a network of asset-recruiting agents, of case officers."

The murmurs rose, but Karp interrupted again.

"I don't care if you came to visit Russia to see family or go to Sochi. You will spend your vacation in training, and at the end of these two weeks, you will be reminded how to be proficient case officers, ready to recruit assets and work them in your city of residence."

The room was silent again, deathly silent.

"To those of you who are now thinking of running to the American Embassy, or boarding the first international flight out of Moscow, I have one thing to say: you have families. We know where they are, who they are, here or in America. You know how the game is played. Don't even think about it."

Karp paused his speech, taking his time to make eye contact with several of the people in the room. A woman on the third row sniffled and wiped her nose on her sleeve, then averted her eyes.

"You have only one choice," he continued, satisfied with what he was seeing. "Serve your country, and serve it well."

The silence continued, his audience watching his every move.

"Good. Now that we understand one another, let's proceed." He paced the room some more. "We'll use technology to home in on areas of interest and conduct our recruiting efforts in a focused manner, going after the valuable intel we need. You'll have cyber support to help you identify weaknesses in our enemy, and the most valuable assets in the field."

Karp resumed his pacing, keeping his fingers interlocked behind his back and continued.

"Case officers are expected to be able to take over new cells with very little notice, and they will be the only ones in contact with Moscow. Lead agents will work the field as instructed, recruit, identify targets, extract the intel, and prepare the transport. You will identify and recruit your assets, motivate and encourage them, drive them, keep them on a short leash."

He paused again, letting them process all the information. "You are here because you have proven yourselves in the years before your departure. Now Mother Russia is willing to forgive your betrayal. You are here because Russia needs you, and because you are tomorrow's heroes, our country's salvation."

Without any transition, Karp started singing the national anthem. One by one, the voices in the room started singing, hesitant at first, then stronger, more powerful, united.

The roar of a jet on an aggressive takeoff climb from Norfolk International interrupted the serenity of the Botanical Gardens, and made Alex pause a little. She and Jeremy were taking the same bench under the old tree, with direct line of sight to Smolin's favorite backgammon game. Alex refrained with difficulty from hiding her face, concerned he might recognize her after he'd seen her on his doorstep. But they were too far, she was safe at that distance.

He wasn't playing backgammon that time, just hanging out, as if waiting for a game partner to show up.

"And?" Jeremy asked.

"And what? Oh, yes," she remembered where she'd left off before the 747's takeoff, "Louie is the one we all go to if we need data. Any kind of data, really."

"So he's a hacker?"

"White hat, and a pretty good one," she chuckled. "When we can't afford to go through channels, or we can't bypass a roadblock, he's always able to find a way to get the job done. Ex-SEAL, and my personal trainer."

"For what?" Jeremy asked. "Computer hacking?"

"No," she laughed. "Krav Maga, weapons, that kind of stuff. You'd be surprised how dangerous corporate investigations can get sometimes," she clarified, seeing how amazed he looked.

Smolin stood up and grabbed his backgammon set under his arm, heading slowly toward the exit. They stayed a decent distance behind, and followed him in the same relaxed pace.

Smolin stopped at a food vendor on his way to the exit, waited in line for another customer to be served, then bought a sandwich. He didn't eat it; he just put it in his pocket and continued his slow stroll through the park alleys.

"What's with this guy and his sandwiches?" Alex wondered. "He's got plenty of those at home, right?"

"Well, maybe they're not that good," Jeremy said. "Remember he threw the one from home in the trash after just one bite. Who knows, maybe he's too polite to tell whoever's making them that he prefers street vendor hotdogs instead."

"Maybe, but I don't think so... It must be something else. Nothing this man does is casual or left to chance."

"Yeah, but we're talking about food here," Jeremy said. "I agree with everything you said, but even spies have to eat."

"True. All right, I'll drop it."

They walked without saying anything for a while, following Smolin as he headed toward the parking lot.

"Do you think he's hoarding food?" Jeremy asked. "How many sandwiches were in that fridge? Four, five? Do you think it's because they didn't have much food in the communist days?"

"Yeah... maybe. But I don't think so," she said grumpily, struggling to hide her irritation.

Here they were, wasting valuable time following a Russian agent who seemed to have nothing better to do than walk in the park and eat. What the hell were they missing?

"How many did you say we had, again?" Alex asked in disbelief.

"There are 142," Jeremy replied. "The entire complement of the *Fletcher*, well, minus Simionov; he's been dealt with already."

"We'll be here 'til midnight," she complained, grabbing the mouse from Jeremy's desk and clicking through sailor profiles.

Jeremy's phone rang, and he picked it up immediately.

"Agent Weber. Yes," he said, "let me put you on speaker." He put the phone on his desk and touched the speaker icon. "It's one of the surveillance teams deployed at Smolin's house," he told Alex.

"Yeah, hi," Alex greeted the caller.

"Good morning, ma'am. Nikolai Novachenko, Smolin's so-called son-in-law, left earlier with a suitcase and a duffel bag and is headed for Norfolk International. What do you advise?"

"Damn," she muttered. "Stay on him, and call TSA and ask them to screen him very thoroughly. Got it?"

"Yes, got it."

"If he carries as much as a safety pin we wanna know about it, OK? And tell TSA to call us the minute they're done with him."

"Yes, understood," the agent replied dryly, a little offended to be treated as if he didn't know how to do his job and some civilian consultant had to spell it out for him.

Alex bit her lip. She wasn't making any friends, that was for sure.

She stood and grabbed her empty coffee cup. "Want some?" she asked Jeremy.

"Please."

A moment later, she was back with both cups refilled to the brim.

"Did they call yet?" Alex asked.

"It's only been a minute," Jeremy said. "Take it easy, will ya'?"

"Yeah, OK."

She resumed clicking through the sailor profiles, a little preoccupied. Her mind wouldn't focus on the work in front of her, stubbornly going over every possible scenario Novachenko could use to transport classified information out of the country. When the phone finally rang, she almost jumped out of her skin.

"Good morning, Agent... Weber," the caller said hesitantly, "this is Shift Supervisor Davidson with TSA at Norfolk."

"Yeah, what did you find?"

"We had to let him go, Agent Weber. We didn't find anything wrong with him, and we checked him thoroughly. We took him in a private screening room and went over everything in detail: clothes, his luggage, everything."

"Anything out of the ordinary? Anything at all? Was he nervous, agitated?" Alex intervened.

"N–no, ma'am, nothing out of the ordinary. He was relatively calm, even apologetic. Most people are a little antsy when we pull them in for private screening, and his behavior was quite normal under the circumstances."

"Why apologetic?"

"Oh, he had a sandwich with him, and he apologized for that, said he didn't know if that was allowed or not. We let him go; they're boarding the flight now."

A wave of adrenaline spiked her heart rate. She hesitated a little... What if she was wrong? Ahh... the hell with it.

"Stop him," she yelled at the TSA agent. "Grab him, and get that sandwich. We're on our way."

She ran to the elevator, followed closely by Jeremy.

"Care to share?" he asked, as they were heading downstairs in what seemed to be the slowest elevator invented.

"Not really," she said sheepishly. "Just a hunch."

Jeremy drove as fast as he could, his siren blaring, zigzagging through traffic like a maniac, and leaving behind a chorus of screeching brakes and wailing horns.

"Call your team for me, get them on the phone," Alex asked.

"Who do you want?"

"Anyone in the surveillance lab, anyone would do."

Jeremy told her the number and she dialed. The car's hands-free system took over, making it difficult for them to hear over the blaring siren.

"Yeah, hi, it's Alex Hoffmann and Agent Weber. Yeah, please go back on surveillance and look for anyone doing anything with a sandwich. What? Yeah, a sandwich. Anything... eating, buying, packing, giving, taking, just anything, any sandwich."

Jeremy looked at her briefly, between avoiding a garbage truck and passing a cab.

She hung up the call.

"I'm starting to see your hunch," Jeremy said, "but it's a thin one, very thin. People eat, Alex. It's just food, that's all."

"I need a mobile lab to meet us at the airport," she continued, unperturbed. "How do I get that to happen? Whom do I call?"

"We have procedures for this kind of thing, you know," he protested. "It's not like a multimillion piece of equipment is at my beck and call."

"Here's how this is gonna go," she said in a low, almost threatening voice. "Either you call your mobile lab to assist us at the airport, or *I* call a mobile lab to assist us at the airport and you foot the bill. Don't care, really. So what's your preference?"

He sighed, made the call, then asked wryly, "Has anyone ever said no to you and lived to tell the story?

Nikolai Novachenko sat at the small table in the improvised interrogation room, courtesy of the TSA. There was one other chair in the room, empty. Both Alex and Jeremy stood, studying Novachenko closely.

On the wall at his left, there was a cheap clock, one of those $9.99 electronic wall clocks one can get from Walmart. Somehow that seemed to be the focal point of interest with Novachenko, who looked at it every minute or so.

"Got someplace to be, Nikolai?" Alex asked.

"Yeah, got a plane to catch," he replied morosely.

"That flight is boarding now, and you're not going to be on it," she said. "So you can relax. The sooner you answer our questions, the sooner you'll be on your way."

His jaws clenched the moment he heard he wasn't going to make his flight.

"You can't hold me here," he protested, starting to get up from his chair. "I haven't done anything wrong," he said in an escalating voice.

"Sit down," Jeremy said, pushing him back into his chair with a firm hand on his left shoulder.

"Who is Evgheni Smolin?" Alex asked.

"Who?" Novachenko replied.

"Cut the bullshit, will you? Or else we'll be here 'til midnight," Alex said, feigning anger, and slammed her hand on the small table. "I'd rather be elsewhere, you know. Smolin, who is he? He lives in your house, so you better know who that is."

"He's my father-in-law," Novachenko replied, stealing another quick look at the clock, and wringing his hands.

"Wrong answer, Novachenko, think again. This time why don't you try the truth for a change? Don't dig yourself into a bigger hole than you can manage."

"No, I swear, he's my father-in-law," Novachenko replied, turning a little pale and biting his lip.

"That's not gonna fly," Alex replied, opening a file and reading from it. "Smolin is from Moscow and has never had any kids. Your wife is from Kiev."

Another quick look to check the time.

"No, no, damn it, your information is wrong. I'm telling you the truth."

"Let's check the facts, one by one," Jeremy intervened. Novachenko checked the time yet again and slouched a little in his chair, more relaxed.

Alex frowned slightly, then looked at the flight schedule. The flight was still boarding. Why was he relaxing now? Made no sense. She had a strong feeling that they were missing something, something of crucial importance.

"Is your wife from Kiev?" Jeremy asked, pushing in front of Novachenko a couple of pictures, one showing Olga's graduation from a Kiev school, the other showing the frontage of a house.

"Y–yes," he stuttered, then glanced quickly at the clock. "Yes, she is."

He had stopped wringing his hands, and his pallor was almost gone. Either the man was an expert in dealing with stress, or something was very wrong.

"Oh, no . . ." she whispered, feeling her blood drain. "What else did he have on him?" she asked Jeremy with an unspoken urgency in her eyes.

"That," Jeremy pointed at a duffel bag left on the floor, in the corner. "And some pocket change."

She grabbed the duffel bag from the corner and made a quick hand gesture to Jeremy to follow her. As she exited the room, she caught a glimpse of Novachenko's pallor returning, together with his upper body tension and hand-wringing habit.

"What's up?" Jeremy asked as soon as they closed the door.

"He was getting calmer with time," she said, going nervously through the contents of Novachenko's duffel bag. "That shouldn't have happened."

"What do you want to do?"

"You keep on drilling him. I wanna run to the mobile lab; they must have some result on that sandwich by now. And I want to give them this," she said, holding a travel-size can of hair spray, "maybe it's got something to do with that sandwich, or maybe it has something to do with time."

"Huh? Do you know you're not making much sense?"

"Yeah, I do," she replied and turned to leave. "But neither does a short-haired man carrying aloe vera hair spray on a flight."

The tractor-trailer took seven parking spaces along the white curb marked drop-off zone only. Black and windowless, the trailer bore the inscription "Federal Bureau of Investigation—Mobile Forensics" in gold lettering.

Alex didn't waste time knocking; she hopped up the two steps and opened the door.

"Ah, Agent Hoffmann," the female lab technician said, "I was just about to call you."

She started to say she wasn't an agent, but curiosity took precedence. "What did you find?"

"You were right, there was something in that sandwich: E. coli SPAM."

"Eww... gross. It looked like ham and cheese to me. How is this helpful?"

"No . . ." she chuckled. "SPAM as in steganography by printed arrays of microbes," the technician clarified, smiling briefly and turning toward an LCD showing luminescent microorganisms, resembling little hot dogs piled on top of one another. "SPAM is an information encryption and transport technique, using fluorescent strains of Escherichia coli treated and arranged a certain way to represent the letters of the alphabet. In these microbe arrays, there are enough colors for anything you'd want to write."

"How would someone grow these microbes and transfer them to a sandwich?"

"You arrange the microbes to represent the message, then grow them in a Petri dish."

"Ahh... Petri dishes, now it makes sense. I've seen those at our suspect's home," Alex added, seeing how confused the tech seemed. "Please continue."

"Then you transfer the cultured microbes to film, and ta-da! Your biofilm is ready for transport."

"But I saw Smolin take a bite from one of these sandwiches," Alex pushed back. "Why isn't he sick, or dead?"

"These E. coli are genetically modified to be entirely safe. In case of trouble, a spy could eat all the evidence and be fine."

"Great," she grumbled. "Tell me please, how does one generate a message, exactly?" Alex asked.

"Seven different strains of E. coli were engineered to glow a different color under the right chemical and light conditions, by triggering fluorescence in a certain protein. The microbes are grown in rows of paired spots, each combination of two colors representing a letter or a number. For example, a yellow and an amber spot could represent the letter A. Here's a sample decoded microbe array I found on the Internet, to give you an idea," the technician said, pointing to a different screen, where chains of little colored circles lined up row after row in a matrix distribution.

"How does one do this? I'm guessing they'd need access to a sophisticated lab, right?"

"Maybe, maybe not. If you want to take the grassroots approach to generating SPAM biofilm, you wouldn't need much; just some Petri dishes, a carefully modified antibiotic solution, culture medium, some LEDs, and... that's about it," the technician clarified, counting on her fingers.

"So how can we decode the message?"

"We can't, not without the original growth environment. We'd need to regrow the bacteria in the same environment, or we would not obtain the right colors and the message would be completely indecipherable."

"What?" Alex said, almost growling. "There must be something we can do to nail this bastard."

"I'm afraid there's nothing we can do. Again, if we use the wrong growth medium, the array will light up in the wrong sequences, and that won't mean anything."

"Could this type of message self-destruct?" Alex asked, suddenly remembering the small can of hair spray she had brought with her from Novachenko's bag.

"Yes, it's time sensitive; the microbe luminescence fades with time if not preserved, or fixated."

"Could this be the fixating agent?" Alex asked, handing the technician the hair spray.

"Let me check," the young woman said, cocking her head to the side and spraying a small amount of substance into a test tube, then inserting it into a gas chromatograph. A minute later, the machine chimed and displayed a chart filled with numbers.

"Yes," the technician confirmed, "this is the fixating agent, that's for sure. I'll treat the biofilm with it and hope it will last enough for us to figure out how to decrypt it. We need to find its culture medium."

"How would that look?" Alex pressed on.

"It could be anything. I'm guessing some kind of liquid or emulsion," the tech added, "although he might not have it on him, that's why SPAM is so secure."

"What are you saying?" Alex asked in disbelief.

"You could have the encoded bacteria here, and have matching controlled growth medium on the other side of the border. No one would be able to grab it and decode it."

"Still, we have to try," Alex replied.

She pulled out her cell and called Jeremy.

"Hey, I need you to bring me everything this guy had on him, and I mean every—"

The trailer door opened and Jeremy walked in, carrying the rest of Novachenko's luggage.

"That what you're looking for?

The technician made room on the table for the luggage, and they all started going through the stuff, piece by piece. Alex almost disregarded a commercially wrapped gift set of cosmetics, containing makeup, lipstick, nail polish and clear coating, all with brand labels. Then she changed her mind and looked at that package in detail.

Alex picked the clear nail protector bottle, opened it and sniffed it. It stunk of acetone... no, that wasn't it. No microbes could live or glow in acetone. She then smelled the nail polish. This one was almost odorless, except a faint, nearly imperceptible fruity smell. She handed it over to the tech.

"Is this it? Could this be it?" she asked impatiently.

The young technician tested it quickly and confirmed it had the chemical makeup of a bacterial growth medium.

"Yes!" Alex said. "Please tell me we can read the message now," she said, clasping her hands in a pleading gesture.

"Yes, we can, if this is the right growth medium, and it is logical to assume it is. Now we can overlay the biofilm on the growth medium and the bacteria will light up, allowing us to read the message."

"But isn't the message encrypted?" Jeremy asked.

"Yeah, it is, but now it's easy, it's a simple alphabet encryption. Any deciphering software will be able to read it. We have CrypTool installed right here," the tech said, turning toward another computer. "It will take an hour or so, Agent Hoffmann."

"It's Alex," she said. "I'm not really an agent, you know."

The technician smiled, a little confused.

"OK, then, let's pick up a Russian spy," Alex said, smiling widely for the first time in days.

"Hey, wait a second," Jeremy said, "weren't you opposed to picking up Smolin until we identify the backup asset, and his entire uplink network?"

"Yeah, I was. But today we almost missed that sandwich. We got lucky, and that's the only reason the stolen intel is still contained. Leaving Smolin out there, regardless of how much surveillance we plant around him, is too much of a risk. We have no choice, they're too damn good," she ended her argument with frustration in her voice.

Jeremy looked at her intently, then nodded and replied, "OK, let's pick him up."

"Gotta hand it to you," Jeremy said as they were arriving at the Botanical Gardens, where surveillance had told them they could find Smolin, "you got some serious skills."

"Thanks," Alex said modestly, then decided to take advantage of Jeremy's state of mind. "That means you'll let me interrogate Smolin?"

"You know I can't do that," he said apologetically. "Nothing changed in our procedure book since the last time we had this argument."

They walked silently for a few yards, then he continued, "Oh, and you need to stay here. You can't come any closer to where he is."

"The hell I can't," she snapped at him. "Yesterday I was able to come within fifty feet of him, today I can't?"

"It's procedure. In case he pulls a gun, or fires it. You could get caught in the crossfire or get hurt. You haven't gone through our gun proficiency. You're a civilian, after all. How about you start behaving like one?"

"We're supposed to be partners; for Christ's sake, Jeremy, don't be such an ass. Can't you just bend the rules a little? There's enough manpower here to arrest a dozen Russians."

"No," he said firmly. "I won't risk it; it's not worth it. You either stay here, or I'll lock you in the back of the car."

"Fine, whatever," she grumbled angrily, splitting the word in half as to make it more powerful.

She watched the three men approach Smolin's backgammon table. He was alone, reading a newspaper. He sensed their arrival and put the newspaper down on the table, then stood slowly, assessing his options. He knew what the three men wanted even before they spoke.

She felt her hair stand on end; there was something about Smolin, something feral. She started walking toward him in a brisk pace, almost running, discreetly clasping the handle of her gun under her jacket.

"Evgheni Smolin?" Jeremy said, wielding his badge. "I'm Agent Weber with the FBI. We'd like to speak with you, ask you a few questions."

As if in slow motion, Alex saw Smolin check his surroundings quickly, looking left, then right, making an assessment of the environment. Then he pulled his gun, lightning fast, and pulled the trigger, aiming for Jeremy's head.

But Alex had already fired her PPK, and her bullet hit Smolin in the right shoulder, causing him to swerve his gun and miss the target.

Smolin's bullet whistled past Jeremy's head, missing it by less than a foot and hitting the old oak tree behind him. The other two agents approached Smolin and disarmed him, then started reading him his rights.

"Whew," Jeremy said, wiping his sweaty forehead, "what kind of consultant are you?"

She smiled and holstered her weapon. "You're welcome."

"I'm getting used to this place," Alex said, looking at the familiar entrance to the Botanical Gardens and following the silhouette of a roaring jet taking off against the sunset sky. "I'm starting to like it," she added, hungrily chewing a bite from a slice of pizza.

They ate near the hood of Weber's car, standing on the sides with the extra large, extra cheese between them, eating as if there was no tomorrow.

"I think we're done with this park," Jeremy said. "With Smolin locked up, there's no reason to visit anymore. Oh, and they'll have your gun returned to you by tomorrow."

His phone rang. He took the call hands free, recognizing the number.

"Weber here, go ahead."

"This is Moore. The team finished reviewing the surveillance tapes again, and there aren't any sandwiches starring in all those hours of film; none whatsoever."

"But did you notice anything out of the ordinary at all? With anyone? I know you've looked before, but now we know more than we did back then. Pull older street video feeds," Weber insisted.

"OK, give me a few," Moore said and hung up.

They sat quietly, admiring how the sunset colors lit the sky, creating wondrous colors and shapes in the exhaust of passing jets.

"You hanging in there?" Alex asked quietly.

"Yeah . . ." Jeremy replied in his typical manner, after hesitating a little. "It's not every day you hear the bullet coming, you know."

"Yup," she replied.

"And when it did, when I heard it coming, it was like it took forever, and all I could think about was my son. He... he needs me to come home every day. He needs me, so I gotta live," he said, watching intently another jet gain altitude.

"And you will," Alex said.

Moments of silence slipped by, as the sky turned darker and the first stars appeared.

"Thank you," Jeremy said after a while.

"Don't mention it," Alex replied.

The phone rang again, almost deafening in the peaceful evening.

"It's Moore."

"Go ahead," Jeremy said.

"We've seen occasional bike messengers pick up and drop off from Smolin's residence, maybe two or three times in the past month. Then one of the agents remembered he'd noticed a couple of bike messengers pick stuff up from Bob McLeod's residence, but didn't think it was relevant."

"Oh, God . . ." Weber said, and hopped behind the wheel of his Charger.

FBI Case # 174-NR-24578

Content of decrypted message on SPAM biofilm

[start message]

Laser weapons system (LaWS) functional and ready to be deployed on naval warships. First hull #DDG1005 in Norfolk. On schedule: DDG136, DDG105. More hull #s to follow.

Technical solution for power source and power storage for LaWS is small enough to allow installation on planes, drones.

Prototype on drone scheduled for early next year. Deployment on fighter jets by mid next year.

Installation schematics, cannon capabilities will become available soon.

Engagement protocol recommends use LaWS to disable, not destroy. Target weapon systems, propulsion, and communications. Keep casualties to minimum.

Recommend effort to obtain power source and storage schematics ASAP.

[end message]

Several Dodge Chargers were parked on the adjacent streets leading to Bob McLeod's street. Two surveillance teams had kept eyes and ears on McLeod constantly since Saturday night, waiting for him to make a move. Finally, he made the anticipated move. He placed a call to FastLite Messenger Service.

A bike messenger, probably eighteen years old, scrawny and crazy fast on his two wheels, appeared from around a corner. He wore a T-shirt and a cap, both inscribed with the FastLite logo. Jeremy waved his badge at him and stopped him before turning on McLeod's street.

"Weber, FBI. I'm gonna need your T-shirt and your cap. And your bike too."

The kid gave Weber a doubtful, amused look. Agent Weber was twice his size.

He read his mind and said, "It's gonna fit, son, don't worry. It has to."

He put on the kid's shirt with difficulty. It would be a miracle if the T did not end up ripped along the seams; it had to be at least three sizes too small.

"Hey," the boy called. "You'll need this too." He handed him the receipt pad and a pencil.

"Thanks."

Weber took the kid's bike and rode it to McLeod's door, then rang the bell.

McLeod opened the door and checked Weber out, frowning a little.

"You're... a little mature for this job, if you don't mind me saying," he commented.

"Yeah... Well, just making an extra buck at night, man, what can I do? Car's broken, can't do pizza delivery no more." He scratched his forehead, then played indifferently with his phone a little, going through his music, giving McLeod the time to make up his mind.

McLeod sighed and handed him a gift-wrapped package.

"It's for my son's birthday. He lives in Smithfield with his mom. Do you think you can take this there tonight?"

"You bet."

McLeod handed him forty dollars and asked him to keep the change. Weber almost forgot to write the shipping receipt.

He turned the corner and stopped, then took the T-shirt off, as soon as he was out of McLeod's line of sight, and handed it back to its rightful owner. Then he opened the package. Wrapped neatly inside a Disney DVD case, several documents marked TOP SECRET were folded in half, all of them unregistered, unauthorized copies of original classified documents. The first page was titled, "Capabilities Assessment for Zumwalt-Class Destroyers." The package was addressed to Smolin's residence.

"Let's bust the bastard," Weber spoke into his radio.

Alex checked her temporary desk, drawer by drawer, making sure she didn't leave anything behind. Hmm... her own office inside an FBI building, who would have thought?

She was getting ready to leave. Her case was closed, and her client, Walcott Global Technologies, happy. Well... as happy as it could have been under the circumstances. She was joining Mason and Sam for dinner later, to celebrate. The next day, she'd board a flight back to her home in California.

"You ready?" Weber asked from the doorway.

"Yeah, ready." She turned to grab her laptop bag, then added, "One more thing I gotta ask you."

"Shoot."

"When you interrogate Smolin, can you ask him... well, about the man, that
Russian . . ."

"You mean the man from the case you said you had no idea what I was talking about?" Weber asked with a crooked smile.

"Yeah, the case we never worked on, that one," she confirmed and winked. "Ask him about a Russian with the initial V, who calls all the shots and plans majestic endeavors of espionage and warfare," she said, almost laughing at how cheesy her description sounded. *But how true...* she thought bitterly.

"You got it. And here's something else that you might find interesting. It's highly confidential; please handle it appropriately." He handed her a manila envelope containing a dark blue brief bearing the insignia of the Central Intelligence Agency.

"What is it?"

"It's a report prepared by a senior CIA analyst regarding Russia's intentions to invigorate its nuclear arsenal and restart the Cold War. It might help you identify your Russian."

She dropped the laptop bag to the floor and flipped through the pages.

"I have to meet with this analyst," she said, then looked on the cover page for the name she was missing. "I need to speak with this Henrietta Marino ASAP. She's missing critical information."

"That's a bad idea, Alex. Hell, no." He ran his hand through his hair in a gesture of exasperation. "See? That's why I shouldn't break the damn rules, 'cause they bite me in the ass every goddamned time," he said angrily. "You're not authorized to know this report even exists. Don't get me in trouble, all right?"

"I won't, I promise. But I do have to speak with her, and it's urgent."

He shrugged, defeated, then added, "Trying to stop you is like trying to stop the damn midnight express. Good luck with that . . ." Weber rubbed his neck as if to get rid of a migraine. "But be careful, all right? Not every agency out there is willing to look the other way on some of the stuff you... didn't do."

"I'll take my chances," Alex replied with a frown. "I have to."

The thirty-six hours Bob McLeod spent in federal detention had left marks on his face, his clothes, and his entire appearance. His hair and beard were grimy and unkempt. He had dark circles under his eyes, and his dirty hands ran through his hair and over his face almost obsessively. He had slept, the little he'd been allowed to, in his suit, and that looked crumpled and dirty, the fine, designer, wool fabric reduced to a rag.

By contrast, the FBI agent seated across from him at the small, metallic table looked fresh and almost content, sipping steaming coffee from his tall cup and showing slight irritation in his eyes when reviewing McLeod's file.

McLeod decided to break the silence.

"You're still not going to allow me my right to an attorney?" he spoke almost defiantly.

"Traitors have no rights," Agent Weber replied indifferently, almost casually.

"How long are you gonna keep me here?" McLeod protested, slamming his hands on the tabletop as much as his chained cuffs allowed him. "You can't keep me like this forever."

"That is correct," Weber confirmed, not even looking at McLeod and continuing to read the excerpt from prior interrogation sessions. "But you seem to be forgetting you were caught in an act of espionage and treason, and that voids all your rights under the Patriot Act."

McLeod fell silent for a while, them whispered, "Gitmo?"

"No. We've recently closed that facility, but we have others, just as capable of handling our country's traitors, maybe even better, because no one really knows they exist. Everyone knew about damn Gitmo... It was becoming such a drag to deal with all that public outrage. That's over, done with. We have new locations." Weber sipped some more coffee, then continued, "For example, we have a new facility specialized for people who won't talk at all, for traitors who just fail to understand their situation. They make things hard for us? Then we make things hard for them... And, of course, we have to keep such operations offshore, in places so deep and dark no one ever hears the screams, and no one ever counts the bodies."

McLeod shuddered and swallowed hard. His defiance was all gone; he sat crouched, with his shoulders forward and head bowed. Then he spoke quietly.

"What do you want to know?"

"For starters, I want to know details on every piece of information you stole, and who you gave it to."

McLeod hesitated. He must have known that an admission of treason was not going to help his case much. For a logical, cold-blooded thinker as he obviously was, he must have known by now he was finished anyway. He might as well cut his pain and get this phase over, done as quickly and as painlessly as possible. Treason carried an unavoidable death sentence. If McLeod didn't know that by now, Weber was determined to reiterate that point and help him make up his mind to talk.

McLeod sighed and started talking in a low, almost casual voice.

"I had access to three classified files—SECRET, TOP SECRET, or above— all about the laser cannon installation on Zumwalt-class destroyers, or about the cannon itself. I copied all three and took the information home."

"Go on," Weber said.

"Then I prepared several deliveries." McLeod cleared his throat, continuing, "I wasn't going to hand out everything in one deal. I milked it for all it was worth."

"So, you're just a regular Judas, a traitor for money?"

McLeod smiled bitterly. "That's what you think, huh? How simple it is for you ignorants to slap a label on someone and find peace with your conscience, no matter how wrong you are. Amazing... Ignorance *is* bliss."

"Then tell me, what am I missing?"

"You haven't asked the most important question: why? Why did I decide to risk my life and my freedom to give these people information? I couldn't care less about their ideology."

"OK, I'll bite. Why?"

"A few years ago I filed a patent for a new navigation stabilization system, one that could be used on Navy vessels, and also adapted to any aircraft. My invention introduced variable geometry controlled by environmental sensors. In short, the vessel would change its hull properties depending on currents and wind direction, bringing significant gains in speed, fuel efficiency, and stability. Do you even know how important that is, how much of a game changer? I guess I'm safe to presume not . . ."

"Yes, you are. Go ahead, I'm all ears," Weber replied dryly, immune to McLeod's biting arrogance.

"The patent was filed under joint authorship, me and Walcott Global. It wasn't the first patent that I filed under these circumstances."

"Then what happened?" Weber asked, while his interest piqued.

"A couple of months ago I heard it on TV, on the goddamn TV no less, that Walcott had sold my patent to Endeavor Aviation for 157 million dollars. Nicely done! I didn't even know about it."

"Then what did you do?"

"At that point I was still a solid citizen," he said with a disgusted scoff. "I went to see my boss about it, then Human Resources. They all said the same thing, that all my work was work for hire, that I was being paid every two weeks, and that they didn't owe me anything. Fucking bastards!"

"I understand you were upset—"

"Upset? I was frantic! What a difference five percent would have made for me, for my life, while they wouldn't even have felt it. Even one percent; I'd have taken that one percent and be eternally grateful. But no... The greedy parasites, the leeches, got away with sucking every ounce of someone's value and paying pennies for it. They had the arrogance to think they could own my brain. They only pay for eight hours of my *time* during each business day. They don't even come close to paying for everything *this* has to offer," McLeod finished his tirade pointing his right index finger at his temple.

"Then what did you do?"

"I decided to make them pay a different way, if I couldn't negotiate with them. I thought maybe there was someone else out there willing to pay me, while I taught the leeches a lesson in humility and fair compensation. That's why I didn't hand out all the documents at a time."

Weber's anger was getting harder to control. He couldn't believe the entitled arrogance in that asshole.

"Did you ever stop to think you were betraying your country, Mr. McLeod?"

"My country can take it, Agent Weber. This country is full of brilliant schmucks like me who'll invent new gizmos every day and get paid next to nothing for it. That's what makes America great, isn't it?"

Weber stood abruptly and exited the interview room, afraid his mixed feelings would cloud his judgment in there. He had spent his entire life serving his country, and nothing disgusted him more than a traitor. He could have wrung that arrogant bastard's neck himself in there, with his bare hands. Yet, in the back of his mind somewhere, he could feel the man's frustration and see his point. Maybe McLeod wasn't the only guilty party in this game... Maybe Walcott could have done things a little differently too, although Walcott had never broken the law; only McLeod had.

But if that were entirely the case, why didn't Mason Armstrong find any evidence of this situation anywhere in McLeod's file, Human Resources debriefings, or during the interview with his manager?

Evgheni Smolin woke up a little disoriented and started looking around his hospital room. The smells of disinfectant and medication were his first sensory input, followed by the whiteness of everything in that room.

He was by himself; always a good thing. His healthy left arm was handcuffed to the bed rail, and an IV line was stuck in it. His right shoulder hurt quite badly, but it was bearable. His right arm was bandaged and immobilized. His mouth felt dry, probably from the anesthetics they had given him for surgery.

There was a chip in one of his molars. He felt around with the tip of his tongue, then grunted angrily. His cyanide capsule was gone, probably removed during surgery. Bastards...

He was hooked up to several sensors. A clasp sensor on one of his fingers measured his blood oxygenation. Several adhesive sensors planted on his chest conveyed electrical signals to the monitors next to his bed. The upper monitor beeped and displayed a healthy, steady heart rate of fifty-eight beats per minute, and a blood pressure of 112 over 74. The lower monitor showed his breathing rate at fourteen per minute, with 98 percent O_2 sat.

The wall at his right was made entirely of glass and had a French door, which was wide open. He took a few minutes to observe the traffic in the hallway, and listen to the sounds—how distant they were and what kind. All was peaceful on that hospital floor, except the MP who guarded his room closely, leaning against the glass. However, that MP was bound to leave his post at some point.

Waiting for that to happen, he started checking out his own body. He lifted his head from the pillow and noted no dizziness. Great. He tensed the muscles in one leg, then the other, restoring a vigorous blood flow and waking those muscles up. He was ready, as ready as he was ever going to be.

The MP looked in his direction briefly, then walked slowly away. Smolin gave him a minute to disappear, then moved into action.

First, he leaned on his left side, reached out, and with a great deal of effort, grabbed the IV needle with his teeth, and pulled it out of his arm. Then he held his breath for as long as he could, sending one of the monitors into a beeping frenzy. After that, he started hyperventilating, and then held his breath again.

This type of respiratory distress finally raised his heart rate above 120 beats per minute and spiked his blood pressure, causing the second monitor to join in the concert of beeps.

A nurse burst in his room and started checking his vitals on the monitors, as Smolin heaved, hyperventilated, and writhed on the bed, making it hard for the nurse to assess his condition. Vaguely, he heard a code call, and then the nurse's voice, yelling from right next to him.

"Hey, you, come on in here and remove his handcuff, stat!"

The MP came in and did as instructed. The moment Smolin felt his hand go free, he grabbed the MP's hand and jumped, headbutting him hard. The MP fell backward against the rack of monitors. The same second Smolin was on his feet, tearing his sensor wires away from his body, and kicking the fallen MP in the neck, sending him out cold.

He turned to deal with the nurse, who was leaping toward the exit. He grabbed her from behind and slammed her against the wall. She fell and lay senseless.

He leaned down, grabbed her ICU access card, and disappeared.

Alex bypassed the line for the public TSA screening and went toward the gate reserved for flight crews and traveling law enforcement. That was her only option, if she wanted to travel anywhere with her weapon.

She presented her FBI credentials to the TSA officer, then she proceeded through the gate, and walked right out of there staring intently at the TSA officer who had just waved her through.

"Is there something wrong, miss?" the man asked, surprised by her intent gaze.

"N–no, nothing," she said. She pulled her cell phone and dialed Weber's number, walking away from the checkpoint.

"Miss? You forgot your bag."

"Shit," she mumbled, then grabbed it and walked away just as Weber picked up the call.

"Hey, Jeremy, it's me."

"Hey, you," he replied. "Ready to go home?"

"Yeah. Just cleared TSA, which made me think we should ask them if they see sandwiches or any other food go by."

"Right," he said, "good point. I'll get right on that. Safe travels, Ms. Hoffmann."

"Thanks. Oh, and by the way, I hated working with you. So you know, Agent Weber," she said, smiling widely. "You're good people, Weber."

"You, too. Hey, could you just hold on for a sec, I have another call coming in."

He put her on hold before she could answer. There wasn't really anything much left to be said, anyway.

"Hey, you still there?" Weber's voice sounded grave and urgent as he picked up the call again.

"Yeah, what's up?"

"Smolin's gone. Escaped, vanished."

"Oh, crap, how the hell did that happen? When?"

"He left the Naval Medical Center in an ambulance, headed who knows where. Left two people down in this wake. "

She suddenly halted her brisk walk toward the gate and did a 180, running in the opposite direction.

"Weber, listen, I think I know exactly where he's going."

"Another hunch?"

"He's going to church."

"To pray?" Weber sounded incredulous.

"Nope... to seek assistance," she said, panting a little from her jog. "I've been wondering how they communicate, how they organize without ever being seen or noticed. Ethnic churches are the best way possible. Even judges resent issuing surveillance warrants for churches. It's the perfect hiding place. There's a Russian Orthodox Church nearby; I'm going there right now. I'm only minutes away."

"Don't engage him until we get there. You hear me?"

"Yeah, sure," she replied, almost chuckling, then hung up and hailed a cab.

Moscow's Ritz Carlton spa knew how to treat its VIP guests. Dimitrov and Myatlev found there exquisite spa treatments in the safety and privacy of dedicated rooms well-guarded by Myatlev's ex-Spetsnaz bodyguards. Rose essential oils and a carefully balanced breeze of fresh air completed a quiet, relaxing atmosphere that both of them enjoyed deeply.

Two masseuses, wearing barely there bikinis, had just completed full body massages for the two guests, then disappeared without a word, leaving their clients happy and content. The men rested naked on warm marble slabs, their skin completely covered in massage oils. They chatted quietly, subdued by deep relaxation, almost dozing off at times.

"You need a lot more massage to deal away with that flab, Vitya," Dimitrov laughed, pointing at Myatlev's potbelly.

"This?" Myatlev asked, pinching his overflowing belly. "This is beyond redemption, my dear friend." They both broke down with laughter.

Myatlev signaled his adjutant, Ivan, for some Perrier water with lime. He drank a full glass, then said, "The goodies are starting to come in, just as planned."

"What do you have?" Dimitrov asked, his interest dissipating his relaxation.

"We have the technical notes for the laser cannon installation on mobile platforms. We have enough to know what we're missing to be able to deploy such weapon systems ourselves."

"What do we need?"

"Power. Our power source for our laser weapon is huge, and our engineers haven't figured out how to miniaturize it, even with the information that's been trickling in."

"So what do you want to do, Vitya?"

"We need to get our hands on the power source schematics, as soon as possible, what else?" Myatlev smiled and winked, making Dimitrov laugh.

"Of course," he replied laughing. "Research takes too damn long."

"I'll send Karp to the field. He's ready."

They remained silent for a while, as their laughter died down and they both became engulfed in their own thoughts.

"You know what else I'd like to do?" Myatlev asked after a while.

"Mmm... What?" Dimitrov replied.

"I'd like to pay a little attention to the American ICBM sites. Rumors have it they're a little rusty, old, and falling apart. I think it's doable and worth checking out."

"We've cleaned ours up," Dimitrov said. "Most of them were bad, inoperable. I wonder if theirs are just as bad."

"Twenty-five years is twenty-five years in both countries, Mishka. That's a lot of neglect. But I'm thinking more than just seeing which ones are operable and which ones are not."

"What?" Dimitrov asked, intrigued, and turned on his side to face Myatlev.

"I'm thinking by now they must know you've cleaned and prepared ours for action, right?"

Dimitrov nodded. "Uh-huh."

"Then they must be getting ready to clean theirs."

"And?"

"And that means nuclear missiles moving from location to location, temporary nuclear test codes available for the right people, and so on. Tons of opportunity for us, Mishka."

"You're a twisted motherfucker! Genius! Let's do that!" Dimitrov said, slapping him hard on the shoulder. "Glad you're on our side!"

"Lady, I've never seen anyone in such a hurry to get to church," the cabbie said, grabbing the fifty-dollar bill offered to him. "Here we are," he said, bringing the cab to an abrupt halt with a prolonged tire squeal.

"Wait here," Alex said, pulling her weapon and heading for the church.

She entered the church quietly, her senses in full alert, taking in the stillness of the place, the dimmed light coning through the stained-glass windows and the strong smell of burned incense. She looked ahead and saw a man walking toward the iconostasis. The man had a slight asymmetry; he walked with his right shoulder a tad lower than the left.

"Smolin, stop right there!" she yelled, pointing her gun at the man's back.

Out of nowhere, a priest approached and smacked her in the head with a prayer book, sending her to her knees and her gun sliding under the nearest pew. She shook her head a little, trying to dissipate the sharp pain, and rubbed her hand against her temple, where the pain was worse. Her hand touched something warm and moist, with a strong metallic smell. Blood. Her own.

She turned while still on her knees and grabbed the priest's legs, throwing him to the floor. Then she sprung on top of him, hitting him hard in the chest with her knee, and in the side of his neck with her right fist.

She reached under the pew and grabbed her weapon. Smolin was nowhere in sight. She ran toward the iconostasis, hesitated a little, then entered the sanctuary just in time to catch a glimpse of Smolin making a clumsy run for the back door.

She holstered her gun then sprinted ahead, jumped, and clasped her hands around Smolin's neck, coming from behind. Then she let all her weight on him, kicking the back of his knees. They fell to the floor, Alex on top of Smolin, and Smolin grunting and swearing, feeling the pain in his shoulder. Her hands still held tight around his neck, squeezing as hard as she could.

"Shoot me," Smolin managed to articulate, in a strangled voice, probably trying to get her to release her grip.

"No," she panted, "first you talk. Then, maybe I will."

He suddenly rolled over on his left shoulder, catching her under his weight, crushing her. She gasped for air. He was massive, and still strong, despite his shoulder wound. She started kicking blindly from underneath him, and finally hit his crotch, while her fingernails dug deep into the skin of his neck, gripping and tugging at his Adam's apple. He yelped and curled on his side, then threw himself against her as she was trying to get up, and slammed her into the wall.

A couple of icons fell off the wall and shattered, and she fell alongside the wall, landing hard. Smolin punched her with his left hand, almost missing, yet hitting her hard.

Her vision darkened, and she felt she was about to lose consciousness. She managed to pull her gun and shoot, getting Smolin in his left shoulder. He yelled in pain and fell to the floor, crouched and writhing.

She stood with difficulty, still pointing her Walther PPK at Smolin, and wiped the blood off her face, grimacing in pain. Her entire body hurt, and a sharp pain pierced her under her ribs every time she breathed. Her head was throbbing, and she was angry as hell.

"Now let's see who's gonna wipe your sorry ass, motherfucker," she said, just as she heard in the distance someone yell, "Clear!"

"Ah... she's got vocabulary too," Weber said, as he entered the sanctuary with his weapon drawn and a couple of agents in tow. "Remove this piece of trash from here," he said to the other agents, then turned to Alex.

"Are you OK?" he asked, then he replied to his own question. "No, you're not. We need to get you to a hospital. Let's go," he said, putting his arm around her shoulder and helping her walk.

"Hey, Jer?"

"Yeah?"

"Did I just break the law of sanctuary?" she asked, feeling a little ridiculous for asking that question. "I chased a man and shot him in a church. I'm not sure how I feel about that."

"And you cussed in a church too! Forgot that already?" Weber laughed. "You'll have plenty of stories to tell your grandkids."

His voice turned a little more serious, as he added, "The law of sanctuary was abolished centuries ago, and all it really stated was that the fugitive seeking sanctuary in a church couldn't be killed, but would still have to be held accountable for his criminal acts."

"Oh . . ." she said, suddenly feeling drained, as the adrenaline washed away.

"The churches weren't meant to be havens for killers and rapists, you know," he continued, speaking as if he spoke to a wounded, vulnerable child. "They were protecting people from political prosecution mainly, like running from an irate king, jealous of one's land, or choice of fiancée. Plus, you didn't even kill him, so you're good."

She looked at him with thankful eyes.

"How come you know so much about this?"

He cleared his throat before speaking and smiled briefly.

"Oh well... I chased and arrested someone in a church one time, and my mom gave me grief about it for weeks."

"No Thanksgiving dinner for you that year, huh?"

"Something like that, yeah . . ." he laughed.

"OK, I feel a little better, thanks. I still feel weird about it, that's all. You know, being in there with my gun drawn and all that."

He helped her sit down on the rear bumper of the ambulance, as an EMT worked on her head wound.

"You wanna know what the punishment was for whoever broke the law of sanctuary in the 1500s?"

"What?" She smiled, wincing from the disinfectant applied to her cut temple.

"They had to pay 120 shillings. That's about fifteen pound sterling, or twenty-three dollars. With inflation and all, maybe a couple hundred bucks would take care of it?"

"That much I can manage," she replied, and they laughed together.

Case # 174-NR-24578
Transcription Excerpt, Interrogation Session #5

[begin excerpt]

Interviewer: "Tell me, what kind of information have you been collecting?"
Evgheni Smolin: "I don't have to say anything to you."
Interviewer: "You risked your life to serve your country; don't you want us to know why?"
Evgheni Smolin: "Whether you know or not, that is irrelevant. Everything I did and do is for my country, for Russia."
[…]
Interviewer: "Who sent you? Who gave you your mission?"
Evgheni Smolin: "Are you actually expecting me to roll and start spilling everything to you, like the lowest of cowards? Then you're bigger idiots than we thought."
Interviewer: "Who's a bigger idiot?"
Evgheni Smolin: "You. All of you, Americans."
Interviewer: "Ahh... I see. Well, you might be right; we might be idiots. Why don't you prove it to me?"
Evgheni Smolin: "Ha! Not worth my time."
Interviewer: "You got plenty of time. You're not going to get out of this alive, you know. We don't trade spies anymore; that's long gone."
Evgheni Smolin: "I took my chances when I came here. I'm proud of what I did."
[47 seconds of silence]
Interviewer: "Here's what I think. I think you work for a bunch of old-timers, still nostalgic after the glorious times of Cold War and communism, some old farts with no idea what the future looks like. I think your country has become weak and cowardly, without its overabundance of slave republics you lost. I think you lost everything you could have been when the KGB fell apart. Guess what? We're not afraid of you Russians anymore!" [brief

laughter]

Evgheni Smolin: "Fucking idiots... Is that what you think? Good, keep thinking that, so you won't see us coming!"

Interviewer: "Yeah, that's what I think. And I think you are a little piece of leftover trash, still clinging to the idea that Russia could do any real intelligence work. Well, not anymore! We caught you on the double, didn't we? And that's because you work for some lame old farts who can't conceive a half-decent intelligence strategy, that's why."

Evgheni Smolin: "I work for two of the smartest people to ever set military and intelligence strategy. What they're planning for you, you'll never see coming. Soon... soon you'll remember my words. So what if you caught me? I'm just a small cog in the great Russian intelligence machine that we've resurrected back to life, and you didn't even know about it! That's how ignorant you are!"

Interviewer: "I'm sure your family would love to hear you're just a cog in a machine when you simply disappear, never to be heard from again."

Evgheni Smolin: "I have no other family than Mother Russia. She will mourn my loss and call me a hero. She'll give me a hero's funeral when I'm gone."

Interviewer: "Russia is nothing these days... you should have picked a better employer. This one's in rags and starving."

Evgheni Smolin: "You—you don't know what you're talking about! How dare you talk about Russia like that? You bastard! Russia will rise again and shove your faces in your own smallness and insignificance. Russia has the greatest leaders it's had in decades, united, ready to fight, ready to wipe you off the face of the Earth. There's no greater mission that I'd rather sacrifice my life for, than the glorious future of my country. Nothing else matters."

Interviewer: "You're just one little cog in a machine, you know? What difference could you possibly make?"

Evgheni Smolin: There are hundreds just like me, already here, working to restore Russia's greatness in ways you can't even comprehend. There are hundreds of thousands more back home, getting ready to strike at a moment's notice. You, and the rest of the arrogant Western assholes who insulted our president, are doomed. Say your prayers and get ready to die."

[end transcript]

Alex checked the time nervously. Her appointment was late, and she wasn't even sure if she was going to show. She went back to reading her notes to refresh her memory, getting ready for a conversation that might not even happen.

"You have some nerve, Ms.... Hoffmann," a woman's voice articulated coldly right behind her. She turned and saw a tall woman dressed in a brown business suit, wearing her hair tied in an unpretentious ponytail.

"Ms. Marino?" she offered and extended her hand. The woman ignored it.

"My first instinct was to blow the whistle on you and have you picked up," the woman continued, the coldness in her voice feeling like a slap to Alex's face.

Alex felt her anger take over.

"So why didn't you?" she asked. "After all, someone like you lives their life under the rule of logic and procedure, right?"

"Don't be presumptuous with me. Yes, I could've had you arrested for a number of things, but that wouldn't have gained me easy access to the information you said you could provide. Your note, although unusual, was quite intriguing."

"Then... can we start over?" Alex said and smiled, offering her hand again. "I'm Alex Hoffmann."

"Henrietta Marino."

"Want some coffee or anything?"

"I'm good, thanks. So, what do you have?" Marino pressed on.

"I read your report. It was very interesting, yet incomplete," Alex said, dropping her voice almost to a whisper.

Marino frowned, then asked quietly, "What do you mean?"

"Your analysis covers the strategic level really well, describing President Abramovich's intentions, and profiling him in detail. Then you analyze the Russians actions and speculate about potential plans of attack. I can give you a glimpse into the type of plans they could be weaving, and an idea about the second layer of command. Well, at least partially."

"What do you mean, partially? What second layer?"

"Have you wondered who helps Abramovich reach his goals?"

"He has a government," Marino said a little hesitantly. "Why? What do you know?"

"There are two other men. One is Mikhail Dimitrov, the minister of defense. He and Abramovich are very close."

"I was wondering about that, seeing that Dimitrov was first 'resigned' by Abramovich, then brought back. The bastard actually spoke the truth for once when he announced Dimitrov's resignation for health reasons."

"Yes and no. Well... maybe," Alex said.

"Could you make any less sense?" Marino asked sarcastically.

"I have another theory. Dimitrov's resignation coincided with the American elections, and the result of those elections was what caused Dimitrov to have his heart attack and temporarily fall out of grace."

"You're saying he did fall out of grace with Abramovich? Why?"

"Well, let's say, hypothetically, that there could have been a conspiracy to thwart the elections, and that failed."

"So it is true."

"What?"

"That you have been involved in a black ops case of sorts... that's the rumor out there," Marino said.

"Hypothetically," Alex said and winked.

Marino rolled her eyes in disbelief. "Jeez . . ."

"When the plan failed, Abramovich got mad, and Dimitrov had his heart attack, so Abramovich ousted him. But a few months later, he brought him back."

"Yeah, but why?"

"Because it's only Dimitrov and this other man who can orchestrate plans of significant strategic importance, and execute them really well."

"Who's this other man you're talking about?"

"I don't know, unfortunately, no matter how hard I've tried to find out. MOSSAD doesn't know either. But we haven't stopped looking for him."

"MOSSAD? Jesus Christ... Who the hell are you?" Marino asked.

"Oh... I'm just a corporate investigator who's had an interesting choice of cases to work on, nothing else, I promise."

"Then how do you know this man even exists?"

"He does. His name starts with the initial V, and he's a brilliant strategist."

"First or last name? And how sure are you about the letter V? Where did you learn that?"

"From the lips of a dying man. And yes, he's real, but we just couldn't find him, not yet."

Henri Marino sat quietly for a few seconds, then asked, "What do you want from me?"

"Nothing, really. Just wanted you to know about these two people, and what their roles could be in one of your scenarios. If V has his hand in any of those plans, expect them to be big, dramatic, of epic proportions and impact." She paused, taken aback by the incredulity reflected in Marino's eyes. "I thought this information might be helpful."

Marino stood, ready to leave. "It might be," she said, reluctantly, then shook Alex's hand again.

"Oh, and if you ever find out who V is, please let me know," Alex asked.

Marino didn't reply, but her cold gaze wasn't very promising.

"Damn," Alex muttered to herself, watching Marino leave. "She must think I'm some sort of nut job."

The familiar driveway was already filled with cars. Steve's matte black M6 was already there, and so were Brian's Lexus and Richard's Benz. Along the curb, there was a rental sedan, most likely Jeremy's. Sam had arrived two days earlier, and his rental SUV was the first car on the driveway.

"Late again," she grumbled, then got out of her car and went straight to the backyard, using the side gate.

She was a little embarrassed to face Tom, considering the last conversation they'd had, and how she'd taken a case without consulting with him first. She felt uncomfortable thinking of seeing Brian; she'd abandoned him mid-engagement and had gone to Norfolk for the Walcott case, a case that wasn't even on the books. Finally, she dreaded seeing Steve, the man she still loved, but couldn't forgive.

She took a deep breath and walked into the backyard, with a wide smile, she didn't feel, pasted on her lips. The familiar yard was decorated with flags, balloons, and ribbons, and the spirit of the holiday engulfed her.

"Hey, look who's making an entrance," Louie said cheerfully.

They were gathered around the four-burner grill, and Tom was entertaining, wearing an apron printed with three lines of text—"The man, the myth, the legend."

Leaning against a tree, Steve smoked a cigar and held a beer in his hand. He raised the bottle to greet her, and she waved back. His eyes were sad, but he was smiling. He frowned when he saw her bruised face and slightly swollen jaw.

Brian gave her a quick hug. "Welcome back!"

"Thanks! And... sorry for everything. I really am, you know," she said. "I can explain what happened."

"No need, we've all gone through these kinds of things. Plus, this guy already explained," Brian replied, pointing toward Agent Weber.

"Hey, Jer," she greeted him, "welcome to California, again," she laughed.

"Yeah... I get great air miles, you know, worth it every time." He gulped some beer. "Good to be here, good to meet everyone I heard so much, yet so little, about. Thanks for having me,"

"Hey, boss," Louie said, giving her a quick side hug. "Did you have time to miss any of us? Or were you too busy playing with the bigwigs of the nation's capital?"

"Sure, you most of all, of course. By the way, I was in Norfolk, not DC," she replied, chuckling. "What have you been up to?"

He threw a side glance toward Weber, then said, "Umm... maybe I'll fill you in later."

Weber laughed and Alex joined him.

"Yeah, Jer, your presence is causing some concern in this group."

She turned toward Tom and his famous grill.

"Welcome back," he said, hugging her without letting go of the barbecue fork. "I'm proud of you, just so you know," he said quietly. "You handled things like a pro."

She looked in his understanding blue eyes and felt a lump in her throat. She was home, with her family.

"Our girl is back," Claire cheered and kissed her on both cheeks. "What would you like to drink, my dear?"

"Stella would be nice, thanks much!"

"I'll get that," Louie offered.

"So, what are we having for dinner tonight?" she asked Tom.

"I'm making us an Independence Day special, burgers cordon bleu, with mushroom and Swiss."

"Umm... not sure I know what that is, but it sounds delish!"

"It's a double cheeseburger really, but grilled differently. I stack the two patties on top of each other on the grill, with the cheese between them. By the time the patties are done just right, the cheese is molten. On the side, I grill the portabellas with a drop of oil in the center, and cover them with a thin slice of Swiss when they're about done. Then everything stacks on a plate, next to the bun, if you still want that. Artery popping, truly American, served with fries, onions, and pickles, and washed down with copious quantities of beer."

"Mmm... mmm... yummy!" Alex said, salivating a little. "And that's why he is the man, the myth, the legend."

"Hear, hear," Steve said, speaking his first words since she'd arrived, approaching the group slowly, hesitantly.

Sam and Richard came out of the house, chatting lively.

"What did we miss?" Sam asked. "Hey, kiddo."

"Hey, Sam," she said and planted a kiss on his cheek. "Hello, Richard."

Louie appeared from inside the house carrying a tray with champagne glasses and a chilled bottle of 1981 Krug Brut. Steve took the bottle and started to uncork it.

"Now that we're all gathered together again," Tom said, "to celebrate our independence and the successful completion of another case, please join me in savoring this champagne and in celebrating another milestone."

The cork popped loudly, and everyone hollered and cheered.

"It's weird and unusual though," Tom continued after taking a sip of champagne, "to have such a celebration without the client present. This is a first, I must say. We do understand the circumstances, and we are grateful we have made a new friend instead." Tom raised his glass to Weber.

"Thank you," Weber said.

"Did we at least get paid on this case?" Richard asked, causing a roar of laughter around the smoking grill.

"Spoken like a true finance executive," Tom laughed. "Yes, this time we got paid, and quite generously I might add. This CEO is very happy," he added with a wink, putting his hand on his chest.

"Whew, I'm relieved. I was afraid I'd get fired after the third unpaid case," Alex quipped.

"I might be the most clueless person in this gathering," Richard said, "but what exactly are we celebrating? What was the case about?"

A brief moment of silence engulfed the joyful crowd.

"It's confidential, I'm afraid," Alex replied, triggering another roar of laughter. Jeremy joined in, starting to feel more relaxed with the crowd.

"Was it hard?" Richard pressed on. "Was it a difficult case?"

"Umm... I'm afraid that's need to know, Richard," Alex replied, still chuckling.

"You weren't gone all that long, were you?"

"Nope, just little over a month, that's all."

"Nice," Richard said. "Nicely done, wrapping a case in a month. I'm impressed."

"Well, thank you kindly," she replied with a warm smile of appreciation.

"Not only that, but Alex sold this case too," Tom added. "I wasn't even involved. Congratulations!"

"Well, can you tell us any details about this case, something to sink our teeth into?" Brian joined the conversation.

Alex looked at Jeremy and they both shared a conspiratorial smile.

"No," she replied, "I don't know what you're talking about. What case?"

"Good one, you guys," Brian said, sipping the last drop of his champagne. "Then, what champagne?"

"And what burgers?" Tom added, turning his attention toward the grill. "So, if we can't discuss the case we've just closed, let's focus on the future instead. Alex, you have a new case lined up, tomorrow morning first thing."

"Huh?" she asked, surprised, then moved next to Jeremy and covered his ears with her hands. "Can you tell me what it's about?"

Tom winked at her and replied, "It's need to know at this time."

The doorbell startled Sylvia; she had dosed off on her couch, and the book she'd been reading had dropped to the floor.

She looked at her watch and frowned. It was late... Who could it be so late?

The doorbell rang again, prolonged, impatiently.

"Yeah, who is it?" she asked and looked through the peephole at the unfamiliar man standing there.

"Ms. Copperwaite?" the stranger asked.

She replied through the locked door, "Yes, who is this?"

"I am here to discuss your gambling addiction and what that will do to your career."

She felt the blood drain from her veins and her heart starting to pound in a deafening rhythm.

"We can do this through the locked door if you prefer," the stranger added unperturbed, "for your neighbors' enjoyment. There's no entertainment like real-life drama, you know."

She removed the chain and unlocked the door, then invited the stranger in. He was a tall, broad-shouldered man with a fierce, uncompromising look in his eyes.

"Come in," she said hesitantly.

The stranger walked in and remained standing.

"Ms. Copperwaite, tomorrow you will be fired from your job, because your employer will learn you stole money to cover your gambling debt. Then you will be arrested for theft.

Fear hit her like a fist in her stomach, almost making her keel over.

"That's... that's not true," she managed to articulate. "I haven't stolen a dime."

"That's not really relevant, Ms. Copperwaite, it's just a minor detail."

She let herself slide to the couch, her knees suddenly too weak to support her. She felt the burn of streaming tears coming from her eyes. She'd always feared she'd hit rock bottom some day, and wondered what that would look like.

"You have a choice though," the man added. "Entirely up to you."

"Who are you? And what do you want?"

"Doesn't matter who I am; only what I want, and what I can do. I want the power source and storage schematics for the laser cannon," the man said calmly, looking her straight in the eye.

She turned pale, as her brain started processing the information in a different light. She suddenly became aware of the man's slight accent that she couldn't place. *Oh, my God...* she thought. *Oh, my God . . .*

She hugged herself and started rocking back and forth, still seated on the side of her couch.

"That's all you want?" she asked quietly, almost whispering.

"Yes, that's all."

The man watched her silently, giving her time to make up her mind. There wasn't much choice. Maybe she could call someone and explain. Would the Feds believe her?

"There's a bright side to your cooperation, if you' decide to help us. Your gambling debts have indeed been paid, every single dime. Cash deposits were made in your name at the ATM, using your bankcard. Incidentally, the same amount of money was stolen tonight. No one can correlate the two events unless you decide to decline my request." The man made his threats with the calm and detached demeanor of a TV weather announcer. He was simply stating the facts.

She swallowed hard, keeping her eyes pinned to the carpet. Trapped. She was trapped, with no way out.

"It's up to you if you continue to gamble or not, but as of today all your accounts are taken care of. All we need in exchange for this generous gift is the power storage schematics. Your call; take it or leave it."

Silence fell between them, interrupted briefly by Sylvia's whimpers and sniffles, as her tears continued to fall, staining her cheeks.

She felt a chasm of fear and darkness open inside her, then heard herself speak quietly.

"OK, I'll do it."

~~~ *The End* ~~~

Did *The Backup Asset* keep you enthralled as you raced through the pages, gasping at every plot turn? Find out what happens next for Alex Hoffmann and her team, in the next unmissable Leslie Wolfe thriller.

Read on for an excerpt from

THE GHOST PATTERN

Alex Hoffmann Series Book Four

THANK YOU!

A big, heartfelt thank you for choosing to read my book. If you enjoyed it, please take a moment to leave me a four or five-star review; I would be very grateful. It doesn't need to be more than a few words, and it makes a huge difference. This is your shortcut: http://bit.ly/BackupAssetReview

Did you enjoy Alex Hoffmann and her team? Your thoughts and feedback are very valuable to me. Please contact me directly through one of the channels listed below. Email works best: LW@WolfeNovels.com.

CONNECT WITH ME

Email: LW@WolfeNovels.com
Facebook: https://www.facebook.com/wolfenovels
Follow Leslie on Amazon: http://bit.ly/WolfeAuthor
Follow Leslie on BookBub: http://bit.ly/wolfebb
Website: www.LeslieWolfe.com
Visit Leslie's Amazon store: http://bit.ly/WolfeAll

...Chapter 1: The Perfect Environment
...Wednesday, March 30, 11:01AM Local Time (UTC+3:00 hours)
...Russian Ministry of Defense
...Moscow, Russia

He glared at the man standing in front of him and clenched his jaws in an effort to control his anger.

"Speak," he growled.

"*Gospodin* Myatlev," the trembling man articulated in an unsure voice, "I think I found the perfect environment for our next test."

Vitaliy Myatlev let the air out of his lungs slowly. This was not one of his multinational corporations... this was the Russian government. People were slow and stupid sometimes. Most of all, people couldn't just be killed on the spot, especially when they couldn't be replaced that easily. Damn... When the hell did he turn from powerful oligarch into a goddamn clerk? A high-ranking one, that's true, but little more than a clerk, serving the almighty Russian president, and running to answer his every call.

The man stood silently, afraid to speak, his back bowing a little more.

Myatlev gestured the man to continue.

"There are 112 men," he said, "all about the same age, height and build, isolated, and vulnerable. It couldn't be better for what we need. They're perfectly contained, and remote. No one will know."

"You're saying this time it will work?"

The man lowered his eyes. "I think so, yes."

"You think...?" Myatlev snapped.

"Umm... sir, with every new pharmaceutical compound there are levels of tolerance, side effects, complications, environmental and metabolic factors to consider. Especially when the drug is aerosolized, the delivery isn't that precise. This hasn't been attempted before," the man added in a timid voice, then wiped his brow with his lab coat sleeve. "We haven't—"

"Save it," Myatlev said. "I've heard it all before, Dr. Bogdanov. Just give me results."

Chief Ramsay paced the room impatiently, muttering curses under his breath and looking out the same window every two seconds, although the view stayed eerily the same. A cold and foggy Aberdeen morning, engulfed in fog so thick it condensed water droplets on everything it touched, including his office window.

He picked up the radio and tried again.

"Nancy Belle, Nancy Belle, this is Shore Base, come in, over?"

He released the radio button, listening intently and hearing nothing. "C'mon, c'mon, where the hell are you?" he whispered impatiently.

His typical mornings were a lot different from that particular one. He'd come in the office a few minutes before 8:00AM, shaking off the humid chills brought by the thick Aberdeen fog, and heading straight for the coffee machine. He'd brew a fresh cup, then enjoy it while making his morning rounds. That was a figure of speech, of course. He rarely left the shore base. Once a rig was in production, barring some unforeseen event, the head of shore base operations had no reason to visit in person. His morning rounds consisted of radio calls with each of the drilling platforms under his purview, making sure everything was running well. He'd check the status of operations for each rig, and receive reports for everything from staff health to outstanding work orders for parts and repairs.

That would have been a routine morning. This time, things were different.

Nancy Belle, or NB64, was one of the three offshore oilrigs he was responsible for, and it was not reading on any comm. The night before NB64 had signed off with a "status normal, nothing to report" code, and now there was nothing, not a single sound coming from the platform on any channel. It was as if the milky fog had swallowed it whole.

A quick rap on the door, and the shift supervisor came in uninvited.

"Boss?" he said, rubbing his forehead hesitantly.

"Yeah, what do you have?"

"Nothing, dead silent on radio, on sat, all of it is dead. I tried a few personal cell phones, none pick up. Even video is down, all of it."

"What?" Ramsay stopped and turned on his heels to face his shift lead.

"Yeah, boss, all video feed is down for 64."

"Damn...bloody hell, what happened to those boys? Have any of the other rigs reported anything?"

"No, nothing," the man replied, shifting his weight from one foot to the other, while the frown on his forehead became more pronounced under the rim of his hard hat. "But they don't have eyes on them either...fog's too thick."

Ramsay went to the window and pressed his binoculars against it, squinting hard against the eyecups, trying to make something out in the milky haze that had swallowed everything like a shroud. His other rigs weren't visible yet either, but NB64 was the farthest one out; it would be a while.

"There's one," he said, pointing in the direction of a familiar shape almost completely hidden in the fog.

"That's 27," the other man confirmed. "If we can see 27, it shouldn't be that long before we put eyes on 64."

"Nancy Belle, Nancy Belle, come in, goddamnit," Ramsay tried again and got no response. "Go try video again, will ya'?"

The man left quietly. He returned within minutes. "Nothing, boss."

Ramsay stuck his face against the cold window and squinted some more.

"There she is," he said, as the fog lifted a little more, enough for him to discern the familiar silhouette of NB64 against the gray mist. "She's still there!"

Ramsay grabbed his binoculars and looked at 64 again. "Yeah, seems to be in one piece, no flames, no smoke."

He made another attempt to raise the rig by radio, then turned to his lead and said, "You know the procedure. We can't wait any longer; it's been almost an hour. We have to assume the worst. Get SAS and emergency response ready, and meet me on the helipad."

Minutes later, the rotor blades of a SA 330E Puma helicopter ripped through the lifting fog as it headed toward the eerily silent NB64.

~~~End Preview~~~

Like *The Ghost Pattern*?

Buy it now!

ABOUT THE AUTHOR

Leslie Wolfe is a bestselling author whose novels break the mold of traditional thrillers. She creates unforgettable, brilliant, strong women heroes who deliver fast-paced, satisfying suspense, backed up by extensive background research in technology and psychology.

Leslie released the first novel, *Executive,* in October 2011. Since then, she has written many more, continuing to break down barriers of traditional thrillers. Her style of fast-paced suspense, backed up by extensive background research in technology and psychology, has made Leslie one of the most read authors in the genre and she has created an array of unforgettable, brilliant and strong women heroes along the way.

Reminiscent of the television drama *Criminal Minds*, her series of books featuring the fierce and relentless FBI Agent **Tess Winnett** would be of great interest to readers of James Patterson, Melinda Leigh, and David Baldacci crime thrillers. Fans of Kendra Elliot and Robert Dugoni suspenseful mysteries would love the **Las Vegas Crime** series, featuring the tension-filled relationship between Baxter and Holt. Finally, her **Alex Hoffmann** series of political and espionage action adventure will enthrall readers of Tom Clancy, Brad Thor, and Lee Child.

Leslie has received much acclaim for her work, including inquiries from Hollywood, and her books offer something that is different and tangible, with readers becoming invested in not only the main characters and plot but also with the ruthless minds of the killers she creates.

A complete list of Leslie's titles is available at LeslieWolfe.com/books.

Leslie enjoys engaging with readers every day and would love to hear from you. Become an insider: gain early access to previews of Leslie's new novels.

- Email: LW@WolfeNovels.com
- Facebook: https://www.facebook.com/wolfenovels
- Follow Leslie on Amazon: http://bit.ly/WolfeAuthor
- Follow Leslie on BookBub: http://bit.ly/wolfebb
- Website: www.LeslieWolfe.com
- Visit Leslie's Amazon store: http://bit.ly/WolfeAll

Made in the USA
Las Vegas, NV
12 February 2024

85680998R00163